HEADHUNTER

*By the same author*

THE TORCH
WHITEFIRE
THE HOUND OF HEAVEN
BLOOD ENEMIES
EIGHTH DAY
SHADOW OF BABEL

# HEADHUNTER

Glover Wright

MACMILLAN
LONDON

First published 1994 by Macmillan London Limited

a division of Pan Macmillan Publishers Limited
Cavaye Place London SW10 9PG
and Basingstoke

Associated companies throughout the world

ISBN 0-333-59533-5

1 3 5 7 9 8 6 4 2

A CIP catalogue record for this book is available from
the British Library

Typeset by CentraCet Limited, Cambridge
Printed by Mackays of Chatham PLC, Chatham, Kent

For my mother, with love

# ACKNOWLEDGEMENTS

I am grateful to the following people for their help, so generously given, in the research for this book:

John, Marian and Tom Mellotte for their warm hospitality and their time in ensuring I had a hard look at Belfast; Jim Taylor, National Trust Head Warden of the beautiful Causeway Coast of County Antrim who gave detail to my inspiration; Jim Shilliday for his efforts and recollections; Captain Will Woodard, for his advice on matters maritime and what could or could not be done in the relevant waters and ports; Dominic Pallot, who persuaded the US Federal Reserve Bank to fit one million US dollars into a backpack; to Dave Neil for his vital contribution which is evident throughout.

Finally and most importantly to John Staunton, musician, gentleman and friend whose persuasive invitation to Ireland, subsequent uncomplaining chauffeuring and on occasion chaperoning – was the start of it all.

*Geoffrey Glover-Wright, Jersey.*

Violence shall synchronize your movements like a tune,
And Terror like a frost shall halt the flood of thinking.

W. H. AUDEN

# PROLOGUE

━━━━━━━━━━━━━━◆▸ ◂◆━━━━━━━━━━━━━━

THE DANCE master wore black: a long sleek leotard that covered torso and limbs like skin.

His tightly drawn-back hair was black, though under the hard lights fine streaks glistened like unexpected traces of silver in coal. His cheekbones were high, Slavic; the hollows beneath deep and interesting to women who believed they showed *hunger*. His eyebrows were dark and almost perfect; growing a little too far over the bridge of his straight nose, making the face dangerous when lowered, as it was then to one long leg stretched to the *barre*.

His complexion was pale; too pale for the condition of his lean, magnificent body to which the leotard clung wetly as he worked. A body made for the sun that the sun never touched. Ever.

His eyes were dark: soft, seductive, or soulless, dependent on the moment: *his* moment; for his every second was calculated: nothing showed that he did not wish seen. He hid his eyes – or framed them – behind long lashes that softened the pupils and completed the lie.

His studio was empty and stilled: varnished floorboards slick and damp from the passage of too many feet; mirrors, running ceiling to floor across the length of two walls (for examining talent and exposing mediocrity), were clouded with moisture, casting the dance master's image back as a dark blur.

He heard footsteps, turned his head measuredly, the artiste's awareness of self clear in the movement, saw the figure at the door and with slow deliberation turned on calloused toes and brought his horizontal leg to the floorboards.

The man showed the large fat manila envelope as if displaying he offered no threat: both arms extended, his apprehension evident – then placed it on the long wooden bench beside him and left.

The dance master waited, quite still, as the footsteps faded to silence. Silence for him. He had long ceased to hear the roar of London's traffic immediately beyond the studio's grimy windows. Had long ceased to hear – or heed – anything he chose not to.

He moved to his battered leather grip, took something from it, sat on the bench, turned sideways, staring at the envelope as if able to read right through the thick manila. With a sharp metallic *click*, a silver blade sprang from his pale left hand. He took up the envelope, sliced expertly with one quick cut and poured two photographs, clipped typed-sheets and money on to the floor between his bare feet.

He smiled.

Not the smile he wore for the women whose indifferent bodies he forced grindingly day after day into a gross parody of art.

The smile of the panther.

# CHAPTER ONE

THEY STEPPED from the brush into his headlights; faces smeared muddy-yellow and brown merging into camouflage gear; brutal automatic weapons held steady despite two tons of steel bearing down on them.

Carter hit the brakes instantly, the pedal pumping beneath his feet as the ABS fought the slide, decelerating the big silver-grey Mercedes 500 coupé hard and straight to a smoking standstill.

He lowered the window, the acrid smell of scorched rubber rising to his nostrils. Leaving dipped headlamps on, he switched off the engine, put on interior lights and placed both hands in clear sight on the padded wheel, watching the tail-lights of Brannigan's taxi fade into the distance.

The first soldier closed in as the second backed off clear of the vehicle, weapon readied, shoulders dropped, not a hint of tenseness in the loose body; but alert, eyes rock steady in the striped face. I'll kill you if you make me, they said and Carter had every reason to believe.

Right then for Carter it wasn't Northern Ireland any more but Nicaragua, Salvador, Iraq or any of the conflicts in between, all of which he had survived and all part of his growing; but wherever, whenever, the covert face of war always hid behind the muddied mask of the tiger.

The pencil beam probed. He dropped his grey eyes to his clothes as the light lanced at them. 'Small arm, automatic, loaded and chambered, shoulder-holster, right side. Legal. Permit's in pants hip-pocket with my wallet.'

'Out of the car, hands on head. *Do it now!*'

Carter swung out of the Mercedes, the door held wide open for him, the soldier standing at arm's length behind it giving his backup a clear line of fire.

'Face the car. Legs spread, hands on the roof. Stretch! *Now!*'

Carter turned, knowing the drill. He grunted as his ankles were hacked further apart, his temper locked deep where it did no harm. He heard the monotonous throb of Army tracking and surveillance helicopters hovering in the murk high above. Belfast's hated heartbeat. For some.

The fierce blow turned his head to ice and the deep throb above echoed, fading slowly in the cold aching blackness.

LEARY'S BAR was packed tight. Brannigan made for where they had dictated he should sit: *Farthest end of the room, by the emergency exit: look for the lovers, they'll be ready for you.* The table became available immediately he ordered his drink. He admired their planning. He settled with his Bushmills before him, they had told him half an hour minimum, not before; they needed time to make sure his back was clean.

They came too early. Barely five minutes had passed. Brannigan recognized them for what they were by the way they moved. And the way others moved for them. He scanned the faces around him for confirmation though he needed none, he'd done his time, he *knew*.

They're not here for me, he thought. This is something else.

The noise from the crowd dipped momentarily then swelled as ranks closed and the Belfast shutters went up. They didn't hear, see, think; they drank harder, laughed louder and kept their eyes in their glasses. A widow would be made tonight; a lover loveless; a mother would lose a son; the old weary story no longer told except by outsiders. This was Northern Ireland and they didn't need reminding.

Poor bastard, Brannigan thought, whoever you are.

They kept coming.

*Not me!*

He saw the soft, dark, killing eyes.

4

Didn't need to see the long silenced Browning.

He knew.

*Me.*

KATE BRANNIGAN knew something was wrong when they held her back on the plane. Then the sight of the heavy man with clouded eyes who was both messenger and protector ducking into the cabin told her all she needed to know even before he spoke. She stared at him; cold, cold as ice; still belted in, not daring to move because her heart, all of her, would splinter.

He sat on a seat-arm before her, the children taken excitedly into the cockpit while he told her the worst news of her life. She felt sorry for him. At least she had the cushion of shock for protection. All he had was his bleak duty.

She sat outside herself, listening, nodding, understanding but accepting none of it. He warned her that the media were out in force – barely held back – that she could outrun them now with his help but they'd hunt her down because this was Belfast, their best hunting ground, and they had half the population in their pay. It was her choice. She could see he hated them very much.

He called himself Reardon and she remembered the name from Patrick's calls. Patrick had said he trusted him, a rare admission from a notoriously cynical man. Was Patrick's death in any way betrayal of that trust?

She wanted to stay where she was for ever, not face reality; sit safe, shutting out all of it in the cotton-wool silence of the airliner's warm cocoon. Outside was a war zone where people were shot, bombed, tortured. Through the window the embattled face of Northern Ireland stared at her from behind a machine-gun in the turret of a grotesque filth-coloured armoured car.

She looked away. 'Now,' she told Reardon. 'I want to do it now.'

'I'll have a stewardess take the children—'

'My children stay with me.'

In the terminal VIP lounge, television crews seemed prepared to burn out her eyes with their white lights. She gathered her children in, not blinking, not daring. She couldn't allow tears; not in public, not for all the world to see; not for her ramrod-spined East coast family to wince at; not for the sake of her children.

Anger blazed as if a furnace opened on her face. Anger at Patrick. She had warned him. Stay home, let others take the risk, *delegate* for Christ's sake. No, he had to go, just as he had to be the last American businessman out of Iraq before it back-flopped into hell. There had been others just as risky. Salvador had almost killed him. Afterwards she'd be there, as usual, waiting tight lipped at yet another airport barrier, kids clinging like ivy and Patrick smiling through the same glib answer: *You don't make real money in Maple Rapids, Michigan, you make it out there on the edge and you have to be prepared to fall off sometime.*

He should never have left Maple Rapids, never met her, lived to old age, hating every moment of it.

They were yelling now, seeming almost to want to break her, the children clawing at her skirt, terrified by their strident urgency, she pressing them to her thighs, hands feeling for their ears, protecting them from the terrible details: the packed downtown bar, the hail of shots, the murder of their father, her husband. And *their* benefactor. It wasn't every day an American businessman planned on investing millions in Northern Ireland. Bastards!

A cruel red-headed girl, fired up by the scrum, her small recorder stuck out like a weapon, shrieked through them: 'How do you *feel*, Mrs Brannigan!'

Like I'm ablaze, bitch! And nothing but the blood of you *bloody* people could put it out.

The questions came from all sides like crossfire with no silence in between for answers:

'The IRA have claimed responsibility, Mrs Brannigan! Your husband was aware of the dangers, surely?'

'Was he satisfied with the protection Westminster promised?'

'Do you feel he was let down?'

'What was his business in *Leary's*, Mrs Brannigan? Is there any truth in the rumour of drugs being involved?'

'That's enough,' barked Reardon, starting forward, straight-

6

arming someone back so hard Kate felt the jolt through the big hand he had gripped across her shoulders.

The red-head's shrill voice cut through the babble: 'You're a wealthy woman, Mrs Brannigan, will you be offering a reward for information on your husband's killers?'

She saw, through the checked flood laying over her eyes, faces, close, distorted, as in a nightmare. *That's what this is.* 'A million dollars,' she croaked fighting to get it out.

'What!'

'What did she say?'

'Mrs Brannigan?'

'*How much!*'

She struggled hard against the pull of the big man. 'A million dollars for the heads of the men – or women, I don't give a damn – who killed my husband. And I don't care who earns it.'

'She doesn't mean that,' snapped Reardon. 'Mrs Brannigan is distraught. Get out of the way.'

'I mean it,' she said and now let him pull her on, pandemonium breaking out behind as she went through a swiftly opened door.

Dark green uniformed RUC officers immediately encircled her, automatic weapons slung across chests swollen by black flak-jackets, high-fronted peaked hats reminding her of Nazi newsreels, the ugly steel-girdered bomb-proof tunnel to the cold night closing around her, her children tripping, unable to match the speed of their passage but held upright by the iron grip she would never relinquish. They were all she had now.

The wind slashed at her as automatic doors slid aside, leaving the opened door of the Rover beyond – and its driver with a matt-black machine-pistol lying across his lap – clear and real and not some tableau behind glass, not some television image; real, as real as death.

Reardon ducked her down into the car fast, tumbling the children into the rear beside her before swinging around the Rover with surprising speed and diving into the front passenger seat, saying breathlessly, '*Drive!*'

One of the RUC officers bent to her closed window. 'We'll get them! Don't you worry about that!'

She heard his hard slap on the roof and the squeal of tyres as though through another's ears: some other person who could do her crying for her.

*I'd kill them myself right now if they stood before me and not feel a thing.* She would cry later when their blood dried. Her anger terrified her but it kept her from sinking.

THE CULLODEN Hotel loomed up in the darkness, half a castle, spired and turreted, standing on Hollywood Hills overlooking Belfast Lough, the lights of the County Antrim coastline trailing behind the former bishops of Down's palace like a thousand candles flickering in holy procession.

Reardon held open the Rover's rear door, Kate Brannigan sitting inside staring up at the looming black silhouette.

'Not as old or forbidding as it looks,' said Reardon, his warm hand around her bicep; the pressure gentle enough to be comforting, but firm, easing her out. 'Nineteenth-century Scottish baronial. Let's go inside.'

She looked at him, eyes bitter. 'Is it any safer than out here?'

Reardon ducked down to the driver, his voice low and quick. 'Anything comes through on the radio let me know – and Ellis, keep alert, this may not be over.' He arose. 'Come on,' he urged, forcing movement into her legs, the children swirling around them like leaves in a storm.

They passed heavy barred gates then through a security checkpoint where the smart blazer-clad guard nodded Reardon through deferentially.

In the lobby she let Reardon check her in and watched the dropped eyes of the team of receptionists, knowing the news had already reached them, hating them for their pity, wanting them to shriek out their anger at the act, not act out reverence like strangers watching a funeral go by.

Reardon came back. 'Get yourself a good night's rest. There's a doctor on call . . . if you need anything?'

'I want to talk.'

'In the morning.'

'Now.' The sharpness in her voice made the children gather close again. One, the youngest girl, cried.

Reardon felt helpless. He stood, feeling threatening, too big for them in his dark, costly overcoat.

'I'll settle them and be right down,' she told him. 'Ask for someone to sit with them a while.'

'Don't you think it would be better if—'

'*Ask!* I'll pay.'

Reardon felt his own anger rise. He wanted to say, *Money won't get you everything here*, but he was as guilty as she of the reverse presumption. For the past weeks he had operated entirely on that basis – her husband a willing partner. He tried to see Brannigan beside her and could not. He saw Brannigan, alone, waiting in the lobby, very American, tall, sky-blue eyes startling in the bronzed face, always first for whatever he had planned; an attractive lazy way about him – and a certain stillness too – that belied his quickness of mind, his intuitive grasp of circumstances, his speed of decision making. He couldn't believe he was dead. He felt betrayed, yet, illogically, still trusting, still prepared to go some way down that disillusioning road. It was in him to be loyal and always had been.

He looked at her. If there had been betrayal it was not her doing. He said, gently: 'Maybe they'll just do it out of kindness? They know about death here.'

She answered wearily: 'Maybe they're too used to it?' She dropped beside the children, comforting them.

'Someone will be up in five minutes,' he told her after making arrangements.

She arose and pointed. 'Wait for me. In there. Don't leave.' She paused. 'Please.'

He walked her to the broad banisters. She turned sharply halfway up, the great ornate stained-glass bishop's window behind her. 'My luggage!'

'It's being brought. Should be here any moment. Don't worry.' He saw her drained face. 'You should rest.'

'Just *wait*, all right?'

He walked back under elegant plasterwork and Louis XV chandeliers into the lounge and settled himself into one of the armchairs, wanting a drink badly but feeling too weary to go through to the bar. He gazed out at the twinkling amber across the Lough and allowed himself a cigarette; the last of the five he had rationed himself daily in his latest purge on his lifestyle. He drew smoke deep, felt the euphoric rush sweep through him and sighed. His heavy chin jutted aggressively. Did it really matter how many he smoked? Pushing hard at fifty-five he would have done all the damage already. Still . . .

'You'll be wanting your usual, Mr Reardon? Bushmills, a touch of water?' The barman offered quietly. 'Spotted you arrive, thought I'd come through and ask.'

'Forget the water – just breathe on it, Gerry.'

'Bad business. I'm real sorry. Just ran it on the box – what she said. That's *trouble*.'

Reardon looked up. 'How did he seem tonight, when he left here? Mr Brannigan?'

'Same big smile. Never much from the eyes with him – not for me anyway. Then, a successful man like that has himself two faces, right? Mind, if I had ten million spare, Belfast would be the last place I'd put it. Still, it was how he lived. Said he enjoyed it. High-risk investment was where you made the real money – the rewards matched the risk. His words, Mr Reardon.'

Not tonight they didn't, thought Reardon. 'Was it you suggested Leary's, Gerry?'

'No, sir! He came into the bar tonight – had a quick one before he left. Asked about the place. I told him . . . well, had a reputation – you know what I mean? Not his scene, I said. He gave me the big grin, said he liked to get about, wanted the feel of the city; the *smell* of it, he called it. Said all he'd seen was what he'd been shown – what you'd shown him, Mr Reardon. Said all that culture was OK but, well, he went, didn't he? Should have listened. Funny him going there when the wife and kids were coming in from the States?'

Reardon might have been made of stone.

'I'll get you that Bushmills then.'

'And a brandy.' Reardon's heavy jaw lifted. 'She'll need it.'

'That's a fact.'

Reardon leaned back against the cushions. He felt a twinge in his stomach and wondered, not for the first time, if he had an ulcer.

10

He closed his eyes. He hated illness. His father had been dying slowly for as long as he had known him. Thank God that was over. No, not hate, he thought. Fear.

Kate Brannigan sat down in front of him.

Reardon stared at her. How can you have three kids and look that good? Three kids turned most women into hags: hard around the eyes, hair brittle, tongues biting. Certainly did where he had been raised: the wrong side of the province for anyone with ambition. He had never forgotten. Perhaps that was why he had never married? It was something of a revelation for him.

'Where was your security?' she demanded.

'He refused it. Wanted to make it plain he was independent. His words. I told him he was being naïve. By accepting the financial package he was already – openly – aligned with us. Didn't do any good. We argued. He got his way. He usually did. I felt he'd have pulled out of the deal if he hadn't and advised London so. They were *very* unhappy.'

'Accepting the deal was good business. He wouldn't see that as accepting your politics. What you term naïvety he'd call cutting the crap. You needed to understand him.'

'I thought I did.'

'So that's it? And he's dead?'

'We tried discreet cover but he guessed – or spotted our people – and told me, *get them the hell out!* Loudly. Said he had Carter and Carter was enough. He'd been in bad situations before. Ulster was just another. He almost convinced me he was right. Tonight proved how wrong he was.'

'I'd forgotten Carter! Is he—?'

'Carter wasn't there.'

'*What!*'

'We're searching for him.'

The barman returned with drinks.

Reardon held the cognac out to her. 'Don't say no. Let it do you some good.'

Her shoulders slumped. 'Is there any good left in this place?'

'There is. But there's few who care. All the world wants is the bad. And that's all the media gives them.'

She sipped carefully, letting the dark gold liquid roll over her tongue, not a hint of wetness touching her lips as she set down the goblet.

Reardon couldn't help watching her. *Class.* I'd have given my eyes for someone like you when I was twenty-five and rising. I might still.

She said: 'That's the first time you sounded like you belong here.'

'I was born here but . . . well, that was a long time ago. That's the problem with Ireland; too many leave it. Both sides of the border.'

She looked out at the Lough. 'Patrick had a bit of Irish in him, diluted, but he felt it quite strongly. Surprised me. Nothing political. Romantic. The *green* of it. The songs, the folklore.'

'Dublin. His ancestry was in the South. He told me over too much of this stuff one evening.' Reardon lifted his glass.

'Does it *really* make any difference? It's just one land mass, isn't it?'

He thought she had beaten her anger but she had barely battened it down. 'Geographically speaking, yes,' he said, lightly.

'Maybe that's the solution. Let geography settle it. Better than the gun and the bomb, surely?'

'The graveyards of this country are full of people who had a solution.' He winced. 'I'm sorry.'

She drank again, avoiding him. Finally she said: 'You think I should withdraw my offer. The reward. Why don't you say it?'

He leaned forward. 'Shock, grief, hits people differently. With you its anger. You didn't know what you were saying.'

'I knew *exactly* what I was saying.'

He indicated the lighted coastline beyond the oily glint of the Lough. 'That's a brutalised world out there and they're all trying to escape it. People maim themselves – blow off their own kneecaps – for the compensation payments. Can you comprehend that? They kill almost daily for a lot less than a million. Even as we sit here they are betraying their own for a fraction of that sum – and betrayal here is an automatic death sentence. You've offered more than money. Much more. You've offered a world they'd no chance of having. Ever. Can you grasp the enormity of that? You've made this a far more dangerous place than it is already.'

12

'Will it get me results?'

'You want that kind of result? Revenge? I really doubt it.'

'What kind of result will *you* get me? Your government? You acted for them, you were their man for Patrick, smoothed the wheels, wined him, dined him, tempted him – but you couldn't keep him alive, could you? So now your job's over? Your responsibilities too? He's dead, the deal is off, you go home and I'm left with the body. Well, it's not enough for me!'

'There's the investigation—'

'And a trial? They're across the border! Long gone. Extradition? You have that kind of pull over there in the Republic? You don't even have their co-operation!' She took one of his cigarettes and brutally snapped his lighter alight, the flame trembling in her clenched fist, her eyes glittering. 'A million dollars buys one *hell* of a lot of co-operation.'

He held her hand steady till smoke came from her lips. 'Blood money,' he said.

'Blood for blood is too old fashioned for you? I thought you Northern Irish were real fundamentalists.'

'And educated, cultured Americans are all liberals with the politically correct Bible tucked in their pocketbook?'

'Listen! They killed my husband, the father of my children; they killed someone who wanted to bring prosperity, jobs, hope. Why? *Talk to me!*'

'Perhaps because only prosperity can defeat the terrorists while poverty allows them to win? Those are my beliefs anyway, my commitment.'

'*Perhaps?* Give me another reason other than sheer bloody murderous savagery!'

He let her come down, let her fight her tears; perhaps putting off the moment he dreaded also. He said, finally: 'I thought he too was committed.'

'Thought? You've worked with him all along, didn't you know?'

He hesitated. 'The routine police murder investigation has already begun. The problem is there may have to be another kind of investigation. One I don't want – and you certainly won't. I'm not certain it can be halted.'

13

'What are you telling me?'

He finished his drink and wanted another, badly. 'They shot him in a bar called Leary's.'

'So?'

'Any idea why he'd be there?'

'He liked bars,' she snapped. 'Men do. Don't *you*?'

'Leary's has a reputation for drug dealing – and I don't mean the amount an addict smokes, sniffs or injects in an evening. There's a serious market in drugs here with serious people organizing it.'

'*That's* what that bitch meant at the airport about drugs!' She looked at him, hard. 'You know what I gave up when my second child came along?'

'You practised as an attorney. I know,' said Reardon. 'Your husband told me.'

'You tread carefully, hear me? So what else did he tell you?'

'All the *good* things I needed to know. What Her Majesty's government needed to know. The deal was we matched his investment. Encouragement for the nervous investor. We were nervous too. We've been caught before by Americans in Ulster. Badly.' Reardon paused. 'He did *not* tell me he visited bars like Leary's.'

She stood quickly. 'Your government even *hints* at drugs in connection with my husband, I'll fight, count on it. I'm going to sleep now, if I can. Tomorrow I'll repeat my offer to as many people as I can reach. And I'll get results. You can count on it. When this is over I'll take Patrick and my children home, not before, and I'll never set foot here again – ever.'

'You're making a bad mistake.'

'I don't believe so. Reardon, be careful how you walk around my husband's memory. Use very soft shoes. Tell your people that.' She turned and strode away.

'The IRA execute drug dealers,' he murmured to her retreating back and leaned back into the armchair.

'Thought you might need a small one, Mr Reardon?'

Reardon looked up. He nodded and let the barman pour. 'Something troubling you, Gerry?' he asked.

'Wasn't listening, sir – but I heard you mention about Mr Carter.'

14

'Yes?'

'Had a beer in the bar earlier – on his own for a change. He left for the airport.'

'The airport? You're sure?'

'Checked flight ETAs on the TV. I thought he was passing time till Mr Brannigan was ready to go, then they'd be off to pick up the lady and the kids – but like I said it didn't happen that way. Mr Carter left then, Mr Brannigan comes in, knocks back a stiff one then takes a cab, alone.'

'You're certain.'

'I called the cab.'

'About Carter too?'

'Pete – out front on security – came by for a natter, said he couldn't believe what he was seeing. The guard sticks by the body, Rule Number One. Asking for trouble, he said. It came too, eh, Mr Reardon?'

Reardon arose quickly, pulled money from his wallet, thrust it on to the tray and made quickly for the car park.

Ellis leaned across and pushed open the Rover's door. 'You've calls from London, sir, urgent.'

'Later. Carter supposedly went to meet Mrs Brannigan at the airport. He wasn't anywhere in sight. There was enough attention on Mrs Brannigan and myself so he could hardly have missed us. I want him found.'

'Never made it, sir. Heard a couple of minutes ago. Got sandbagged. Not the airport road. Heading into the city.'

'You're sure?'

'The Army is. They found him.'

'Why didn't you come and tell me!'

'Didn't feel I could interrupt, sir. Anyway, he's in the Royal Victoria, injury, he's not going anywhere.'

'Right. Hospital. Go.'

'London, sir?'

'London can wait.'

Ellis backed out fast; the body of the machine-pistol wedged by one thigh against the swing of the car, its trigger-guard clear and ready.

Reardon felt the deep surge of power press him back in his seat, the innocuous saloon – like most things in Ulster – not quite what it appeared to be.

MARCUS CARTER was the most controlled man Detective Inspector James McAlister of RUC Special Branch had ever encountered. Those who passed through his experienced hands usually protested vehemently – often physically – if they had to repeat their tale too often, yet the American's patience, despite mild concussion and immersion in the cold-water ditch from which the cautious crew of a passing Army armoured patrol vehicle had lifted him, seemed infinite. He might never have signed the statement – given earlier to a CID detective sergeant of the Royal Ulster Constabulary – now lying ignored on the bedside table of the guarded private room in Belfast's Royal Victoria Hospital.

McAlister had seen Carter's military record – that part of it cleared by the Americans over the electronic information link – and it was certainly impressive, but he doubted if even Brannigan's highly qualified hired gun had any idea how hard Northern Ireland was. He suspected Carter found both him and his Detective Sergeant, Danny Keegan, parochial. Hadn't America's great cities set the benchmark for violence?

McAlister smiled softly. You've been here a month, laddie, and you don't know anything. The tension, the ruthlessness, the brutalities break even the toughest. You've felt the tickle of the whore's tongue on your handsome face while she took your money, that's all. Now you're feeling the drive of her knee into your privates.

Keegan leaned over the bed rail. 'They were Provos. The UDA used Brit uniforms and weapons for one of their hits: August eighty-six. UDR man did the selling. The Provos just nicked the idea. Better late than never. But they'd never get the weapons right unless they'd killed a couple of squaddies and lifted theirs and we'd know about that. So they used Armalites, right?'

'SA-80s, standard British Army issue,' stated Carter.

McAlister's manicured fingernails tapped the signed statement. 'So they're the genuine article? British soldiers?'

'I said *soldiers*. Trained, disciplined, cool. They were good. Very good.'

'You should meet some of the new Provo units, Major. They're not all unruly leather-jacket and jeans long-haired unshaven hoods.'

Carter glanced up at the Scotsman. 'Drop the "Major". I've been out of the US Army for two years.'

McAlister smiled. 'Of course. Any other observations?'

'They could have been Special Forces.'

McAlister sat carefully on the edge of the bed. 'Here, that translates as Special Air Service. Dangerous thought. Now why would you think that?'

'Gut.'

'Ah! With your background you should know? That's your contention?'

The telephone by the bed buzzed. McAlister lifted it, listened, sighed, replaced the receiver. 'Whitehall's representative is here to speak to you. They've just lost ten million sorely needed dollars' worth of investment in this godforsaken city. Not too pleased with you, I'd imagine. What do they call it in your game when your client gets killed? Losing your name?' McAlister drew on his overcoat, untucking and smoothing a creased pocket flap carefully. 'Well, everyone loses after tonight's bloody work: Westminster, Ulster, the unemployed. The question is, who gains?'

'How'd you let your boss talk you into letting him roam free, unminded, in a place like this?' asked Keegan.

'Like you, I take orders, Sergeant. Read my statement.'

'But you didn't follow them,' observed McAlister. 'You followed *him*?'

'I had enough time to do both.'

'Barely. He wanted you out of the way and you weren't having it? That's how it was – more or less?'

Carter looked up at him.

'Wrong place for silence,' warned McAlister.

'I'll talk to Reardon.'

McAlister smiled gently. 'Who has influence in high places. Yes, I can see you would. Are you really out of the military, Major? One never knows with you Americans – no offence meant, just speaking from my experience round about your submarine bases in Scotland.

17

Plenty of civilians got themselves saluted when they didn't warrant it
– or so they maintained. You take my meaning?'

'I'm out. Right out.'

'Well, if anything springs to mind, talk to us first. That's good
advice in this city. We're the ones with our ears firmly to the ground.
If anything is happening – or about to happen – we usually know
first.'

'Not this time.'

McAlister nodded, grimly.

'They weren't IRA.'

McAlister stood directly above him. 'If that's the case – who
killed your employer? Have you thought about that?'

Keegan came around the bed impatiently, counting off on thick
fingers: 'Provos gave the correct code to the TV station when they
called in . . . they admit the hit . . . their trademark's all over it . . .
the drunks and druggies in Leary's we've questioned aren't talking,
which means it's the Provies. You're blowing smoke to cover yourself.'

'And if you *are* it makes it difficult for us to see,' added
McAlister, moving to the door. 'CID might think it's drugs related
but you say it's not – to your knowledge – which means there's
something for *us* to eat here. So if you think of a convincing reason
your boss was in that bar – not counting dealing in narcotics to make
a few million to improve his cash flow – you be sure to let me know.'

Carter nodded at the transcript of his statement. 'You forgot
something.'

'The guv'nor doesn't read fiction,' smiled Keegan.

'Fact,' said Carter. 'That's why you're leaving it here. The last
thing you want is me in a courtroom. I'm what they call an expert
witness. I don't think your people would want the press reporting
what I had to say.'

'There'll be a man outside watching over you through the night,'
advised McAlister.

'Keeping someone out – or me in, Inspector?'

Keegan grinned and closed the door.

'How serious is his injury?' enquired Reardon, exiting the lift with Ellis.

McAlister said: 'He'll be out in the morning. Unless we can stop him.'

'What are you talking about? What happened?'

Keegan answered: 'Says he got pulled by an Army foot patrol in full warpaint, sir. Stepped from the brush in front of the car. Claims he played it right – warned them he was carrying – they had him out of the car fast . . . and goodnight.'

'Mistaken ID? That's happened here before. Anyone taking responsibility?'

McAlister shook his close-cropped head. 'No Army patrol on that road at the time.'

'That's been confirmed?'

McAlister nodded and glanced at Ellis. 'Of course Hereford's boys wouldn't admit if they were there.'

Ellis said: 'We don't make ID mistakes.'

'When you do they're fatal, laddie.'

'He's alive, isn't he?'

'What are you implying, Inspector?' demanded Reardon.

'Nothing. We assumed it was the Provos who ambushed him – disguised. He says they were Army. Special Forces. It's in his statement.'

'SAS,' said Keegan.

McAlister sighed. 'His military record confirms he'd have knowledge of their techniques.'

Keegan grinned at Ellis. 'Takes one to know one.'

'He's off his trolley,' said Ellis.

McAlister nodded Reardon aside. 'You'll be speaking to London, sir?'

'Of course.'

McAlister waited for the rapid muffled thud of a helicopter to pass, low, somewhere overhead.

'What is it you want, Inspector?' urged Reardon, impatiently.

'The press will have a field day with Carter's story – fact or not. His background guarantees they'll push it to the limit. Even hint at SAS involvement in a killing here – doesn't matter if there's a logical reason or not – and the place will go up like a tinder-box. We can't

19

have that kind of talk. Spreading SAS horror stories is an IRA game and they're good at it – so we can do without an American adding to them. Someone might believe him. Like the media?'

'I *do* understand, Inspector.'

'Then understand why I need Carter under protective custody. At least until the furore dies down. Then we can fly him out. London could order his detention?'

'Out of the question. He's an American – there'll be hell to pay if we use those tactics. The issue is delicate enough – politically – already. And with Mrs Brannigan's offer of a reward! You have heard about that?'

McAlister nodded, curtly. 'More reason for getting *both* of them out of play. We'll never get anyone on our books again if that kind of offer is taken seriously on the streets. Who's going to risk a lot of pain and a bullet in the back of the head touting serious information long term for a few thousand tax free and a new face later – maybe – after this?'

Reardon shook his head, forlornly. 'I'll talk to her again tomorrow but I don't hold out much hope.'

'She knows about the drug connection?'

'I had to warn her of the direction the investigation might take. The very mention of drugs had her practically filing a lawsuit there and then. She's a former attorney.'

'Does she know the IRA caller claimed the killing was down to drugs?'

'Absolutely not. London had a hard job gagging the press agency who took the call but we made them see sense – finally. His investment plans were reason enough for the murder. And there's absolutely no proof – or suspicion – that Brannigan even *used* illegal drugs, never mind traded in them. Has Carter explained why he allowed Brannigan out alone?'

'Brannigan's orders, he claims. Which he half obeyed. He followed him instead, in the Mercedes – Brannigan took a cab.'

'No, Carter left first. The hotel barman confirmed it.'

'Carter must have waited somewhere and watched Brannigan leave.'

Reardon shook his head. 'The ambush on the Mercedes was meant for Brannigan. It's obvious.'

'Never trust the obvious in Belfast,' McAlister said, heavily.

Reardon grunted, then questioned: 'Why the charade with the Army uniforms?'

McAlister's thick eyebrows lifted. 'Would *you* stop, suddenly faced with armed civilians? Here? Anyone with sense would take the chance and put their foot down *hard*. A speeding car with a determined driver is difficult to stop, even with automatic weapons. Carter would have taken evasive action, then driven right over them. He's trained for it.'

'But he'd stop for an Army patrol, of course. Clever.'

'We only have his word that Brannigan ordered him away,' commented McAlister.

'You don't believe him?'

'I can't exactly confirm it, can I, sir?'

'You don't think *he's* involved in the murder!'

'That's CID's job to discover. What you don't want is having the *really* bad news confirmed.'

'Isn't Brannigan's murder bad enough!'

'Not as bad as discovering that maybe he *was* setting up other business interests in the province that had nothing to do with industry and that the Provos got wind of this and made their well-known attitude to drug dealing apparent to him?'

Reardon tightened his jaw. 'I can't believe he was dealing in drugs. For God's sake, man, we'd have known! Downing Street had him fully vetted. We've learned our lesson the last time an American had a free hand with British taxpayers' money in Ulster. Much of our intelligence effort these days is geared to defeating illegal drugs trading. We'd have *known*!'

The helicopter thudded again overhead. 'Night shift,' observed McAlister. 'You know they've got the most sophisticated electronic surveillance equipment in the world up there – and they still don't see or hear everything.'

'It's not the same, Inspector. This was a personal thing.'

'It's personal with Carter too. He's lost his man. And I guarantee he's looking for someone to blame. He's that kind. I'd say he's planning to go freelance.'

'Freelance?'

'Wants to set the record straight. Get his name back.'

21

Reardon stared at him. 'You mean go after the IRA, *alone?*'

'You haven't understood, sir. He doesn't believe it *is* the IRA who killed Brannigan. He thinks it's *us.*'

A cold irrational fear touched Reardon and though he pushed it away it left a sickening feeling of suspicion deep in his stomach. He thought of the brutal world outside which he had for so long stood aside from; had been protected from: and another, forbidden to him, which he had, under protest, fed. 'I'll talk to Carter,' he said.

'Then to London, sir?' pressed McAlister.

'Then London.' To the one man who won't lie to me, thought Reardon, with relief.

THE CROWDED hotel lounge was designer hi-tech cold, with hard composite surfaces, dark glass and nineties minimalist lithographs facing down grey, grainy photographs of dead poets and legendary film stars.

At its rear, a guitarist, with ghostly self-playing midi-controlled keyboards beside him and a control console perhaps from NASA, took his break and flicked the remote for the large TV screen showing the international being played live at Belfast's football stadium.

If not for the news break headlining the arrival at Belfast International airport – to a chaotic media reception – of a pale, shocked, darkly attractive woman in her thirties, eyes bright and fixed in anger, choked voice almost drowned in the babble, it would have been impossible to believe cold-blooded murder had taken place earlier, a few blocks away from the lounge.

Her biting words – hastily curtailed by her escort – dispelled any doubt. *One million dollars for the heads of my husband's killers.*

'You hear that? *Rick?*' one man pressed his companion when it was over; his accent flat, anonymous, its origins thoroughly ironed out by training for just such a situation. He might have heard his instructor's resolute voice right then, in English, the only language that existed then – and now – for any of them: *To hear is to remember, son, so give them nothing to hang on to: no broad vowels, no colloquial inflections, nor, if you're a nancy boy, no delicate lisp. Hear what I'm saying? You'd better, because one day, sure as a whore breaks wind you're going to owe me your life. To hear is to forget; that's your aim.* 'A million US? That's freedom, Rick. For all of us.'

They sat away from the bar on curved banquette seating, cups of coffee before them; the main entrance to their left – one of them facing it – an emergency exit front right, only one table between them and instant escape. The people between were not a factor; they were moveable, predictable, expendable; not necessarily in that order.

His companion sipped black coffee silently, soft brown eyes with long almost feminine lashes resting lazily on the entrance.

'Rick?'

'If we live to spend it.'

'You'll work it out, Rick.'

'They're back.'

Two men joined them, smiling easily, pink faces looking freshly scrubbed.

'Half-time? What's the score?' One sat while the other bought beer. 'What's wrong?' he asked, suddenly alert.

The one called Rick inclined his head at the bar. 'Wait.'

The man returned and placed two pints on the table.

'OK, what's happened?'

They were told of the news flash. For a while they sat in silence, watching but not seeing the game.

Finally one leaned forward, warily. 'But *who*?'

'Rick?' urged the other newcomer.

'Who is easy, when is easy. Afterwards is the problem. They'll *all* be after us.' Rick locked his fingers behind his head and stretched his long dancer's legs. 'But we've been there before.'

'We'll do whatever you say, Rick,' said the blond one who had waited with him for the others.

Rick smiled.'You will.'

THE HOUSE stood behind Queen's University Belfast on a darkened street lined with tired cars and exhausted trees; its façade of worn red brick matched in any British mainland city from Portsmouth to Edinburgh.

They chose their hour calculatedly, when even hardened insomniacs and the most vigilant succumbed to sleep, choosing entry through the front door because it was the simplest and safest way. From experience they knew front and rear windows would be screwed to their frames and devices to injure or maim those who chose clandestine entry from the rear would be in place.

They had instruments to defeat the door's double locks and used them swiftly and precisely.

Inside, the smell was of too many living together for too long with too little air and small regard for the niceties of cohabitation; or of countless itinerants leaving only their odour as mark of their passage. The three knew the smell; it's distinct pungent masculinity a familiar, acceptable part of covert urban warfare.

They chose the ground floor to lessen their chance of discovery, killing swiftly with silent weapons, each an act of practised efficiency; only afterwards when the one with the soft eyes held out his gloved hand for the final tool was there any noise at all and then only that of dead meat: no cry, no anguish, no farewell for life was already extinct.

Those above who slept dreamlessly, or dreamed fitfully or heroically of the Cause, would awake to a nightmare.

# CHAPTER TWO

K ATE BRANNIGAN broke the surface in the Culloden Hotel's octagonal pool, swam powerfully toward the steps and sat wringing out her auburn hair.

'Leave me alone,' she said, curtly, avoiding looking at the male figure who had moved behind her in the otherwise deserted Elysium.

'I'm Marcus Carter, Mrs Brannigan.'

She watched her children playing in the clear water. 'They don't know he's gone,' she said, dully. 'Not really. Where the *hell* were you?' She tossed a fat plastic ball toward the children. 'You failed, Carter.' Now she turned and looked up, eyes hard. 'Or is there more to it than that?'

His flat grey eyes held her.

She said: 'If I were a man you'd kill me for that?'

'Only fools kill over words, Mrs Brannigan.'

She looked away. 'I'm sorry.'

'I was following your husband. He ordered me to the airport – to meet you. I figured I had time to cover his back then make it to you. I was wrong. Badly wrong.'

She looked up at him again, measuring him, judging his strength, his heart. He looked young – but something in his eyes aged him so she guessed late thirties – and fit in an underplayed way; his clothes loose, a touch too big, hiding or perhaps disguising the strength in his lean body. She used to be good at faces and better with eyes; a criminal lawyer needed to be – to separate the real killers from the posers. She decided he was hard, probably ruthless. She needed someone formidable. Someone who would protect them all and to hell with the consequences. Someone who wouldn't lie to her.

She asked, sharply: 'What stopped *him* from coming? What was so important he wouldn't take time to meet his wife and children after not seeing them for weeks? This is one of the most dangerous places on Earth! What was so goddamn *vital* about that sleazy bar?'

Carter bent beside her, scooped up a handful of sparkling water and let it run through his fingers like quicksilver. 'I don't know.'

'Tell me what happened. All of it.'

'He told me he felt lousy – something he ate downtown at lunch, he said. Wouldn't have a doctor. Said for me to meet you off the plane and bring you here. I left him in his suite lying on the bed, figured he'd sleep till you arrived.'

'Instead he went to that bar.' She stood, almost as tall as him, walked to where her robe lay, drew it on and towelled her hair brutally. 'Patrick had a digestion like iron. He'd eat stuff that would make a goat throw up.'

'Are you OK, Mrs Brannigan?'

She stopped, head tilted, auburn hair scattered. 'You mean am I bottling it all up inside and not allowing myself to grieve? Damn right I am! I've the rest of my life to grieve. My husband always used to say – when there's business to take care of you put other matters to one side. It's too late now but finally I agree with him. It's time to act, not grieve.'

'You've got the pot boiling here – the reward offer? The Brits keep it simmering most of the time – lid tight down. You're not popular.'

'Do you care what the British think?'

'I'm not paid to care. I'm paid to guess what people are thinking and stop it becoming action. Making enemies is not good policy. Your offer will make you more than you need.'

'Are *you* going for the reward, Carter?'

His eyes fixed on her. 'No, ma'am.'

She finished her towelling, then said, 'How is your head?'

He fingered the stitched wound and shrugged.

'I saw a report on local TV news about what happened.'

'But you didn't believe it.'

'I'm having a hard time believing anything right now. Don't take it personally. How come they didn't kill you? They killed Patrick.'

'Maybe it wasn't necessary? Don't believe news releases over here, Mrs Brannigan.'

26

'They're lying?'

'They're controlled.'

'Go on.'

'There's nothing more.'

'Sounds like there's a lot more.'

'Remember where you are. You haven't been here long enough to learn about this place.'

'Teach me.'

'There's a permanent high-security condition operating. Everything bows to that. This isn't the US – you can't dig too deep for the truth. You can try but access is denied. It's about the closest you'll get to a police state. They'll lie if they have to.'

'*Are* they lying?'

He looked at her.

'My husband lied. Lied to you and maybe to me. Was he being controlled?' She walked to the poolside and called the children in, pulling them easily from the water with strong swimmer's shoulders, drying them carefully. 'You've met Reardon?' she asked.

'He's been with us start to . . .'

'Say it, *finish*. Except it's not. Not yet. Not till I'm ready. Have you seen him since it happened?'

'Last night. In the hospital.'

'He puzzles me. I can't make out where he stands in all this.'

'He's London's man. A decent one.'

'The world is full of *decent* men who get stomped into the ground every day of their lives. The last thing I need right now is a decent man.'

Carter crouched close beside her. 'You should get out of here, now.'

'Is that professional advice? Run?'

'It's the correct reaction under these circumstances.'

'No. I have business to take care of.'

'Waiting around to pay someone a million bucks?'

'You don't approve?'

'It's your money. My advice is wait someplace else.'

'You don't mean run, you mean hide. Any other suggestions?'

'Fly the kids home.'

'The children stay with me.'

27

'Then let me find a place out of the city. Somewhere rural. Enough clear ground around it for me to be effective.'

She stood. 'You're assuming I want to retain your services.'

'I don't want your money. I want my name back. My reputation. You were right, I failed. I want the truth as much as you do.'

She gathered her children in. 'And I want to make damn certain *Patrick's* name isn't dragged in the dirt. The only way I'll do that is to find the truth behind his death. I'll be frank with you, Carter, this started as anger and very real desire for vengeance. I'm not ashamed of that. What I heard from Reardon last night changed those emotions. Tempered them from burning rage to cold resolve. My children are *not* going to grow up haunted by the story of their father's brutal slaying in a Belfast drug den as if he were some low-life hood. He was an honourable man. For me, now, this is a matter of honour. That may sound anachronistic but that's how it is.'

The golden-haired girl tugged at her robe, pointing urgently. 'Mommy, look!'

She turned, seeing two men enter the Elysium grasping four pieces of luggage. 'Clean clothes, I don't believe it! Come on everyone. Carter, you're still on the payroll if you want? Will you get those bags.'

'No, ma'am.'

She glanced at him.

'I need my hands free – always.'

'This'll only take a moment.'

'A moment is all it takes.'

'What's the major qualification in your job, Carter?'

'There's only one. Readiness to step in front of whatever is meant for you.'

'Or them,' she said, indicating the children.

'That might mean losing you, Mrs Brannigan.'

'Yes.'

He nodded.

The children had reached the men already, yelling, tugging at the cases. '*They're ours! They're ours!*'

'Enough,' said Kate Brannigan sweeping them aside.

'Mrs Katherine Brannigan?' one enquired.

28

She read the offered RUC warrant card. 'Does our luggage really need a police escort, Inspector Harland?'

'You confirm these are your cases, Mrs Brannigan?'

'Confirm? I bless them. You too. They were supposed to be here last night. I have three children with not one change of clothes between them since leaving Boston yesterday. Do you have a family, Inspector?'

'I must ask you to open them in our presence, please.'

'Why?' asked Carter.

'And you are, sir . . . ?'

'Mr Carter is in my employ, Inspector.'

'I see. This does not concern you, Mr Carter.'

'I'm responsible for Mrs Brannigan's life, Inspector. I decide what concerns me.'

Harland put his warrant card back into his jacket breast pocket. 'As you wish. Mrs Brannigan, if you wouldn't mind?'

'You want the cases opened here?'

'In your suite, I think.'

'Why?'

'Just do as we say.'

'Are my bags impounded, Inspector?'

'No.'

'Are they viewed as material evidence for any investigation you're conducting?'

'I don't see that has any bearing on—'

'Inspector, before I touch those bags I want to make absolutely certain they haven't been tampered with. They've been out of my possession for the last . . . why, almost thirty-six hours!'

'As you can see the locks are unbroken.'

'Unbroken certainly but can you guarantee they haven't been unlocked?'

'Are you refusing to open your bags?'

'Are you insisting I do?'

'If you refuse, I must insist, yes. You leave me no choice.'

'Then you must have reasonable suspicion that those cases contain – what? An illegal substance? Narcotics, for example?'

'Why would you assume narcotics, ma'am?'

29

'Because I was informed my husband's murder last night may have a narcotics connection.'

'By whom? Not the police.'

'By a representative of your government, Inspector. A senior representative. Mr Alan Reardon.'

Harland hesitated. 'Mr Reardon shouldn't have raised the matter while inquiries were still in hand.'

She smiled drily, indicating the bags. 'The inquiries in hand being the ones you are holding right now, I presume? I'm an attorney, Inspector, weren't you warned? I'm perfectly willing to open those cases right here, right now, with Mr Carter as witness to the contents. However, Mr Carter is also witness to my reservations made clear to you regarding the security – the integrity – of my baggage since last in my possession. You understand all that, Inspector?'

'Just open the bags, Mrs Brannigan.'

She found keys and unlocked each case. 'Which do you want opened first?'

Harland pointed.

She complied, then lifted the lid. 'Children's clothes, as you can see.'

'Please remove some.'

She looked up at him.

'Remove the first layer, Mrs Brannigan.'

Her fingers felt the firm plastic even before she lifted the clothes out. Despite herself, despite her outrage, despite even half-expectancy, her hand reached for one of the twelve exposed, bloated, shiny white slugs.

Carter's grip on her wrist was like a serpent's strike, his face suddenly close to hers. He pulled her hand back. 'Fingerprints,' he breathed.

She looked up. 'You're going to have to do better than this, Inspector. I warned you, this material – and I claim no knowledge whatsoever of its content nor presence here – could have been planted anywhere between the Boston baggage check-in, the transfer at Heathrow and the Belfast airport luggage bay where I assume the bags have lain, probably unattended, all night.'

'And the journey by road to here,' added Carter. 'Unless you came in by chopper?'

Harland warned: 'That is a serious accusation, sir.'

'You're about to make a serious charge, aren't you?'

'Not necessarily.'

Kate stood. 'All right. Let's hear the deal. I withdraw my reward offer? Have I completely blown the *status quo*? I'm truly sorry. Go to hell!'

'Leave Northern Ireland, Mrs Brannigan. It's safer for you.'

'For me, Inspector? Or for those who sent you?'

'We're taking your luggage to the airport. Travel arrangements have been made for you and the children. Mr Carter can be included in those. I think that would be wise.'

'You can't force me to leave, Inspector. You haven't a hope of holding me on the evidence you've got – you've planted – in those bags. You'll have to prove I handled at least one of those packages to make any charge stick and Mr Carter was quick enough to stop me being foolish. It would have been just too easy for a third party to have placed them in there. You've never heard of drug smugglers planting narcotics on unwitting, innocent-looking travellers – usually a family – when their baggage is unattended? Retrieving – stealing – it later at their destination after customs? You *are* a drugs squad officer?' She sighed. 'Well, that's one scenario the courtroom will hear – even if it isn't the correct one – and I think they'll seriously consider it. You'll never get a conviction. That's if you really are prepared to go to trial? Go back and tell your people they've got the wrong woman. They'll have to try harder.'

'We're taking the cases,' growled Harland.

'I expected nothing less.'

'You'd be well advised to change your mind.'

'Goodbye, Inspector. I have some shopping to do.'

ALAN REARDON had taken the 7.10 a.m. flight out of Belfast earlier that morning, the weather turbulent, even severe.

His usual flying cold sweat would have had him limp and ragged by the time the tyres of the 737 scorched the runway at Heathrow but for the turmoil in his mind; instead he disembarked tense and driven, and, using controlled security channels, made rapidly for the secure area where the promised Downing Street Jaguar waited, engine thrumming in near silence.

The chauffeur drove him immediately to the guarded rear entrance of Admiralty House overlooking Whitehall, the old naval headquarters building from where Britain's fleet was directed at the height of the Empire. Here he followed an armed Marine escort to the dining-room and waited alone, overlooked sternly by great naval figures of the past canonized in dark oils.

'Sorry to have kept you waiting,' said the Prime Minister, entering after ten minutes had passed, hand extended. 'The latest rounds of work over there seem to be going on for ever. Not been in here before? We used this as the Cabinet room the last time work was done at Number Ten.' He smiled indicating, above the marble chimney-piece, a painting of Hercules scorning Pleasure, in the shape of two nubile females, for Virtue. 'Can you see that above a full-blown cabinet – ladies present! Still it's a relief from all this heavy naval history. Now there's someone you'd think out of place here unless you knew he doubled as diarist and secretary to the Admiralty. Recognize him? Samuel Pepys.'

Reardon looked at him. 'Any double interests *I* had in the matter of Patrick Brannigan were not through choice, Prime Minister. I have acted completely professionally in my capacity as an adviser to the Cabinet Office – reporting directly and confidentially to you.'

'Aren't you being oversensitive? I know you've not been happy with the situation but my comment wasn't barbed in any way. Reardon, you're not responsible for his death! Calm down. There was absolutely nothing in any of your reports that need cause you sleepless nights.'

'Nevertheless I wish my objection to the fact of my reports being passed to other government agencies to be made a matter of record. I was dealing with a foreign national! I will not be responsible for any consequences resulting from such distribution.'

'That sounds ominously like you're distancing yourself from Brannigan? Is it this drugs business?'

'On the contrary.'

'From me?'

'Of course not.'

32

'Reardon, you have no illusions about the ways of government, I'm certain. One does what one must when one is placed in a particular position. I value your advice and your judgement. I trust you. You don't need me to say any of that. Brannigan may be dead but I shall continue needing your commitment to the province – to our shared ideals for Ulster. I know you had developed a good – even close – relationship with Brannigan in a relatively short space of time and you're feeling his loss. That's obvious. He was the kind of man who was very easy to like. I think this entire drugs thing is nothing but an IRA smear to make their unemployed supporters – who are now going to stay that way – accept this atrocity. I've made my feelings clear to the RUC on the matter. We've also hit the media hard following the IRA's coded message accepting responsibility. Thankfully, they are co-operating. Mrs Brannigan will appreciate that, I'm certain.'

Reardon remained silent.

'You must have come all this way to say something important? I know how you suffer, flying.'

'Will you answer a very direct question, sir?'

'I hope I can?'

'Would you know of any reason why we would want Patrick Brannigan dead?'

'*We?* That's outrageous! No, of course not.'

'I don't believe the IRA killed Patrick Brannigan.'

The Prime Minister leaned back against the great mahogany dining-table and crossed his arms. 'All right, assume you are correct. Who are we looking at as an alternative? I don't mean *us*, for God's sake! INLA? UDA? One of the crazier loyalist groups? UFF? We have our choice of enemies over there, as you well know.'

'The most dangerous enemy you can have, sir, is within your own house.'

Light flared on the Prime Minister's spectacles. 'If that is an accusation, you'd better have some strong evidence to back it up.'

'No evidence. Fears. And one man's intuition. More than intuition, his experience. Also my knowledge of him.'

'Who?'

'Brannigan's bodyguard. Marcus Carter. Hear me out, please. Carter was ambushed when he disobeyed Brannigan's orders and followed him instead of going to meet Mrs Brannigan flying in from Boston.'

'I've seen the faxed RUC report. He states his attackers were an Army patrol. The RUC insist they were IRA in disguise. Surely with their sources and experience they should know?'

'Carter is a former US Special Forces major, sir. He says the men who ambushed him were trained professional soldiers. Special Forces. Probably British. Forgive me, sir – but *he* should know.'

The Prime Minister studied him carefully. 'Let's say he's correct? Let's say an SAS unit made an identification mistake. They were after someone but got the wrong man. Or the wrong vehicle? They were in a hide for hours, even days, tired, stressed . . . mistakes happen, they're not infallible as some people like to believe. It is possible. Look, Carter obviously wasn't killed – nor even badly injured, was he? The SAS can be rough. He's aggrieved. His pride is hurt. He's a former Special Forces officer. Yes? *Point?* Reardon, litigation is the most virulent disease among Americans and compensation is the medicine that cures. If there's clear proof of a mistake I authorize you to offer compensation. Within reason, of course.'

'There was *no* military nor paramilitary patrol near the area at the time: SAS, regular Army, RUC Special Support Units, nothing overt, nothing covert.'

'If you really trust Carter's judgement so much I'll have thumbscrews used and we'll see if anyone owns up.'

'You're missing the point, sir.'

'Am I? I'm often told that but I rarely am. However, please enlighten me.'

'I didn't mean to be rude. I'm just eager to establish facts.'

'No offence taken. Go on?'

'Carter told me that Brannigan had made an excuse – mild food poisoning from a meal that afternoon – and ordered him to the airport alone instead of going along as well, as originally intended. Brannigan lied. He took a cab to that bar, not the act of a sick man.'

'This wasn't in Carter's statement to the RUC.'

'He doesn't trust the authorities over there. Not under these circumstances.'

'He obviously trusts *you* – or perhaps he has reasons of his own

34

to use this route for his information?' The Prime Minister watched Reardon, closely. 'Have you any idea why he told you this?'

'He's a bodyguard. He lost Brannigan – hence his reputation. *You* must know how bodyguards feel about that happening? He wants the record set straight. He knows I have direct access to the top. To you, Prime Minister. He wants the truth. So do I. I want to draw a straight line under this before I walk away, black on white. I too feel responsible. I encouraged Patrick Brannigan's involvement in Ulster.'

'Reardon, the truth is that Brannigan exposed himself and we may *never* know why. The truth is there are no straight lines and all colours are grey in this particular world. You may have encouraged Brannigan's interest in the province – that was your job, your responsibility, and you did it very well indeed – but his involvement was all his own, right from the outset. The initial approach was his.' The Prime Minister glanced at his watch. 'I have a Cabinet very soon. I'm sorry.'

'Prime Minister, please! If Carter is right about a Special Forces unit – perhaps even our own SAS – ambushing him, then—'

'No! Stop there. Overlooking the absurdity, even the insulting nature of your speculation – not to mention the danger – just consider the facts. No one knows them better than you. The IRA wanted Brannigan – or for that matter anyone like him willing to invest in the province – dead. They don't want investment in Ulster. We do. We needed Brannigan alive. Why would we want him *dead*?'

'I don't know. That's why I'm here. I want your assurance that we are not involved. I do know the IRA would think long and hard before they killed an American. An *Irish* American? That's totally illogical or completely stupid and these days they are neither. *You* know how much money is raised for the Cause in the United States!'

'Too much. So maybe this is a case of the lesser of two evils? In a war you must expect expediency – and this *is* war. They did what they had to do to halt the setting up of a major industrial project?' The Prime Minister pushed himself firmly from the table. 'Reardon, return to Ulster, talk to Carter, get him to see the realities involved here. These accusations – if that's what they are – will get him nowhere and could cause severe damage. The last thing we need is an altercation with the United States. We've built bridges that have taken time, patience and a great deal of diplomatic skill. I don't want them undermined. You understand me? The President and I spoke in the early hours. It was not an easy conversation.' He paused, thoughtful, then looked at Reardon. 'It's important you persuade Mrs Brannigan to leave the province. We're responsible for her and her children's safety and after her outburst on television I can't guarantee that. Does she fully realize what she said? Offered? One million dollars for the heads of her husband's killers?'

'Every word. I talked to her last night. She won't leave, Prime Minister; I'm certain of that.'

'You've never married, Reardon. Women under pressure can say the most outrageous things yet the next day it's as if nothing happened. I must end this now. Contact me when you've spoken more to Carter. I'll put some fire under the Army to see if we can clear the business of this patrol that attacked him. I'm sure it'll prove to be the IRA – and if it *was* a mistake by the SAS or some other covert operational unit of ours then it was an untimely coincidence, nothing more. Carter can't blame himself – he was sent away by his employer. Whatever happened to him on that road wouldn't have made the slightest difference to the tragic outcome. He would – could – never have saved Brannigan. Make him see that. Buy him off if necessary, we don't want him talking to the media – not if he's as convincing as you say. That could open a hornets' nest. If it *was* the IRA who killed Brannigan that does them considerable damage across the Atlantic and us no harm at all. You understand me? I don't need to warn you how damaging sensationalized speculation would be for us.'

The Prime Minister took Reardon's arm, leading him out. 'From what I've learned of Brannigan he operated alone, took on areas in the world very few businessmen would touch – which of course is why he hired bodyguards like Carter wherever he went. It's a pity he didn't allow them to do their job! He liked living dangerously. Perhaps he had a death-wish?'

'No,' Reardon said, firmly.

'Carter didn't say why Brannigan went to this place Leary's?'

'If he knew he'd have been with him – wanted or not.'

'One of the tabloids had picked up – bought probably – some story about Brannigan being seen with a woman in a taxi before he arrived there. A young woman. Lies, no doubt. Anything to juice it up. I nailed the editor's hands to his desk on that one. Sex and drugs are food and drink to those people.'

'If you saw Mrs Brannigan, Prime Minister, I believe you'd have no doubts about Patrick Brannigan's fidelity.'

The Prime Minister's eyebrows lifted above his glasses. 'She's obviously made an impression on you.'

Reardon made an embarrassed, dismissive gesture.

'Three children?'

Reardon nodded.

'Tragic. Thank God they're well provided for.'

They walked in silence toward the lift.

The Prime Minister ushered Reardon inside and started their descent. He spoke quietly. 'Brannigan had reason to be in that place. It may be that reason that killed him. You're not an investigator – don't forget that – but you're the best evaluator of any situation I know. Do we understand each other?'

Reardon gave the briefest smile. 'People still express surprise you won the leadership.'

'Do they? How do you react?'

'I smile, Prime Minister.'

'So do I. Do what you can with both Carter and Mrs Brannigan. It's sensible they leave Ulster. Let me know the outcome, soon. Incidentally, why is a man of Carter's calibre working as a private bodyguard? A former major of Special Forces? I know this may sound perfidious given our standing *sensitive status* agreement with Washington on Ulster . . . but could there be any possibility of their having an interest beyond their usual awareness of the situation? I do have a reason for enquiring.'

'Carter being Washington's man? I doubt it. From what I understand he's a virtual exile now. Based in London. From what Brannigan told me he was a casualty of US foreign policy; Central American policy, to be precise.'

'There have been a few of those.'

'Carter has *views*, as Brannigan once put it, regarding Washington.'

'Hence his wariness of conspiracy, I suppose?'

'Possibly in this case, *awareness* of it?'

37

The lift shuddered, then stilled. The door opened.

'Goodbye, Reardon, safe journey. I won't come outside.'

Outside, the temperature had dropped, the chauffeur ready, smiling briskly, the Jaguar's door opened. 'Back to Heathrow, sir? What a life!'

Reardon fell into the soft hide, unresponding. *I don't believe you wanted to die, Patrick. So who gains from killing you?*

Watching from above, face set, the Prime Minister recalled the telephone call he had made in the early hours informing the White House of Brannigan's murder. Afterwards, badly shaken by the President's reaction of barely suppressed anger, he had lain awake for hours, trying to recall either the President – or Brannigan – ever mentioning they had known each other in any way that might, even loosely, be called friendship?

His memory was excellent; he was renowned for his attention to detail: the answer, he was certain, was negative.

He recalled Brannigan once, in answer to his gentle probing over dinner only one week before, half-joking, blue eyes twinkling: *I'm as conservative as you are, sir: hell, I'd ride to the right of John Wayne if he was still in the saddle.* Yet this Democrat President whose liberal stance was so open it was virtually celebrated had reacted as if he had lost – if *not* a good friend, then someone of considerable importance to him. Importance in presidential terms meant high in the pecking order and the pecking order, no matter how you viewed it, was political; overtly or otherwise.

*He blames me. For what? Negligence? Or has he suspicions of something worse?*

Bullets of ice hit the window. He fought his doubts with their hard reality. *This* is what's really happening. It's hailing and the day goes on. The early hours breed demons of doubt: their time has gone, this is now. This is real.

Still, the quiet calculated part of him that made him what he was warned: Brannigan's planned investment in Northern Ireland was chicken-feed in American business terms. Wider US investment in the province had dried up with the escalation of violence and what there was, had, in one infamous incident, cost us dearly. Brannigan was important to *us*. To *me*. I needed this show of foreign confidence desperately and nothing denotes confidence as well as good old

American dollars being waved – even if half would have been our own.

So why barely disguised presidential anger? Why – in retrospect certainly but he was sure it was not his imagination – the underlying note of suspicion in that smooth Southern voice? Politics? There *had* been the threat of intervention during the presidential election but that had been shelved with other vote-gathering hypes. Was there something going on now? Something he had been kept in the dark about by his own people? Was it really possible that Brannigan's activities were some kind of front – that he was the vanguard of a White House backed fifth column in the province? Brannigan *was* of Irish descent.

He shook his head sharply. He was becoming paranoid!

Reardon's dark question hovered ominously like the low clouds overhead. Would you know of any reason why *we* would want Patrick Brannigan dead, Prime Minister?

He saw the Jaguar drive away; the deep blue coachwork whitened with hail.

This was a man he could not ignore. If he must draw from the miasma of information that spewed out of Northern Ireland he would rely without hesitation on one objective, utterly reliable source: Alan Reardon.

He knew that no matter how strong his own position, how firm his power-base, in the darker recesses of government there were decisions made upon which he had no direct control and sometimes little, if any, knowledge. He feared the chill that seeped from the secret corners of his world – his little protection the warming constancy, though not fealty, of those closest to him – feeling the chill now as he turned from the window.

He moved to a secure telephone, hesitated over it, uncertain.

There were those in the Palace of Westminster who viewed the SAS as no more than a deadly instrument of the secret world. State executioners. He knew that in certain expedient circumstances that view was an axe-edge from the truth. Had the axe fallen on Patrick Brannigan? He could not believe it. Yet . . . ?

Would he dare throw meat for the radicals to devour, no matter how rotten, how unpalatable for his own table?

He touched the telephone but still did not lift it.

Come on! You're a pragmatist. The deed, if it *were* done, is done. Ulster is a murky world where few things are visible. If Reardon's fears and Carter's judgement are right – and the President's reaction gives every reason to believe they might well be – you have to find out why and fast.

He pushed back his glasses on his nose and lifted the telephone. If there *were* lies, he would shake his secret mandarins so hard the truth would fall out through their lying teeth.

*Truth is rarely pure and never simple*, Wilde warned him.

'T HEY MUST have found them by now,' said the soft-eyed one called Rick: a name so much a part of him now he had almost forgotten any other he once had; forgotten who he really was. This mattered little to him. There was no going back.

'Maybe they found them and ran a mile!' grinned one of the others who they knew as Max, the youngest among them but still years older than the boy soldiers crouched on Belfast's streets or ducked into armoured cars against the sniper's bullet.

Rick glowered. 'They should have called in one of their top men. Someone to take a decision. Either claim the killings were SAS or sectarian. They've done neither. They missed good propaganda.'

'You can't predict everything, Rick,' said the blond called Dave.

'The unpredictable is always the most dangerous.'

'Yes, Rick.'

'If they do nothing, there is a reason,' said the one named Arnie who one life before, because he had never quite mastered being who he was supposed to be, had finally been made a Pole. *Poles are mongrels*, the dictum had come from on high, and where they were bound was packed with mongrels. *Mongrels are readily accepted; be grateful.*

They had been right. Arnie was happier than the others: he had Sandy and the baby while Dave and Max had only their Saturday night lays who did it with anyone. And Rick?

Rick needed no one.

Arnie was worried about Sandy, he wanted this over, quickly:

wasn't certain he wanted to be part of it . . . but it was unthinkable for him to be outside the group. And once the decision was made he had no choice. Once Rick had spoken, no one had a choice.

'We take the reason from them, Rick?' he offered. 'That way we *know*, OK? You'll feel easier knowing their minds. Just let's do it, quickly.'

'*Take*, Arnie?'

'Take one of the *Irish*. Get the truth from him. What the hell!'

'We take only the money. We're not fighting the Irish.'

'Rick, if they do not report the killings, they are hunting us for sure. We butcher their people – soon we must fight them!'

'They don't know who we are. *We* don't even know who we are any more!' Rick laughed, the others joining him; Arnie too, disguising his troubled eyes.

They settled to their fishing from the rocks on the Antrim coastline where, upon the low cliff above, stood the cosy inn whose bearded proprietor had earlier welcomed his unexpected off-season sporting guests with warmth and a generous tot of Bushmills against the cold. Arriving with well-used fishing equipment bought from stalls in Belfast's Smithfield market and clothing from second-hand stores on the Dublin Road first thing that morning, they might never have been the same four men who had flown into Belfast buried in one of several football charter flights from Birmingham two days before.

Rick watched the sun flicker like gold tossed on to the water. Soon he would be free. Begin a new life somewhere. Somewhere with style where he could stand *out*; not stand back where the shadows of the ordinary concealed him in necessary mediocrity. Rick needed to shine.

*Another* new life, he reminded himself, turning away, smiling secretly; wind as chill as a winter morning's razor on his skin, pleased that the booming sound of waves crashing on the great hexagonal stepped rocks of the Causeway blanketed his thoughts from the others.

He wondered what the American woman would be like, close to? He would smell her grief: moist, pungent, like new-turned earth by a fresh grave. There had been no tears on television but he could bring them forth. Let her see her husband's fearful last moment

41

reflected in his eyes – held for ever – as his beautiful mother swore, fearfully, she could after his first killing had been accomplished at Krasnodar.

He would like to be inside her when she did. In his special way. He needed that very badly right then. It didn't have to be her. It didn't have to be a woman.

Deep down inside him, the other secret voice he kept locked away whispered: *I am the widow maker and the headhunter; fear and chaos and destruction are images of my creation and I of theirs.*

# CHAPTER THREE

DETECTIVE INSPECTOR James McAlister believed there was no
such thing as a safe house. For him house meant static, static
meant easier to find and, once found, certain death for whoever was
inside the site, including himself.

Instead, through various ingenious means, he kept his *little birds*
– he hated the IRA's derogatory *tout* for informers – constantly on the
move, always meeting them personally, allowing no one, however
insistent or senior, to perform this duty for him. He would call off
any meeting, routine or crash, mundane or critical, if he could not be
there to control it. No other business was as important as listening to
his little birds and none of his informants would have it otherwise.

McAlister listened with his heart first; his head he left for later
when the machines turned in the sound-room nestling in the heart of
Palace Barracks in Hollywood, East Belfast. There, protected from
eavesdropping by a silent outgoing electronic tide, he heard disembodied voices, listening only for content; not timbre, not tremor
disguised by bravado, not the clear quake of terror – only *words*
stripped of everything but meaning. He had heard their emotion in
various vehicles earlier.

For the ones who were not as hard as they believed and
afterwards cried in the dark with regret, McAlister was father
confessor; to frightened boys just the right side of breaking – and how
he kept them hovering there was a mystery – he was the gentle caring
mother who would soothe, scold, cajole, somehow always get them
back into the cold. He held them all in his carefully constructed cage
of promises, small deceptions, flattery, grudging admiration, controlled amounts of money and, vitally, his devout vow of salvation
when it was over and he opened the door to a new life.

Naturally, each had his own vision of this blessed release,

revealed in half-believed whispers or sharp, petty demands, until finally McAlister knew more than their secrets; he knew their dreams.

His control was total but never physical, never violent, and *never* sexual, although James McAlister was gay.

Violence he accepted as part of his world while not personally resorting to it, and, acknowledging the emotional precariousness of shared danger with frightened, dependent young men, he abandoned his sexuality the instant he slipped beside any one of his charges with his gentle opening: *How has it been, laddie?* Only thus could he close out the very real probability of hurt or, given the dire circumstances, loss. Personal vulnerabilities he reserved for his solitary private life where he could contain hurt, bear pain, heal and recover from wounds without affecting another.

Though he performed routine Special Branch duties, McAlister was primarily an agent runner: the RUC's best; a fact acknowledged at the heart of their considerable power. While his private life caused concern to his superiors they recognized that his complete awareness of his survival – necessarily more so than his fellow officers – depended on his personal actions: his care and discretion, his recognition of literally placing his life in another man's hands each time he considered a personal relationship. They were, nevertheless, grateful he lived more the life of priest than paederast.

On a lower level, where others might face ribaldry or contempt, McAlister had no such problems. Indeed, he was held in awe, not least by Danny Keegan, his Detective Sergeant, who now drove him back toward Belfast after his mobile meet on the Londonderry Road.

'It's him! You said he'd call, boss,' grinned Keegan.

McAlister took the telephone. 'What can I do for you, Major?'

'Do I have to repeat myself?' said Marcus Carter.

'Somehow the rank has not separated itself from you in my mind. Bear with me a while. In time you'll become used to it again or I'll remember you're no longer involved.'

'McAlister, I don't care if the US Navy ran you in circles around your Scottish glens; *I'm* not CIA, NSA, DIA, nor any part of their games. I'm plain Marcus Carter who just lost his employer. That's it.'

'Retained, I hope, by the widow?'

'The two Narcs you sent got that message, loud and clear.'

'I sent no one. I take it you mean our Drug Squad? Their purpose?'

'Brought Mrs Brannigan's luggage from the airport. Fully loaded. Packages of the heavy white stuff jammed in with the kiddie-clothes. If it was the real thing we could all be millionaires.'

'If?'

'Never found out. Offered a deal: next flight out, first class, hired help included. Mrs Brannigan declined. Said she'd see them in court.'

'Where are you now?'

'In the Mercedes.'

'Alone?'

'With one angry lady, three tired kids and a trunk full of new clothes. We just emptied your best department store. They kept the luggage. Nice people, your colleagues.'

'I'll say it again. I sent no one. Why the call, Major?'

'We're moving out of the city.'

'Where?'

'We don't need more harassment.'

'I'm not giving you any.' McAlister tapped Keegan's arm indicating more speed. 'We need to talk. You've checked out of the Culloden already?'

'Not yet.'

'How close are you?'

'Five minutes if we don't hit any more road blocks. You're really strangling this city today.'

'Losing Brannigan cost the government dearly. It's necessary to show others it won't happen again.'

A woman's voice snapped down the line. 'You shouldn't have let it happen the first time!'

'Mrs Brannigan? We should talk.'

'I've done my talking to the police.'

The line went silent. 'Carter? Are you still there?'

'The pressure isn't working, McAlister.'

'Carter, this is Belfast. You'd do well to stay inside the fortress – if you take my meaning. It's a war zone beyond.'

45

'I know about war zones.'

'Not this one. I'll be at the Culloden as soon as I can. Don't leave.'

The line went dead.

Keegan frowned. 'What was all that about, boss?'

'Someone's playing games on our patch.'

'Provos?'

McAlister shook his head tentatively. 'They didn't hit Brannigan.'

'The little birdie told you that today? They've figured out it's going to cost them too much in the collection plate over the water! Republican trash, boss, you can't believe one fuckin' word.'

'Insult your enemy, Danny, and there's no honour in engaging him.'

'There's no *honour* in those Provie bastards!'

'There is in us. That's the point of all this.'

Keegan murmured an obscenity and lit a cigarette. 'So *what* then? What did the little bugger say?'

McAlister watched the highway ahead, silent.

'When you decide, boss, you tell me all about it, OK?' Keegan muttered.

McAlister said, quietly, 'Was Brannigan careless, crooked or just stupid? Or something we proles haven't got brains enough to be consulted on?'

'Politics, boss? There's too many bodies left lying on that road,' Keegan warned.

'I know. The Culloden, Danny, fast as you can.'

'Mrs brannigan, you had a telephone call from the United States. The gentleman insisted we had you call back as soon as you returned.' The Culloden receptionist handed over a message slip with the suite key. 'He said to tell you it was urgent.'

She read the slip and turned to Carter. 'I've never heard of any Eugene Parriss?'

'Business associate?'

'Patrick never brought work, nor business colleagues, home. He always took business calls in his study – *strict* rule – so I never got familiar with names. Our Vermont home was a complete escape for him and he kept it that way. That's over now. I'm going to have to find out about everything – fast. I'll call Parriss right away.'

The duty manager came over. 'I've had to keep the press out, Mrs Brannigan. They were becoming a nuisance to other guests.'

'Good. I've said all I want to say.'

'A package was delivered for you. It's in your suite.'

She nodded. 'I'm expecting store deliveries.'

'This came by cab. If there's anything more we can do—?'

'You've all been very kind. Everything's just fine. I can dial the US direct from my suite?'

'Of course.'

'Would you have someone bring my shopping from the car?'

'Right away.'

Carter said: 'I want to check that delivery.'

She saw his look. 'What?'

'You took on the best-organized terrorist group in the world last night, live on TV.'

She blinked. 'I hadn't thought of it that way.'

'I'm thinking for you. That's my job.'

She breathed. 'I should let you do it.' She gathered in her children. In the suite, she flopped against the bunched pillows of the vast double bed, lifted the telephone and dialled, long legs stretched out, the children sprawled around her, exhausted by all that had happened. In three days her life had been changed for ever.

'Mr Eugene Parriss? Katherine Brannigan. You called me?'

Through the opened bedroom door she could see Carter sitting at an antique desk carefully untying string around a large package.

'Thank you for calling back so promptly,' said a deep, New England voice.

'Your message said urgent, Mr Parriss. I have no idea who you are. Please tell me what this is about?'

'You're in a dangerous and vulnerable position. It's vital you are fully informed of your circumstances. And your options. This can't be done on the telephone. Other arrangements are being made.'

'What are you talking about?'

'Your offer of a reward has endangered your life and the lives of your children. Under the circumstances we accept responsibility for protecting your lives but we cannot under existing arrangements cover one million dollars.'

She moved the telephone to her other ear and tugged the smallest child back from the edge of the bed. 'Insurance? Patrick took out special cover for Northern Ireland? Mr Parriss, I'm not expecting you or anyone else to pay. This is personal. And this is hardly the time to discuss other arrangements!'

She could see Carter had disposed of the string from the box and now had his fingers under the flap, slowly easing up the sealing tape. He thinks it's a bomb, she thought, and felt momentary panic, but knew he would not try opening it in the suite if he had serious doubts.

'Mrs Brannigan, you don't have personal funds to cover that amount,' Parriss said, in her ear.

'I'm sorry?' she said, detachedly.

'You don't have the funds. I know your current financial position to the last cent.'

'That's absurd. I don't understand? Just *who* are you?'

'You should move from the hotel right away.'

She snapped: 'Now *wait*, damn you!'

Carter had stripped away the wrapping and was working on the box-top directly and very cautiously. He glanced up at her.

'My husband—'

'Your husband conducted business on our behalf many times. I'm afraid all is not as it may have seemed. You must come to terms with this, your safety depends on it.'

The box-top was opened, Carter standing directly above it, staring into whatever lay inside. He closed the flaps, looked at her, his face a mask.

'*Who* are you! Is this some sick joke?' she snapped into the telephone.

'Mrs Brannigan, better this conversation is not continued on the telephone. As I said, other arrangements are being made.'

'Damn other arrangements, you talk to me *now*.'

'You've made yourself too vulnerable.'

'I'm protected,' she retorted.

'You have more enemies right now than one man can deal with – no matter how efficient. You have your three children's lives to consider. Can Carter protect you all?'

She looked at Carter, perplexed.

Parriss said: 'Is he there now?'

'Yes.'

'Call him.'

She signalled Carter closer, pulling him to the telephone, his face almost touching hers. 'He's here. Right by me.'

'Your husband had a metal shell attaché case. Is that there?'

'In the closet?'

'Have Carter open it and use the equipment inside. He knows how. The opening combination is your youngest child's birthday. Tell him.'

She recited the numbers flatly to Carter who wrote rapidly on the bedside notepad: *Agree – whatever he says.*

She shook her head, obstinately.

'You've no choice,' he told her, flatly.

Parriss ordered: 'Hang up the phone, Mrs Brannigan. When Carter is ready have him call my number using the device in the case.'

Carter had the case open on the dresser. 'Call the desk and have your account made up. Do it now. Then get the kids ready.'

She still held the purring receiver, stunned. 'Why?'

'Your husband didn't just tell lies; he lived one.'

'Oh, God, it *is* drugs.'

'You want me to keep you alive? Don't ask questions. Not now.'

'*Carter!*'

He took a travelled Samsonite from the closet, tossed everything belonging to Patrick Brannigan inside, and snapped the locks shut. 'Move!'

She gathered the drowsy children to her, not moving. *'Patrick! What have you done?'* she murmured.

Carter said: 'Don't break now. You haven't the time.'

'Go to hell! Just leave us alone.'

'I can't do that.' He pulled her away from the children and out of the room, locking the door behind, took her to the package he had opened, holding her over it, his hand clamping instantly over

49

her mouth – turning her shriek into a strangled wide-eyed moan of terror.

'You asked for heads,' he reminded her; his lips jammed to her ear as she writhed under his grip, away from the dead, upturned faces. 'They want one million dollars or three heads in exchange.' He swung her around to face the bedroom door. 'Yours and two of theirs. You can choose which.'

She bit his hand and shrieked.

He turned her fast and jabbed her soft middle, dropping her gasping to her knees, then crouched beside her as she fought for air, speaking quickly, close to her ear. 'I'll keep you alive. I'll do that even if it costs my life. But you have to do what I say when I say it. Do you understand? You have the brains and you think you're a tough woman who can handle anything but you have no conception of what some men are capable of. I'm capable of doing everything they've done and everything they'll *do* if they take you. And I'm capable of stopping all of it. But it has to be my way. *Do you understand?*'

She nodded, eyes streaming mascara. 'You bastard,' she gasped.

'That's why I'm the best chance you have.' He sighed. 'You can't offer a million dollars and hope to walk away.'

He released her.

She lay on the carpet feeling its texture beneath her wet cheek, feeling humiliation, pain, anger, but mostly terror; through it all hearing Reardon's warning of the night before: *You've made this a far more dangerous place than it is already.*

She had brought this on herself and her children and now all their lives were in Carter's hands. She hated giving up so much, unequivocally, to another person. How much more *could* she give than complete trust to a virtual stranger? She felt naked in her fear. She pushed herself away from him. 'I'll do whatever you say. Just get those *things* out of here.'

'We leave those for the police.' He stood over her. 'I have to call Parriss.'

'Who is he, Carter?'

'Who do you think is powerful enough to have people snagged in a web like this? Who *uses* people in foreign countries – sometimes without them knowing it? Langley. The CIA.'

She stared at him, aghast. 'I don't believe it.'

50

'You will.'

Banging came from the bedroom door. She rushed to unlock it and grasped the child standing inside.

'Why are you crying, Mommy?' asked the golden-haired girl, from the bed.

'I'm crying for Daddy, sweetheart.'

The child moved and clutched Carter's hand. 'Daddy's dead,' she told him.

He rested his hand on the golden curls. 'I know.'

Kate Brannigan looked up at him, bleakly: 'Parriss said there's no money. I don't know whether to believe him.'

'Believe him.'

'If it's true, I can't pay you.'

'This is nothing to do with money any more.'

She looked at the box. 'Tell them that.'

R EARDON SAW McAlister and Keegan exiting the Culloden's security hut just as Ellis drove him into the car park from meeting British Airways' weather-delayed London shuttle.

'Catch them before they leave!' ordered Reardon.

Ellis punched the horn twice and swung toward the two Special Branch detectives.

Reardon dropped a rear window. 'I want to talk, Inspector. Get in out of the rain. Only you, please.'

Keegan shifted the weight of the box he carried. 'I'll dump this in the car, boss.'

McAlister peered in at Reardon. 'Are you all right, sir? You look ill.'

'Bad flight. It's always a bad flight for me. Ellis, go get yourself a damn drink or something.'

'I'll be right outside, sir. In the rain but out of earshot of course.' Ellis grinned.

'Cheeky bugger sometimes,' murmured Reardon as McAlister climbed beside him into the Rover's rear. 'Over-trained and over-confident.'

'But over here, thank God. They're about all we've got that still makes the Provos tremble. Used to be different before they learned how to manipulate the media. Now we walk on eggshells: RUC, UDR, Army, everyone. That's maintaining law and order in Ulster for you.'

'Everyone except the SAS, perhaps?'

'Marcus Carter still on your mind, sir?' McAlister leaned back against leather. 'How was London? Or is that indiscreet?'

Reardon watched Keegan unlock the boot of a weather-beaten grey Ford. 'Looks as if you've been travelling.'

'Around and about.'

'Anything to tell me?'

McAlister pointed. 'That box he's just put in was left for us by our American friend.'

'Brannigan!'

'Carter.'

'He's gone? With or without Mrs Brannigan?'

'All of them. The family.'

'Where?'

'No idea.'

'Why so suddenly?'

'You recall Mrs Brannigan's words on television? I mean her precise words?'

'I was right beside her. A million dollars for the heads of—'

McAlister nodded toward Ford. 'Literally executed. In both senses.'

Reardon turned, disbelieving.

'Don't jump to conclusions about Carter, sir. He simply left the box. Looked inside of course. Left a message telling me his prints were all over the packing and warned *me* not to jump to conclusions.' McAlister reached into the silk lining of his hand-tailored jacket and took out a transparent evidence bag containing one sheet of paper with large uneven print sprawled across it. 'No envelope used, so they didn't lick anything. I'd say they know what forensic science can do these days. The Provos are very up on that. Part of their training. What *not* to do.'

'This is the IRA's work?'

McAlister might not have heard. 'Cut and paste typescript;

from a magazine in this case, not newsprint. There'll be no finger-prints.' He read, flatly: ' "One million US dollars or we claim in kind. Three heads. Yours and two children. You choose." Calculatedly ambiguous, that last part. Choosing to pay or survive? Or choosing who survives? She does have *three* children?'

Reardon snapped: 'She's already stated she's willing to pay. That's an unnecessary, inhuman, threat!'

McAlister wiped condensation from the window and peered out. 'Do you feel any better, sir?'

'I did before reading this. They can't mean it?'

'Rain's stopped. Better come with me.' McAlister got out of the car, led Reardon over to the Sierra, opened the boot and lifted the flaps of the box. '*That's* inhuman. They mean it all right.'

Reardon backed away from the three distorted faces pressed against thick polythene; a zipper closed across them like a shared diagonal scar. No terror nor rictus; eyes closed, relaxed; they might have been sleeping or dreaming still – not disembodied heads – and more terrible for this.

McAlister ducked into the Ford and came back with a silver hip-flask. 'Brandy. Drink some.'

Reardon swallowed, then wiped his hand across his mouth. 'Dear God.'

McAlister said: 'They've made her face the hardest of all possible choices for any mother. Which of her children should survive? If she had second thoughts about paying the reward – or if pressure was put on her to reconsider – their threat stopped all that dead. The heads are as much proof of intent as of the deed.'

Reardon leaned against the car; sweat beaded on his brow. 'What the bloody hell is going on, Inspector?'

'I can only tell you what I've been told – and that does *not* mean it is the gospel according to Sinn Fein, or the Northern Command, or Dublin, or whichever section of the IRA is playing the strong-man this week. My informants are good, they serve their purpose, they save lives but they're not at the *heart* of things. The boy I met today – like all of them – is just a scared little bird in a very big cage. If you want something political, something from someone close to the top, you need to ask *them*. Box 500 to us, MI5 in your language. They'd deny all knowledge of owning such an asset, of course. Even to you,

53

sir. They tend to write their own rules. But you're Whitehall: you know that already.'

'Not that side of the street,' Reardon said, badly needing a cigarette. He decided two of his daily ration were left, took one and proffered the case.

McAlister shook his head. 'Only as company for my little birds.'

Reardon said: 'Let's walk.'

They passed through the security gate and on to the lush grass sweeping down past their eyeline to the Lough below.

Reardon said: 'So tell me what you heard today?'

A sudden gust whipped them and McAlister brushed a sprinkling of cigarette ash from his overcoat. 'It wasn't IRA nor the mad dogs of INLA that killed Brannigan. That's the word for what it's worth. My source is usually accurate. Neither are officially denying it, which isn't unusual; they'll usually accept responsiblity even by default. Any media mention will do. What *is* strange is that there's rumour of manic anger at the top over the murder. Tout-fever seems to have taken hold too. Although I don't see any direct connection between that and the murder – bar the synchronicity of the events? Why start a hunt for informers when it's something you didn't do? I've some nervous ears listening out. I want to know what's going on but I'm not pressing. I'm not prepared to jeopardize positions – maybe even lives – for this.'

Reardon shuddered. 'How do they keep it up? Informers? My insides couldn't take it.'

McAlister answered without humour. 'I keep them supplied with the right pills. Too many visits to the lavatory is something the Provos watch for.'

They walked on in silence.

Reardon said: 'If it *wasn't* the IRA, that eliminates drugs, doesn't it? That was their supposed motive given by the caller, after all? If their involvement in Brannigan's murder was a lie then by implication any involvement he may have had in drug dealing was also. So do the IRA know who killed Brannigan? And perhaps what is more important, now, *why*?'

McAlister turned in mock surprise. 'Know? No one *knows* anything here! Not even priests hearing confession. My own confessor will vouch for that. Even the truth here can be a lie – if government policy dictates it be so. What few understand across the water is that, here, truth is negotiable. You must excuse my cynicism, sir, it develops naturally alongside sore knees from crawling under cars, cricked necks from checking house-callers from windows and recurring night-sweats – none of which count as grounds for additional pension rights.'

'I accept it must be hell.'

'Hell is eternal. Here you know you're on limited time.'

'You're Roman Catholic? Must be difficult for you? Here? Your job?'

'It doesn't make me lose sight of anything, if that's what you mean?'

'Not at all. I simply meant—'

'I know.' McAlister stopped, folded his arms and gazed at the opposite shoreline. 'It works for me sometimes – with the little birds. They miss going to the priest, you see. They can't, can they – with some of their sins? The leadership is Marxist of course so God is as dangerous for them as the British. Perhaps more so? The lads find that difficult to handle – being brought up with Him and the Holy Virgin virtually as part of the family – the icons right up there with the family photographs. It amazes me sometimes how easy it is to get them talking until I remember why – then it's not surprising at all. I'm just proxy confessor.'

Reardon let the silence between them hang, then, walking on, reminded him: '*Do* they know who killed Brannigan?'

McAlister sighed. 'The Provos? They think it's *us*. The question is us here or us over *there* – if you see my distinction?'

'You mean London?'

'And all its works.'

'You know something else, McAlister. Out with it.'

McAlister shook his head. 'Supposition. Worse, dangerous supposition. Detectives are meant to work only with the available facts.'

'I'm not about to haul you to London in chains, if that's what you fear?'

McAlister smiled. 'No.'

'Well?'

'Carter telephoned me, told me Mrs Brannigan had her luggage

55

brought to her from the airport by two RUC Drug Squad officers who insisted she open the cases in front of them.'

'This was last night?'

'This morning.'

'I don't understand? Her baggage was to be taken immediately to the Culloden. I ordered direct clearance as soon as I arrived at the airport. I was quite specific: no formalities. My task was difficult enough already.'

'It turned up today. Carter called me.' McAlister stopped and faced Reardon. 'One case contained packs of white powder. If cocaine or heroin, enough to make us both millionaires, he said, and I believed him.'

Reardon suddenly seemed defeated. 'She asked about her luggage when we got here last night. I said it was on its way. Naturally I assumed her concern was normal. *Damn!* She's been arrested?'

'You're forgetting she left with Carter – barely an hour ago. No, she's not on bail.'

Reardon gave him a hard look. 'The RUC doesn't leave million-dollar drug traffickers running free. What's going on?'

'Do you see her as a drug smuggler, sir? Or her husband?'

'I'm an adviser on whether to give foreigners British taxpayers' money. Not a bloody detective.'

'Were you sent back with orders to detect?' enquired McAlister, measuredly.

A cold blast blew off the Lough. Reardon thrust his hands into his overcoat pocket and began walking again. 'Come on!'

McAlister followed. 'No one from our Drug Squad paid a call on Mrs Brannigan. They have no interest in her or her luggage. The officers were bogus. I'll leave you to consider who they might be. They took all the luggage away – drugs too, if that's what the bags really contained.'

Reardon felt queasy and wondered if he should have refused McAlister's brandy; there was nothing but bile in his stomach after the flight. He was certain now he had an ulcer.

He passed a handkerchief over his clammy face. 'The *quid pro quo*, Inspector? Obviously they were there to do more than frighten her?'

'The deal was, take the next plane out and charges would be dropped.'

Reardon stopped dead, as if he had walked into a wall. 'You're not treading on eggshells any more, McAlister. Broken glass. You understand me?'

'Perfectly.'

Reardon nodded curtly, embarrassed by his vehemence.

'Do I voice any of this conversation . . . upward, sir?'

'Not until I've taken advice. Can you manage that?'

'I'll do my best but I can't delay too long.'

'I know. How public will the contents of that box become? Difficult surely to keep a triple killing quiet? There are bodies belonging to those heads out there somewhere – surely it won't be long before they're discovered?'

'The thought has struck me. I think because of the Brannigan background any investigation will be kept very tight. No press releases. Not yet, certainly. Forensic investigations take time and we have to establish identification. The main problem is we'll need to interview Carter and Mrs Brannigan. If they've gone to ground somewhere and we instigate a search the media might become aware. You could use your connections to pull a complete blackout over everything connected with the Brannigan murder?'

'I said: I'll take advice. I need a little time. Not much. Any idea who they might be?'

'The heads? We'll find out. There's few slip our net in this city.'

'I assume this sudden disappearance of Carter and the family means the reward is still going to be paid? She was prepared to pay for revenge, she'll certainly pay to protect her children. Perhaps it's been paid already? Were there any instructions for payment?'

'Not that Carter let us see. Couldn't have been paid today though. Carter said they'd been shopping all day, replacing the luggage. The box wasn't handed to them until their return around four. Too late for the banks – even if any were prepared for such an extraordinary demand. The equivalent of a million dollars, cash?' McAlister nodded at lights flickering now on the opposite shoreline. 'I'd say our headhunters are waiting, somewhere out there.'

Reardon drew himself up. 'The Prime Minister asked me to persuade Mrs Brannigan to leave Northern Ireland.'

'She's been offered that option already, sir,' reminded McAlister, steadily. 'I assume there's no connection?'

'Of course not! I gave him Carter's views regarding his attackers. And voiced my own fears. He accepts the circumstances warrant an inquiry. Damn it, McAlister, *whatever* else may be involved here she *is* safer out of the province. Hasn't the butchery we witnessed today proven that?'

McAlister grasped his arm, turning Reardon. 'With her gone it'll be over. You know that?'

'I don't think so. I don't think the truth here is *negotiable*.' Reardon shook himself free and stalked away, heavy shoulders hunched. 'Not if I have anything to do with it,' he called back.

*How much longer will that be?* McAlister bit back the words.

'Give your contact number to Ellis,' Reardon called. 'I'll phone you.'

McAlister watched him enter the hotel. Why is it so important to you? he asked silently. All this for an American you could hardly have known? Was his betrayal yours also? Were you the tool used to cut him down and you've felt the cold from a murderous hand on you? You've been used? Is that it?

He cursed himself. Come on, *march*, don't debate the issue; act – before that poor bastard lines himself up for a place behind Brannigan.

He walked briskly back to the car park.

# CHAPTER FOUR

————•✦•—✦•—————

T HEY WERE close to the border, the troubled lights of Belfast far behind, the darkness of the countryside complete. Here the long battle was engaged in silence and discomfort with weapons which an earlier generation from either side would have considered impossible. On the ground night had become day and a bullet's course as true as the laser pinpoint of red fixed on its victim's heart. Above, as constant as the stars, machines equipped with infra-red eyes hunted the heat-signature of terror: the glow from a weapons cache, the trail of a crawling man, the pool around men in hiding, the consuming heat of corruption – from the fox on the wire to the tortured final resting place of the traitor.

As he drove, Carter saw none of this but knew and believed all because he had served, hard, on the proving grounds of the technology.

He drove fast but defensively, aware that this close to the fortified border town of Newry roadblocks and foot-patrols halted traffic without warning and failure to stop could mean bullets through the rear of the Mercedes where the three children lay sleeping.

Before leaving the Culloden, he had called Eugene Parriss back as ordered, using the device in Patrick Brannigan's attaché case. *They're expecting her*, Parriss had said through the electronic warbling, giving an address over the border near Newry. *Get her there, Carter, safely. She needs us.*

And you need her, Carter thought. 'Soon be at the border,' he murmured to Kate Brannigan who lay back in the reclined seat beside him.

She had shut herself off throughout the journey, her mind in turmoil, wanting him to swing the Mercedes around and head back for the airport and the flight to the one place she felt safe, felt secure:

their Vermont home. Except it was no longer secure: after Parriss's call nothing was secure any more. She had never felt so stripped in her life, everything dissolving around her and she powerless to stop it. She knew it was futile to run, worse, it meant certain defeat and she could not afford to lose. She must fight; face the facts whatever they were, Carter had some of the answers and she knew she must use him, ruthlessly.

'What are we here for?' she asked, wearily.

'They want something. They always want something.'

She straightened the seat and faced him. 'If Parriss *is* CIA – what are they doing here? How was Patrick involved?'

'He was either CIA all along or they sucked him in for this. Doesn't matter which. He was part of an operation they had running here in Northern Ireland. A vital part. He wouldn't have been killed otherwise.'

'I'd have *known*.'

'You wouldn't. Not unless he wanted you to.'

'I feel used.'

'I know.'

'But this is British territory. Our allies?'

'You don't have to be an enemy to get CIA attention. Langley's had a watching brief in Ulster for years.' He glanced at her. 'But this is something more. They want something from *you*. Maybe something your husband didn't do – or was stopped from doing? I can't see any other reason why Parriss called. Why he gave you the truth so hard after what you've suffered. Except breaking you down to put you together again – their way. They can do that. I've seen them do it.'

'Me? I can't even see *Patrick's* role in this!'

'He may have been more but I'd guess he was a fixer. The CIA does more than simply spy on target countries – they play the political game, cover the whole field: government, opposition, revolutionary underground movements, anything likely to break through or cause trouble, politically. Ideology doesn't matter – *presence* does. Theirs. That's how they become powerful. Power they exercise ruthlessly when necessary. Langley makes and breaks leaders and regimes. Where did your husband operate? Central America, the Middle East? To be effective they need legitimate cover and they need it to be credible. You need me to spell it out? Everything points

60

to his business interests having CIA funding. Possibly total control. Investment right through to profits. If Langley's got a stranglehold on your purse-strings, they hooked him years ago.' He turned. 'You've been living Langley's dream.'

She stared past the sweep of the windscreen wipers at the wet night. 'I just woke up. I called my bankers before we left. There's a legal problem over what constitutes company assets.'

'Suddenly they include just about everything?'

'Even our Vermont home. It's going to take a fight to get enough even to live on. How can they do this to people?' She closed her eyes. *Oh, Patrick.*

'There would have been a special reservoir account set up somewhere – regularly topped up – to finance your lifestyle . . . and shell companies for the various deals. Everything had to look legitimate – *was* legitimate – but the big money was always Langley's and they'd have made damn sure whatever it was spent on ended up as theirs. Your husband probably made profits on top – he was an operator, that was obvious – but the real money and the properties were never his. He only had *use of* for the duration and Langley just called time. That's how I'd read it.'

She shook her head incredulously. 'I never questioned any of it. Patrick lulled me into trusting everything he did. Everything that happened. The success, the expectation of more, the security. I never once asked how much money there was. I just spent it. Jesus, I was a *fool!*'

She felt panic rise, the prospect of raising three small children with no husband and fragile security suddenly terrifying. She forced it down. She would do anything to protect her own; to safeguard their future. Whatever the CIA wanted from her – however dark – if it offered security, she would co-operate without hesitation. 'Damn you, Patrick,' she murmured.

Carter said: 'Don't hate him. Whatever his reasons, he was doing his job. A job that got him killed.'

'I don't hate him! I just don't understand why he – *goddamnit* why did he have to lie? For so long? Couldn't he just tell me the truth? He made me live the lie – the lifestyle – like some brainless bimbo. *Shit!*' She turned quickly to check her children. 'It's all right, sweetheart,' she soothed the youngest. 'Go back to sleep.'

Carter said, quietly: 'Arabs and Latinos expect a millionaire to have all the trappings: cars, house, beautiful wife.' He saw her face. 'Just telling you how *they* see it.'

She laid her head back, silent again. After a while she asked: 'What turns an educated man into someone prepared to sacrifice his life for money?'

He smiled. 'Are you still talking about your husband?'

'I'm talking about you.'

'What did your husband say?'

'Not much. You were West Point, had enough decorations for a Christmas tree, didn't seem to own a thing and didn't care.'

'That's it?'

'He trusted you with his life.'

'That's all that matters. The rest is irrelevant.'

'For Patrick, perhaps. I'm a woman. A mother. I want to know what drives the person in whose hands I'm placing the lives of my family. What happened?'

'I need to live, just like everyone else.'

'You're not like everyone else, though, are you? Don't misunder-stand me; I'm grateful for that. Grateful to have you here right now. But there's more reason for your being here than simply putting food in your belly? You know so much background to all this? Maybe you're doing what Patrick did? Lying to me?' She turned, gripped his arm, the lean muscle astonishingly hard beneath her fingers. 'I need to know who is real. *Are* you part of all this?'

'I know their world. Special Forces duties put you on the fringe of it. I know what they're capable of.' He glanced sharply at her. 'Be grateful for that. You've got too many enemies right now. Keep your friends close.'

'Are you my friend, Marcus?'

Now he looked at her. 'I'm better than your friend. I'm your enemy's enemy.' He shrugged as if tired of explanations. 'You want reasons for me ending up being a bullet catcher? Sometimes Washing-ton's policies are wrong; sometimes the military fouls up implement-ing them and someone gets canned, OK? Read the papers, it happens all the time.' He turned back to the windscreen.

After a moment she said: 'You left that box for McAlister – why

62

hasn't he called? Here – in the car? He really *is* police. He *must* want answers.'

'McAlister doesn't have the right questions – yet. I've given him enough to make him think. Make him doubt. He'll worry at it and maybe come up with answers. What he'll be allowed to do then . . . is another matter. Anyway, it suits McAlister to let us disappear. You're bad news, bad publicity – bad *business* for people like him. You just hyperinflated the information market.' He tapped the car phone. 'Switched off. Don't use it unless there's no other way. The easiest form of communication to intercept. Don't give them the gift of knowing where we are – let them work for it.'

'Them? The ones who brought my luggage? You think they're following us?' She turned quickly to the stream of headlights behind.

'If it *is* the Brits—' He looked upward. 'Their eyes and ears are up there. Choppers packed with electronics that would give you nightmares. You thought *Blade Runner* was only a movie?'

'They could be watching us *now*?'

'Now. That's Newry ahead. The border. After that they're blind.'

NEWRY HAD great holes exploded out of its body leaving raw brick wounds with dusty-red rubble flowing down to wasteland, each bound in wooden fencing and razor wire – a temporary measure as permanent as the continuing savage battle.

The pre-border checkpoint had another fence, this alien, even satanic: dark, tall and deep, constructed from steel and reinforced concrete, with sensors and cameras and bomb-proofed observation positions jutting like cancers. Behind, like some bizarre aviary, caged above in steel netting against mortar attack, was where the serious business of security continued, unceasingly, night and day.

Outside, checking vehicles, exposed and vulnerable, youthful soldiers in combat camouflage and seasoned RUC men ballooned in body-armour moved apprehensively: alert, weapons readied, circling, side-stepping, turning as if performing some practised but lethal dance, keeping their backs to whatever protection was offered, their eyes never stilled, readied constantly for any movement or action which would ignite the next round of violence.

Carter let their lights shine on him, let their hidden cameras photograph him and the car, let their computer file the Mercedes' registration before he was waved through to a landscape that might have been created by Orwell or Wells in darker moments.

'It's terrifying,' Kate whispered. 'I never realized.'

'You don't until you're here,' Carter murmured and drove on.

They circled a man-made hill where trundling heavy machinery continued constructing whatever lay beneath, despite the hour, rain and death threats to their operators; where a steep-sided narrow road climbed, bearing dire warnings and razor wire and other, unseen, lethal deterrents to even the most fanatical bomber; where towering lighting pylons flared like star shells over a Great War entrenched command position before the hidden enemy burst into view.

*Except they never do,* thought Carter. This war is fought in befouled ditches and savage streets and defeated terraced houses with convenient upper windows and back exits to more of the same. And the face of the enemy is a defiant scowl; or lying in a road, field or ditch, open eyed to the interminable rain.

The Mercedes bumped as the road surface deteriorated.

'Welcome to Eire,' Carter said, seeing the Carrickdale Hotel coming up to his left, and high and behind to his right, a blink of light from the final British Army border observation post as a helicopter circled to touch down.

R ICK COULD be anyone he wanted.
Now he was an American: the studious type with the glint of spectacles and a diffident smile welcoming you to his lies.

The boy soldier at the Newry checkpoint stood no chance.

'Are you entering the Republic, sir?'

'You bet.'

'Tourist?'

'Sure. Digging up old bones.'

'Sir?'

'Ancestors. Do you realize how many US presidents come from Irish stock? I mean *both* sides of the border? Over one dozen! Can you believe that? Saw the Ulysses S. Grant homestead yesterday up by Dungannon. Day before we did Chester Alan Arthur – Culleybacky? We'll take in Andrew Jackson on the way home. My partner and I, we're having a really great time.'

The soldier ducked his head to view the good-looking blond beside him in the car, grinned. 'Have a good trip.'

'You bet. Stay safe now!'

Dave closed his eyes.

Rick smiled.

CARTER SLOWED and took the turn-off he needed. Kate watched the road in silence, leaning away from him; her depression deepened by the sight of the grotesque armed encampment. She rested her face on the cold glass, rain beating uselessly against her cheek like tears she refused to shed. She felt alone, desperate. 'What are we going to do?'

'We listen to what they have to say.'

She turned, fear in her voice. 'There are killers out there waiting for money I don't have!'

'No one is going to harm you.' He glanced backward at the children. 'None of you. Trust me.'

'I trusted a man for seven years. Trusted him enough to bear him three children. It takes his dying to show me that I only knew half of him. Which half? The *real* Patrick Brannigan or the façade that made the rest work convincingly?'

'Let it be.'

She blinked sudden tears away. *I don't hate you, Patrick, but you've hurt me enough to blunt the pain of losing you a little. Is that your gift to me? Was that why you never even hinted that there was this other life? That someday Parriss would have to call as he did today?*

She had once seen herself so clearly but barely recognized the gullible, dependent, used woman she now was: everything she had despised, even pitied, she had become. She felt ashamed and angry. She must get back her steel. For herself, her children, for Carter. And the CIA: whatever their plans for her.

Carter swung the long blunt nose of the Mercedes between thick stone columns bearing opened, railinged gates then continued up a long drive deep in long-dead leaves.

'This isn't what it seems,' he said, not looking at her.

'You've been here before!'

'I took him wherever he ordered.'

'What are you hiding?'

'I'm preparing you.'

'For what? What's in there? *Carter?*'

Carter halted the car before a rambling, run-down house. A glow appeared in strangling ivy above the arched stone porch. An ancient studded wooden door opened and a flame-haired, beautiful woman moved under the light, smiling slightly, caught there as if by Titian.

Kate felt sick. 'Another of Patrick's secrets?'

'She's not what I thought she was,' Carter said. 'Be grateful for that.'

'God damn you, Carter!' she whispered.

She looked directly at the woman. If he spent time alone with *you* I don't even want to think about it, she thought despairingly.

Carter got out and opened the door for her.

'I'm Hannah Armitage. Whatever Carter may have told you is wrong.'

Kate smiled bitterly. 'In that case that makes you what I think you are.'

Carter said: 'I told Mrs Brannigan this probably wasn't what it seemed. What I thought it was.'

Armitage grimaced. 'I'd better get some damage limitation working quickly, then? Kate, Patrick needed cover to visit me. I ran him.'

'I can believe that.'

The heavy red hair swirled as it was tossed aside impatiently. 'You're not listening, Kate. Damp those emotions down and hear me out. You can handle this.'

66

'I don't want to hear!'

'You have to.'

'God *damn* you people! Couldn't you leave me with *one* illusion intact?'

'Kate, I'm not going to let you believe Patrick's death was anything less than honourable. We're here to do a job. You can't know how vital that is. Patrick risked his life every minute he was here. He was scared sick most of the time – even if he didn't show it. If it would have helped him I damn well would have bedded him – but that never came up, OK? I can't prove it to you so you'll just have to take my word.'

'What was he doing?'

'That's better. Come inside and we'll talk this right through.'

Inside, a plump, dark girl, wearing denims and a top that hung loosely over her large breasts, smiled broadly from a doorway off the dark panelled hallway. 'Hi!'

Armitage said: 'This is Brenda. She'll have the children bewitched in minutes.'

'The children stay with me,' said Kate.

'Kate, they're exhausted! So are you. I promise you they'll be completely cared for and loved.'

'Care and love I can give them. I want them protected. I'll hold you responsible.'

'I believe you.' Armitage glanced at Brenda who went outside to the Mercedes.

'Fire's in there,' Armitage pointed. 'You both look as if you need warming. Kate, *food*, you have to eat!'

They entered a heavy-beamed low-ceilinged room furnished with deep overstuffed settees and armchairs grouped around a vast blazing fireplace. Armitage indicated a heavy Elizabethan sideboard laden with dishes.

Kate shook her head, tightly.

'Later then. You'd better meet Henry.'

A man arose from behind an armchair facing the fire, hand already extended, hair sleek, swept back hard and bound into a small tight pony-tail. 'Henry Melsham.'

'Henry's my agent. I'm a writer.' Armitage smiled. 'It makes

67

movement – and enquiries – easy, Kate. People rarely question the motives or the curiosity of a writer. The Irish less than anyone.'

'And it makes installing electronic communications a breeze,' added Melsham. 'She has to have direct comms out to anywhere in the world. Research never stops, does it, Hannah?' Melsham grinned. 'We have a satellite dish out there on the lawn? Might as well be a sundial for the attention it gets from locals. Great location, this. And *old*. Jesus! Rented. I park my car Stateside for what we pay for this place!'

Kate glared. 'Is there anything – *anyone* – in all this who really *is* what they seem to be? How did Patrick get involved in this – charade?'

'It's no charade, Kate. This is real. All of it. It's a matter of what is *visible*,' said Armitage.

Melsham dipped his sleek head. 'We're sorry about Patrick. He was loved, truly.'

Kate looked at them, her temper fierce but controlled. 'I'm not usually given to profanity but as you've taken my children out of earshot I'll just ask what the *fuck* is going on? My husband gets himself shot to death for you people and you're having a weekend house-party here!' She rounded on Armitage, unable to control her animosity, her blinding jealousy, any longer. 'What are you? Irish? English? American? *What?* What is this place? A CIA *station*? Isn't that what they're called? Shit!' She felt the tears spring to her eyes and bit her mouth hard. She tasted blood.

Armitage came close but Kate raised her hands defensively. 'Don't! All right?'

'Kate, we understand. You've been faced with so much in no time at all. You're handling it really well under the circumstances. Kate, listen, I'm American, like you. Irish mother. The hair's a give-away?' She twisted a red curl, ruefully. 'Uncontrollable.'

Kate chose a chair deliberately and sat, forcing control. 'What was my husband doing for you? Or am I not allowed to know?'

'Kate, you *have* to know.' Armitage glanced quickly at Melsham.

Melsham said: 'Kate, we want you to carry on Patrick's work. We have to ask you to deal with people we can't directly associate with. That's what Patrick was doing for us. He laid himself on the line all the way: his reputation, his life. He was a courageous man,

Kate, he knew right through that none of what he did could be recognized. No medals, Kate. No glory.'

'And he was murdered.'

Melsham looked at his hands. 'There was nothing we could do, Kate. I swear to you.'

'They've got something going with the IRA,' Carter said, flatly. 'Patrick fronted it for them. Walk away from this, you don't need it.'

'Stay out, Carter,' warned Melsham. 'You're not involved.'

'Don't count on it, Henry.'

'Is it the IRA?' Kate demanded.

Melsham nodded cautiously.

'Say it, damn you!'

'Yes,' Armitage admitted.

Kate leaned back against the cushions. 'Dear God, this gets worse by the hour.'

Armitage said: 'Patrick had established a basis of trust. Can you imagine how difficult that was in a climate where hate has been the norm for centuries? That's the calibre of man he was.'

'You don't need to sell my husband to me!'

'We're not selling him to you, Kate, we're establishing whether you understand what is expected of you.'

'Me? For God's sake, why? Do it yourself! Or send Carter, he's got the background for this kind of thing.'

'Carter is precisely what we don't want. We need someone so far from what we do that their cover – and their life, Kate – is never compromised by any doubts over their . . . authenticity. Patrick was a businessman. He could use that role to the limit. He could haggle – he could *bend*. He could compromise his principles and not be doubted. No one is ever surprised when a successful businessman is ready to do a deal which might be *not quite* legal.'

'Are you saying Patrick was acting illegally here?'

'Highly. But his role was vital if we were to achieve our ends.'

'Which are?'

'You don't need to know, Kate.'

'You need to know what we want – not what we want it for,' added Melsham, coldly.

Kate glimpsed, for a moment, the ruthless professional behind the polished manners and fashionable grooming. Melsham would sacrifice her if it became necessary. Or if she was a threat. She knew it. She drank wine from the glass Armitage placed by her elbow. It tasted as bitter as aloe. She wondered if that was from fear. Her situation appalled her. These were her *compatriots* yet she was as afraid of them as any enemy!

She found her voice. 'Who killed Patrick? I have to know that before we go any further. Was it the IRA? Had they found out what he really was? Is that what I'll be walking into if I co-operate with you? Suspicion?' She could not believe she had said what she had. It was like walking through a dream – but being able to control it. She didn't want control. She wanted to believe none of it was happening. Patrick was alive and she was . . . what she had allowed herself to become. She knew she would never be that person ever again. And part of her was glad. Even at such dreadful cost.

'We're not sure,' admitted Armitage. 'It's a mess.'

'It's a fuck-up,' growled Melsham.

'And you want me to follow Patrick?' She stared at them, disbelievingly.

'We establish contact at arms' length, Kate. That way you're out of harm's way. Telephone first – we have all the contacts – then if that goes well we . . . we'll need you to make physical contact. You have to allay their suspicions, first. If they did kill Patrick you have to make them believe they've made a grave error. As callous as this may sound, this tragedy should work for you. If they believe they've made an awful mistake they'll feel a natural sympathy for you.'

'The Provos don't know what the word means,' said Carter. 'She won't last a minute.'

'Don't tell me what I can't do,' Kate snapped.

Carter smiled. 'They're playing you like a fish on the line.'

'Are they? We'll see. Tell them what happened today.'

'What?' Melsham demanded.

'All of it,' she ordered.

Carter took an apple from a bowl on the sideboard and bit into it, moving close by the fire. He dipped his head at Kate. 'You know about the reward, Henry?'

Melsham jabbed a finger at a television set. 'CNN ran it clear through the night.'

'Someone took her at her word. Delivered a box to the hotel. Three severed heads. They weren't taken from the city morgue. They're waiting to collect. *You* know the money doesn't exist – not in the real world. They don't. The problem is their threat is real.'

'Threat?'

'One million US or they collect in kind.'

'Kind?'

'Come on, Henry.' Carter gave a weary shake of his head and nodded at Kate.

'Fuck.'

'And she gets to choose which of the kids make up the numbers. How's that for pressure?'

'When was this?' asked Armitage, watching Carter, intently.

'This morning. After the police came by with Mrs Brannigan's luggage – packed with ten k's of heroin. Maybe cocaine?'

'*What!*' Melsham blurted.

'You just don't know what's going on, do you?' snapped Kate. 'It's not surprising you lost Patrick!'

'Just tell us, Kate. Calmly,' Armitage urged.

'They planted narcotics in my luggage. They wanted me out of Ulster. I told them to go to hell.'

'Wait. They knew which hotel to make their delivery to? How?'

'I don't know! They called around? Checked five-star hotels, I'm *supposed* to be a millionaire's widow. Does it matter *how*?'

Melsham rounded on Armitage. 'They knew *exactly* which hotel. It's what Langley feared right from the start. It's a Brit operation! The heads are perfect. They want Kate out – they tried the narcotics scare, that didn't work – so now it's straight terror.'

Carter said: 'That assumes they know she hasn't got the one million dollars – otherwise there's no threat, is there? She wanted revenge and she was prepared to pay, she believed she could. The threat only really exists if they knew already that she couldn't.'

'What's your point?' growled Melsham.

'They knew what Brannigan was all along. Which means you're blown. Time to move on, Henry.'

Melsham studied him. 'You knew it was the Brits all the time, you son-of-a-bitch.'

71

'I wasn't taken out by Provos when I followed Brannigan. I knew that.'

'I'll call Langley. *Fuck!*' Melsham strode out, fast.

'Where are the heads, Carter?' asked Armitage.

Kate answered. 'We left them for the police.'

Carter tossed the apple core into the fire. It sizzled then flared. He watched it burn.

Armitage watched him. 'Reardon came by the hospital when you were being treated? I need to know what you told him. Carter?'

'Exactly what I told McAlister – the Special Branch cop who interviewed me.'

'You told Reardon you thought the *British* were responsible! You know who Reardon reports to?'

'I told him I don't believe the IRA are. That's not the same thing.'

'He believed you?'

'He listened. I think McAlister believed me – though he blew smoke.'

'Reardon flew to London this morning and met with the Prime Minister. NSA has an intercept order on Reardon's calls.'

Carter looked up, quickly. 'Slipstreaming past GCHQ? That order must have had *some* signature on it! Or does Langley have that kind of leverage over Fort Meade these days?'

'I shouldn't have told you that. Forget I did. Let's just say there's complete co-operation on this. Look, our analysis has Reardon as legitimate: clean, no intelligence or security connection whatsoever. That doesn't mean he's not dangerous. It's better you hadn't spoken with him.'

'Dangerous like a loose cannon on your deck?'

'Something like that.'

Kate watched, disturbed, aware of the tension between them.

Melsham came in, briskly. 'Do the deal, Hannah.'

Armitage moved beside Kate. 'Forgive us if we've seemed insensitive to your loss. All I can say is there's a lot at stake here. More than you can imagine. Matters were delicately balanced before Patrick's death. We hope we can retrieve our position. We have a dangerous – unstable – situation here and we need to get it back on

72

line. You're stressed, we understand that, but we need your help and you need us. You have to trust us, Kate.'

Melsham said: 'Patrick's gone. Gone for you; for us too. A great loss to both sides. All right, that's life. There's nothing more I can say about it. Accept the role we're offering. We can't force you to act in your own best interests but I advise you to. You have three children to house, feed, educate. These are tough times. All it needs is you taking Patrick's place. Follow through what he started. After this you're clear of the Company.'

'I just want to get out of this nightmare. I want to get back to Vermont, safe, with the children. I want security. I want what I thought I had. Give me all of that and I'll do whatever you want.'

Melsham said, 'You get us what we want you can write the cheque yourself.'

Kate chilled as Patrick's words returned to her. *You don't make real money in Maple Rapids, Michigan, you make it out there on the edge and you have to be prepared to fall off sometime.* And he had. Now she tottered on the brink of the same precipice, unprepared. She was not Patrick. Never would be. Yet she *must* be. She had no choice. Somehow she had to go through with whatever they ordered.

'What do I have to do?' Her voice seemed miles away.

'Right decision,' said Melsham, firmly.

Armitage silenced him with a swift motion. 'Kate, listen carefully. You don't realize it but you have a legitimate role in your husband's business activities. Patrick had you sign a document once that you didn't read thoroughly. Unforgivable for an attorney but understandable – you'd quit practising and being a mother of three is demanding. Don't blame yourself. So legitimately you can make business decisions – you can take over where he left off, Kate. Carry matters through. Matters important – *vital* – to us.'

'I want guarantees. Hard legal guarantees. I want the financial side tied up before I do anything.'

'No problem. We're very fair.'

'I want more than fair. I want what I *had*. And I want any threat to me and my children removed. Either by direct action or settlement – I don't care which. That's your problem.'

Armitage said: 'We'll deal with the threat, Kate. We can make that commitment.'

Melsham said: 'Sorry, Carter. We need to secure our interests here. Keep your wine glass, there's a cellar full where you're sleeping.' He directed the automatic he held toward the door. 'Move.'

'Just until this is over, Kate,' said Armitage. 'Carter understands the rules. He just breaks them.'

'Keep using your lawyer's mind, Kate,' advised Carter as Melsham directed him out.

Armitage poured two glasses of wine and put one in Kate's hand. 'Don't worry about him. I need your complete attention. We need to brief you and there isn't too much time. In a moment you can check you're happy with the children's condition – set your mind at ease – then we'll get down to it.'

Kate sat stunned by Carter's swift removal – and the manner of it. Her fear had receded with the promised return of security for her family but now it gripped her once more. She felt utterly alone. She had not quite realized how much she had come to depend on Carter's presence. 'Can't we leave this until tomorrow? I hardly slept last night.'

'Tomorrow is impossible. You have to be put back into play right away. You're fatigued Kate, we understand that. Shock, grief – everything that's happened. It's expected. We can keep you going with some medication. Don't be alarmed, we're not into addicting our people. Afterwards you can sleep for a week. You're going to need something. You have to drive back to the Culloden tonight.'

'Tonight? I've checked out!'

'We've fixed that. Your suite is on hold.'

'Do you organize your man's life this way? Ruthlessly. *Fait accompli?*'

'I don't have a man.'

Kate met her eyes. '*Did* you have my husband?'

'I told you, no.'

'I couldn't tell if you were lying. You'd be too good at it.'

'I'm not lying.'

Kate drank some of the wine. It still tasted foul. 'Carter helped me,' she said. 'Why do you have to do this to him?'

Armitage looked at her. 'Carter will kill whoever he believes killed Patrick. He'll go after them if we let him – and we can't allow that. We need to keep this controlled. We can't have a rogue running loose.'

'There's something else. I sensed it. Something you know. Tell me.'

'There's another possibility, Kate.'

'I don't understand.'

'How much do you know about Carter?'

'Very little. I trust him. Patrick trusted him.'

'Patrick trusted his *abilities*. Patrick had no illusions about the situation in Northern Ireland. He knew his life was at risk from any number of factions here. We couldn't supply protection, it was too risky, would have endangered his credibility. So he hired Carter.'

'What are you trying to tell me?'

'Carter is a killer. A cold, ruthless, utterly efficient, highly trained killer.'

'He was a soldier. That's what they are.'

'The Army eased him out of their back door. Did you know that?'

'He told me.'

'Did he? The whole story? Or some vague statement about being a victim of Washington politics? That's the line he usually gives prospective employers. I'll give you the real story. Langley had an operation running to solve the problem of the drug barons in Colombia. Deals were being made ... we could have shut them down: we had the muscle, we'd got them on the run by closing off their money-laundering operations one by one – Jersey to Jakarta – but we didn't want a war, we wanted them together and talking to us, we wanted to reason, to give personal safety guarantees, even arrange amnesty, if they complied with our conditions. We didn't want to smash one syndicate and have another grow from the remains. We wanted termination and we wanted control all the way to the wire. Marcus Carter was leading a Special Forces unit in the mountains, hunting the same drug barons we were dealing with. His team was on loan, routed through Drug Enforcement to the Colombian government, and they weren't there to play games. They'd been in there for months. Tough conditions. A lot of waiting. A lot of aborted missions. Then they lost a couple of men the hard way.

Torture. Castration, blinding. Warnings of course. Yanks go home. A different world, Kate. *Serious* money. Enough to topple – or control – governments. In Langley's terms that's unacceptable. Carter wasn't just fighting drug barons. He'd taken on the complete corrupt system. With so much money in the pot every covert operation was blown before it started. Only an organization as powerful as Langley could do the job he was trying to do – and even we had to compromise. Carter doesn't know the meaning of that word.'

'He found out what you were doing?'

'Langley had rented a villa outside Bogotá to wine, dine and whore the barons. Real life, Kate, that's how it runs. Someone got in there one night – God knows *how* past the guards – and finished them off while they were sleeping. All of them. Decapitation, Kate, their heads were found in hanging flower-baskets by the pool next morning like fruit. It's a Khmer Rouge terror trick and Carter has more red bandannas hanging on his belt than maybe even he cares to remember. I've seen his record – the real one, not the PR printout. Of course it was never proven it was him – with or without his team – but they'd dropped out of sight in the mountains for days so the logistics were easy.' Armitage sighed. 'The military were persuaded they'd be better off without him. Carter doesn't care too much for Langley, and it shows.'

Kate sat stunned. 'You're saying he's responsible for what's happened here? To me?'

'*Possibility*, Kate, Langley has this credo that coincidence is another word for conspiracy. This is a big operation, Kate – if I draw their attention to what's happened here they'll do more than order his detention. You understand me?'

'But Melsham will have told them.'

'We're people, not computers. Melsham doesn't know about Colombia – there's no reason he should. *I* know because I was involved in that theatre at that time. Without Carter's knowledge, of course. Langley will make the connection, given time and their Cray mainframes, but by then this should be over and they'll be interested in other matters.' Armitage emptied her glass and looked at Kate. 'You've formed an attachment to Carter. Understandable given the circumstances. You're vulnerable and he's a natural protector. Just keep an open mind, all right? That's all I'm saying.'

Kate glanced involuntarily at the door Carter had been taken through.

Armitage smiled. 'Melsham isn't going to kill him, Kate. Carter wouldn't let him.'

'He *can't* be involved in this! Even if he knew Patrick was going to be killed. Even – my God! – if he was involved in his *murder* he couldn't have known what I was going to say – to offer – when I arrived? How could he? This is just more pressure, isn't it – removing Carter makes me completely dependent on you. I'm not a fool!'

'We wouldn't want you if you were, Kate. Someone once said, chance favours the prepared mind. Perhaps he heard and took his opportunity? *Someone* did – and Carter had it all going for him.'

Kate protested. 'He stayed with me when Parriss said there was no money. I couldn't pay him – so what was the point? He knew there was nothing for him. That's not the behaviour of a murderous extortionist?'

'Carter didn't stay with you. He *brought* you here. He knew we'd have to pay if we wanted your co-operation and it was plain as daylight to someone like him that we did need your co-operation badly.'

Kate stared at her. 'I have to leave my children here, with you? That's part of the arrangement?'

'It's safer.'

'Not if you're right about Carter, it isn't.'

'*If* I'm right it's not their heads he wants – or yours. He wants one million dollars.'

'If you're wrong?'

'If I'm wrong then there's people out there he'll hunt down and kill and I don't want that.'

'People who killed Patrick. Maybe *I* want that.'

'If it *is* the British that's politically unacceptable, Kate. Also disastrous for this operation. He's neutralized – here. We can't afford another Colombia. And remember, you have every reason to want this to be a complete success. Just put Carter out of your mind.'

'What do I have to do?'

Armitage smiled. 'Make some ruthless – but gullible – men believe you. Be a woman, Kate.'

77

'Then?'
'We need some names. Names we believe they have.'
'Why?'
'Never ask why, Kate. It could kill you.'

# CHAPTER FIVE

RICK LAY on his back; cold mulchy earth pressed against him like something long dead. He breathed deeply, the smell of rotting vegetation, fungi and the earth itself completing, for him, the illusion of lying in a grave.

He felt content.

Almost content.

He wished the murk above him would clear and he could see the stars, not just the blurred, floating, pitted ball of the moon – which he considered imperfect.

Rick had a deep longing for the stars. An almost orgasmic yearning. Sometimes – *those* times – it was orgasmic.

'How long, Rick?' asked Dave, teeth chattering, very cold. 'She could be in there all fucking night.'

Rick saw a gap in the clouds and a sprinkling of stars peeking through. He smiled.

'*Rick?*'

'You recognize that, Dave?' He lazily pointed a finger over his head.

'Satellite TV.'

Rick turned, his face so close his breath was warm on the blond head beside him. 'Remember, Dave?'

Dave licked his cold lips. 'Sure, Rick.'

Dave mainly remembered the screaming. *Afterwards* was something he had to shut out for ever. Except Rick was there beside him always there, a constant reminder. He stared at the small upward-tilted grey metal dish caught in the dull moonlight barely twenty yards away on the ragged lawn, shook his head, apprehensive now, knowing the signs.

'Don't look for things, Rick. Let's go for the money and blow,

OK. I don't know what the fuck we're doing here anyway. *Jesus*, crossing the border! It's crazy! Come on Rick, let's get back. She'll find the message we left and she'll pay up. She's got kids, she won't mess around. Shit, she *offered* the money! Maybe we shouldn't have threatened her, Rick? She'd have let the minder go if we'd played it easier.'

Rick swung over fast, grasping the back of his neck with immense strength, his fingers buried to the vertebrae. 'You're alive because I always know.'

'*You're right! Rick, you're right!*' Dave gasped, his voice quaking as much from fear as pressure from the steel fingers.

'Always.'

'*Always*, Rick.'

Rick smoothed the blond hair gently.

'We couldn't do without you, Rick.'

Rick kissed his ear, his tongue probing the ridged, resisting folds. 'You wouldn't be alive without me,' he whispered.

They lay silently for a while.

'What are you going to do, Rick?'

'Ask questions.'

'No, Rick!'

'No?'

'Rick, it doesn't matter. *Does it?* It's over.'

'It'll never be over.' Rick's hand clamped hard over Dave's face as the lamp shrouded in ivy over the doorway of the house glowed and Kate Brannigan stepped outside, Hannah Armitage close behind; red hair aflame in the pooled light.

'Drive carefully.' Armitage's voice carried clearly in the night as Kate climbed behind the wheel of the Mercedes.

'Remember what I said about the children,' came the reply, warningly.

'I'll remember. Wait for their people to contact you, Kate. Just relax at the Culloden. Heal. It's in play now, all you have to do is go with it. This will soon be over and you can get back to Vermont.'

The Mercedes roared, then pulled away, lights blasting at the undergrowth.

Rick ducked fast, pushing both their faces into the earth, his eyes tightly closed until the sound of the engine faded, preserving night vision. Opening them, he saw the red-head still standing, thoughtful, under the light before she turned and went back inside.

'Beautiful,' he whispered, releasing Dave.

'Come on, Rick – we'll lose her!' Dave hissed.

'Where? At the hotel? Didn't you hear?'

'I heard,' Dave murmured, real fear building now.

Rick pulled himself up lithely, silhouetted against the bleak moon, stretching like a panther in the darkness. '*Now*, Dave.'

'Yes, Rick.'

H ANNAH ARMITAGE unzipped her skirt and sat on the bed in her underwear. She felt flat, recognizing the come-down from the pills she had taken immediately the call had come through from Langley ordering her to move on Kate Brannigan. She tried to remember how many she had taken since. Four? Six? It would be hard to sleep now without barbiturates. She decided she *had* to do something – seriously – about what was becoming a habit every time the pressure started.

'You're scared,' she said, quietly. *Admit that and you're halfway there*. She found a hairbrush and dragged it roughly through her hair. Bullshit! Admitting it made things worse.

She had never felt so exposed as now in Ireland. In other – more openly dangerous – locations the enemy had a *different* face; here it was as familiar as her own. Part of her – her own blood – was the enemy. They're not *your* enemy, idiot! The Brits can take that responsibility.

*When you're exposed everyone is the enemy*, she remembered Patrick Brannigan saying when they had lain on that bed together – after his hurried taking of her the first time.

Sorry, Kate, bare-faced lies come with the job.

She barely saw the black blur before an arm was locked around her throat, choking her cry. The strong *click* of the stiletto blade erupting millimetres before her right eye stopped her heart, dead.

She gasped in one sharp breath and lived again as the pressure eased slightly before a steel hand crushed her mouth. 'Any sound – *any* sound – and you're blind for ever, hear me?'

She tried to nod but the grip was awful. She smelt mustiness and earth and death and quailed inside. *Oh God let me speak! Yes! Yes!*

'Affirmative,' the smooth voice purred. 'That's what you people say so I'll believe you said that. All right? Now, when I take my hand away I'll put it between your legs and you won't make any sound except maybe from pleasure which might – or might not – please me. Whatever you decide to do, do it very softly. Understood?'

She grunted.

His hand lifted. Free air moved across her face, blood flooded back and a thousand needles pricked at her bruised skin. She felt faint and knew she must stay conscious to stay alive.

He cupped her and she shuddered.

'Repulsion? I don't like that,' said Rick.

She gasped as his hard finger tore through her underclothes, penetrating her brutally.

*Anything. I'll do anything. Just let me survive.* Nothing else filled her mind. No who, how, why: no thought of duty, no protection of the operation, only survival and the staggering, sickening, thought of that needle-blade piercing her eyes.

Rick whispered. 'I'll ask things and do things at the same time because you're tempting and you're clever and you'll respond perfectly because you're trained for this. They prepare you for the worst.' She felt his smile rise beside her ear. 'The worst they could think of is where I begin.'

Dave blurted. 'Rick, for fuck's sake! The minder's still here.'

'He won't hear, will he?' He shook her. 'Will he?'

'No!' she whispered.

'Then again, maybe he will?'

'*No!*'

The slim stiletto blade moved and lay across the bridge of her nose, covering her eyes, still warm from where it had been cosseted next to his skin. She wanted to vomit.

Rick said, 'Kill him, Dave. Just don't wake the children.'

She squeezed her eyes tight, closing out everything. She wished she was a child again. Had never grown. She wanted to be with the children, be as small as they, lying nestled between them, as safe as they were. He wouldn't kill them. Not when he didn't want to wake them. She clung to any small glimmer of hope. Don't kill me. Don't hurt me. Please!

'I want you to turn over,' the soft voice purred in her ear. 'On the bed. Kneel, bent over, like a Muslim. Pretend you're praying to Allah.'

The blade moved away and down. She flinched as it touched her hip and she felt soft material slip from her.

'Now,' Rick said. 'Kneel. Do it now. Say *I will*.'

'*I will*.'

'You will.'

She pressed her face into the bedclothes but his fingers twisted it around so she could see him with one terrified eye. Her skin felt cold, she had never felt so open, so vulnerable, so degraded. She bit her lip hard and shut down everything inside her like a light being switched off. *Nothing*. She was nothing. Meat, on the slab. Nothing.

She heard the dreadful click and her eye opened wide – but this time the blade had been withdrawn and relief flooded through her. Until she felt hard metal touch her. *There*.

'*Oh God! Please no!*'

'God would fuck you if he saw you in this position,' Rick said.

He was mad: she knew he was mad. 'What do you want?'

'Everything.'

'Do whatever you want. *Anything*. Don't hurt me!'

'Tell me everything.'

His thumb found and pressed into her.

'Everything you know.' The *click* was hard and jagged, like bone snapping. She strangled her scream as she felt the length of the slim blade rest warmly, safely, on her coccyx. She wanted it to stay there for ever, not lift, not—

She told him all she knew and he stroked her back right through it as if she were a loved animal.

She felt something drop on her, warm and wet, and felt disgust, recoiling inside; then his thumb moved and the wetness was *there*.

She screamed from the sudden searing pain but his clubbing blow stopped it dead inside her, numbing her mind, her body and, mercifully, most of the dreadful pain.

Let me live, came the thought – perhaps even the words – gasped into the bedclothes. She heard roaring in her ears, felt the warm flood of the sea over her, then nothing.

AT FIRST, Carter thought it was an animal. A whimpering animal scratching at the solid wooden door of the cellar Melsham had locked him in. He sat loosely, legs stretched out, only the chair cushion Melsham had tossed in as an afterthought between him and the cold stone-flagged floor. Overhead two bare light-bulbs glared tauntingly, as if highlighting his impotence.

He had resigned himself to his incarceration. There was nothing he could do. Not yet. And burning up inside was a waste of energy. An opportunity would arise and he would take it. He would need all his energy, all his resources, soon enough.

He was determined to free Kate Brannigan from Langley's web and knew from harsh experience that whatever they had told her of the operation there would be more, much more; and all of it dangerous.

He watched the handle move, slowly.

No animal.

He arose, moving swiftly, soundlessly, to the door – positioning himself, elbow raised to jab the wood back into the face of whoever was beyond.

A small gap appeared and he heard his name, gasped, but unmistakably his name.

Hannah Armitage slumped through, naked, blood pooling around her – too much, too quickly – a trail of it down the narrow wooden steps marking her desperate passage. He searched quickly for wounds, finding none.

Then he saw, and recoiled.

He knew she was a breath away from dying.

She gripped him with extraordinary strength which told him she knew too.

'*Listen.*'

He watched her gather herself, every last second of her extensive training going into the moment. *'Melsham's laptop. Distant Thunder. It's all there.'*

He knew immediately that Melsham was dead.

'Tell me. All of it.'

She did, with him forcing it from her like an inquisitor, even torturer; ashamed but resolute.

Afterwards, she gripped him harder, pulling his face close. *'He's taken the children. I promised her! Get them back!'*

He felt himself go cold. But there was relief too. He had thought they were dead. Not daring to ask. It was something for another moment. His own to discover. To deal with.

He nodded.

*'Say it!'*

'I'll get them back.'

He held her, there was nothing else he could do. He cradled her head, his lips close to her ear. 'Who did this?'

She rested her head against him and sighed. He shook her but she lay slack against him. He pinched her cheeks, breathed life into her. 'I've got to know what I'm facing.'

Fear was alive in her dying eyes. 'He's evil.'

'Who!'

She had gone without him knowing.

He felt alone. Alone but for faceless evil he knew was no longer there, only the throb of it remaining like the echo of a furnace deeper even than where he lay. Or perhaps it was just fury pounding at his mind.

He stayed with her for a while, letting her blood seep into him.

*One day it will get to you, son; that's when it's time to walk*, advised a weary military long ago, long dead voice.

'Not yet, sir,' murmured Carter. Not yet.

M ELSHAM'S BODY lay under the bedcovers, broken like a bird, head flopped too far over – identical to the girl who had looked after the children.

Carter left it alone – not stripping back bedclothes as he had from Brenda's body checking expectantly, but, thankfully, negatively for more of what had been done to Armitage – and went immediately to the IBM laptop on the heavy dark wood dressing-table.

He sat on the low upholstered stool before the ancient browning mirror.

*You don't look like the guy I used to know.*

'You'd better be,' he murmured.

*Somewhere out in the night there's a butcher running wild and sure as Hell burns you're going to be blamed for this bloody work.*

He knew the CIA would soon be wanting him, badly. The police too, on both sides of the border – if Langley wanted to play it straight and hand them his file, which was by no means certain. He knew Langley well. They might want him in play – for themselves – because he was *there* and alive; they might want him dead; or, ideally, in now and dead later. He had no time for the complexities of their games. No time for explanations; no time for questions, no time at all before the woman he had sworn to protect opened herself to some of the cruellest terrorists in the world. No time before he must hunt the animal who had stolen her children.

He had to move, fast, but he needed some answers before he took another step forward.

He flipped the laptop open, keyed in DISTANT THUNDER and looked into Langley's mind.

Finally, it made sense.

It was a nightmare.

He closed the computer, stripped off his bloodied clothes, showered in Melsham's bathroom, found clothes in his wardrobe that more or less fitted then burned his own in the old boiler-house next to the cellar they had locked him in.

Then he covered Langley's back for them.

He had his reasons.

One million reasons.

THEY TOOK the back lanes, where the Army patrols were stretched the most. One moment they were in the South the next in the North. Nothing warned them, no one stopped them, nothing changed except registrations on cars tucked close to neat bungalows with tidy fences – and the road surface which improved once the invisible frontier had been crossed.

The children slept, deeply, mouths agape. Rick had fed them downers from Hannah Armitage's bedside table – helping himself liberally to her other supplies.

They made the main highway to Belfast quickly, Dave driving, Rick bright eyed beside him, smoking steadily from a pack of menthols he had found with the amphetamines. Rick was not a smoker but, just then, drawing cooled air through burning ash pleased him. The concept of opposites existing together – inseparably – was one he enjoyed. He had read Fitzgerald once – they had fed them a little of everything in Krasnodar – and he remembered something about an artist being someone with diametrically opposing views yet still able to function. Rick had always been an artiste. The world was his stage and nothing, and everything, was real. Which was why he loved the stiletto in preference to the crude carbon-bladed knife they had supplied at Krasnodar . . . another lifetime before . . . loved the artistry, the *entrance* of the secret silver blade readied in his closed fist to spring, startle, terrify, kill.

*Like me.*

The soldiers were there in the road, waving them down with torches, the unmistakable red line of a laser targeting-sight slicing through what remained of the night.

'Stop or run, Rick?' asked Dave, urgently, tilting his head back at the children.

'Stop. Watch the eyes.'

'Yes, Rick.'

'Ready?'

'Ready, Rick.'

They stopped on the hard shoulder, one trooper from the four-man patrol peering in beside Dave, his torch probing. 'Whose kids?'

'Uncles' outing,' smiled Rick, perfectly Irish. 'Early start. Too early. Finished before we even get started.'

The trooper looked at him. 'What's your plans?'

'Oh, some fishing, bit of paddling for the children, you know.'

'Where'll that be, then?' The torch flicked on to Dave, blinding him.

Dave flinched. 'Er – Giant's Causeway—'

Rick seemed to sigh, his right hand came up from where it had drooped slackly between his thighs, a silenced Browning automatic filling it, the double thump like pillows being pounded, the camouflage-smeared face at the window exploding, the body punched back on to the road, legs jerking – Rick already out of the car, killing swiftly, silently, except for the *thump-thump thump-thump* in the night.

'Drive!' he snarled, and hauled the door closed, hard.

The car lurched and crunched down on its springs, the exhaust clanging on the tarmacadam.

'Drive *around* them!'

'Sorry, Rick.'

Rick lit another cigarette, turning to the rear. 'Little lambs,' he cooed. 'Not a murmur.'

'*Why*, Rick? What'd he see?'

Rick laughed. '*Heard*, Dave. You told him where we are.'

'I—'

Dave was trembling. Rick caressed his neck. 'The eyes, Dave. He'd filed us away. Had to be – all right?'

'They'll find them!'

Rick laughed and pitched the glowing stub into the night. 'You think the Provos will let anyone else take the credit for killing four British soldier boys? Steal their glory? We can kill Brits till Lough Neagh runs red. It's open season. Come on, faster, I'm tired. Think how you'll enjoy spending all that money.'

Dave drove harder, watching the night slowly die around him, his eyes still. *I want to live to spend the money, Rick.*

THE FIRST hint of dawn cast an ominous glow over the primeval basalt rock formations of the Giant's Causeway on Antrim's coast as Arnie stood gazing at the dark sea from the window of the cramped dormer bedroom of the cliff-top inn he shared with Max.

It came not as revelation but growing certainty: whatever he had agreed with the others he had no intention of giving up his modest but respected single-bay London mews garage-workshop and the comfortable flat above for another start somewhere; no matter how pleasant, how tempting the location, or how much money was put in his pocket.

The truth was, Arnie had reached the height of his life's expectation. He was as content as he could be under the circumstances; immune now to the strain of his *black* existence; performing duties forced upon him with cold, detached efficiency. He was mortal, he would not live for ever, what he had was good enough to see him through to his end, whether tomorrow or forty years on – which was all the time anyone could expect.

Above all, he had Sandy who loved him *crazily*; crazily enough to have his child with no proposal of marriage forthcoming, nor expected.

Marriage was something Arnie dared not contemplate; not as matters stood with the serpent Krotkov in London who they all knew was once a Directorate S *illegal* but now, with face and allegiances changed, was Kramer, who had them all in his relentless grip; even Rick.

Arnie shook his head wearily. How could *he*, a forgotten soldier from a lost war, resist the will of one who slipped so easily from his own into his enemy's nest? One so clever he was rewarded with position and influence, gaining absolute power over those he once merely controlled.

Kramer who once was Krotkov: Arnie's nemesis for deceiving the country that now was truly home. A good country; whose essential defences he had been carefully placed to destroy when the call came from the bitter school of dissimulation, sabotage and silent killing in Krasnodar in the Transcaucasus that had spawned him. *A call as certain as history!* They had trumpeted day and night for two years, numbing his mind into final submission. A call which, if answered with courage, sacrifice, their twin doctrines of *aktivnyye meropriyatiya* – active measures in hostile and denied territory for subversion, disinformation, target acquisition and sabotage – and *aktivnyye akty* – direct action, including assassination and abductions – would guarantee victory.

How they had lied! How miserably they had failed. They could not win one battle on their *own* streets.

When the revolution was done and their countrymen took their freedom, no one from Arnie's *Spetsnaz* cell had been set free. Kramer had ensured that. There was no freedom while he held their future in his hands. Not until his – or his new masters' – use of them was done. If it ever was?

Arnie's cropped head dropped into his permanently oil-ingrained mechanics' hands. What would he do to safeguard what was now his life? Become traitor? He almost laughed aloud, waking Max who snored like a beast opposite him. Betraying *what*? Country? Party? Ideology? All that was finished. *Over*. The rulers there now were gangsters, profiteers, carpet-baggers who had switched sides and stripped the country when the long Cold War ended with a whimper. And beneath these pariahs, laying low, were the hard ones who trusted history, waiting with the timeless patience of the committed for the world to turn their way again. And perhaps it would? Either way, there was nothing there for Arnie: nothing to go back for; nothing to betray. It was over. Now he stood for nothing; achieved nothing for anyone. Except Sandy and the baby. What would he do for them? To protect them. Safeguard what he had built for them. What *dare* he do?

He skirted a dangerous option tentatively, as he might a trembler switch on a bomb, not daring to approach directly; barely touching it with his mind. He allowed the probing fingers of dawn's light to lift the dark cover off his fears.

Arnie feared but was not afraid of Kramer who he would have enjoyed killing personally long before if the serpent did not provide continuing protection against deportation or long-term imprisonment for them all. He knew their actions over the last hours had certainly jeopardized Kramer's position with his new masters – an irrelevance, even a source of pleasure, for the others but for him a catastrophe. Without Kramer's protection he was doomed.

Unless he found a more powerful protector.

And if he, Arnie, could halt further action.

The moment was *now* when Rick was not there.

The thought turned his bowels to liquid.

Childhood images filled his mind: a chill, cavernous, candlelit church in the Ukraine; a mural that held a mystery: a face painted on dry stone that the towering bearded priest spoke of fearsomely as the Deceiver – calling him *Satana* and *Diavol* – yet he was darkly beautiful, outshining even the fairest angels congregated above.

Rick had stolen his eyes.

Arnie was deeply afraid of Rick.

Rick was beyond redemption.

He remembered the scathing words of an instructor at the main *Spetsnaz* training centre inside General of the Army Sergey M. Shtemenko Military School at Krasnodarsoye: *We drive ignorance from the peasants among you with education but nothing drives superstition from your souls.*

Many of his comrades had laughed. Arnie knew their laughter; he used it himself to cover his terror of forces darker than any enemy he was being trained to face. They had trained his mind and honed his body but after everything he still had his peasant's soul.

He had long accepted that some things were as unchangeable as others were inexplicable. As now, with the lassitude in his muscles and the deep, near crippling foreboding that even the thought of going against Rick brought upon him.

Rick would kill for a whim. Arnie had seen it. For betrayal he would keep you alive. At his pleasure. He would leave you skinned, screaming on the wrong side of death's door with the empty, bloodied, pale thing lying beside you like some ghastly twin.

Yet there was no other way. Except losing Sandy and the baby, for Kramer would make certain he never saw them again. And that for Arnie was no way at all.

The pay-phone was downstairs under the staircase outside the cramped bar. He knew who to call. The important one. The serious one in the photographs Kramer brought to them, hissing there must be no mistake: under no circumstances was *he* to be harmed. The target was the smiling American who would go alone like a lamb to the slaughter if they followed his orders to the letter, with Rick doing the speaking, because Rick could sound like anyone he wanted to.

He knew *where* to call. The hotel where he had taken the box

Rick had lined carefully with polythene and newspaper before sealing the zippered plastic suitbag containing the strangely peaceful dead faces inside.

Arnie looked out at the breaking dawn. Call, and all would be well. Any man whose possible death made Kramer tremble *must* have power to make things right. Such a man could arrange for him to stay with Sandy and the baby, could do what Krasnodar – even illegally – could not do; could make him an Englishman. Not a *fucking* Pole.

All he had to do was call.

Then run into the night.

He could not face Rick's eyes afterwards.

Rick would know.

Rick saw inside him.

Rick saw fear as others saw light.

Yet, for Sandy and the baby, Arnie crossed the divide. Went down the creaking stairs leading to the telephone in the dark well outside the bar, moving as light as a cat, his heart stopped dead with his held breath. There, he made his call to his saviour, whispering, breathless from fear, quaking from it, shamed by it, standing in the dark, whispering, cursing himself for being so cowardly.

The creak behind him seemed like a rifle shot; the numbing silence afterward, a bomb blast. He cut the call and stood still, the rank odour of stale beer stronger than anything he had ever smelled in his life, the far-away crash of breakers on ancient stone matching the erratic thump of his heart, waiting for Rick's soft touch to begin killing him.

The sound of a shotgun hammer snapping back was like angels singing for Arnie. Rick was a silent killer. Always. You barely heard his weapon. For Rick a shotgun was an obscenity.

'I'm real sorry,' the landlord's deep Ulster burr grumbled. 'Couldn't help but hear. They'd never forgive me. Ye have to understand the way things are over here.' He shifted the double-barrel. 'Away from the telephone now. I'll use this if I have to. Keep back now! And don't try waking your mates or it's over for ye.' He dialled quickly, stabbing in the digits. 'It's Cochran,' he growled in the mouthpiece. 'Ye'd better come over here. Now. This is your business not mine. I want it out of here – that's what I pay ye for.'

He put down the telephone and pushed the door to his private quarters open with his bare foot, found the dome of an old light switch and dropped it. 'In there and sit. Ye've some waiting to do. If I were you I'd get your story straight or make your peace with Him.' He closed the door, ducking his head at the picture of Christ on the wall.

Arnie felt his bowels turn slowly to melting ice: Rick would return soon and kill them all; kill him too – when he was ready – because Rick watched and listened as close and as silent as the night before he struck. He would hear everything.

*If you're lucky you'll be dead before he steps from the shadows. If you're lucky they'll kill you out of anger and stupidity.*

He looked at Jesus.

*Are you really stronger than Satan or is that more priest's lies to keep our heads to the ground?*

He would tell them everything, quickly. Lie that *he* not Rick had severed the heads. They were peasants, had no control – surely they would kill him?

But Rick might come before they did.

*He saw Rick's perfect sculpted torso, ablaze in firelight like some ghastly martyred angel, nails hammered through his scrotum into the cruel wooden frame, forced up on his toes as they stripped half of him away; saw Rick's dark eyes seeking him out as he lay silent as death in the rocks with the others, not daring to move, barely daring to breathe. Silent, watching, listening, tortured Rick who saw and heard all; saving their lives with his silence while killing them with his eyes.*

You can't save me from Rick, he told Jesus. Rick owns me.

He told himself: This is an old man before you. A grandfather. An innkeeper. He surprised himself thinking in Russian. His best chance was now. Before the *Irish* arrived and lowered the odds.

Before Rick returned.

He made his goodbyes to Sandy and the baby – in case – and leapt for the gun.

# CHAPTER SIX

———————◆▸◄◆———————

JAMES MCALISTER was used to telephone calls in the deep watches of the night. This was when his *little birds* suffered most from fear of living another day or of dying before its end.

He never ignored the insistent ring; he knew and understood the reasons: his own day-to-day existence being only marginally less dangerous than that of his informers. The vital difference was McAlister, while not conquering fear which he knew had its purpose, had learned to respect it; using it against complacency born of the grim routine every member of the police or security forces performed constantly to stay alive and whole in Northern Ireland.

He was not expecting Reardon's deep – unapologetic – voice.

'McAlister? We need to meet, urgently. I'm already up and dressed, I'll come to you.'

McAlister glanced at his watch: five thirty. 'Not a good idea.'

'Don't worry. I'll be safe enough, I have Ellis with me.'

'It's not you I'm worried about, sir. I don't want your face around here. Anything that draws attention is dangerous.'

'Understood. The Culloden, then? When can I expect you?'

'Soon.' McAlister pushed himself out of bed; shaved, dressed, had coffee and a crusty bread roll inside him and was ready to leave within twelve minutes: a routine as practised as his strict adherence to personal security measures before leaving the house and entering his car.

Prepared, he scanned the darkened street from his unlit upstairs bedroom window for unfamiliar vehicles or shadowed figures. Satisfied, he armed himself, switched off the garage alarm, stepped outside to chill darkness and confirmed with his fingers that tiny wedges he placed in the garage door were undisturbed. Now he switched on a pencil torch and scanned the door's edges for the deadly softness of Semtex or the fine trail of wire.

*Another day you've left it, laddies; another life used up.*

Inside the garage he checked the tuned engine bay, wheel arches and underside of his anonymous grey saloon with torch and mirror before climbing behind the wheel.

The passenger-side door opened and a handsome Celtic face ducked beneath the roof-line. 'You'll not need that, Jamie. Can I join you a while?' The Belfast accent was pie-crust thick.

McAlister kept the snub-nosed Smith and Wesson revolver he had drawn in clear view. He tipped his head backwards a fraction: 'Who have you got out there with you, Bobby?'

'Couple of lads. Not bad. They'll stay where they are.'

'*Very* bad, I'd imagine. I wondered what had happened to you – whether you'd finally taken the big step? Seems you have.'

'You don't wonder about anything, Jamie – you make it your business to know. You put the word out to the uniformed lads the minute the force dumped me: find Bobby Harding and get him to call me. You wanted me whispering in your ear like one of your tame Provies.'

'You never did call.'

'I never did. I'm no tout. I believe in what I'm doing, Jamie. Just as I believed in you.' Harding looked straight ahead, his pain as transparent as the glass windshield before him.

'Don't say it.' McAlister replaced the revolver in its shoulder-holster and spoke gently: 'I can't walk with you when your chosen path is fanaticism. And that's what it is, Bobby.'

'It's our country!'

'The Irish say it's theirs.'

'The Irish are *that* way!' Harding's fist smacked into the door beside him, the car shuddering under the impact.

'I know where South is, calm down.' McAlister took his hand. 'All right, that's the drama and the passion over with. Now tell me why you're here? UVF business? Have you been sitting out there all night waiting to catch me at first light? I must be slipping, I shouldn't have missed an unfamiliar car.'

Harding smirked. 'I know the hours you keep, Jamie. I don't

95

have to wait on you. Anyhow, I know most of the reserved registrations, don't I? It's nothing to have a plate made up. You don't walk away from the RUC after five years without taking something with you.'

'You didn't walk away, they pushed – and you deserved it.' McAlister gave a hard look. 'And using any one of those numbers is a sure way of getting yourself killed.'

'Only if they know I'm doing it.'

'Testing me is the act of a child, Bobby. I have to report it, you know that.'

Harding's jaw jutted. 'I shouldn't have said anything then, should I?'

'Those words might well prove to be your epitaph, someday.'

'Don't say that, Jamie.'

'It's getting light. Tell me why you're here then go away and destroy those plates. And don't use any of those numbers again. I'll give you an hour before I make my report.'

'Let me stay with you, Jamie. Please?'

McAlister shook his head firmly. 'It's over. Should never have begun. In any case you're involved with an outlawed organization now which kills any chance it might have had. Tell me what you've come to say or go. *Now*, Bobby, I'm not waiting on you!'

Harding glowered, sullenly. 'It's about the big Yank. The one who just got hit.'

'Brannigan? What about him? Out with it.'

'There was this meeting. Them and us. *Business*. You know.'

'Slow now,' McAlister warned. 'Business? Provos and UVF? Protection?'

'Like a bunch of sodding bankers they were, round that table. Suits and fucking calculators! Demarcation, they called it. Settling who was paying what to who. Seeing there was no treading on each others' toes.' He turned, angry. 'It's all about *money*, Jamie! What happened to the patriotic heart of the struggle? Ours *or* theirs? It's a bloody disgrace!'

'A minute ago you were talking about believing in what you were doing! Make up your mind. Or is this the voice of disillusionment I'm hearing?'

'Don't mock me.'

96

'I'm sorry, but you knew all this before you started in with the UVF. Unless you've been walking around with eyes and ears closed these last few years?'

'But hearing them discussing it *cold* like that over a few jars . . . then off out the door killing each other—!'

'They don't kill *each other*, Bobby: they kill the innocent. And the naïve, like you. Face it, that's what you are. They're evil and you don't qualify for their game. Get away from them – if you can.'

'No.'

McAlister sighed. 'Then I can do no more to save you from yourself.'

'Yes you can, Jamie. I'll leave them for you.'

'No. Tell me about Brannigan. Come on!'

Harding stared at his hands. 'I overheard something.'

'At this meeting?'

'I was baby-sitting our people with a couple of the lads and this team of young Provies were down the corridor doing the same – only acting like Billy the Kid and the James boys rolled together. Drinking. Stupid fucks. We're better than they are, Jamie; we have the training, the discipline—'

'Of course you have, we gave it to some of you. Hurry up.'

'The Provies are bubbling like a kettle on the boil, so I'm listening hard – but not so's you'd notice – because that's what five years in the RUC does to you, right?'

'You're talking about the minders now?'

'Sure. The big boys are inside now, door locked.'

'So what was said about Brannigan?'

'Not *what* was said, Jamie. How they *were* about him. Up! You know? I'm thinking: You *eijits*, he's not pouring dollars into your kitty! So what's got you going? I'm beginning to ask myself. I mean *investment*, that's bad news for the Provos, right? Then one brags about how he knows the Yank took a black-cab ride with a couple of their fixers a couple of days before.'

McAlister made himself go loose; taking one step back to keep it running slow and easy, despite what he felt inside. 'On his own, with the fixers, Bobby?'

'The Yank and the fixers in the cab, that's what he said.'

'You're sure?'

'I'm not deaf – or thick. I heard what I heard.'

'A Catholic black cab?'

Harding laughed harshly. 'The only time you'll get a couple of Provos in a Prod cab is when the ride's free and one way. Right?'

McAlister nodded. 'Anything else said?'

'That's when it happened. One of their runners brought a message up: wee kid blowing like he'd run half the city to get there. Whoever sent him didn't trust the phones.'

'And rightly so. Time?'

'Seven thirty; bit after maybe. Didn't check.'

'News of the hit on Brannigan? That was the message?'

Harding turned, fast. '*They* hadn't hit him, Jamie. I could tell. You could too if you'd been there. Door was open now and I could see them all around the meeting table inside. Ours and theirs – and theirs were burned up about it. You should have heard them! Had a real go. Said it was us. Cursing like no tomorrow! I thought for a bit there was going to be blood flying and how there'd be a slap-bang RUC party up at Castlereagh afterwards because half the top boys from both sides had wiped each other out.'

McAlister sighed resignedly and leaned against his door. 'Unfortunately tempers cooled and we have to continue the fight? What a shame. And you've been sent to tell me it wasn't the UVF either? You're *their* messenger boy, are you?'

'You don't have to put me down, Jamie.'

'I do. To make you see sense. Get things into proportion. I'm wasting my time, I can see that. So is this official? Official and bloody *true*? It's vital I know. This is too important for factional games. Bobby?'

'I said so, didn't I?'

'They sent *you* in particular. Why?'

Harding picked savagely at a calloused knuckle. 'They said use my connection with you.'

'Your connection?'

'They knew Jamie. They've got people inside the force – you know that.'

'They may know about me but that doesn't mean they know a damn thing about *us*. Unless you told them. Did you?'

Harding shrugged, nonchalantly.

McAlister's eyes were ice. 'You couldn't keep your mouth shut. I swear you're going to die talking your head off. You *fool*! The Provos will use that information.'

Harding laughed, scornfully. 'We wouldn't tell the Provies!'

'Dear God – grow up! You think the Provos haven't got someone inside the UVF? They're not thick Paddies any more. Just when are you people going to face that fact?'

'No way. We'd sniff one of theirs out in five minutes.'

McAlister reached across and pushed open the door. 'Tell your masters your message has been delivered. On your way, now.'

'I could be good for you, Jamie.'

'You sound like a worn-out song. Out you go. I'm in a hurry. Go on, Bobby!'

McAlister drove away from the house, watching Harding in his rear-view mirror, standing forlornly in the road, the early morning light glowing behind him, a pathetic figure who once had seemed so young, vigorous; *alive*. Love is worse than ageing, he thought: at least age gives you time to decline; not diminish you in moments.

*Damn!*

He felt ashamed. Cruel. Yet what choice had he? He brushed a trace of the crisp roll he had eaten from his moustache and smelt cologne: Bobby Garvin's, when he had held his hand. He drove faster, keeping the stubby magnum close, excising sudden memories, relinquishing responsibilities. Life or death? He could only control his own and even that was seriously in doubt every day of every week in the wet grey hell of Belfast.

With the road almost entirely clear of traffic at that hour he arrived at the Culloden within fifteen minutes, completely missing the grimy grey Mercedes coupé parked in a back-slot of the jammed car park.

In the security hut the officer in the death throes of his night shift heaved himself up and gave a weary salute.

'Leave that for the Army, laddie,' muttered McAlister, his humour rarely good in the early hours.

He found Reardon in the Culloden's deserted, darkened lounge and gratefully accepted coffee the big man poured from the pot brought by the blurry-eyed night-porter.

'I was delayed. Business. Sorry.'

'You've heard something?'

'First tell me why I'm here, sir.'

Reardon sipped coffee, his eyes on McAlister. 'I shouldn't be speaking to you, of course – not at this level.'

'You should, sir – if you're as worried as I am about what may be being done under the cover of the law.'

'Then you're convinced—'

'I'm convinced of nothing, sir. Not in my world.'

'You *have* heard something.'

'I had a caller before I left. My information is that neither Republican nor Loyalist factions were responsible. Another – disturbing – matter regarding Brannigan came up. Seems he made contact with the Provisional IRA. I know you don't want to believe that but it has to be investigated. I'll check with my other informants. If I learn anything I'll let you know immediately.'

Reardon looked out at the iron-grey morning. It seemed he had never left that armchair since facing Kate Brannigan barely thirty-six hours before. He breathed: 'Who *do* you trust in your precarious world, McAlister?'

'My sergeant, Keegan, my superiors of course – unless, or until, my trust is dashed. That's all I can do.'

'That's the quandary though, isn't it? It takes betrayal of trust to prove it was unworthily given.'

'You can trust me, sir.'

McAlister waited, the conflict inside Reardon plain, thinking: *It's always this way for the ones who can't bear the responsibility of secrets.*

'Does the term *Spetsnaz* mean anything to you?' Reardon asked finally.

'Soviet shock troops.'

'Rather more than that. The equivalent of our SAS – except we would never place our people inside the territory of a potential enemy years in advance of any possible conflict. We, thank God, don't indulge in such political – nor I hope military – terrorism.' Reardon paused. 'Imagine you're someone highly trained, highly motivated, indoctrinated, sent to penetrate the fabric of your country's enemy, becoming illegally domiciled there for many years. Becoming, in time, indistinguishable from the crowd. In a cosmopolitan society such as ours that's no great difficulty, is it – being absorbed?'

100

'No.'

'Suddenly, there's revolution at home, your masters are ousted from power, you daren't return because you've seen how they've been treated. You're not stupid: you're the sharp end of all they stood for, so if you return your chances of keeping out of some freezing prison camp, or worse, are not brilliant. Even if you somehow manage to stay free, you know your quality of life will be reduced. There's clear evidence of that almost daily on TV newscasts you see in the country you've infiltrated. Given those circumstances, what would you do?'

'Probably take my chances where I was?'

'With your forged papers and your fabricated life? Waiting constantly for the hand on the shoulder? Living a twilight existence, prey to the worst kinds of blackmail and exploitation? What choices are there for you if you're suddenly squeezed? Run? Where? You wouldn't have been trusted with a passport once you were in the target country: otherwise what was there to stop you bolting immediately or at your leisure? So you'd have to apply for one. Which means close scrutiny of yourself and your forged documents by enquiring, suspicious bureaucratic minds. It's a near perfect trap, isn't it? If someone wanted to make use of such people? Once caught in it, there's little choice but to do as you're told for as long as you are told. It's like having a trained killer dog on a secure leash – released at will. The question is *who* grips the restraint? Whose will?'

McAlister looked hard at him 'You're describing the men who ambushed Carter. You'd better tell me all of it.'

Reardon placed a Culloden notepad on the table between them – filled with brisk writing. 'A very frightened man called me earlier. His English was good enough but *he* was all over the place. He whispered frantically – barely coherent – throughout his call. All I could hear with any accuracy is written there. His real name – as near as I could get – is Anatoly Demurov; cover name, Arnie Kawolski: Polish *émigré*. Claims to be *Spetsnaz*-trained for a KGB deep-penetration sabotage and assassination unit in the event of war, code name *Spartan*. Infiltrated into the UK in 1982. He offered target names as proof. He named his KGB controller – resident in London: Oleg Krotkov.'

'Former controller?' questioned McAlister.

Reardon forced a thin smile. 'Krotkov is now called Kramer.

Works for, and I quote Demurov precisely – I had him repeat this – the *English secret police*. In my language that's MI5. Yours too, I'd imagine.'

McAlister made no response.

'You're not surprised?'

'We have a term for it. Appropriation of assets. When a Provo blots his copybook really badly – something criminal, or worse, talks too much to the wrong people – we usually get the word, move in fast and take him over. Sometimes they come across without an approach. No other option. If it's bad enough it's us, or, in Provo-speak, a *head-job*.'

'The difference is at least they can run.'

McAlister smiled. 'These lads are hooked. Couldn't live an ordinary existence. They'd die of boredom. They'd die in their beds and for them that's *waiting* to die. They're used to forcing the issue. In the end it's simply a matter of being *involved*. I'd be very surprised – assuming this Demurov's story is genuine – if they don't suffer from the same disease. The question is, why has he decided to jump *now*, after all these years?'

'He's had enough. Needs my help desperately. Wants to stay in England for ever and run his garage. I'm not entirely clear if this exists, is his dream, or even a demand. Whichever, it's very important to him.'

McAlister shook his head, firmly. 'Not enough reason. He's admitting to murder and conspiracy. There's more. A relationship?'

'Yes. A girl. Named Sandy. And a child. Born or unborn, I couldn't quite get.'

'More like it. He wants you to do what, precisely?'

'Save him from Kramer. His exact words.'

McAlister twisted Reardon's notes toward himself. 'Where is he?'

'Hung up before I could find out. He was clearly terrified of being overheard – wanted to get off that line the second he started speaking. I'm not sure he *knew* where he was. He might have been playing safe of course. I pressed him but it was hard enough just keeping him on the line. I've never heard anyone so scared. Like a child whimpering in the dark. What could scare a trained saboteur and killer so?'

'Maybe being out there too long?' McAlister pointed. 'What's this refer to? Legananny?'

'I wanted his location. He was chary. Probably afraid I'd send in the SAS and he'd have no bargaining position – if any position at all! I pressed and he mumbled something about being close to *big stones*. Wouldn't say any more. Afterwards I thought, the Dolmen? Legananny, County Down?'

'I'll have the local lads nose around discreetly for strangers.' McAlister put the notes down and studied Reardon's heavy face. 'You've spoken to anyone else about this, sir?'

'I called an Army friend on the mainland. Ministry of Defence. An old friend.'

McAlister poured coffee carefully. He pushed Reardon's cup toward him. 'An old and *trusted* friend?'

'Certainly.'

McAlister sipped. 'Carter said two soldiers stopped him on the road. We know from information received at Leary's that Brannigan was gunned down by two men. The time scale makes these two different groups. No way were they the same. So there's a four-man team out there. That's SAS style – as Carter implied.'

'I know. *Spetsnaz* use the same formation – according to my information.'

'Did Demurov actually *admit* they'd hit Brannigan?'

Reardon indicated the notes. *'Was not you, sir; the American was always the one.* Can't shake the inference there. Brought home the fact of being a target over here myself – though not in this case. Demurov was quite firm on that. Repeated it: *Was not you, sir.* Had to convince me I suppose – if he wanted my help – that I wasn't a target also.'

McAlister tapped the paper.

'What?' demanded Reardon, watching his eyes.

'He differentiates between you and Brannigan quite clearly, doesn't he? As *I* read this, the emphasis is: was not *you*, sir, the American was *always* the one. Making it clear you were never in the frame. Indicating they were warned who *not* to hit?' He looked up. 'Mistakes can be made. Two big men, similarly built. Under pressure there might have been a mix-up. They're trained pros so they'd have been thoroughly briefed. Wouldn't have gone in any other way – not if they're what Demurov says they are. So they'd have seen photographs of Brannigan – and you because you were with him so often. Would have been given movement details, location and so on. *You* were to be kept alive. Was that what he was telling you?'

'Possibly.'

'By inference, then, you were important to whoever sent them. Or whoever *ordered* them to be sent. Which logically implies something – someone – political. I'm widening the focus. You have to be prepared to see things you're not going to like.'

Reardon glowered at him then drank coffee, gloomily. 'Go on.'

McAlister thought: *You've reached the stage when you'd like it all to go away. It won't. I won't let it.*

He continued: 'Supposition: Demurov's in a noose. He's worked out, if he doesn't slip it soon it's going to strangle him. Maybe Brannigan was one twist too much. He remembers his briefing: realizes that whoever ordered the hit was worried a mistake might be made. So they're scared of you, of your influence, your direct access to Downing Street – the media haven't exactly been vague about your role, have they? He'd have been aware. You're his way out. Classic stress reflex: reaching out for the one who threatens whoever threatens him. In the early hours when he's at his lowest ebb.'

'So you believe he's genuine?'

'Czechs and East Germans were over here with the IRA for years. A hard game Moscow played with MI5 – stopped only by the collapse of the Soviet bloc. They were supposed to be mercenaries but few believed that. The SAS dealt, terminally, with any they found – so legend has it. That doesn't mean there aren't some out there somewhere, still, given cover by a lover, whatever? Anything is possible. No reason why the same shouldn't apply to left-behind *Spetsnaz*.' McAlister paused. 'How much did you tell your MOD friend?'

'As much as I had to, to get answers.'

'And his opinion?'

'*Spetsnaz* units are dug in deep near vital defence installations or political targets. Settled into our way of life. English speakers with low-profile jobs. Fully assimilated, yet in limbo. Waiting for orders that, now, will never come. Afraid, disillusioned. A cocked, loaded gun – with no finger to pull the trigger. He believes we may have to announce an amnesty to coax them out.'

McAlister leaned forward. '*Someone's* finger is on the trigger.'

'I know. What do we do?'

'Flush out Demurov and his team. But they're only the *weapon*. We need to know *why* Patrick Brannigan was murdered. If it wasn't IRA or UVF or any other local faction and Demurov's tale is fact and not disinformation we're into murky territory.'

'Disinformation?'

'You said it yourself: living permanently under cover, threatened constantly with exposure and arrest, anyone who knows the facts about these people has them completely at his mercy. This alleged controller of theirs . . .'

'Kramer.'

'. . . might *claim* he's working for the English secret police but could just as easily be in business for himself. Or for someone else. That's the thing about the secret world: anyone can say they're part of it and no one who isn't can prove otherwise. The truth is that Demurov and his team have little choice but to believe what they're told.'

'You must find Demurov,' urged Reardon. 'He'll give us answers.'

'He won't have any. Not to the questions we'll be asking.'

'He could give us Kramer.'

'Do you really believe that Kramer is that exposed? Or that he's the controlling mind here? If Demurov's "English secret police" *are* MI5 – with their own hidden agenda in all this – you can guarantee that Kramer's buried so deep we'll never unearth him.'

Reardon's fist smacked his palm in frustration. 'I keep asking myself the same question. Who gains by Brannigan's death? What would MI5 gain? Nothing. They lose face, credibility – they *lose*, McAlister. Everyone loses! Even the IRA: killing an American *must* cost them – if only in contributions! Yet, still, he was murdered.' He leaned back, wearily. 'So what do we do? Nothing? Let it fade? Yesterday's news?'

'If Demurov makes contact again tell him – no, *order* him, be authoritative, he may need that from you to make the jump – order him to come to you here. If for whatever reason he can't do that, order him to go to some alternative point – easily identifiable – and go and get him yourself. I'll make sure there's backup.'

'Is it possible to check on Demurov? His background? A Polish *émigré* might possibly be on your files?'

'There'd have had to be a reason for our interest in the first place – and the whole purpose of deep cover is to avoid official interest so I very much doubt that anything will turn up. I'll check – discreetly – but don't expect much. If we don't have anything I'll try Immigration Intelligence at Harmondsworth. There's OTIS – Overstayers Tracing Intelligence Service – but that's Home Office and if Five *are* involved we'd be plugged right into them.'

Reardon grimaced. 'What do we do if Demurov doesn't make contact again?'

McAlister arose. 'Sir, there's one factor in all of this that we can't ignore. We're dealing with the murder of an influential, well-connected, wealthy American. We're in danger of losing sight of that among all the other issues involved: drugs, the million-dollar reward, Brannigan's alleged contact with the IRA and now Demurov with his *Spetsnaz* story.'

'You think we're being . . . deflected?'

'I don't know. I *do* know that the man who was closest to Brannigan here – besides you – has disappeared after sowing some very nasty seeds in both our minds. I want a long, hard talk with ex-major Marcus Carter.'

'And I've planted those same seeds in the Prime Minister's mind,' murmured Reardon. 'Can you find Carter? There's a car phone in the Mercedes – have you thought of calling that?'

'Switched off. No matter, no one moves far in Northern Ireland without us knowing. If he's still here we'll find him.'

'And if he's – they've – left?'

'Then whoever is behind this has won. But if I read Carter correctly he's going nowhere – except for someone's jugular. I'd guess he's out there trying to find out *whose*. From what you've told me of Mrs Brannigan – and my brief encounter with her – she isn't likely to discourage him.'

Reardon added sombrely: 'Aren't we – less emotively – attempting the same thing?'

'We shall stay within the law,' McAlister replied, sternly.

'And they won't?'

'Mrs Brannigan doesn't believe we can deliver justice. Depending on how deep this goes – perhaps I should say *high* – she may be right. Let me put it brutally to you, sir. You have me, an officer of the law; she has an executioner.'

'I think you had better find Carter – quickly.'

C ARTER WAS a few feet above them.
He had arrived back in Hannah Armitage's car, looked for the Mercedes, saw it parked in a back slot of the Culloden's packed car park, deliberately found the furthest, tightest corner under a tree for himself then made for reception and had the night porter ring her suite.

She took a while to answer, sounding drugged, her speech slurred. '*Carter!* They let you go? I'm sorry, I've taken a pill. What's happened!'

'I'm coming up. Take a cold shower. I need you completely awake.'

She had unlocked the suite doors for him. Inside, he could hear the hiss of water and her hurried movements in the bathroom.

He saw the note on a table beside a savagely torn envelope and read the cut-and-paste lettering. ONE MILLION DOLLARS TODAY. WAIT FOR COMMAND.

He went to the bathroom door with it. 'When did this come?'

The rush of water stopped. She opened the door, a towel loosely clasped to her front. 'The desk gave it to me when I got back.'

'Delivered when?'

'Immediately after we left. To the security hut. I asked for a description of whoever delivered it but that particular guard had gone off duty. I insisted the desk call him. He remembered the man.'

'That's what he's paid for.'

'Fair, slim, late twenties, maybe thirties. Young looking. He said nothing. It was over in a moment. He was in a hurry. The guard thought he was with the security services.'

'Why?'

'Because of Patrick, I suppose. He said he had the *look*.' She

107

turned away, staring blearily into the steamed mirror, uncaring about her nakedness. She pinched her cheeks, fighting the numbing effects of the barbiturates.

Carter left her and dropped tiredly into one of the armchairs: he hadn't slept in almost twenty-four hours. He stared at the ransom note, one word holding him.

*Command.*

Not instructions, not directions; not even orders.

He remembered figures in camouflage stepping out into the speeding Mercedes' headlights; painted faces; confident barked commands; almost *felt* the deliberate blow to his skull with the assault rifle which he knew, ill judged, could have killed him but instead left him with no more than mild concussion and a few stitches. He had few doubts then and none now: their carriage, authority, confidence – and something only the French managed to put into words, *esprit de corps* – marked them indelibly for him as professional soldiers from an élite unit. Or had been; once. Carter knew. He'd been there too.

The British knew about DISTANT THUNDER.

It was the only possible explanation.

But still not enough.

There was more he couldn't nail down.

He understood them being mad as hell if they knew what he now knew. He knew them well – and this wasn't how they reacted under threat. This was *mad*, mad. They were cold, calculating; they might – probably would – kill Brannigan the CIA negotiator and, yes, try and shift the blame on to the Provisional IRA – the natural patsies – but the demand for the offered reward? The severed heads?

*Whose* heads, goddamnit?

The paradox continued relentlessly. The cold, professional, silent killing of the sleeping Melsham, the perverted, bloody, *obscene* thing done to Armitage, the taking of the children before being given any chance to pay what had been freely offered – taking them before being given commands as to *how* to pay!

A line of insanity seemed to run through the succession of events, as though someone had gone off the rails.

Carter knew how easy that could be for a particular type of soldier. The kind he had been. Waking one day to find the blood on your hands veiling your eyes, your everything; seeping into your

108

mind until all there was, was blood; asleep or awake. You watch for it in your comrades, hoping to God they're watching *you* because if they weren't . . .

He remembered the blood pooling thickly around Hannah Armitage, the smell of it.

'Tell me,' Kate Brannigan said, sitting opposite him, wrapped in a thick towelling robe, seeming smaller than before, hair wet and straggly; apprehension, fear, vivid in her barbiturate-dulled eyes.

*You're too vulnerable right now.*

There was no other time. He knew it had to be now.

'For God's sake tell me!'

'The children have been taken.' He nodded at the note. 'I'd guess by those people. They killed everyone. Brenda, Armitage, Melsham. All of them. I couldn't do a thing. Couldn't save any of them, couldn't stop it. They locked me up and condemned themselves. I could have stopped it. I know I could.'

He sat watching her disintegrate and could do nothing; her head fell, she buried her face in her robe over her thighs, a small wail rising from deep inside, seeming to come from all of her, through her skin, her wet hair, all of her. He moved and she threw an arm straight out, fingers splayed, rigid, holding him at bay.

He could do nothing.

Except kill for her.

Which he would do.

Eventually.

*Absolute certainty.*

With a little something added for Hannah Armitage.

He saw Brannigan's dull silver attaché case beside her new and still unpacked luggage – went to it, removed the connectors, set it up, touched in a number on the panel and watched the digital display flash rapidly, settling momentarily then continuing until, finally, making the secure connection with Langley. He pressed the control so that she could hear.

'Parriss? Carter. Don't interrupt. Your assets in the South have been liquidated. All of them. I've cleared all company stock. I have it safe. Better for you – and for me.'

'We'll want it back. The *matériel*. All of it.'

'In time. You won't get your people back.'

109

'You *have* evaluated your position, Carter?'

'It wasn't me, Parriss. They'd taken me out of it. Understand that before you make more mistakes.'

'So who?'

'Distant Thunder,' Carter said and listened to the silence. He heard the distant electronic warbling as the microwave frequencies rapidly changed, resisting tracking.

'What do you want?' asked Parriss finally.

'One million dollars. Now, today.'

'You're being unrealistic. Over-ambitious.'

Carter didn't disguise his contempt. 'It's not for me.'

'Really?'

'The children have been taken. We have the demand. Same as before. One million US. Parriss, hear me, I'm not prepared to stand by, not prepared to get *their* heads in a box. I'll help or I'll destroy your operation. I did it in Bogotá – September ninety-one – check it out. I'll do it here too. Choose. Right now.'

'There is no choice. Will she go along? Go through with it? Distant Thunder? She knows?'

'She'll do anything.' Carter looked at Kate who stared at him like someone out of their mind.

'Carter?'

'I'm here.'

'She'll *have* to go through with it, Carter. There's no other way. There's no time to set anything else up. It needs to be done now whilst Brannigan's collateral holds with them. They're open to her if she can do it. Is she up to it?'

'She's up to it.'

'You're sure.'

'I'm sure.'

He watched the tears roll down her face. She trembled as if she were freezing. 'The money, Parriss. Today. Don't stall. You can arrange anything, anywhere, any time. Do it or I'll blow this apart. I mean it.'

'There's a private merchant bank there we can deal through. They can handle it.'

'If you own it, sure they can.'

Parriss gave an address in Belfast's financial district.

'When?'

'You said immediately. Someone will be waiting. Frankel. Carter, listen: you know what we want, we don't get it we'll get you. It's only a matter of time.'

'And if the Brits know too?'

'They don't.'

'How can you be sure?'

'Because if they did, you wouldn't be talking to me right now and Mrs Brannigan would be with her husband – the children too if it was unavoidable. The British are the most ruthless people on God's earth when they have to be.'

'Then start worrying, because if it's not them, there's a rogue out there rampaging through every move you've made – and you don't have a goddamn idea *who*.'

'We assumed you, Carter. Maybe we still do.'

'So why am I calling you, telling you all this?'

'You're not calling, you're negotiating.'

'For what?'

'One million dollars, of course.'

'Which you're willing to pay?'

'If it keeps you silent of course we're willing to pay. That's sound business.'

'And the children? You don't care about them?'

'Have they *truly* gone, Carter?'

'You son-of-a-bitch! Yes!'

'You're the bodyguard. You lost them. They're your responsibility.'

'I'm not behind this, Parriss. Make that clear to your people. I've enough problems without your hired guns on my back. You send any I'll send them back, black-bagged.'

'You're safe, for now. Meantime we'll check out your "rogue". If one really exists we'll find the beast and cull it.'

Carter heard Hannah Armitage's last gasped words: *He's evil!*

He put down the hand set, disconnected and closed the case.

*I'll* cull the beast, Parriss.

He was still a soldier and a soldier could only act when he was certain of his objectives. He knew what they were now. End her pain, spare her from danger: achieve those, then . . .

111

'Sleep some more,' he told her. 'I'll get the money.'

'I'll never sleep again.'

'You will.'

'I'll only wake to this nightmare.'

'Then you'll have to do something to end it.'

'What? Tell me. I'll do anything.' She stared at him. 'I'll kill to get my children back.'

'What did Armitage want you to do?'

'Make contact with *them*.'

'IRA?'

'Yes.'

'*That's* what you have to do.'

'I'm scared.'

'Good, that'll keep you alive.'

'Do they have my children?'

He shook his head. 'I don't believe so.'

'It *can't* be the British?'

'It can.'

'What did Patrick do to them?' She shrieked, rising: '*What could be so bad they'd take my babies!*'

He grasped her, pinning her arms. 'You have to hold on. I don't know what's happening out there. Not all of it. I know something's gone bad.'

She stopped struggling, her face close, he couldn't shake Armitage from his mind, even her hair smelled the same. He released her.

'You said *rogue*?'

'It's off the rails somewhere. It happens. This is the real world, people plan, people fuck up, sometimes intentionally, sometimes *inside* . . . they lose control and you get what we have here, a kind of madness. I know what I'm talking about.'

'Bogotá? Is that what happened? To *you*? Armitage told me. She was there. She told me about the heads.'

He pulled her face around to his. 'I'm not the rogue, Kate.'

'I believe you.' She freed herself from his grip. 'Will you get my children back?'

'I've got you the money. Right now that's all that matters. Right now that's all you can take. You have enough to do.'

112

'What am I getting in to?' She nodded at the satellite communications equipment he had used. 'What is Distant Thunder?'

He shook his head firmly. 'No. If you *have* to know more, I'll tell you. You won't thank me for telling you.'

'It's bad?'

'It's bad.'

'Why would Patrick get involved? He—'

'Didn't have a choice. Not with Langley. When you're in, you're in for ever, for all of it. You don't get the option.'

She closed her eyes. 'Don't let me down. *Please.*'

'Count on it.'

'Marcus, could *Langley* have taken the children? Making certain I co-operated?'

'Langley will kill – even kill their own – if the circumstances demand it. I was there, Kate. No, Langley didn't do it.'

His stillness, his certainty, were terrifying.

Her fear took her breath away. She gasped: 'What kind of people have my children?'

'I'll get them back, Kate. I swear I'll get them back.'

A dreadful vision sliced through her mind. *'Dear God, not their heads in a box! I couldn't live!'*

She gripped him, desperate for his strength as her own failed. She had to go on, whatever it took to make that next step forward. If she faltered it was over. He felt like rock. One rock in a sea of anguish threatening to sweep her away. She clung to him, hard; her life depending on it.

# CHAPTER SEVEN

T HE SHOTGUN blast shook everything in the rickety dormer room. Max jerked awake, catching sight of himself in the weary mirror of the old wardrobe; a dark shuddering shape, bedclothes bunched at his tight waist, hair spiked, eyes wide.

The mirror stilled but not before he was up and moving for the Browning they had all been issued with by the still-eyed armourer who had opened the boot of the dirty Ford at the airport and pointed out the jack tucked behind the spare wheel with a soft, mocking, '*Now don't start a war.*'

He was at the top of the stairs, hard naked belly on the floorboards, then slipping like water down them, head first, the heavy 9mm ahead and raised, one-handed, the other his brake and he didn't give a *fuck* about splinters. Arnie's bed was empty. Maybe the war had begun.

He smelled the cordite. Smelled the direction of it. The door, to the right by the telephone, a meagre stripe of light at its base. He smelled what the shotgun had done. He gagged. He always gagged even though he had smelled enough exploded shit in his time to cover half the cliff they were perched on.

Max was naked and even in the dark of the stairwell, very white.

The landlord opened the door, shotgun in hand, barrels down, seeing him instantly; his jutting buttocks, muscular back, hands raised, black gleam between them; then the sudden flare, the explosion of stars, the fire at his own chest, the smell of burning which he knew was himself.

He felt no pain, slumped against the foot of his bed, waiting for Max to finish him. He felt bewildered. Tired. *Jesus* he was tired.

Max never came. He had died instantly, a reflex tug on the

shotgun's trigger discharging the second barrel barely two feet from his upturned face.

As the morning light grew, the landlord could see what was left and turned away.

Arnie whispered. 'Finish me.'

'Only had the two shells, son,' murmured the landlord, looking at the gutted form thrown down by the opposite wall. 'You should be gone.'

'Max's gun. Get it.'

'Do it yourself.'

'I can't move. Please.'

'They'll want you alive.'

'They're dead already. *Please.*'

'Ye're not making sense.'

'Hide yourself. But give me Max's gun.'

'I'll not move. I'm bleeding to death.'

'Then pray it comes soon.' Arnie closed his eyes. There was no pain. No sensation. Nothing. *Only your head is alive and your head is all Rick needs.*

A car crunched on gravel outside.

'You're a fool,' Arnie murmured.

'Your other two friends aren't here, are they?'

'They will be, old man.'

THE PRIME Minister sat alone, wading steadily through the official red boxes he could never escape from – nor wanted to – though he often wished their contents would show some sign of reducing after the hours he regularly put into dealing with them. They filled his life and, like his ever growing responsibilities, someone was always waiting to add to them.

'Come!' he snapped, irritated by the interruption so early that Saturday morning – contrary to his instructions not to be disturbed.

The Director-General of the Security Service (MI5) entered briskly with a flustered Downing Street secretary in tow.

'I know this is irregular, Prime Minister, but I must speak with you.'

He nodded, dismissing the secretary, then arose. 'Director-General?'

She turned, waiting for the double doors of the cabinet room to close.

He had guessed why she was there. 'You've heard I've been asking questions?'

'Sir?'

'The Brannigan business.'

'Everyone is asking questions, sir,' she replied, cautiously. 'We still are.' Her mouth tightened. 'If you have questions concerning my Service why haven't you approached me directly, sir?'

'Why are you here?' he countered, determined to keep the higher ground. His admission had been foolish. She had caught him unawares: half his mind on his red boxes, half still on his second early hours and unpleasant telephone conversation with the American President within two days. He had to tread carefully. This was a tough professional before him. He needed loyal allies not strong enemies.

She gazed at him with veiled eyes.

He never had been able to read her. Closing the red box before him he indicated one chair in the row lining the long coffin-shaped cabinet table. 'Whatever you have to say must be important?'

She had a stillness he found unnerving and a directness in crises which – he bore witness – could cut his senior ministers down like wheat under the scythe. 'Prime Minister, something is going on. I want to know precisely what!'

'That is what *I've* been asking.'

'Then I repeat, you should have come directly to me.'

Silence hung.

He nodded. 'It's obvious you know something.'

She passed over a document folder taken from her slim leather case. 'Telephone transcript. You'd better read it.'

He did.

Done, he closed the folder. 'Does Mr Reardon know you keep a verbatim record of his calls?' Say it, he scolded himself. *Bug. You bugged my personal representative.*

'It's essential we have advance knowledge of his movements. Especially after Brannigan's murder.' She nodded at the folder. 'He's suddenly taken to acting rashly. Almost left for the airport yesterday without his bodyguard! He came here, I understand?'

He stated, brusquely: 'Reardon was – *is still* – directly responsible to me. He reports directly to me. I would have thought this guaranteed total confidentiality. He has a right to expect that under these circumstances certain . . . organs of state . . . are kept, if not at arm's length, then certainly out of earshot. He is already sensitive about his reports being distributed to other government departments. He would be furious to hear that his every word is being recorded. Quite frankly, Director-General, *I* am!'

'If we had been allowed to – monitor – Patrick Brannigan's calls he might not be dead today,' she said, steadily.

He had expressly forbidden that action. He remembered, clearly, signing the order: could see himself doing it. *Damn.*

She was gazing above his head, her eyes apparently on the portrait of Walpole above the mantelpiece behind him.

Comparisons? he wondered. Did she care about history? How little he knew of her – or of any of the heads of his various intelligence and counter-intelligence services. *Heads.* A good word. Heads wearing masks concealing faces he never truly saw. Did anyone? You worry too much, he told himself. Probably she was only looking at the clock.

He opened the folder again. '*Improbable* . . . don't you think? Former Soviet troops lurking behind English identities – killing Americans?'

'You're missing the point, sir.'

'You're the second person to tell me that in two days. Reardon was the other. What *is* the point?'

'You saw Sinn Fein's press conference last night denying IRA involvement in the murder?'

'Of course.'

'They could be telling the truth. We believe they are. Which means a very dangerous game is being played here.'

He glanced up.

'I think you're in danger of being the ball, sir.'

He met her eyes, wanting her unreserved co-operation, wanting to trust her, wanting the monolith she controlled firmly behind him

117

and not – as was rumoured with at least one past premier – scheming to destroy him.

She asked: 'Are you at liberty to tell me the state of our relationship with America – at this moment?'

'I hope no worse than it was at four o'clock this morning – which was when I last spoke with the President. Then, it was icy. Yesterday it was cool. Tomorrow? Well, perhaps you could advise on that? You seem to be running ahead of me!'

'Thinking ahead, Prime Minister: doing what I was appointed to do.' Her eyes were searching. 'I would like you to be frank with me, sir?'

'Within the limits of your need to know, I shall be.'

'This may be outside those limits. In my judgement the situation demands—'

'I'll decide that,' he interrupted. 'Go on.'

She spread her fingers over her briefcase and looked at them, her fingernails trim, colourless, her hands tanned and strong. He noticed small calluses and wondered if they were from a racquet sport or one of her service's harder courses he had heard gossip about. She was certainly still young enough to survive them.

She asked: 'Do you have knowledge of a current MI6 operation in Ulster?'

He frowned, annoyed. 'I will not get involved in your rivalry with SIS. In these dangerous times it should not exist!'

'It doesn't. Certainly not in that theatre of operations. They lost Northern Ireland to us. No longer have a charter to operate there. *Your* government's decision, sir.'

'You're implying they are?'

She indicated the transcript. 'Reardon's caller – this man Anatoly Demurov – claims he works for the "English secret police". By implication *us*.'

'And you're here to assure me he does not?'

'Absolutely.'

'So? He's SIS? That's what you want me to believe? He's Six's man?'

'Six's agent, yes. Or recruited by one of theirs. Probably this *Kramer* he mentions. Recruited under a false flag. *Our* flag. Demurov believes he is working for the Security Services when in fact he's SIS every step of the *bloody* way. Literally,' she added, heavily.

Her own anger – checked hard but still glowing behind her eyes – surprised him. And disturbed him. He had never seen it displayed before. She had always presented herself – convincingly – as emotionless.

'Supposition,' he countered. 'Unless you've proof?'

'Not yet.'

'When?'

She shrugged, not nonchalantly, weightily; burdened by reality. 'Any move we make could ring alarm bells at Century House.'

'*If* it is Six.'

She looked at him, silent; confident.

'You felt you should talk to me first.'

'The final responsibility is yours, sir. If a scandal stemming from this broke, you are the Prime Minister . . .'

He leaned back in his tall chair. It creaked loudly in the dead silence. 'And the prime target?'

She gave a small hard smile.

He cleared his throat. 'I had a meeting with the Cabinet Secretary last night. I asked to be apprised of any operations mounted by SIS which might – however remotely – involve him. Brannigan was, after all, a well-travelled man, a great deal of his time was spent in world hot-spots.'

'*Asked*, sir? Forgive me, but you could have ordered—'

'You don't knock holes in your own boat in rough seas.'

Her eyebrows lifted fractionally at his coded admission. 'Why did you seek this information? Suspicion? Or something firmer?'

He felt the need to confide in her, felt hemmed in, felt the weight, the dreadful responsibility, of losing an historic, centuries-old relationship – and with it the country's most powerful ally both militarily and economically. He had the British Ambassador in Washington's terse reply to his overnight enquiry as to the President's present disposition toward Britain beside him:

*. . . The American sun is shining on Germany and Japan which means the old Axis shadow falls on us again – perhaps not militarily, but in these harsh times a trade war can be as catastrophic as the real thing. Efforts must be made to safeguard what remains of the Special Relationship. I sense – from my cool reception at last evening's party at the White House – that matters are currently at a low ebb; something must be done . . .*

He felt the cold grip of failure clasp him, readying to cast him aside – like others who once sat where he sat now.

He told her what Reardon had flown to London to tell him. That Marcus Carter believed the British, not the IRA, had killed his charge and that his ambushers were Special Forces personnel – possibly SAS. That Reardon had begun, seriously, to believe a conspiracy was in full flow. Full *bloody* flow, he thought, echoing her. The worst kind of conspiracy, he said: formless, apparently motiveless; only violence on the surface warning of deeper undercurrents beneath.

When he was done she leaned toward him across the table. 'What will you allow me to do, Prime Minister?'

'What *can* you do? You only have suspicions. If I'm to believe it *is* the Secret Intelligence Service behind this – running some covert operation – then I *must* have motive! What have they to gain? Your service's discomfiture? My downfall? That's what you're hinting at, isn't it? So . . . what? And *why?*'

'You have preconceptions about us and Six, Prime Minister,' she stated, flatly. 'They blur the issue here.'

'*Disregard* them!' he snapped.

'Very well. Operation: kill Patrick Brannigan and blame the Provisional IRA for the murder. Objective: destroy the on-going very lucrative relationship the IRA enjoys with a healthy proportion of Irish Americans – and all those other sympathetic groups: liberals, leftists, revolutionary or otherwise, campus radicals, the list goes on. Brannigan had Irish blood. He was perfect. The perfect target.'

'The man was dealing personally with *me*! They surely wouldn't risk the possible consequences?'

She looked at him, unflinching.

'If this is true I'd have to admit to the President that—' He faltered, appalled at the thought.

'Six have no great love for the present American administration, sir. You're aware of that I'm sure. If further damage is done to your personal standing with the President they wouldn't weep in their pink gins.'

He stared at her.

She pressed him. 'Sir, *we* exist to stop trouble, to protect, to defend the realm. Six exists to *foment* trouble if or when such action is considered to be in the national interest. Who decides what is the

120

national interest? You? Cabinet? Privy Council? Parliament? All of these *and*, if they so chose, your Secret Intelligence Service also. So easily. You need never be consulted. Need never know. They don't exist, yet have almost unlimited power, secret funding – and a very long arm. They enjoy the highest responsibility and the least accountability – until parliament does to them what they did to us: gives them a foundation in law. SIS can and I believe *would* do whatever they considered most expedient – if the stakes were high enough. They are – here.'

'But to begin such an investigation would have terrible repercussions. I don't need to explain to *you* what happens when you drop a stone into the waters of the secret world. The ripples . . .'

She raised both hands, quickly. 'No! No investigation. We have to deal with this in a way which suits our purpose. We need to get to the centre of the conspiracy. And nail it. Nail *them*, hard.'

'Someone said that nailing down the Secret Intelligence Service is like trying to nail jelly to a wall.'

'Freeze it first,' she said, unsmiling.

He breathed. 'How?'

'We have Demurov.'

He indicated the transcript. 'You don't.'

'He'll make contact again with Reardon – or this RUC Special Branch officer, DI McAlister, Reardon's confiding in will find him. We need do nothing. When the time comes we act. Get the information we need from Demurov and his comrades. Then it will be up to you how you deal with it, Prime Minister. How many ripples you cause.'

'This man McAlister? How good is he?'

'He'll do the job, sir. He's the man with the contacts, the man who knows what's rumbling over there.'

'And how long before those rumbles become heard?'

'McAlister doesn't appear to be passing very much on to his superiors. There appears to be a tacit agreement – discretion – made between himself and Reardon.' She nodded at the small machine. 'Reardon isn't even certain of you, sir.'

'I heard,' he said tightly. 'We need to know what's going on between them. *Away* from telephones.'

'We have a man close to Reardon. Couldn't be closer. His

121

bodyguard, Ellis. We know everything that passes between Reardon and McAlister. You don't need details of how.'

He frowned, annoyed. 'I ordered the *SAS* to provide a man for Reardon. I made the call myself!'

'He is Hereford's man, sir – via Curzon Street.'

'Your world!' He pushed the transcript away from him. 'Why wait for Demurov to contact Reardon? From the sound of that he may have been apprehended making that call. With your resources surely you could mount a discreet search for these people?'

'As I said, sir: if Six *is* involved, we'd risk alerting them of our interest. Any official action will do precisely that. Reardon is an economist. His actions – if anything blew up from this – could be construed as, well, paranoia. As you said yourself – he seems to be blaming himself, for Brannigan's death.'

'This man McAlister is a Special Branch officer. That's as official as you can get!'

She nodded. 'But known as something of a maverick, sir. Generally plays things very close to his chest. Their best agent runner. The way he is handling this won't appear at all strange – or out of the ordinary, believe me.'

'I hope so. You have to understand what's at stake here. What I need.'

'You need the truth. Discreetly. You need to limit damage between us and the United States; between Downing Street and the White House; between yourself and the President. I understand fully, sir. That is why Reardon – with McAlister behind him – must be allowed to run free. They're your hounds; let them run the fox to ground. Once that's done . . . well, then you must decide what you wish to do.'

He protested: 'I've read MOD reports in the past. *Spetsnaz* are highly trained assassins and saboteurs. Reardon, by any stretch of the imagination, is no *hound* to their fox!'

'Reardon has Ellis for protection and McAlister, well, he takes risks every minute of every day in Northern Ireland. You need to know what's going on here, Prime Minister. *You have to know.* I appreciate your concern for a civilian but the only question you need ask yourself is: Does the greater issue here justify putting a life – or lives – at risk?'

He breathed.

'Do I let it run, Prime Minister?'

'Have I an alternative?'

'You could do nothing, of course.'

'And it might go away? There is that school of thought in politics currently. Do you believe in this instance that might work?'

She shook her head, firmly.

He stood. 'I want to know exactly what's going on at all times. And I don't want Reardon's life put at risk, *unnecessarily*. No risking him to get it over faster or cleaner. He trusts me. You understand?'

'Of course, sir. I'll report directly to you.' She moved briskly to the doors.

'If Reardon contacts me shouldn't I at least tell him—'

She turned, fast. 'Reardon mustn't know! I wouldn't discuss the matter at all, sir. Even on a secure link. If he does call or come to see you – and I don't believe he will the way he's apparently thinking now – I'd take the line with him that you're not pursuing the matter personally any further. That you've every confidence in the Security Service. You've placed the matter in our hands.'

'That may push him into more rash action! He already suspects you.'

'Rash actions often produce *reaction*, sir. At this moment we need that. *You* need that.'

He watched the double doors close then sat, pondering all of it. Had he just found answers or just added more questions to the pot? Whichever – the pot was close to boiling and he was holding it. And he couldn't let go. He hadn't the option. Leaders never had: great, or otherwise.

He stared ahead bleakly, his red boxes discarded.

He was scared.

And still alone.

*Power is silence, with no counsel but your own*, Walpole might have whispered behind him.

He looked at his secure telephone line. There were others who shared the burdens, the loneliness, of power. Grateful friends, once enemies; past masters of the secret world and keepers of the greatest secrets, still. Deals were currently in progress: favours were owed. The fleshy face of the Russian leader hovered temptingly. Would you unlock this box for me, *tovarishch*? Reveal for me the new lives, the real faces of your abandoned warriors: your Spartans who sit on our sea-wet rocks and destroy our endeavours?

CARTER HEADED for the south side of Donegal Square in Belfast's city centre, making directly for the address of the small merchant bank Parriss had given.

'You've been here before. Like the house across the border,' said Kate Brannigan. 'With Patrick. We're doing all the things he did, aren't we? How much do you know that you're not telling me?'

'I got as far as the door. Hired guns don't get invited inside banks. Especially private banks.'

'You haven't answered me.'

He halted the Mercedes. 'Not now. Stay in the car, I'll deal with this.'

'No.'

'I've got some hard questions to ask,' he warned.

Her jaw was set, anger defeating the despair she had felt barely an hour before. 'Carter, I know *everything* that happens from now on, all right? I see it, I hear it for myself! I'm not going to be fooled any more, not going to be sent away again. I can ask as hard as you can, maybe harder, I've got more at stake – *my whole life*. You hear me?'

'I hear you.'

The street was deserted. Nobody left vehicles overnight on Belfast's city centre streets.

A gleaming BMW coupé drew up behind them. The driver got out: small, dapper, bald; as polished as his car, nothing about him suggesting he had been ordered from his bed before dawn that Saturday morning.

'It's on,' said Carter, exiting the Mercedes, opening the boot and removing Patrick Brannigan's travel-worn suitcase – emptied for the money. The man did not offer his hand. He said: 'Frankel,' then glanced uncomfortably at Kate Brannigan.

An Army helicopter thudded somewhere overhead.

Carter nodded. 'Mrs Brannigan.'

'I know. The TV. Terrible. My condolences.'

'You've met with my husband before, Mr Frankel?'

His eyes were pebbles in a cold pool. 'Inside is better I think.'

His office was perfect: minimalist, nothing out of place, nothing that could be hidden left in view; his desk six square feet of smoked glass without a finger mark on it. He indicated soft beige leather chairs then took his own – identical but larger – and switched on the black NEXT computer beside him, his eyes flicking momentarily to the scrolling numbers on the screen before settling on Kate. 'I met your husband once, Mrs Brannigan. We would have met again . . .' He glanced at the screen as if for a prompt, then fell silent.

'Why? Why did you meet?'

'I don't think I can discuss that.'

She said: 'Carter, please put your gun on Mr Frankel's desk.'

Frankel looked at Carter who laid his dull ceramic automatic on the smoked glass, making a dead *clunk*.

Frankel stared at it. He said flatly: 'It's out of the question. You don't quite grasp the situation here, Mrs Brannigan. You're dealing with something way beyond—'

'Mr Frankel, let *me* make a statement about the situation here. I have just been widowed. My husband suffered a violent, brutal death. Murdered in cold blood. I am also a mother whose children – *all* of them – have been kidnapped overnight by people who may be reacting to acts the people you represent are responsible for. I am, at present, unstable. I am not well disposed to you or your masters – who seem to be the motivators of these tragedies which have fallen on me. If you don't give me answers to my questions I can't be responsible for my actions. I *will* not – afterwards – be held responsible. Any court of law would concur. I am a lawyer, I speak with authority.' She looked at the hand gun. 'I might kill you – or, more likely, as I'm not used to handling firearms, maim you for life. I will suffer no remorse. Do you understand me?'

Frankel licked his lips. 'Mrs Brannigan, I hear what you're saying. But *you* must understand we're not dealing with *private* matters here. This—' He winced as if saying the words were going to hurt him. 'This is government business. You've been made aware of that I understand. There are laws I must abide by. I have American citizenship. Dual citizenship actually.'

'For services rendered or convenience, Mr Frankel? Never mind. I repeat: why did my husband come to see you?'

Frankel's rounded shoulders lifted. 'Money. Why else?'

'Money for his business? The project, here in Ulster?'

'Of course.'

'What else? Specifically.'

He stared at her, defiance – or perhaps disbelief in her ability to carry out her threat – in his small eyes.

'Don't doubt me, Mr Frankel. I am close to the limit of my control, if not my sanity.'

Frankel shifted. 'There was a possibility funds might be needed in – another – direction. In the event this was not the case.'

'Which is why he's holding so much cash,' said Carter. 'They didn't want paying. Not in cash.'

'I know no more.' Frankel laid both scrubbed pink hands on the smoked glass. 'That's it.' He lifted his hands, blinked at the glass and passed his spotless linen handkerchief over the blemish.

Carter growled. 'I think you know a whole damn lot more. What would have satisfied them? What *will* satisfy them?'

Kate glanced at him. 'The IRA?'

Carter nodded. 'Patrick needed information from them for Langley. Desperately. The Provisional Northern Command wanted something money couldn't buy, but which they knew Washington could supply if pressure was applied – hard. They had plenty to squeeze with.'

Frankel's pink face had paled. 'I swear I know nothing of any arrangements other than financial!'

Carter smiled coldly. 'You never heard the word *Stinger*?'

'I don't know what you mean.'

'SAM, Frankel. Surface-to-air missile. They bring down choppers in the kind of pieces you can sweep up by hand. The IRA have been after one – as many as they could get their hands on – for years, but no one's been crazy enough to deal. Not until now. The Brits have a blanket warning out in the arms market: supply Stingers to the IRA and face summary execution, no question. Washington has the same threat out on supply to all terror groups, that's why airliners get brought down the difficult, risky way – smuggling bombs on board. If the Brits got word that someone even breathed the word

126

Stinger in the ear of the IRA the SAS would be deployed fast with orders not to take prisoners. Helicopters are the single most important weapon the Brits have here. Eyes, ears, trackers, the whole surveillance ball game which is the only game there is over here. They'd obey no conventions, show no mercy, if that situation was threatened. They would even kill an American who promised to relieve a chunk of their economic troubles over here. I believe they did.' Carter looked directly at Frankel. 'They would *certainly* kill anyone who aided in the arrangement of a Stinger deal if they were given his name.'

'I don't know a damn thing!'

'Hurt him if you have to,' Kate Brannigan said. 'Just make sure – afterwards – he can open wherever he keeps my one million dollars.'

Frankel froze.

Kate glared.'You *do* have the money?'

He stuttered: 'The delivery of the money is subject to a condition, Mrs Brannigan . . . not mine personally you understand!'

'Get Parriss on the line,' growled Carter. 'And don't tell me you haven't the facilities!'

'He's not available. No one at Langley is. They won't talk, I swear. You have to do what they want. I've been instructed to tell you the money is here. I guarantee that it is. As soon as you've complied with the condition I will *gladly* hand it over. Today, as agreed. I swear. Please just do what they want.'

'We don't have time for this, Frankel,' Carter said. 'There's three small lives riding on us having that money.' He reached for the automatic, cocked then pointed it. 'Open the safe.'

'I can't. It's time-locked until Monday morning.' He nodded at the black terminal on his desk. 'Langley can over-ride. I can't. I'm telling the truth!'

Kate Brannigan's voice was flat, resigned: 'What do I have to do?'

Frankel leaned forward, eagerly. 'Do what you agreed.'

Her eyes flicked to his telephone.

'No! Not from here! Use public phones. *Definitely* not your car phone.' He glanced at Carter. 'Alone, Mrs Brannigan. You must go alone. You have to take a taxi. A black cab. Their procedures are very controlled. Once you have been picked up I will hand the money to Mr Carter.'

Kate looked at Carter. 'Oh God,' she whispered.

Carter said: 'Where's your bathroom, Frankel?'

'Just outside the door.'

'It has a lock?'

'Certainly.'

'Use it.'

'I don't need—'

'You do.'

Carter marched him, the automatic at his back, to an outer lobby. Frankel unlocked a door. 'How long am I going to be in there?'

'As long as it takes.'

Carter took his leather key pouch from him, pushed him inside, turned the key, went back into the office, leaned over the desk, tapped a sequence into the keyboard and switched off the computer.

'Erasing his recording,' he explained, facing her. 'Kate, I thought I'd be able to save you from this. Get the money, make the pay-off, take the kids and go. I was an idiot. Parriss went along with what I was saying to give himself time to think.' He nodded at Frankel's chair. 'And act.'

She drew her shoulders up. 'I can do whatever they want. If I *have* to I can.'

'I know you can.'

'So let's do it. Let's do it and *go!*'

'You don't know the cost.'

'Cost? I don't care. I want my children back. They're worth any cost.'

'How many lives are your children's worth, Kate?'

'I don't understand?'

'Yes, you do. How many lives would you be prepared to sacrifice to have them safe? It might come down to that.'

'*I don't know!* How could I? Don't ask me!'

'I'm asking you if you really want to know what this is all about. It's up to you if you hear it from me, now – or the Provos later. They'll expect you to know. If you react badly they might too. I can't be there to protect you.'

'I don't care *who* tells me. I want my children back. That's all!'

'Did Armitage tell you what you're supposed to get for Langley?'

'Names. A list of terror groups the IRA are in contact with. What's so damn *bad* about that?'

'Langley already knows the names and locations of every active terror group in the world today and shares that information with the world's intelligence organizations. They're after names of *specific* terror groups. Groups – or individuals within groups. They're compiling a hit-list. They want you to get it.'

She snapped: 'I can live with the deaths of a few terrorists on my conscience.'

'It's not as simple as that. Nor as limited. Innocent people out there on the streets may die. Men, women, children. Maybe not here, in Belfast. Maybe London? Manchester? Birmingham? Some major British city. Langley is prepared to risk sacrificing one British city for four American ones, that's the bottom line. It's running scared that what happened to the New York World Trade Center might happen there again but magnified ten thousand times in destructive effect – or spread across four cities anywhere in the States.'

'What are you talking about?'

'What Armitage died telling me.'

'Tell *me!*'

He did, living it over again.

The freezing cellar: Armitage's ghastly white face looking up at him, her freckles becoming deep blemishes on her skin, her blood pooling around both of them, joining them, her choked rasp

*Carter, listen! Melsham's laptop. Distant Thunder. It's there. All of it. Arms shipment. Ukraine. Maybe criminals, maybe political . . . we don't know who supplied . . . don't know who bought.*

She was passing him her torch because there was no one else. No one else for her. Ever. Melsham was dead, dead in reality and dead in her mind immediately she gave the operation's code name.

It was all still with him. The sweet scent of her hair against his face, her sigh; his cruelty, shaking her, wanting all of it, demanding it even as she was slipping away.

*ADMs. Five. We bought information the IRA were offered one. Turned it down: too risky, too crazy. Carter they know who have them!*

Her eyes closing, body shivering; colder than she ever had been, colder than she ever would be again; he stroking her hair, holding her, warming her, pointlessly, as it all began to make sense.

ADM. Atomic Demolition Munition. Battlefield atomic weapon: a man-portable nuclear land-mine designed to block valleys or take out major *autobahn* junctions, stopping NATO forces' forward roll. Obsolete but deadly. In the confines of a city, catastrophic. Made for the once upon a time war that never happened. Chickens coming home to roost. With the chaos over there it was always going to happen. Some chickens.

*Hannah! No one told the Brits? Right? Talk to me! I've guessed it but I need to hear it.*

Bloodless lips, affirming, silently.

*Because Langley's buying names? At any cost? In case the ADMs are meant for us?*

Her eyes opening, his answer clear in them – with her shame.

*We know they're meant for us.*

He shaking her again, more cruel than he had ever been to anyone: *Brannigan was dealing for Langley? So what's the price? What's on offer to the IRA for the information? For the names? Clean money?*

*They've got money, Carter.*

A limp rag-doll in his arms; her shivering ceased; he willing her back. *Hannah! Their price?*

A long wait, then, whispered: *Stingers.*

He, leaning back, drained; crumbling brick, damp and cold through his jacket.

Stingers to bring down the choppers: the Brits' eyes in the sky. The Khmer Rouge had a saying for everything and he knew most of them. They had one for this: blind your enemy and he walks the path you choose.

*He's taken the children. I promised her! Get them back!*

His promises, the anonymous evil she could not describe, all of the rest of it which was too dark too dreadful to really see straight any more.

His last words perhaps spoken, perhaps only thought: *The White House will crucify Langley.* Kissing her forehead when she had already slipped from him leaving him with silence and a charnel house and the hideous thought that all of it was already known in that high

130

place but burying *that* immediately: wanting to believe in something, still; wanting to believe in right beyond the distortion of expedience – for he was a soldier of the heart, not simply of the flag.

Kate Brannigan heard it all, silent throughout, and silent afterwards.

From outside Frankel called, protesting: indecipherable, muffled, ignored.

'She said the IRA turned it down.'

'They were *told* they turned it down. That's exactly what they want to hear. Langley's gambling that the IRA know their limitations. Home-made mortars, vans packed with barrels of industrial fertilizer spiced with a few kilos of Semtex, that's their style. Gambling they don't have the technical expertise needed to handle an ADM – nor the nerve because ADMs are old, obsolete, probably unstable; that at least they're halfway stable and don't have Allah and Paradise engraved on their hearts and their minds like some; that they're really only interested in intimidation and collection of protection dues and the propaganda benefits of some Brits dying every year; that they're very comfortable with the status quo and the next generation can worry about the Revolution.'

'Well, damn it, they're probably *right*! That means what I'm doing is right too! I'm stopping a catastrophe in *my* country. What are you trying to do, Carter? Scare me? Stop me!'

'I'm telling you Langley doesn't have to be right.'

'So what can I do?'

'Tell the British.'

'The British? The British killed my husband. Probably kidnapped my children! Are you out of your mind?'

'The British people didn't. If Langley's wrong they're the ones who'll have to suffer. Maybe they have a right to know what could be? Know the nature of the threat at least?'

'I don't *want* to be here. Don't make it worse than it is.'

'You are here, Kate.'

'You can't ask me to *choose*!'

He looked at her. 'It isn't a question of choice. Only knowledge. Right now – under the circumstances – you haven't considered it. You will later – if things turn out the worst way. To live with that you'll need to have faced the possibility now. You'll need to know in yourself you made the only decision you could. Any other way and you'll end up crazy.'

'How many? How many people?'

'An ADM detonated in the confines of a city? Right place, right time? After the first thousand who keeps counting?'

'God *damn* you, Carter.'

'He probably has.'

She stared at him. 'Get Frankel.'

'What are you going to do?'

'I'm a mother! What do you expect me to do? Let my children be butchered! I'll do whatever I *have* to do.'

THE CLIFF-TOP hotel was a dark silhouette against the morning glow. Somewhere downstairs, at the rear, a dull glow shone like a secret welcome.

'Drive past,' ordered Rick.

Dave asked. 'Why?'

Rick looked at him; sighed: 'He lives there alone, rides the moped propped by the front door. Has one girl working at the bar, lives out, comes by bicycle, I chatted her up. We have the only rooms. There's him, there's us – and there's a car parked around the side. You're not looking, Dave.'

'I'm tired, Rick.'

'Tired of living?'

'How far do I keep going?'

'A mile, then we go back along the cliff-line on foot. They'll be watching landward.'

'Who, Rick?'

'Doesn't matter. I told you at the start. Once this rolled, they'd *all* be after us. We'll soon know.'

'They'll have seen us drive past.'

'They saw a car drive past in bad light. Maybe. But we'll let them sit a while. We can enjoy the walk back. Watch the sunrise.' He turned to the children. 'Little angels, still sleeping.'

'They OK?'

'Dead.'

Dave turned sharply.

Rick smiled. 'To the world, Dave. I wouldn't kill our future.'

Dave drove on.

'Stop here.'

'Yes, Rick.'

'Leave the children in the car. Lock up in case they wake.'

'Better leave a gap at the window for air?'

'We won't be long.'

'Sure, Rick.'

They stepped from the car into a chill grey-gold glow.

Rick ran to the cliff edge. He called: 'Breathe that!' Then clasped a lean, powerful arm around Dave as he came up beside him. '*That's* a sunrise!'

'Easy, Rick!'

Rick leaned over the precipice, gripping Dave. 'Do you think I would?' he whispered.

'Of course not.'

'You'll always be safe with me. Even this close to the edge. You always have been. Remember that.'

'I remember, Rick. That's why I'm here, with you.'

Rick pulled back and kissed him on the lips. 'You're here because half of you loves me, half hates me and all of you fears me. But I can forgive you all of that.' He laughed. 'Just as long as you never ask *why* of me. Those who know *why* they do anything are locked to this planet, body, soul and mind and nothing will ever free them. They're pitiful; sitting at the bottom of their dark pits wondering why the world isn't aware they've fallen through. What's the best thing to do in the morning, Dave?'

Dave grinned. 'Fuck?'

Rick walked the edge, backward, soft dark eyes half closed, moist earth crumbling like marzipan under his shoes.

'Rick!'

'*Kill*, Dave. The long dark night leaves the soul unprepared for dying: trembling like an animal, uncertain and primed for the trap. Come on.'

The wind tore tears from Dave's eyes. 'I'll never ask why of you Rick. I swear!'

Rick smiled.

Inside.

*I am the widow maker and the headhunter; fear and chaos and destruction are images of my creation and I of theirs.*

# Chapter Eight

McAlister had declined Reardon's offer of breakfast at the Culloden, wanting to be alone, to think, to *be* whoever was controlling the maze he had entered.

He drove into the city centre in the brightening morning gloom and sat alone in the Europa Hotel coffee shop, watching the traffic through new plate-glass windows – replaced after yet another bombing – his mind working steadily as he sipped black coffee and chewed absently at an unbuttered croissant, shuddering at other early-risers ploughing through the traditional highly calorific Ulster Fry.

Feeling vibration from the cellphone in his inside breast pocket he laid down his cutlery, made for the far side of the Europa's spacious lobby and took the call.

'McAlister? Reardon. I've just heard from one of the staff here: Mrs Brannigan's checked back into the hotel.'

'And Carter?'

'Yes.'

'I'm coming. Hold on to both of them.'

'Wait! They're out. I checked with security here. Left in the Mercedes, not long after you. I felt weary – went back to my room, fell asleep again – missed them. I'm sorry.'

'You weren't to know, sir. Any idea where they've gone?'

'No. I checked at the desk. All they know is she's expecting an urgent message or call from someone, left them with instructions to pass on the car phone number. No return time. They said she looked unwell.'

'I'll have a call put out on the Mercedes. We'll find them. The children are with them, presumably?'

'No. That's something I wanted to tell you. They didn't return with either of them. She's probably flown them out. Very wise.'

McAlister glanced at his wristwatch. 'Too early. I can't see her dumping them at the airport, not in her state of mind. Can you, sir, realistically? Remember what she's just received in that box. And the threat that came with it.'

'She's hidden them?'

'I'd guess that's what she and Carter were doing last night. Good, they're better out of it. She's expecting the demand for the money. It had to come soon. That must be why she's left the car telephone number. Can you stay there until they return? Until I can get someone in place? Will your man Ellis help?'

'Of course. You're still coming back here?'

'On my way,' McAlister confirmed and ended the call. The small unit purred again immediately.

A relieved – and immediately angry – Danny Keegan snapped: 'Boss? Where've you been? You didn't call in any destination before you left your house. I've had half the force out looking!'

'Sorry, Danny, rush call.'

'That's the kind when they get you.'

'Not this time. What's so urgent?'

'Four squaddies went down last night.'

Nothing shocked McAlister any more. Now it was just the cold feeling of inevitability. Worse: resignation. 'Where?'

'Your favourite road.'

'Newry? And I'm supposed to get the *little birds* singing? Tell them I'll do what I can.'

'Four down? They'll want better than that, boss. What's up?'

'*I'm* up. Up to my nostrils in something odoriferous.'

'If that means what I think it does – you've got something on the Yank?'

'Not on this line, Danny boy. Look, get them to pass this to someone else. I have to play this *close*. Understand. I need some time to myself.'

'I'll do my best.'

'Who's doing the leaning?'

'Full-blown colonel, breathing fire.'

'With four of his lads dead are you surprised? There'll be some broken hearts over the water today.'

'Three dead, one survived. Well, alive . . . just. A couple of hours – tops – they reckon. Just time for us asking the big questions and the priest telling him he's off to a better place.' Keegan snorted derisorily.

'You're with the laddie, now?'

'Just down the corridor. Army's got a battalion around him. Funny one, this, boss. Bastard Provos had kids in the car. Wee babies. Squaddie got that much out.'

McAlister felt cold rising from the small of his back, like ice melting upward. 'Three kids?' he asked, half of him knowing the answer already.

'You're doing it to me again, boss.'

'Danny listen, have they operated? Or isn't that an option?'

'If you're asking what they took out of him – a couple of nine-millies. Close group. Tap-tap. Inch apart. Left cheek. Imagine what that felt like. Jesus! Some shooter. Army says they were all hit with the same gun. Browning Hi-Power.'

'SAS gun.'

'I didn't say that.'

'You've had a small walk around Major Carter's views, though?'

'You don't seriously think . . . ?'

'I don't. But maybe someone wants us thinking that way.'

'This is going to be one of *those*, isn't it?'

'It already is. Danny, I need that laddie kept alive.'

'I'll tell the priest to put a call through to his boss.'

'Is he still conscious?'

'Drifting.'

'Whisper in his ear that someone's coming who can *do* the ones who did him and his oppos. If I know my Brit squaddie that'll keep him alive for a while.'

'Do *I* get to hear this too?'

'You get to lift Bobby Harding. Check the Malone road first – he'll be drinking along there somewhere. Has an early morning thirst when he's nervous.' McAlister gave a vehicle registration. 'One of our reserves he's had made up. Thinks he's being clever. He's stupid. And a born procrastinator. I'll lay a year's salary he's still driving around with it up. Just has no idea how dangerous life can be.'

'Here beginneth the first lesson,' snarled Keegan. 'What condition do you want him in?'

'Talking.'

'Walking?'

'That's up to him,' McAlister replied heavily, thinking: *Better broken bones, Bobby, than a bullet in the head, which is what you're down for.* As is everyone who attended that 'business' meeting. IRA godfathers don't get deeply, visibly upset, Bobby, it's not their nature. Unless something portentous was in motion and had just been derailed. They'll be wondering who sniffed the wind that night and maybe they've been keeping their eyes, ears – and options – open. You visited me in the wee small hours, Bobby. There'll be some serious thinking being done about that visit right now – if you had yourself a shadow you didn't spot.

'Bring him in any way you have to. Right away. And Danny, do it *quietly*. There'll be some dying done today if it's known we have Bobby Harding.' He breathed deeply, controlling fear; using it. A dark moment of hopelessness rushed him. It was all – all of it, all the years of constant, grinding alertness, of violence, of death – suddenly too much. 'Maybe it's going to happen anyway,' he said in a low, burdened voice.

'What's going on, boss?'

'Get Bobby, keep him somewhere deep. Unofficial but secure. All right?'

'I'll do that all right,' Keegan said, flatly.

'Do it now. And let me know when it's done.'

'See you later, then?'

'You will.'

McAlister immediately called Reardon back at the Culloden.

'I can't make it there, sir. Not yet. Can't explain on the phone. You have my number. Call me if anything happens. Something might have broken. I'm *sure* it has. Wait for my call, sir. We must know exactly where Mrs Brannigan is at all times!'

'Carter too?'

'I have a feeling that Carter is not vital to what's happening here. He was taken out of it. The pressure is all on her – planted drugs, harassment, and, now, I'm afraid for her children.'

'I don't understand.'

'They're not *there*, sir. You told me yourself.'

'You thought she'd taken them somewhere safe?'

138

'Sometimes I trust my instincts more than my judgement. This is one of those times. I believe a lot happened last night and some of it may concern your early morning caller.'

'Demurov? What have you heard!'

'I can't talk now. I'll be in touch as soon as I can. I have to go.'

'McAlister!'

'Listen to the news. And don't let Mrs Brannigan go again.'

'Is she in danger?'

'We're *all* in danger, sir.'

'*Damn it, McAlister!*'

McAlister pocketed the cellphone, turned his back, took his automatic from its shoulder holster, pumped a round into the breech, released the safety and tucked the gun butt inwards in his waistband – inches away from hands on a steering-wheel. He stepped outside, very alert, signalled urgently for the barrier-posts barring vehicle entry to the Europa's patrolled forecourt car park to be cleared and drove his grey Cosworth-engined but unbadged Sierra out fast, heading immediately for Victoria Hospital.

He had no illusions: Bobby Harding had almost certainly condemned him to death.

'LADDIE'S NAME?' McAlister asked the hard-eyed Paratroop officer towering over him in the hospital corridor, jaw jutted, absurdly small silver-winged beret pulled hard and tight over his cropped head as if capping his anger.

'Corp'r'l Higgs.'

'Colonel, right now your lad doesn't need a copper, he doesn't need you, he needs his mam – more than he's ever done before – and I have to go in there and be her substitute so don't expect me to call him *Corporal Higgs!*'

'He's a soldier.'

'He's a dying boy. Soldiering is over for him. Right?'

The broad camouflage-clad shoulders dropped a fraction. 'Thomas Albert. Lads call him Tommo.'

'His mum doesn't, I guarantee.'

'Hell, how'm I supposed to know?'

'You're not. In my world it's the first thing I learn.' McAlister eased him aside. 'Don't worry, I've done this before. Too many times.'

He showed an expressionless Para NCO his warrant card and entered a cool private room, the air-conditioning whispering distantly, and sat beside the deathly still, prone figure, wincing as he saw the dreadful wounds and the distorted face. He seemed to be looking at two different faces overlapped on the same skull. One side reasonably normal, the other a drooping, deeply discoloured, swollen, unreal mask.

The male nurse in attendance saw McAlister's expression and bent close to his ear: 'Left side is completely paralysed, that's why he looks like that.'

McAlister nodded and sat beside the bed, gently taking the lifeless hand before him. 'Tommy? It's all right, son. You're hurting but you're in good hands. You just lay still and rest. You need your strength. All your strength.'

One side of the face moved, the mouth half lifting into a snarl. McAlister knew it was a smile. He squeezed the hand. 'That's right, a little smile cheers things up no matter how hard it all seems.'

A coarse sound came from the twisted mouth.

'No need to talk. Just rest.'

'*Barshtard!*'

McAlister stroked the hand, seeing the gravel burns on the heel. He saw the falling body, hideously gun-shot, the hand striking the road first.

His voice was firmer now, even stern. Strong. 'One man only, Tommy?'

'*Tchoo!*'

'Two? From the North or South?'

The close cropped head moved sharply, impatiently, a cry of agony immediately coming from the twisted mouth.

'What is it, Tommy?' McAlister's soft voice returned.

The nurse tugged at McAlister's arm, shaking his head disapprovingly.

McAlister nodded.

'*Lisshen.*'

140

McAlister moved very close. 'I'm here, Tommy.'

'*Corshhway. Shiantscorshway.*'

The cold crept again over McAlister but with it now came exhilaration. *Big stones.* Not Legananny Dolmen, not stones; great hexagonal primeval rocks.

'He said that before, a few times,' whispered the nurse.

'*Ghoin' shere. Barshtard shed sho. Other whun shot me.*'

'Tell me about the children. How were they, Tommy? Alive? Frightened but alive?'

A small flicker of humour touched the one opened eye. '*Bhabes in the whood.*'

'Sleeping?'

The eye closed. '*Umm.*'

'But alive. Definitely alive?'

The destroyed face gave a small nod. '*Ahh!*' The cry was agonizing.

'That's enough,' said the nurse, firmly.

'I won't ask any more questions,' McAlister assured gently. 'Let me sit here a while.'

'No more questions?'

'None. I've got the answer I came for.'

McAlister sat silently for some minutes, offered a hopeless prayer, holding the cold hand in both of his, as though warming it.

The life-support system emitted an unbroken wail. He stood and left as frantic activity began around the still form. They would try to save the shattered young body but he knew the soul had flown. He had seen it all before, too often. He wept gently; only with his eyes, his face unmoved, seeming more defeated than distressed.

The Colonel stopped him outside, concerned. 'You didn't *know* Higgs, did you?'

'Did I need to?' McAlister asked and kept walking.

T HE MERCEDES' phone trilled. Carter lifted it, his eyes not moving from Kate Brannigan using the pay-phone a few feet away on the west side of Donegal Square, her expression bleak.

'Mrs Brannigan?' a cool, arrogant, upper-class English voice enquired in Carter's ear.

'Who wants her?'

'None of your damn business.'

Carter saw fear flare in Kate's eyes as she saw him holding the car phone. 'Wrong,' he said.

'You're who?'

'Carter.'

Silence.

'I've been misled,' said the voice, tightly.

Carter sensed anger. 'How?' he asked.

'Not important.'

'Who are you?'

'Don't be stupid. How's the head? No permanent damage?' A sudden smile, a taunting lilt, drifted through the voice. An actor's delivery, thought Carter; flirtation with reality. Detachment from it.

Kate ended her call hastily and dashed to the Mercedes, heaving the heavy door shut. 'Oh God! The children?'

Rick said: 'That's what I want to hear. Maternal concern. Put her on, Carter. Unless of course you've taken advantage of the situation and screwed her and her money which means I'm dealing with *you* now? Was it good? A little *loose* after three children?'

Carter offered the receiver; silent.

Kate grasped it like a lifeline. 'I'll pay! I swear. Don't hurt my children. The money is here – in Belfast. Dollars. As much as you wanted. I'm sorry, it can't be released until—' She looked at Carter. 'Later today.'

Silence.

She pushed back her falling hair, bent forward, one arm clutched around herself to contain the pain. 'For pity's sake, you *have* to believe me.'

Carter pulled her close so he could hear, an arm around her shoulders. She leaned into him, head down, half broken but fighting.

Rick sighed. 'I don't recognize pity. Like so many received values it's an encumbrance in this age. I like this age – there's a certain *louche* freedom to it. A hint of things being out of control. I open myself to you so you realize, if it came to it, that slaughtering

142

your children would mean no more than . . . oh, choose any meaning-
less thing.'

Carter clearly heard Hannah Armitage: *He's evil.*

'You're *sick*!'

'*You* asked for heads, Mrs Brannigan.'

'It wasn't what I meant! You know that!'

'I believe in absolutes.'

'God *damn* you!'

'God has deserted *you*. Bring me my money, Mrs Brannigan.'

She covered the mouthpiece, whispering urgently to Carter. 'I
have to meet *them* at seven. They wouldn't agree any earlier.'

'Tell him the money will be released at seven.'

She did.

'Using the motorway and the Mercedes it will take one hour to
come to me, Mrs Brannigan. Come alone. Used notes only, no
sequential numbering, no dyes. I'm not a fool. And I want a document signed by you. Written confirmation of your offer and payment
of the reward. Legal. I've earned the money, no one takes it away.'

'I can't come! Carter will have to bring the money.'

'Can't come for your own children? What could be more
important?'

'You know damn well!'

'Do I?'

'You didn't kill my husband because it *pleased* you!'

Silence.

'Are you there?'

'I've always been here for you, Mrs Brannigan. Tell Carter if he
even *looks* at me aggressively tonight I will kill your children before
his eyes. Beginning with the little girl. I shall split her like a peach:
anus to navel. Primitive but satisfying and ecologically sound – giving
her life's juices back to the earth. Then I'll kill him. He's dangerous.
I'll do that quickly. Tell him.'

'You're mad!'

'Pray I am not, Mrs Brannigan. If I am, your children are
already dead and only my sick mind is speaking here.'

'*Oh, please!*'

'Carter drives to Antrim, heads seven miles west of the Giant's
Causeway, waits on the mainland side of the fishermen's rope-bridge

at Carrick-a-Rede until I'm satisfied he has no surprises for me. After that, we'll see? I hope you trust him because if he runs with the money you have a lifetime of pain ahead. Unless I decide to be merciful and end it for you. Sweet relief or unimaginable pain? You choose. Don't let Carter decide for you.'

'Who are you?'

'Everything you ever feared.'

The line died.

She closed her eyes, her voice a coarse whisper. 'You heard what he said he'd do to Alice?'

'I heard.'

'He couldn't!'

*He did*, Carter remembered, but shook his head. 'Threat. Making sure you obey. He gets off on control – and fear.'

'Don't do anything to him. Give him the money and bring me my children or he won't have to kill you. I will. I swear.'

'I believe you,' said Carter. *And I'll cull the beast.*

THE DAWN chorus had begun, pleasing Arnie. He listened, glad his head was alive. He knew it wouldn't be long now and was glad. Glad too there was no pain.

'You're done,' the man in the worn green corduroys told him, squatting before Arnie. 'Problem is we're not done with you.' He put his hand to his face against the stench.

The landlord was on his unmade bed, deep red staining the sheets beneath his shoulders. He gasped, angrily: 'Get me seen to! I've done my part!'

'He's not a player,' Corduroys said to Arnie. 'Only a watcher. You and I we're in deep, right? Know the score. Who's winning, who's losing. We're winning.'

'Finish me,' said Arnie.

The second man – a youth, uncombed, neck raw with boils – kicked Arnie. 'You just tell the man what he wants then I'll put one where it counts.'

Arnie forced a bloodless grin. 'I'm only a fly, OK? I come with the shit but I didn't make it.'

The youth kicked him again.

'Do it some more, mother's piss. You're killing me a little every time and it don't hurt one bit, OK.'

Corduroys shoved the youth back with one arm, still squatting, still watching Arnie. 'You have to learn which ones you kick and which you respect.'

'Pile of shit!' spat the youth.

'Where's home you're so far away from?' asked Corduroys quietly. 'What's that old bugger talking about?' He aimed a thumb at the bed. 'Russia? You're a Russian?'

Arnie laughed, fever getting to him now. 'Fucking Pole.'

Arnie realized that Corduroys was astonishingly like one of the Aggressor Group commanders at Krasnodar, who existed only to hunt down trainee *Spetsnaz* and break them, like the real enemy – only worse.

Corduroys laughed with him. 'And the Brits loved you like they do all the itinerant Paddies.'

'He's crazy old man.'

'So why're you here in this vale of misery?'

Corduroys put his hand on Arnie's leg encouragingly. Arnie was glad he could not feel it. Right then the last thing he needed was encouragement. He wanted it over. Yet to feel human touch – even ill-meant – would have been good at that moment of supreme loneliness.

He breathed deeply to lift the two-ton lead weight that seemed to lie on his chest. 'For the fishing, OK?'

'What'd you leave behind?'

He was breathless but he got it all out in one burst. 'Good job, great girl, baby coming. That's me, OK. Anything else you want, that's big questions and I don't have no answers. Sorry.'

The thumb wiggled at the bed. 'Patrick over there says you sang a great song down his telephone.'

'Old man like that! What's he know in the middle of the night? Maybe he's completely drunk? Maybe dreaming?'

'Had a nightmare so bad he blew your mate's head off?'

'He's completely crazy. Got scrambled brains like mother's piss over there.'

The youth had a revolver. A big Webley on a lanyard around his neck. He bent quickly, jabbed it at Arnie's knee, the cord taut. He tugged at the heavy trigger, the blast deafening, stunning, in the confines of the small room.

Arnie shook his head against the ringing in his ears and stared, marvelling, at his leg, now almost completely severed. No pain. Nothing could hurt him. He began laughing, the note rising, howling, to the pitch of hysteria. No pain. I've cut out the worst part of you, Rick! He looked down on himself. *Dead. Only your head is alive and you're out of that now.*

Somehow he came back from wherever he had been and saw the youth cowering as Corduroys' hard measured slaps punished him, over and over, like branches snapping.

Then the silence became long.

Too long for Arnie.

Too complete.

The birds had stopped singing.

Don't ask me anything, Arnie commanded silently. Not now.

The landlord moaned: 'I need the doctor.'

'You'll get one,' Corduroys answered pushing the youth away. 'He definitely used that name? You're absolutely sure.'

Arnie's eyes pleaded: *Die now, old man. Let your last drop of blood leak out now.*

'Reardon. Like the snooker player. Sure. I heard everything. Right by that door. No mistake. Christ, help me!'

The youth coughed blood. A thick gout of it down his grubby denim shirt. He stared at it. 'Fuck,' he coughed. '*Oh fuck! Oh, Mother!*' Then slumped on the bed staring at the hole directly beneath his chin.

Corduroys' hand flew for the fallen Webley but toppled with the hard punch which caught his shoulder, knocking him back against the youth's feet, feeling warmth but no immediate pain. Missed the bone, he thought, his brain surprisingly clear despite the shock. Rick put the heavy silencer under his chin and lifted the mottled face. 'Watch what I do to my friends and wonder what I do to my enemies.'

'Let me die, Rick,' Arnie said.

'There's a time for dying, Arnie.'

'There's no pain, Rick. I'm dead all over.'

'Your head is alive, Arnie.'

The click of the stiletto was like teeth gnashed together.

Arnie squealed and spat out his tongue.

Rick sighed, 'Now we'll never know,' touched his silenced Browning to the shuddering head, murmured 'Goodbye, Anatoly Mikhailovich,' squeezed the trigger, then stood still, reflective, in the flat silence. He turned and shot the youth and the innkeeper dead in rapid succession.

Dave leaned on the door frame as though bone-weary, his own silenced weapon dangling like a weight in his fingers.

'We can't leave this mess.'

'I'll sort it. Rick.'

Rick dropped to his haunches before the shocked, now grey-mottled face of Corduroys. 'It begins,' he murmured.

McALISTER SLUMPED into his car and closed his eyes. It's getting to you, he warned himself. Time to move on. Take some brain-dead job walking the glens where the only violent crime might be the murder of some unfortunate animal.

His cellphone denied him even the thought of escape. 'McAlister? Tom Slattery.'

McAlister sat up. 'What's the Garda doing this time of the morning?'

'I opened up a butcher's shop here by the border a couple of hours ago. South of Newry, just west of Aghnaskeagh. Three bodies: two women, one man. Visitors, not locals, leased the place a couple of weeks back. Heard the news you had an Army patrol put down a few miles north of here in the early hours. Time frame and proximity makes it worth a look. If you saw what's been done to one of the women you'd look at any possibility.'

'Tell me.'

'Ripper country. This one likes extending what God began. Get the picture?'

'Graphically. You said *one* woman?'

'That's the strangeness of it. Other one's dead but unmarked. No molestation, no mutilation. Neck snapped, clean as you like. The man too. Same technique.'

'Professional?'

'Takes a certain *assurance* to get close enough to kill a sleeping soul with bare hands, Jamie – wouldn't you say?'

The ice crept further up McAlister's spine.

'You there or gone back to bed?'

'I'm in my car.'

'So what's *your* early start?'

'Talking a squaddie through the gates to St Peter. Only survivor of the four. He's gone – minutes ago.'

'I'm sorry.'

'So am I.'

'We've a connection here, haven't we, Jamie? It's in your voice.'

'If we haven't, Tom, we're both too old and too tired for this job and we can't see straight any more.'

'Want to meet?'

'Not time enough. On the phone – but not this one. I'll call you. First I need to collect an autopsy report I've been avoiding. Half an hour?'

'I'll be here.' Slattery gave the number at Hannah Armitage's house.

'Who found the bodies?'

'Milkman. Extra milk was ordered. Lady of the house – the one cut up – had nephews and niece arriving for a short stay.'

The ice reached McAlister's neck; his head hurt. 'So what made him suspicious – this morning?'

'The girl was usually awake; rose first, early, took in milk and groceries from him and made breakfast for the others. He'd get a mug of tea from her regular – maybe something more; we're working on him still but I don't have him in the frame. The lady's car – always left out – was gone. Fancy TV satellite dish on the lawn – brought with them special the girl had told him – that's gone too. Milko got himself a ladder and took a look upstairs. Saw the girl in bed, blankets pulled back, naked, real big tits, couldn't take his

148

eyes off them, realized she wasn't breathing – elbowed the glass and got in. Called us after taking a good look around and throwing up his breakfast. He wasn't the last. I've a couple of boys doing the same.'

'Quickly, Tom. What were they? The victims?'

'You mean nationality? Yanks. We've got the passports.'

'Yes,' McAlister murmured.

'You knew?'

'Feared.'

'Get to that safe phone soon.'

'Tom.'

'What?'

'Listen. We're walking the high-wire here. Somewhere along the line we may be asked to forget everything. So keep it tight. Absolute minimum personnel and resources. If the gag goes on you don't want to be calling sixteen junior constables into your office for the heavy hand because they'll have told wives and girlfriends already and nothing will shut *them* up. This could be heavy.'

Slattery hesitated. 'Right, I hear you. Thanks.'

'You'd thank me more if I'd put the phone straight down on you when you called.'

'Jamie, come over and take a look what's on the floor of the cellar here. There's an animal roaming out there I want put down. I'll see this through best I can and if I'm stopped I'll want some hard reasons *why*. Heavy or not. Make sure you call me. Here, take the missing car reg, just in case. Put it on your computer for me.'

McAlister put down the phone. He stared through his grimy windscreen but all he saw was three sleeping faces, upturned in a box, packed carefully with tissue paper and polythene. Like displayed fruit.

*Takes a certain assurance to get close enough to kill a sleeping soul with bare hands, Jamie.*

And if that cool assurance becomes cold contempt and that dreadful divide is crossed when the ability to kill becomes the power to kill and the power becomes need? What is left, then, of humanity in that teetering mind?

Drive, he told himself. *Drive*, damn you, don't sit!

But he had to go back into the hospital, the depths of it, where death was dissected to determine those last few moments of life.

Had the executioner's axe fallen on three sleepers' necks? Or had expert hands twisted and snapped life's cord first?

M cALISTER REACHED the Culloden within the hour, Reardon pacing the lobby in waiting.

'Your room,' McAlister said abruptly and followed the big man up the sweeping stairs.

There he wasted no time. 'I have a maze in front of me. I'm trying desperately to find a way in. Let me give you some facts and think aloud at the same time.'

'I'm listening,' said Reardon and sat on a chair, McAlister pacing before him.

'Fact: Carter and Mrs Brannigan crossed the border last night. The Mercedes was photographed and registered on the computer at Newry. Obviously there'd been a meeting set up.'

'Not too fast. Meeting? With whom? Stick with facts for now.'

'I'm assuming the meeting but I'm damn sure it was on. The Mercedes had crossed there before. Almost certainly Brannigan and Carter in the car.' McAlister gave a date.

Reardon protested: 'She was still in America.'

'I meant Patrick Brannigan, sir.'

'Oh,' murmured Reardon, unhappily, remembering. 'That was a day I had to report to London. Go on.'

'There were three Americans renting a house over the border – close to Newry. One man, two women. Information I have confirms they were prepared for the arrival of children. It's just too much of a coincidence not to be the Brannigan children. Some time very late last night or in the early hours of this morning the three were killed. Brutally. One of the women was sexually mutilated. The Gardai are there now. The investigating officer is a friend. He contacted me.'

'Does he know of your suspicions regarding the Carter-

Brannigan connection? The first visit – or this second border crossing last night.'

'Not yet. I wanted to speak to you first.'

Reardon stood. 'Wait! Let me get this absolutely clear. There's been multiple murder in a house in the Irish Republic which you're alleging Carter and Katherine Brannigan were heading for? You're not telling me they're responsible—!'

'They both returned across the border safely – but without the children. The children were not found in the house.' McAlister stopped and rubbed his eyes wearily. 'I'll come to the children in a moment. No, I don't believe Carter or Mrs Brannigan killed those people. I *do* think they were involved with them. I want to find out how. And why.'

Reardon sat again, his heavy jaw determined. 'You know more. Who killed those people? For God's sake, man, *sit*.'

McAlister stopped, then sat on the big double bed. 'Facts end now.' He saw the opened diary to his left, the entry, the telephone number, the name, the time of the call, the double underlined letters NA after.

'All right. So what do you *think*?' insisted Reardon.

'I know – I'm certain I know – where Demurov and his group are holed up. The Giant's Causeway, Antrim. Not Legananny. *Rocks*, sir, not stones. Demurov meant rocks.'

Reardon looked at him, astonished. 'How did you discover that?'

McAlister told him.

'You're saying Demurov's group killed that patrol? Not possible. The killings were near Newry in the early hours – around four o'clock according to the news, and they're close on the time because of the patrol's call-in schedule. Demurov's call to me was around the same time – and you're saying he called me from *Antrim*?'

'Not necessarily. He could have called from anywhere. Even right after the patrol was hit – which *might* explain his nervous state.'

'But you don't think so.'

'If he's what he's supposed to be – a highly trained Special Forces soldier – an armed confrontation with an Army patrol wouldn't put him in the state you described. I think he was holed up somewhere waiting for the ones who hit the patrol to arrive

151

back. His comrades. He took the opportunity to call while they were away. Betraying them. I think his anxiety was not of capture but of what he's involved in. *Who* he's involved with. These aren't Boy Scouts.'

Reardon lit a cigarette, drew deeply, coughed immediately and stared reproachfully at the cigarette. 'You're connecting the murders in the Republic with Demurov's group? But you said it yourself – assuming Demurov's story is true – these are trained soldiers, not sex fiends, not female mutilators?'

McAlister looked at him. 'You've seen news reports out of Bosnia, sir, surely?'

'Of course, but—'

'That was there and this is here?' McAlister smiled tightly then shook his head. 'These aren't soldiers any more. Not in any disciplined sense. They've been trained – very well – but if I'm right, there's no longer any control on them. They're outlaws. And if it *is* their trail we're following they're *way* outside the law. Any half-qualified psychologist could give you pat reasons for their behaviour: abandoned by their own after a lifetime of indoctrination in preparation for sudden, swift acts of destruction and assassination; taken over by *us*, or a secret part of us who utilize their darkest skills. Now . . .'

'Now?'

'Breaking free of their chains? Wanting freedom? Complete total freedom. Wanting – demanding – part of the society they were pledged to destroy. Or the fruits of it. The problem is the only skills they're equipped with to achieve that end – *swiftly*, which is their entire ethos – are the skills they were trained in: treachery, destruction, murder – and almost certainly torture. This is without the possibility of stress from years of apprehension – waiting for the call that never came – snapping already strung-out, manipulated minds.'

Reardon stared at him. 'My God! They're responsible for the heads? They claimed the reward for the man they killed themselves! That's what you're telling me?'

'Yes.'

'Then who were the victims? The heads?'

'Might have been random choice – but in that case they *had* to be reported. Three violent deaths? Three headless corpses laying out

152

there, undiscovered still? I don't believe it. There's a deathly silence on the streets. Might never have happened. Someone knows but they're keeping quiet. There's a reason for that too – connected or unconnected with all of this. If we ever get to find it!'

'Can you prove any of this?'

'I've just been to the morgue. Met the pathologist who examined the heads. I suspected – hoped – I'd find the necks had been snapped expertly. As were two of the victims in the Republic killings.'

'And they were?'

'No. The only similarity – and I believe this is vital – is that all five were sleeping. To kill one person without waking them is not as easy as it may sound. Killing isn't easy. Not cleanly. To kill five silently as these must have been needs an expert in the black arts. Silent, swift, sure, icy nerves, supreme confidence. Life, death, over, walk away, no turning back, no regrets: next one.'

'Everything *Spetsnaz* are. How *were* they killed? The three men here in Belfast? Decapitation? Or something before that?'

McAlister arose and moved behind Reardon, his fingers gently finding a soft place at the base of his skull. 'There. One precise thrust: a very slim blade directly into the centre of the brain. Death instantaneous. Heart stopped, no blood pumping so no pressure. Then a butcher's meat cleaver, or something with a similar length of weighted blade, and the job's done. The pathologist suggested that if they were all done together, which is likely, each was killed in turn with the blade, then the first was returned to for decapitation – allowing time for blood to settle. No mess, no blood showered on the perpetrators. Live decapitation is a messy process. There'd be a fountain of blood with each. Pints of it.'

'Dear God!'

McAlister moved away. 'I'm guessing. Informed and, I think, close. But to be sure I need to get some hard background on Demurov and his comrades. I have to ask you to use your influence, sir.'

'How?'

McAlister indicated the opened diary. 'Call the Prime Minister.' He glanced at the opened diary. 'Looks like you've been considering it? Perhaps you've done so already?'

'I struggled with myself over all of this. I mean it's not my position to be involved . . .' He waved dismissively, obviously angry with himself. 'I couldn't get through.'

'Couldn't?'

'Not available,' Reardon growled. 'Look, I thought we agreed there's the risk of alerting whoever is responsible for all this? Just a couple of hours ago?'

'A risk we have to take. Now.'

'Why?'

'Only he can do what I want. *Get* what I want.'

'Which is?'

'Old Soviet military records. They're accessible these days, aren't they, to the right people? Even KGB records?'

Reardon frowned deeply. 'If it's *vital*.' He paused, unhappy. 'I'll have to give reasons. Explanations. There's every chance his enquiry will alert the very people behind this. We'll be exposing ourselves. They killed Patrick Brannigan – cold-bloodedly, even contemptuously when you consider the political level he was dealing at – you think they won't do the same to us? McAlister?'

McAlister had pushed himself up and had walked to the window. Outside it was raining hard, the clouds overhead mountainous and black.

'Doesn't that cause you any apprehension?' demanded Reardon. 'It does me. I'm fifty-five and I'm beginning to realize I haven't done one-*quarter* of what I want to do before I move on to whatever else is in store – if anything!'

McAlister did not turn. 'I'm convinced there's a conspiracy. No proof, no understanding of why, but it's going on out there. *Now*. Maybe we'll break it. Maybe they'll break us. It's a situation we can do little about. We can do our best to protect ourselves – that's about it.'

'No, it isn't. We can walk away.'

'We can't. We've six murders – ten when you add the Army patrol. Three involving decapitation and one sexual mutilation. I suspect kidnapping can be added to that list of crimes. The Brannigan children. I think our *Spetsnaz* comrades have them as insurance against receiving the one million. If there wasn't the political aspect

154

to all of this I'd believe Mrs Brannigan and Carter might have gone across the border to collect or perhaps deliver the money – or both? That these Americans were high-flying negotiators of some kind. Insurance, that kind of thing. That something went wrong. One million was no longer enough. The children would be worth that each to their millionairess mother. That the murders were carried out because of a refusal by the negotiators to pay more. As punishment – and as warning to Mrs Brannigan: find more money or else the same happens to your children.' McAlister blew out. 'God, I'm tired.'

'But you don't believe any of that? It's convincing. I'd believe it.' 'Tell me what you do believe!'

'I warned you earlier about not losing sight of the American element in all this. That's coming into harder focus now. The victims in the Republic killings were all Americans. Americans with sophisticated satellite TV equipment for their leisure time. I doubt if they had any leisure time. A communications satellite dish closely resembles a satellite TV dish to an untutored eye – and all the eyes in the country area the house was situated in would be untutored. And they'd been staying there for too long. Arrived before Brannigan was shot. Before the reward was offered. I'd like very much to look in the boot of the Brannigan Mercedes at this moment.'

Reardon blinked at him. 'What's going on, McAlister?'

'We're in the eye of a hurricane with the truth so lost in the debris spinning around us we can't see it. Perhaps we never will. Perhaps we'll never be allowed to. There's politics and Intelligence involved and that's a combination I've learned to back well away from.'

'You can still do that.'

Now McAlister turned. 'We can't. We have to stop the butchery that's going on out there. We have to find – and stop – the killer. Right now the rest of it is out of our control. The investigation of the murders in the Republic is beyond my influence and news of those must break. Perhaps nailing the killer will draw other matters into the open.'

'You really believe so?'

'Either that or my colleague with the Garda will receive an

order to close his investigation. In which case we'll know the strength of what we're dealing with.'

'I fear we're not *dealing* with anyone, McAlister. I fear we're more in danger of being *dealt with*.'

'Will you call the Prime Minister, sir?'

Reardon breathed. 'No.' He looked at the ominous sky, sickly. 'I'll ask him face to face. Even if I have to fly through that.'

# CHAPTER NINE

D AVE FINISHED his work at the rear of the cliff-top inn, ran to the front and leapt behind the wheel of the car parked by the entrance.

'Done?'

'Sure, Rick. No problem. Gas cylinders, two full, one halfway. I rigged the feed. They won't twig it until they go in with the tweezers and plastic bags – if they bother. It'll look like straight negligence. Lot of that about. Two minutes. Better get going.'

Rick turned to the rear. 'Enough time to put our friend back in there.'

Corduroys recoiled, smelling the fumes from Dave. *'Jesus!'*

'Rick, let's go.'

'Wait.' Rick leaned on the seat back, soft eyes enquiring. 'Go where, friend? You have a name? A home? We need looking after.'

'Go fuck yourself. You're bluffing.' Corduroys glared defiantly but nothing could hide his fear, his eyes flicking to the inn, panic building visibly.

'Something in there we don't know about? Put him back inside, Dave. There's time. Just.'

Corduroys blurted: 'Murphy.'

Rick laughed.

'It's Murphy, blast you.'

*'Rick!'*

'Ask Murphy, where?'

*'You want to burn, you stupid Irish fuck?'* Dave spat.

'All *right*! Go left, follow the coast road *but get out of here*!'

Dave accelerated hard, tyres spitting gravel chips like bullets.

The bang from behind was metallic, like cannon fire, then a massive *woomph* shook the car violently, lifting it, heaving it off line, debris rattling on the roof, the rear window crazing, collapsing in a thousand crystals, Murphy already down cowering between the seats.

'*Shit!*' Dave blurted. 'What was *that!*'

Rick laughed. 'Little explosives cache.'

'You're fuckin' crazy!' Murphy yelled. '*Fuckin' crazy!*'

Rick grasped his hair, pulled him upright, dug steely fingers into his cheeks, forced his mouth open, fed glass crystals into it. 'You talk when I want you to.'

Dave grasped him. 'He's got to direct us, Rick.'

'So he has.' Rick slapped Murphy hard on the back, crystals spewing out over the seats.

'I'll kill you,' Murphy gasped.

'Stay alive, Murphy, that's your priority: don't increase your chances of being killed. Aren't you people *trained?*'

'You're fuckin' SAS, aren't you? Bloody glory-boys.'

Rick's voice was icy. 'We're better than SAS. Better than all of them. Sit still and stay alive.'

Murphy's mouth was full of blood. He spat sideways over the seat.

Rick turned away in disgust. 'Change cars when we get the children. They can't lie on that!'

'Yes, Rick.'

Their car was where they had left it, windows opaque with condensation. Dave halted beside it, got out and opened all the doors, checking the comatose forms inside, the smallest child – the fair girl – half-conscious and crying. He lifted her out, soothing her.

'What you doing with those kids?' demanded Murphy, getting out, brushing glass crystals from his clothes. 'You perverted bastards!'

Rick jabbed the silenced Browning to his belly, marched him to the cliff-edge, tipped him forward, only the rigidity of the gun and the strength of his wrist stopping Murphy from toppling to the rocks below. 'This is all your life is worth: a bullet in the balls before you fall – or just the fall. That's it. No other expectation. Your time is limited – or extended – by what you say to me. You understand?'

'*I'm going to fall!*' Murphy gasped.

'You're going to die.'

'Please, no. I understand. *Yes!*'

158

Rick swung him away from the edge, marched him back to the cars and pushed him toward Dave. 'I'll sit with the children in the back, maybe sleep a little. He'll direct you. If you think he's running you in circles, wake me.'

He climbed into the rear, lifted the small girl on to his lap, fed her another pill – closing her mouth until she swallowed – slid low into the seat, closed his eyes and warned softly: 'Murphy, I wake faster than you can move and kill faster than you can think. Ask Dave.'

Murphy glanced at Dave and saw, starkly, for a brief elusive moment, his own fear reflected back at him.

'Yes,' murmured Dave.

Dave drove in silence, occasionally grunting as Murphy grudgingly gave directions, the road dipping and rising like a roller-coaster, the view seaward spectacular, the fifty-million-year-old hexagonal basalt formations of the Causeway behind them now, the cliffs already wearing the early russets and fawns of autumn. He watched goldfinch and linnet foraging for seed-heads and longed to lie – just *lie* on his back on the cliffs and gaze at them, maybe for ever, never moving from that spot, never doing another thing ever again. Just watching. Waiting to die. Not rushing toward death as he seemed to have been doing for as long as he could remember.

A migrant red admiral butterfly tempted by late blooms of mayweed struck the windscreen, and fluttered, stunned, pinned there by the passage of air. Dave reached out and flicked it free. He saw it in the mirror, fly, fall, fly again. Go home, he told it.

'It's beautiful country,' said Murphy. '*Irish* country. All of it. You'll never own it. Never!'

'Shut up,' Dave murmured. 'It's not my fight.'

Murphy's farm was peaceful. Sheep grazed, close together, shifting slowly like a white cloud on a rolling green sky. A Range Rover squatted on fat tyres before a rambling, well-built, surprisingly modern single-storey house.

'Terror pays, Dave,' said Rick, perhaps waking.

Dave halted the car.

From inside the house came the strains of country music.

'America comes to Ireland,' smiled Rick.

'That's Irish,' muttered Murphy.

'Then Ireland bends to America, offering its asshole like all the rest.'

'Fuck you.'

'Been a long time since I've met one with such fight, Dave. This will be interesting.' Rick got out and breathed the morning air deeply, stretching.

Dave said, quickly, not turning. 'Do anything he wants. *Anything.*'

'Murderous bastard! I've faced worse,' growled Murphy.

Dave's eyes locked with his in the mirror. 'You haven't.'

'Who're you then?' a woman called, lightly from the porch.

'Who are *you*?' smiled Rick.

'She's not part of this!' snarled Murphy, leaping from the car, Dave grasping him, hard. 'Leave her out!'

'She's *here*,' said Rick.

Bobby harding sat on the iron bed, angry, a bruise developing on the left side of his face.

McAlister entered, pulled the folding chair around and sat, arms folded, on its back. 'They hit you,' he observed.

'Bastard Keegan. Hates me.'

'You've betrayed all he believes in. Does it surprise you, Bobby?'

'All he believes in is himself.'

'Don't tar others with your own brush.'

'Save the Scots homilies, Jamie, makes me want to puke.'

'That's early morning drinking – not me.'

'What's all this about, then?'

'Just some questions.'

'We did our talking this morning.'

'You began talking. You haven't finished.'

'I'm not saying another word.'

'Yes you are. And I'm going to do you the biggest favour anyone will ever do for you. I have an identity going free, a bit of money in

160

the slush fund and a halfway decent start on the other side of the world where nobody knows your face.'

'I like it here.'

'Here doesn't like *you*, Bobby. You're going to be very dead within days.'

Harding looked at him. 'You're dreaming, I can handle myself.'

'No, you can't. You never could; not as a copper, not as a person – and I'm damn sure not as a terrorist.'

'I'm a patriot not a fucking terrorist!'

'*And Terror like a frost shall halt the flood of thinking.*'

'What's that supposed to mean?'

'It means your brain's seized up. You're a terrorist as far as the law is concerned and that's all that counts, patriotism isn't even in the equation. Wake up, Bobby, I've warned you before, you're a wee lad trying to play big boys' games and you don't even know their rules.'

Harding fingered his cheek and winced. 'He shouldn't have hit me.'

'I'm sure you deserved it. Come on, I want an answer.'

'What's the question? Not what you're offering – I mean what are you after?'

'Something's going on out there and I need to know what it is. You're a scheming lying little turd but you're the best listener I've ever known and I can't believe you haven't heard a lot more than you've told me.'

Harding shrugged, but smiled.

'That really pleases you, doesn't it? Being told you're good at something. *And* being able to withhold something from me.' McAlister turned. 'Danny. Bring that in, will you?'

'What?' demanded Harding.

'Wait.'

'What's going on!'

'How's the face, *Booby*,' grinned Keegan entering, grasping a box.

'Don't call me that, you fuck.'

'It's what you are.'

Harding wrenched at the handcuff which linked him to the bolted down bed-frame.

'You can tug harder than that!' smirked Keegan. 'Or does it hurt too much?'

'That's enough,' McAlister murmured. 'Let him see.'

Keegan flopped the box on to the mattress beside Harding and lifted the lid with a flourish. '*Voilà!*'

Harding shrieked and leapt back on the bed, both legs coming up under his chin. 'Jesus, fucking Mary! Get them away!' He kicked at the box but Keegan deftly swept it out of harm's way.

'Know anything about them, Bobby?' asked McAlister, gently.

'You think I'd do *that*? Jesus!'

'Look at the faces. Closely. Calm down and look at the faces. And you tell me, Bobby, if you've heard anything about three lads going missing? Get them closer to him, Danny, let him see properly.'

'No!'

Keegan thrust the heads under Harding's eyes.

Harding turned away and vomited.

Keegan sneered. 'Little sod.'

'Let him calm down,' said McAlister and made a discreet gesture toward the door.

Keegan left.

'Now I need you to take a good look, Bobby. Then we'll talk about your future.'

Harding raised himself, avoiding the pool of vomit, and sat on the edge of the bed, the heads on the floor at his feet in the box. 'Jesus, they stink.'

'Of formaldehyde, not corruption. Think of them as evidence. You remember your training? Detachment. Just look and tell me what you see.'

Harding gulped and drew a sleeve across his mouth. 'I could murder a drink.'

'Afterwards.'

'Oh, *Jamie!*'

'Just *look*.'

'The one on the right does a bit around the bars. Rough trade.'

'You're sure?'

'I've *had* him, for fuck's sake!'

'Connections?'

'He's a Catholic, lives where you'd expect him to, mixes with his kind – and I don't mean *gays*, all right!'

'He's a Provo?'

'Could be. Not serious stuff. Distracts the squaddies, maybe. He's a bit outrageous.' Harding gulped. 'Was. Jesus!'

'The others?'

'I can't know *everybody*, can I?'

'Look. Look closely. Try and see them alive.'

'How can you see *that* alive!'

'Try.' McAlister took his hand but Harding snatched it away.

'Don't work your magic on me, I *know* you, remember?'

'Try, Bobby. Your life depends on this.'

'I think I've seen that one, there, the curly-head.'

'Where?'

'University district. He's a Provie runner. Courier, you know. Walks messages or bits of weapons through the checkpoints. Cool. But small fry. These aren't shooters, they're not even waiting in line. They're slime. Living like shit, doing drugs—' Harding waved dismissively. 'Rubbish. Who's gonna kill me for them! Shit!'

'I'm after who killed them. I'm after finding out why no one has reported that two, probably three, lads with Provo connections – serious or not – have been butchered. Butchered right in the heart of the city. Right there in bed-sit land where there's plenty to notice they're not around.'

'I'll want money,' Harding said. 'Lots of it.'

'You'll get what's available, nothing more.'

'How much?'

'Enough to see you all right until you get yourself on your feet and find work. You'll have the papers to be able to. *If* you have the inclination. Come on, what else do you know? I'm not waiting on your pleasure.'

'Just a story.'

McAlister nodded. 'Once upon a time . . . ?'

'Maybe it's not enough for you to stick to the deal.'

'I'll decide that.'

Harding breathed, then shrugged. 'The next afternoon, after the Yank had been topped – I told you about the Provo lads, Billy the Kid, the James Boys, remember?'

'Bodyguards, talking too loud, I remember.'

'They were drinking. Lunch time. I was cruising. Head down, leathers, heavy-metal wig, all the gear, *you* wouldn't have recognized me.'

'Yes, I would. You're stupid.'

'Don't. That really hurts.'

'Just go on.'

'They looked sick. Sick as pigs. I was still thinking about what had happened with the Yank – so naturally I figured the way they looked was connected. So I wanted to hear what I could and take it back with me. Get some respect.'

'Of course.'

'They'd been called out. I thought then – still did until just now – they were talking about a hit they'd made. Retaliation. They said three dead. For sure three. It sounded like things had gone bad. Messy.'

'They hadn't made the hit. They were called to clean up. Disposal of the bodies belonging to those heads. That's what they were talking about. You couldn't get it.'

Harding stared at him. 'I didn't know. I was listening across a bloody bar crammed with Catholics who'd have cut my balls off if they'd twigged me. It was fucking *dangerous*, Jamie!'

'So what happened?'

'Nothing, that was it. They huddled, looking pukey, I couldn't hear any more – and maybe I was getting a few looks. I left.'

'You reported this – to the UVF?'

'Sure. They said, great.'

'And you wanted to be loved.'

'I just wanted respect. I deserve respect.'

McAlister stood. 'All you deserve is a boot where it hurts. I'll do the best I can for you. In the mean time stay here. There're people out there who want you – and me – dead. In fact anyone who was at the meeting when Brannigan's shooting was announced who isn't IRA.'

'Why?'

'If I knew that I wouldn't need you. But I imagine – no, I'm certain – Brannigan was involved in some deal with the Provos. Something big. Nasty. Bad enough to have him killed.'

Harding sat bolt upright. 'Jesus! You think London did it!' He tugged at the handcuff – hard, ripping skin and drawing blood. 'I'm a fucking sitting duck here. I want out. You've set me up!'

'I'm saving your life.'

'I don't want it saving. I'll save my bloody self. Let me out of here!'

'You'll not last a day out there.'

'So I wait here for a couple of London's hard men to finish me? Fuck you, Jamie!'

McAlister walked out.

Keegan was waiting. 'Well?'

'I'll buy you an early lunch.'

'What about him?'

'Send him on his way. He's more afraid of us than of them out there. I'm afraid he'll hurt himself if we hang on to him. They'll kill him, of course.'

'And you'll let him go?'

'I can't be responsible for every weak fool in this world, Danny. If I tried I'd die myself just from the weight of it.'

'I HAVE to sleep,' Carter told Kate Brannigan.

'Back to the hotel?'

'We stay away from there until this is over. Stay low all day. We've left a trail to and from what happened last night. If someone discovers what's in that house over the border we could have a big problem. You have to be free to do what you have to do tonight – and so do I.'

'They couldn't link us with that, surely?'

'I told you at the start, this is the closest you'll get to a police state. Knowledge of people's movements is routine here. If they need the information they'll soon find out we crossed the border at Newry last night. Every number plate at that checkpoint is photographed and fed into their central computer. They'll soon connect that with the earlier "sightseeing" trip I took across the border, same crossing place, with your husband. There's good co-operation with the Irish police here – no matter what you read – and with *that* kind of murder they'll be in close contact. Especially as it happened a couple of miles from the border. How did you recross the border last night?'

'Same place. Is that important?'

'Stopped you?'

'Slowed me, then waved me through. Smiled, both sides of the border, even at that hour.'

'Lonely men, beautiful woman, expensive automobile. So I could have been sleeping – in the back? They wouldn't have seen?'

She shrugged. 'I guess. But you crossed back yourself last night. They'll have that on computer.'

Carter shook his head. 'There's plenty of unchecked crossing points. That's what makes it so hard for Brit security to keep the lid on this place. Terrorists making a hit don't come and go through checkpoints.'

She gasped. 'Carter, you took *their* car. That puts you there, in that house.'

'Yes.'

'Oh God! Where is it? Abandoned somewhere?'

'You want a car discovered fast in Ulster you abandon it. Any abandoned vehicle – even something parked for too long – is suspected of being a car-bomb. No, it's in the safest place possible under the circumstances. Amongst a whole bunch of others – many with Republic plates. The Culloden car park. Right at the back under a tree – probably deep in bird shit by now.'

'But that links you *directly* to it! To the murders!'

'By the time they make all the connections – and maybe discover it – this will be over. What we have to do is break the direct line to *this* car. We'll lose the Mercedes. Hire something – maybe buy something.'

She looked at him.

'What's wrong?'

'They wanted to know where the Mercedes was.'

'Who?'

'*They.*'

'Say it, don't hide from it. The Provisionals?'

'Yes! If that's who I was talking to, yes! I spoke to a woman. She sounded like a goddamn school teacher.'

'She probably was. What's their interest in the Mercedes?'

'She asked where it was, I said right outside. She said, fine.'

'What else?'

'Nothing about the car. Just told me to call at quarter to seven and order a cab. Gave me a number. That was it.'

Carter scanned the car's interior.

'What? What is it?'

'I don't know. But they do.'

'And Patrick did too?'

Carter frowned. 'Maybe.'

'I don't understand. He was one of them? CIA. Langley. Whatever they like to call themselves?'

'Yes.'

'So he knew! This was his car, wasn't it? He bought it in Europe. Stuttgart. I remember him raving about it on the phone. A school kid again.'

Carter tapped the dash. 'No one really knows all of it. Even at the heart of it. There's always someone who knows more than you.'

'What are you saying?'

'That if the IRA show an interest in this car, it isn't because they're school kids again. They've a reason. A serious reason.'

'So what do we do about that?'

'We find someplace I can look it over carefully. Thoroughly. Afterwards we find somewhere to sleep a few hours – without filling any register – then we do what we have to do.'

'How can you say it like that! "Do what we have to do"? I've got to meet with hardened terrorists and you've got to get my children back from a psychopath! This is happening. Real. It's a nightmare!'

'There's no other way of putting it. You're right, it's real. We have to do this. Both of us. You have to get the money to save your children and I've got to deliver it. We do what we have to do. Now let's get this car off the road.'

THE PLAIN-CLOTHES woman Special Branch officer sat in the Culloden's lounge with the lobby in clear view. She saw Reardon come down the staircase and hand his key to the desk.

The hard figure of Ellis, his bodyguard, strolled toward her. 'I'm taking him to the airport. I'll be back soon as I can. If Carter or Mrs Brannigan arrive, hold them.'

'How?'

Ellis grinned. 'Offer to make up a threesome! You work it out. Arrest them.'

'I can't do that. There's no warrant.'

Reardon walked over. 'What's the problem?'

'Question of how to hold Carter and the lady, sir.'

'I've no warrant for arrest, sir,' the officer repeated.

'You stay, Ellis.'

'No way, sir.'

'For God's sake, man, I got myself to the airport on my own once, I can do it again. It's far more important we hold Carter and Mrs Brannigan than have you driving me around. Besides I'm fed up with your sense of humour.'

'It's against the rules.'

'Bugger the rules. No one else seems to be taking any notice of them at present. I'll take a cab. Get the security guard to check him out when he arrives.'

Ellis stood his ground. 'From what little you've told me about all this, Mr Reardon—'

'Ellis, if they'd wanted me dead they'd have done it by now. They were after Brannigan, not me, I have that verbatim. Now just do as I ask. Keep Carter here, by force if necessary.'

'I can't be involved in that kind of action, sir,' interrupted the officer.

'You bloody won't be,' growled Ellis. '*I'll* check out the cab driver, sir.'

Reardon hated taxis. Their drivers always talked. Talked drivel. Usually reactionary and offensive. He buried his face in the newspaper he had snatched from the Culloden's security guard-house, the moment they were out of the gates and on their way.

What rubbish, he thought angrily, turning the pages of the tabloid.

A bare-breasted young woman smiled widely at him.

I could be your father, he told her. Possibly your grandfather.

He felt utterly depressed. Just the thought of the flight, he decided. The bloody dreadful thought of the hour or so in that silver cylinder too close to eternity.

'Weather's bad,' observed the cabbie, accelerating on to the motorway.

*Shut up!*

Reardon read, something inane, taking in none of it.

Just think about what you're going to say. No, think *why* you're going to say it. He'll take some convincing. He's not a man who makes sudden decisions. None I've seen anyway.

*Russians!* he thought. He'll think I've gone mad.

'Got someone to pick you up the other side, sir? I've a brother works the rank at Heathrow. I can call him, get you a good deal?'

'I'm going to Birmingham,' Reardon lied.

'You've a long wait for the flight, then!'

Reardon raised the tabloid higher, shut his eyes, closed himself off from all of it. He saw Kate Brannigan sip, *beautifully* sip, cognac. I'd give my eyes for a woman like you, he remembered thinking, sitting giving her the bad news. He smiled, reliving the moment. *I would still.* He rested his head against the seat back, fell asleep.

They drove alongside at speed, heavy-calibre automatic fire punching pieces from the taxi like paper ripped and tossed into its slipstream, concentrating on the rear side window and the spread newspaper; then accelerated away, leaving the half-destroyed careering vehicle to plough into the barrier and erupt with flame.

It was over in moments.

Reardon never knew.

THE PRIME Minister took the call in his private office on the secure line, dark coffee at his elbow.

The Kremlin interpreter came on first. 'The President wishes to inform you of his pleasure in being able to aid you. We have the information you required, sir.'

'Tell the President I am most grateful – and impressed by the speed of your reply. It's been so few hours since my enquiry!'

'We have efficiency still in some areas,' the interpreter said, sombrely. 'The President asks again how is your charming wife? Her flu?'

'No change from this morning. Thank him for his concern.'

'He also asks – he hopes, sir – that matters regarding certain financial proposals already discussed will pass quickly through the bureaucratic process.'

'I am giving the matter my full personal attention.'

There was a pause. 'The President is most pleased to hear this, sir.'

'You have the information for me?'

'Faxed already. Your staff will bring this to you soon I am sure.'

'Please thank the President very warmly for me.'

'It will be done, sir.'

'The information? Will it be in English?'

'I have personally made the translation, sir.'

'Thank *you*, then. Goodbye.'

A deep, gruff voice rumbled in the background.

'Sir!'

'Yes?'

'The President reminds you that . . . these individuals – and naturally their mission – are from the *former* regime. In no way can we be held responsible for their actions. We regret their presence in your country.'

'That is clearly understood. He should have no concern over the matter.'

'Very good.'

The background voice rumbled: 'Goodbye.'

'The President says goodbye, Mr Prime Minister.'

'I heard. Tell him goodbye from me.'

He replaced the receiver, sat back, closed his eyes, thought: God, why do I feel so tired! and waited for the knock on his door.

He awoke with a start to find one of his secretaries before him, grasping a neatly cut and stapled series of faxed pages to her bosom.

He shook himself. 'Please leave them.'

She left immediately.

He read.

Done, he sat back, staring at the sheets.

Brave men all – and dedicated, he thought, wonderingly; wondering most about the one called Karelin: not least because, if war from the East that had threatened for decades *had* come – came now, at that very moment – here, named in black and white before him, was his personal executioner. Prepared, according to his *Spetsnaz* oath, to fulfil his orders or die trying. It was an eerie feeling. And uncomfortable.

Of course the war had not come.

He was alive.

His executioner's hand had been stayed by the course of history.

Only Patrick Brannigan was dead.

The sleeping killer had awakened. *Been* awakened. Was a killer still. Peace or no. And out there, now.

*Killers*. Four in all.

Under whose command?

He sipped his cold, forgotten coffee, grimaced, put down the cup.

He stared at the papers, Karelin's shadow seeming to fall across him even though the personal threat was no longer there. Valentin Vasilevich Karelin – or Richard Steven Cain as his KGB *legend* had him. Strangely, an artiste among artisans. A choreographer of serious dance. *Avant-garde*, his legend read; *a refugee from rigid Soviet orthodoxy certain to be welcomed by Western liberals and inevitably cocooned by their selfish, eager claim to his talents . . . talents providing access to high places and also opportunity when the time comes . . . with the excuse of temperament to cover excesses . . .*

*Excesses* was not a word the Prime Minister was ever comfortable with. Now, especially, when related to a highly trained, undoubtedly expert, silent killer and saboteur. The contradiction was obvious – and viewed in the light of the horrific incident detailed in Karelin's combat and subsequent medical record – disturbing.

The others' cover-lives were more mundane and thus appeared safer; ridiculously so – for all three who completed the Spartan unit were certainly as deadly as Karelin, the master of dance.

Anatoly Demurov, otherwise Arnie Kawolski, Polish *émigré*, occupation mechanic; Sergei Fedashin or Max Goldman, second generation English born, of Lithuanian-Jewish immigrants, tailor; Yakov Lobjanidze or David John Ryan, trader, English, a bit of Irish history too far back to be viewed as dangerous. All self-employed, all with small inconspicuous businesses that never grew, never went under, just ticked over, unchanging. Unlike their heartbeats? he wondered – for these were strangers in a strange land, forever expecting discovery. Or perhaps not. Perhaps they were trained so well, they never were strangers. Even if they were, what difference would it have made? Walk out there on the streets now, he told himself – how many nationalities would you walk past in five minutes? In *one* minute. And most would be domiciled. Here. How easy it must have been for the KGB. What a soft touch we must have seemed.

He sat back in his chair. It was only a question now of reeling them in.

*So do it. Get on with it!*

That was the easy part.

It told him nothing of who was behind them. Who woke them. Who controlled. Who was so contemptuous of himself, his authority, of the law, that they would unleash secret killers at will. Who protected them. Financed, now – for someone must – their other passive roles. Who kept them like whores for their darker needs.

There was a knock on the door.

'Come.'

He saw his secretary's face. 'What is it?'

She laid a faxed sheet before him.

His eyes moved swiftly, then closed. 'Oh, dear God,' he whispered.

'I'm sorry, sir,' she murmured and left.

He swallowed the coffee dregs in one gulp as if bitter medicine: punishment – and cure – for his lack of drive to end this conclusively. For not ordering Reardon out when Brannigan was killed; for using him; for forsaking him; for thinking, *acting*, with political aims – and ends – in mind and not the safety of his trusted servant.

Well, it was done.

Now, without restraint, he must discover – if not publicly *un*cover – the conspirators and put them to the sword. As their

172

Spartans would have done *him*, had fate, and history, not abandoned them and favoured him instead.

Not kill of course.

Destroy.

Force from office.

Which, in a way, was a kind of death.

He stood, resolved, angered that killers trained for *his* execution had been used against Brannigan. Somehow that made this personal. Very personal. Reardon's murder compounded his outrage. *Whoever* had carried that out, it was still a personal attack.

His tiredness had evaporated. He would act. Swiftly, decisively, ruthlessly. He was the most powerful man in the country. He would use that power. Trust his own judgement. Certainly he trusted neither of his secret houses. Not *utterly*, which was how it should be. They both had something to gain and – in those bewildering times – much to lose.

He remembered his predecessor's firm advice, given with brimming eyes at the moment of crisis and despair he gained from; heart speaking, not brain: If you *have* to trust someone, always trust a British soldier. They're the best in the world. They'll never let you down.

He reached over the desk for the telephone. 'Get me Hereford,' he ordered. 'Officer Commanding. Yes, immediately.'

A cool voice came on the line. 'Prime Minister?'

'Reardon has just been murdered in Ulster.'

'I've heard, sir. From our man, Ellis.'

'Ellis wasn't with him?'

'Unfortunately not. Reardon ordered him to stay behind. There appears to be something going on we've not been briefed about – sir.'

'Yes.'

'Ellis said Reardon was coming to see you. Were you aware of that?'

'I guessed from the report. But I didn't order him back over here.'

'What do you want done, sir?'

As easy as that? he wondered. All our travails over there, all the killings, the sorrow, the politics, the shame, the inhumanity? And it comes down to the man commanding the élite of élite forces asking: What do you want done?

So be it. 'I want the men who did it.'

'We all want the men who did it, sir. I require precise orders. Rules of engagement with the enemy.' The cool voice hesitated, the tone subtly changed: harder. 'If you require there to be any?'

'We may not be discussing the same enemy. Colonel, meet me here. How long will it take you?'

'Chopper to Chelsea Barracks, car to you, no time at all, sir.'

'Discreetly, please.'

'Tradesmen's entrance, sir.'

He put down the telephone.

*And executioners'.*

B OBBY HARDING found the nearest working pay-phone, called the crash number they had given him for dire emergencies.

'What?' demanded the hard Belfast voice.

'I've got word there's some hits going down soon – maybe today.'

'Who is this?'

'Harding.'

'Who?'

'Bobby Harding!'

'All right. Talk, make it quick. On who?'

'The main players.'

'You're dreaming. They wouldn't try it. Too much to lose.'

'Listen! Jesus! Not the Provies. The Brits. They're setting us up against each other.'

'We *are* against each other, you stupid fuck! Now get off this line.'

The receiver purred in Harding's hand. He smashed it. Then crouched on his haunches in the box, feeling done, strung out. Maybe he should have taken Jamie's offer.

*Shit*, he wasn't running. He was going to be somebody and this was the place to be. It was his struggle. *He* could be a main player given the breaks – like this one: knowing something was going to happen when no one else did. Except Jamie. And Jamie was right most of the time. Except about *me*.

Saturday, he thought. They lunched on Saturday. Business. Respectable. Looking good. Keeping the public face right. Never the same place, naturally – but he'd minded them enough to know the circuit. He'd cruise it, find them, tell them face to face, tell them he heard it straight from the mouth of Jamie McAlister who knew all there was to know about Belfast. And they'd know the name Bobby Harding first off.

He found them by the river. A favourite place. Upstairs overlooking the rowing club, members sculling by fast, like long-legged water-boatmen.

In fact he found their cars. BMWs, all of them. Two men lounging by them, smartened and slicked for the outing.

All's well then, he thought, entered and walked up the stairs.

They were by the window, the best table naturally – kept for warlords of both sides – protected by a table of four, of whom Bobby recognized three.

'What you doin' here?' one of the four demanded, wiping his mouth of tomato sauce from his spaghetti.

'Want to talk to them – important.'

'What do you know that's important?' grinned another. He grimaced. 'Looks like you've pissed yourself.'

'I was sick. Cleaned it up. It's still wet.'

'They're talking,' said the one he didn't know.

'I can fuckin' see that. They'll want to hear what I've got, OK.'

'Tell us.'

'I tell them,' Bobby's jaw jutted. 'It's important. Just ask.'

'Better be good.' The man arose, tossed his napkin on the table and moved away.

The others looked at him. He could feel their contempt. It hurt him. He couldn't help being different from them. Being gay. This was his fight as much as theirs. He put in as much. Risked as much. He could see the car park. The minders had gone. Peeing it, he thought, or getting out of the drizzle.

'They'll hear you out. Come on.'

Bobby approached the table, stood there, feeling his knees touch each other, quivering as if a current was being passed through. Get this right, he told himself. Don't overdo it. Just tell it like you think it is.

'Give him a chair,' said one, the most powerful. 'All right? What's got you in that state?'

Bobby felt the chair strike the rear of his knees and flopped into it, too hard.

They laughed.

He looked at them. They weren't that frightening. He could be any one of them. Could be better. He'd had the training, knew all the tricks – and knew all the faces.

'Come on, we haven't got all day.'

Without me you haven't even got today, thought Bobby but only said: 'Sorry. Just getting it all together.'

The shots were like hammer blows striking sheets of steel. Echoing off flat surfaces of stone and hardwood, then swallowed by long reverberating tunnels – one of which Bobby felt himself slide into, clasping his back where the bullets struck, seeing the juddering forms before him exploding in reds and greys and pink-whites of bone as he slid away from them into muzzy grey darkness which held, not quite becoming black.

He felt something at his head and looked up. The foot was huge, the leg above it reaching for ever to the machine-pistol. Ingram, he thought. *I know, I've the training*.

'Recognize this fucker?'

He recognized them. The James Boys. The giant with the Ingram was Billy the Kid.

'He was there. Used to be a sodding copper, someone said.'

'Used to be.'

'Finish him.'

The Ingram barely moved.

The flare from its barrel took for ever to reach him.

# CHAPTER TEN

———◆►◄◆———

RICK WATCHED the TV midday news lying on a sofa, black hair wet from his shower, feet bare, legs curled under him, the long-barrelled silenced Browning across his thighs, Murphy's wife directly opposite on a deep, leather armchair where he had positioned her, pale with fear, Murphy himself seething, gagged and bound to a heavy wooden garden chair to his left. The children drugged and silent in one of the four bedrooms.

The announcer paused, took paper from an unseen hand, scanned it and read a brief report of the fatal M2 shooting, naming Reardon, describing him as a Treasury economic adviser. The taxi driver's name was withheld until next of kin were informed.

'You know who that is?' blurted Dave, eating a sandwich.

Rick looked at Murphy for a long moment. 'Was.' He uncurled, leapt up and ripped the tape from the mottled face, tearing the skin.

Murphy gasped. 'You bastard.'

The silencer pressed firmly between his eyes. Rick whispered. 'The gun is everything. When I hold it, I am everything, you are nothing. If you held it you would still be nothing because you kill at a distance. The only way to kill is close, as close as a kiss.'

Rose Murphy screamed.

Murphy's eyes were wide with fear, as if seeing deep into Rick and finding only horror. 'What do you want from us?'

'I want to know why.'

'Why what?'

'Why?'

'For fuck's sake!'

Rick backed away. He held out his hand to Rose Murphy. 'I'll give him time to work out the answer.'

'Leave her alone, you bastard!'

'He doesn't know what you want!' she pleaded. 'Tell him!'

Rick smiled. 'I can't tell him. I don't know. *He* knows.'

Murphy struggled like a man demented but his bonds and the heavy chair defeated him. He slumped. 'For fuck's sake tell me. I can't guess what's in your sick mind.'

Rick swung one leg in a perfect arc, graceful, balletic, his bare calloused foot striking the side of Murphy's head, knocking him over. He placed an arm around Rose Murphy's slender waist, and led her away, whispering in her ear: 'Don't look back. I'll kill him before your head turns.'

The tears fell from her, her lips quivering, numbed by fear, by the menace hiding like a serpent coiled for the strike behind his soft caressing eyes.

Murphy roared, on his side on the thick carpet, battling furiously with his bonds again.

'Pull him up and shut him up, Dave,' Rick called without turning at the door of the master bedroom. 'Inside,' he said. 'And don't do anything. Just stand. You can't buy me with your body. *Yes*, you've thought it, women always do, it's their first and last resort.' He tore a strip off the masking tape and wound it completely around her head: mouth, neck, hair, everything.

She stared, petrified.

He held the stiletto before her eyes and pressed the release, the razor-sharp blade thrusting out so close she felt the small rush of air on her skin. She felt wetness on her nose that was not tears. A small red globule formed, fell, Rick catching it in his palm, tasting it, savouring it.

He kissed her nose, licked it.

He said: 'They made me eat my friend.' His voice held torment; and awe.

Her scream was deep inside, a voice lost in a hole too deep, too dark, to climb from. Even through the gag it was loud.

Murphy, righted again in his chair, heard it. He howled like an animal.

Dave hit him, a chopping controlled blow to the apex of neck and shoulder, Murphy's head whipping back in reaction, face raised. Dave clasped it, shook it, the heavy jowls wobbling. 'I warned you in the car: *Do anything, say anything*. Not to stay alive, to make him kill you, quickly. You'll be praying for it soon.'

'Help me!' Murphy gasped.

'I can't. It's gone beyond . . . everything. This is how it is. Rick is all there is. You don't understand.'

'I don't want to understand – I want my wife away from that maniac. Just tell me what the fuck he wants!'

'He wants to know why we're here.'

'Jesus, if *you* don't know, *who* does!'

'We know we were sent to kill the American.'

Murphy froze. '*Brannigan?*'

'Brannigan.'

Rose Murphy's muffled squeal came down the corridor. Real pain, now.

'Get him. I'll fuckin' tell him *why*! Just get him *off* my wife!'

MCALISTER, FOR once, used his office. He sat forward on his chair, forearms bare, planted on the steel desk. He looked at Ellis as he would a criminal. 'If there's anything I should know that you haven't told me – and I don't care if it's down to Defence of the Realm, Official Secrets Act or some other high-flown muzzle – you'd better tell me fast because I seem to be treading blood already and a few pints more isn't going to make any difference. You hearing me?'

'I'm hearing.'

'Speak.'

Ellis stared at his calloused hands.

McAlister snapped. 'He's dead, boy. You lost him. You and Carter ought to form a bloody club.'

Ellis glared. 'He ordered me to stay. Your sodding tart couldn't handle Carter. She couldn't handle my dick if I'd put it in her hand!'

'*Officer*. And I'll make the professional judgements,' McAlister snarled. Then softened. 'I can guess how you're feeling. He's gone. You can't change the play. You *can* change the outcome.'

Ellis looked at him.

179

'Well?'

'My position isn't good right now, I don't want to make it worse, OK.'

'It isn't getting any better, laddie – and you know it.'

Ellis shrugged. 'I was pulled by Five soon as I got assigned to Reardon. They read me the riot act. Told me I do what they say from then on. I mean, they *are* in control!'

'What did they say? Want?'

'Everything. Every word that was spoken between Brannigan and Reardon. Every word either one said to *anyone*, period. I got to place the telephone bugs, do the business – Christ, *you* know!'

'And you heard any of this? The conversations? Were you enlightened? If so, enlighten me please because I need a ray of *something* bright here!'

Ellis breathed out heavily. 'Brannigan either was a pro himself – or he was being minded bloody well. Bugs picked up zilch.'

'He found them?'

'Someone jammed them.'

McAlister considered this, then said: 'Carter was doing the minding? I mean the mission – not just the body? That's what you're saying?'

'Maybe. Or Brannigan was a real smooth operator who did it all solo? James Bond with microchips. Sometimes I saw the ice in him. I reckon if I'd had to take one meant for Mr Reardon he'd have watched me go down and not blink. For all the big smiles he was a hard bastard. *Calculated*, you know?'

'Do *you* know Reardon spoke directly to Downing Street? On the phone you bugged.'

'They *are* ours, you know – Five – not the sodding Russians'.'

'You're behind on your enemies, son. They're ours all right but that doesn't give them the right to pick up the ball and run when the rest of us plodders are kicking the damn thing according to the rules. So what's their game?'

'How the fuck do I know?'

'They had to tell you something. Unless you're so dim you never questioned any of it. And *that* I don't believe. Hereford doesn't let dim-wits through the gates. Come on, they gave you some line, truth or not, I want to hear it.'

'Brannigan was a front. He had Irish blood way back but you know how the Yank Paddies see that – like it was yesterday.'

'*Front* as in IRA money?'

'What else? Once he'd set himself up over here, NORAID funds could be channelled through company accounts – and laugh: the Brit government would be financing half the deal!'

McAlister's lips tightened. He leaned back.

Ellis's muted Welsh lilt was suddenly very clear. 'Well then? Does it play? I mean, what do you think? Bullshit or gospel?'

'I don't know. Yes, it plays all right. I'd believe it.'

'Thanks!'

'The question is, is it the right game?' He pushed himself up, turned away, looked out of the window at his view of drainpipes and the building's inner well. I live a life of back walls: places no one else wants to be, or see. He peered down into the grubby gloom. *Quite.* One day I'll walk out the front door, wear a dazzling shirt, smile, wave, give the world more of me than I give myself. And you'll be shot down like a dog. Get yourself back where you belong. Live. Live another day.

'They'll want you home now? Hereford?' he enquired.

Ellis hesitated. 'I'm waiting on word.'

'You'll have a hard time.'

'Sling my hook probably. Unless Five come clean.'

'Don't count on it. As the US Navy used to say up at Holy Loch when I was there: "You've been drafted, shafted and rafted." In Queen's English, up the creek without a paddle. Unless I help you.'

'How?' Ellis asked, despondently.

'I'm not sure – yet.'

'You tell me what you want.'

'Stay on a couple of days. I'll say we need you for the inquest. Hereford can't argue with that.'

'I can't stay at the hotel. Not on my pay. I'm off expenses. The car's gone too.'

'Stay with me, I've space.'

'OK. Thanks.'

'One thing. Before you get the story elsewhere, I'm gay. But my interest in you is professional. Strictly. Understood?'

'I wouldn't have known.'

181

'You would if I'd wanted you to.'

Ellis stood, offered his hand. 'Sorry about what I called your officer.'

McAlister shook it. 'If you *had* put it in her hand she'd have broken it off.'

Ellis grinned. 'I'll get my kit from the hotel. Meet you here?'

'I'm that side of the Lough, I'll pick you up. Can't say exactly when. I'll call when I'm on the way.'

'See you later, then. Thanks again.'

McAlister sat, almost feeling the presence of Reardon there with him, urging him on. 'I'm not giving up!' he muttered aloud, angrily. He looked at his three telephones. *Straight. Secure. Secret. Like Me. Appearing to be the first, will never be the second, am the third.* He lifted the secure line and dialled the private number he had read – and remembered – from Reardon's open diary on the bed.

The familiar flat voice gave his name.

Unreal, thought McAlister. I'm dreaming.

'Who is this?'

'Inspector James McAlister, sir, RUC Special Branch. I've a need to speak with you. An urgent need.'

'You're doing that already, Inspector,' said the Prime Minister. 'Well?'

McAlister told him the purpose behind Reardon's fatal journey: the need to acquire old KGB records.

'I'm ahead of you, Inspector. Give me a safe fax number and I'll send you everything personally. Your eyes only, understood?'

'Perfectly.' McAlister gave a number.

'You realize if Reardon had called me he wouldn't have been in that car riding to the airport?'

'He tried, sir. You were unavailable.'

The line fell silent for long seconds. Finally the flat voice said: 'I heeded bad advice. Well, we all have to live with our mistakes, don't we? Unfortunately, at this level, others die for them. I'll send this material immediately. Keep me informed, McAlister.'

CARTER PULLED the Mercedes into the small garage.
'Problem?' asked the blue-overalled mechanic. 'Nice motor. You'll need the main dealer there on the Lisburn Road if it's serious.'

'Knocking. Not engine. Underneath. Need to get it on the ramp and take a look.'

'Why not? I'll drive that heap off, you get on there, OK?'

'Sure.'

Kate Brannigan got out, stood looking emptily at the car.

The mechanic pointed. 'Coffee machine in there. TV too if you want – while we take a gander?'

She nodded, entered his glassed office and fed coins into the machine, sipped the hot tasteless mixture, staring at the two men working their way along the bottom of the raised car, the television murmuring in the background.

The name Alan Reardon swung her around, his heavy face staring at her, still, like death, the next pictures confirming the illusion: the burned-out wreck, the trail of metal along the highway as if the car had torn itself apart before crashing.

She barely heard the commentary, words seeming to spring out of the blur – *economic adviser – taxi – airport – M60 machine-gun – terrorists* . . . then, quite suddenly, Patrick's blue eyes stared at her, directly at her, he smiled, turned away, ducked into a car and was gone.

*Come back!* She almost called it out aloud.

She stood stunned, the commentary droning on, advising the world of the connection between the two men.

Death is the connection, she spat silently. Death is how you people live here and I've had enough of it. She saw a pack of cigarettes on the cluttered desk, greasy matchbox alongside, she took one, lit it, drew deeply, her eyes flooding with tears. '*Shit!*'

'You all right?' Carter asked at the door.

'Reardon's dead. Murdered.' She dipped her head at the television, the picture already changed to languorous thoroughbreds led by bored handlers past eager, greedy, addicted faces. 'He was on his way to the airport. Maybe he'd quit. Too damn late!'

'I'm sorry.'

'Why? I didn't know him.'

'But you liked him. Patrick liked him. I heard him tell you on the phone.'

'Patrick liked anybody who agreed with him.'

'That's not true.'

She stabbed out the cigarette. 'I know. I'm just sick of it. Sick of it all.'

'It'll be over soon. By tomorrow it'll be over.'

'I'm not holding my breath.'

'Trust me.'

'You I trust, it's all those other evil bastards without faces out there.' She gasped, fighting emotion. 'Jesus, I'm scared.'

'You're human.'

'That's a comfort?'

'It's a fact.'

'Great. So was Patrick. How come he did it all the goddamn time? Year after fucking year!'

'He wasn't you – and you don't want to be him. This is a one-off, do it and run. Don't even look back when it's over.'

'Are you *kidding?*'

He looked at the ramp. 'The car's clean.'

'Clean?'

'Nothing attached, concealed, modified. Not that I could see.'

She gave a hard, dry laugh. 'Maybe the IRA just want the car? That's their price? One Mercedes 500 coupé!'

'They can have it.'

'Sure. If only! Let's get out of here.'

Carter aimed a thumb at the mechanic. 'His aunt Doris has a guest house. Clean, small, somewhere back of all the main action. I said we'd take a couple of rooms for a day or two. There's a lock-up garage there with an old Jaguar sedan inside. I've rented the Jag for tonight – store the Merc in its place. He'll call her right now if it's OK with you?'

'No.'

'No?'

'*One* room. I'm not going to lie alone all day waiting for tonight. I'm not going to fall sleep and wake with no one there. All right? Doesn't affect your statutory rights.'

'I'll tell him.' Carter turned.

'Marcus.'

'Yes?'

'Thank you.'

He nodded. 'Save it for when it's over.'

'SIT DOWN, Colonel.'

The SAS commander wore civilian clothes – well-cut tweeds. He sat, looked around him.

The Prime Minister remained standing. He gave a wan smile. 'Not exactly the seat of power. I'm glad my wife's got flu and dozing, she'd think I'd gone quite loopy having the SAS to tea in our private rooms. There is a reason.'

The Colonel looked up at him, silent.

'You people have a certain stillness about you, if you don't mind me saying. Reminds me of those lizards with the long tongues sitting on some tropical rock waiting for the next meal to fly by – then *zap*!'

The Colonel gave a tight grin. 'If we're *still*, sir, it's because we spend our lives waiting in a high state of readiness. That's our purpose as you're aware – being on permanent stand-by. Wildlife comparisons? I'd say we're more like swifts – letting our temperatures drop to save burning unnecessary energy.'

The Prime Minister laid the MI5 transcript of Reardon's telephone call from Arnie and the faxes from the Kremlin on the low coffee table. 'Read those. The profiles from Moscow will interest you. One in particular. Not often you get a chance to see the enemy's view of his own? Even a former enemy. Especially when they've had to put one back together after some damn *hard* bites have been taken out of him. An interesting study our own tame witch-doctors would give a great deal to get hold of – and they never will! I'll make tea in the mean time. That do you?'

The Colonel chuckled. 'My wife won't believe I'd been made tea by the Prime Minister.'

'You know, I never think of you people as being married. I'm sorry, that sounds terrible.'

'People do tend to view us as emotionless killers incapable of meaningful long-term relationships. It's not true, of course. A married man in our job tends to be circumspect, measures all the options

185

most carefully, and we value that. We don't crash through windows without thinking very hard about it beforehand.'

'I should hope not. Your tea? Milk, sugar?'

'Hot, white and sweet, sir.'

'Sounds like someone I once knew,' grinned the Prime Minister, keeping things light. 'Shouldn't say things like that, of course. Breaks just about every rule in the politically-correct handbook. When you've read, come into the kitchen. Best place for a chat.'

'I will, sir.'

The Prime Minister made tea, cut slices of banana cake from a tin, then sat, watching sports on a hand-size colour portable, thin buzzing cheers coming from it like static.

After a while the Colonel entered, sat across from him on the plain table, laid down the faxes. 'I'd not like to occupy *that* mind,' he said, steadily, tapping the clipped top sheets.

The Prime Minister made no attempt to switch off the set. 'I thought the same thing.'

'Who are we . . . avoiding, sir?' The Colonel's browned hand swept the humid kitchen air briefly.

'If I knew that, Colonel, we wouldn't be in here.' He sat forward. 'When your major intelligence agencies declare war on each other there's every reason to believe or suspect – even *expect* – that they'll each want to know what's being decided about them at the very highest levels of power. And if you're thinking: *My God! The bloody PM's gone paranoid*, don't feel too bad about it. I've had a few on those lines myself over the last day or so.'

The Colonel sipped his tea, gave a tight smile.

'Of course that's only background to why you're here. I don't expect you to mount raids on Five or Six.'

'I'm grateful for that.'

The Prime Minister offered cake, his eyes shifting to the fax. 'I want you to find *that* mind – the body that goes with it, of course – and his comrades, too.'

'Yes.'

The Prime Minister looked at the cake. 'Then kill them. All of them.'

The Colonel paused; measured, like someone awaiting a signature. He said: 'You're certain of that, sir.'

The Prime Minister met his eyes. 'Caught alive, placed on trial, the repercussions will be appalling. We're currently developing our relations with the Russians into something really worthwhile. Long term. Trade, investment, influence, all are important – but the most vital issue is their nuclear weapon destruction programme and their determination to have their former satellites follow their lead – which is the only sure guarantee of non-proliferation there can be. This is a new era of understanding. Ghosts from the past – especially violent ones – are precisely what we don't need. Either us or Moscow. You understand me? The importance of what I'm saying?'

'Perfectly.'

'*Dead*, Colonel. Stone dead. And no graves. No bodies either, if you can manage that? In a sense they don't exist anyway. If you act quickly it might get blurred by the sectarian blood-rites that have been taking place today. Five gunned down by lunch time? Civilization – if that's what they call it over there – really *is* in one of its downward spirals!'

He reached back and took a slim buff folder from the work-surface behind him. 'Inspector James McAlister, RUC Special Branch, Belfast. Everything there is to know about him. Professional, personal, the lot. He and Reardon were deeply involved in all this. Had a – pact, I'd suppose you'd call it. Their own private investigation into the American Patrick Brannigan's murder over there. I'm afraid I encouraged their activities – after Reardon flew to London to voice his suspicions personally, and confidentially. Suspicions that perhaps the IRA were not the perpetrators. That some deeper purpose was behind the murder. Possibly involving the Security Service. The telephone transcript you read was a part of all that. The Director-General of Five came to see me as soon as she received it. Obviously Five had their own suspicions to have mounted the bugging operation in the first place.'

'You implied a war between Five and Six a moment ago. She points the finger at Six?'

'I'm not going deeper into that, Colonel, but you understand the kind of fog I'm stumbling around in? I'm not certain we can afford to clear that fog. Too damaging. Sometimes one has to be pragmatic in government. You'll have to take my word I'm acting for the best here.'

'McAlister?' the Colonel prompted.

'Called me earlier. Told me everything he knows. If anyone can track down these *Spetsnaz* it's him. You have a man over there – Ellis?'

'In trouble right now, abandoned Reardon.'

The Prime Minister raised a hand. 'He'd been suborned by Five. That's how Reardon was bugged so effectively. They recruited the man nearest to him – his bodyguard. Ellis told McAlister all this, today. McAlister offered to help him ride out problems with you. In a way it was McAlister's doing – Ellis's not being with Reardon at the critical time – so don't view your man too harshly. McAlister's keeping him over there for a few days. I suggest you don't object. Let Ellis ride McAlister's coat-tails. When he's been led to Karelin and the others . . . he can do what must be done.'

The Colonel skimmed McAlister's file. 'Not alone,' he said quietly but firmly. 'I know you want knowledge of this restricted but Ellis must have backup. These aren't run-of-the-mill terrorists, they are – or certainly were – élite Special Forces troops. Even a few years on from their best – and out of a military environment, which means discipline and fitness are probably below par – they're still bloody dangerous. I know *Spetsnaz* methods. After their kind of training – or ours for that matter – there are two critical things never forgotten. One, survival: technique and instinct never leave you, ever. Two, killing: the expertise to do it swiftly, effectively and, when necessary, silently, will always be there. Only the *readiness* to kill diminishes.' He tapped the faxes again. 'Reading those I seriously doubt it has.'

He pushed the faxes away a little. 'Providing effective backup for Ellis won't be easy with someone as aware as McAlister constantly in his company. A senior Northern Ireland police officer *lives* by being aware. Of course if he's to be advised of the hidden agenda . . . ?'

'Absolutely not. From what I've read on him – and viewing his stand with Reardon – there's every chance he'd feel compromised. Might even intervene. With tragic results, I'd imagine – caught between SAS and *Spetsnaz* fire! You're the expert. Make whatever arrangements are necessary. Clandestine if necessary, just make certain there's no publicity afterwards.'

'One can't always control these things, sir.'

'One can *redirect* if control is lost, Colonel.'

The soldier gazed at him.

188

The Prime Minister sipped tea. 'Ellis lost Reardon? Allowed him to make that taxi-ride alone? He must be pretty cut up about that?'

'Certainly.'

'Enough for revenge? Enough anger?'

The Colonel stiffened. 'I don't sell my men down the river. Even after they've messed up.'

'I don't expect you to. Be straight with Ellis. Warn him what could happen to him if things turned sour. If the media got hold of this. I'd do my best for him – behind the scenes, of course. Ellis is perfectly placed and motivated. You agree? The media will latch on to that instantly. They're well aware the public expect motive.'

'And the noblest motive is the public good?'

'You have no illusions that this is a debate, Colonel, I'm sure.'

'Prime Minister, I'm only called in when every last word and the very last expellation of breath in the debate is done.'

'Speak to Ellis as soon as you arrive back at Hereford. Colonel, you'll follow this through personally.' It was an order.

'WHAT ARE you, Murphy?' enquired Rick as they were led down wooden stairs to a basement, Dave following with Rose Murphy.

'Quartermaster,' Murphy responded, cowed.

'So you need to know a little of everything, who wants what, who gets what, the where, the how of all of it – but not necessarily the why? *Why* is reserved for decision makers. Are you a decision maker, Murphy? Or just their storekeeper?'

'I do my bit.'

'And do you share your bit with the lovely Rose? Whisper your secrets when they get too much for you, spill them into her when you come?'

Murphy squeezed his eyes tight as if that might shut all of it out, even the dreadful smooth, mind-devouring sound of Rick's voice.

'I thought so,' Rick whispered, close.

'Do it to me, not her,' Murphy murmured back as if they were sharing a secret.

189

'The *dance*, Murphy, not the dancer. Do you understand?'

'God save her from you.'

'He can't save *me* from me, Murphy.'

They entered the secret room through wall-length wooden shelving, hinged and concertinaed from the centre, the joins concealed by clever beaded construction and dozens of hanging tools.

There was a map on the wall, stabbed by pins of various colours, some flagged, others anonymous. Rick reached forward, removed one pin at the top of the map – the inn near the causeway – and tossed it over his shoulder. 'We could work right through this and change history, Dave. You realize that?'

'Sure, Rick.'

'But that will take time, which we don't have.'

'*Tell him whatever he wants*,' Rose Murphy pleaded, the thin, perfect cut on the swell of her full left breast like an artist's fine brush stroke.

Murphy looked at her. 'They'll kill us.'

'*He'll* kill us!'

'I will,' agreed Rick.

Murphy sagged. 'What're you after?'

Rick found a folding chair, set it up, sat. 'Patrick John Brannigan? I want everything.'

'Why? You killed him, didn't you? What's the point?'

'We want to gain something from his memory, don't we, Dave?'

'Whatever you say, Rick.'

'We've begun to believe he was worth more than the amount we were paid. Which I have to tell you was meagre.'

'You're private,' Murphy said, revelation in his eyes. 'Fucking contractors.' He laughed. 'You *are* bloody Russians. Free enterprise, is it? What are you? Moscow Mafia?'

Dave hit him very hard, a massive blow to the temple; explosive anger behind the balled fist. He barked something which was not English.

Rose Murphy screamed as her husband dropped, lifeless.

Rick watched, unmoving.

Dave said: 'I'm sorry, Rick.' He lifted Murphy, slapped his cheeks lightly. 'He shouldn't have called us that. We're soldiers.' Defeat, shame, filled his eyes. 'We *were* soldiers. The best. I'd like to go home, Rick.'

'I'm your home.'

A thick bubble of blood formed on Murphy's lips.

'He's bad, Rick.'

'He's dying.'

Rose Murphy shrieked and hurled herself at Rick despite her bonds. He caught her fast, easily, twisted her. 'Watch. This is death. Blood. Stink. Waste pouring from you like a drain.' He pressed his lips to her ear, whispered: 'I'll die like an exploding star. A morning star brighter than day. Nothing left to bubble and rot. Nothing but the soft rush of vapour like my breath on your cheek.'

She wept, deep hopeless sobs, turned away from the slumped form Dave still held up.

'He's gone, Rick.'

Rick turned her face up to him. 'Welcome to the dance.'

ELLIS WAS propped against a car, a large athlete's equipment bag at his feet for luggage.

McAlister leaned across and pushed the passenger door open, smelling whisky instantly as Ellis swung in beside him then turned to toss the bag into the rear. 'How many?' he asked.

'Not enough to be belligerent.'

'I trust – with your training – belligerent is not the way you get when you've had a few.'

'Not usually.' Ellis glared at the windscreen. 'Just pissed off. Feeling a bit sorry for myself. Bloody Welsh get that way.'

'As long as it's nothing specific. I mean specific to this investigation?'

Ellis turned. 'That's what you call it? Seems like you and Mr Reardon were kind of running your own show there for a while? *Unofficial*. Before the curtain dropped on him.'

'You are feeling sorry for yourself. I'll feed you well on the way – that'll lift the Celtic gloom and dilute the alcohol.'

'Way where?'

'Where giants race before the flood.'

'Oh, yeah!'

'The Causeway.'

'What's there?'

'Answers. Maybe?'

Ellis edged himself lower in his seat. 'It's all sodding maybes right now, isn't it?'

'You are armed?'

'From puberty, Mr McAlister.'

'Well, at least it didn't stunt your growth.'

Ellis chuckled.

McAlister glanced at him. 'Don't you want to know what's up there? What we're up against? *Who?*'

'You're going to tell me, aren't you?'

McAlister dropped the glove box cover, revealing a sheaf of paper bound by an elastic band. 'If I told you the Prime Minister fed those into a fax machine himself would you believe me?'

'Mr McAlister, if you told me they're recycled from the Queen's bog I'd believe you. The shit I'm in I'm with you all the way.'

'Read, then tell me what you think.' McAlister started the engine and drove cautiously through the tight ranks of parked cars. He cursed, seeing there was no space left to swing into the next row and snapped the gear-lever into reverse. Then stopped.

'What's up?'

'Stay there,' McAlister got out and walked to a car bearing Eire number-plates tucked well back in the furthest corner beneath the thick foliage of a tree. Only the filthy rear end of the Renault saloon showed, the Eire registration almost completely obscured by grime. He bent, took a handful of leaves from the ground and wiped it. He came back, pointed. 'Can you get into that?'

Ellis grinned.

'Do it.'

'What's in there?'

'An expensive piece of American high-technology, I suspect.'

Ellis delved into his bag, came out with a small box and followed McAlister to the car, the security guard already running toward them from his hut.

McAlister thrust his ID forward.

'It's a guest's car, not a bomber's job.'

'American guest? Name's Carter?'

'Right.'

'When? The car arrived when?'

'Last night – well early morning, really. Wasn't my shift. It's logged to him, though.' The man ducked his head at the security hut. 'I've the exact time back there.'

McAlister swore. 'The bloody obvious always gets missed. Well, this puts him *right* in the frame.'

The security guard hovered.

'On your way,' McAlister said. 'This is police business.'

The man looked nervously at the car.

'Don't worry, you're right, nothing explosive in there. Not the kind you're worried about, anyway.'

Ellis had the boot open in seconds. 'Well, that didn't fall off the back of a lorry,' he breathed.

'Seen one before?'

'*Used* one before. Iraq. Smaller – but the same purpose. Satellite comms. Very sophisticated. For people who don't trust telephones – even the ones they call safe. I'm talking heavy traffic here, Mr McAlister. *Command* decisions. Spook country.'

McAlister thrust his hands into his pockets, for once oblivious to the cut of his clothes. 'It's time I made *my* decision, laddie.'

'What's that?'

'Walk on or walk away.'

Ellis shifted, frowned. 'Which affects *me*, right? So what's it going to be?'

'Before Reardon I might have turned around and walked. I can't do that now.'

Ellis looked at him, hard. 'No more than I can.'

'That's settled then. You transfer everything to my car, I've a call to make.'

McAlister got back in his car, rapidly stabbed digits for Slattery's cellnet number in the Republic into his handset and waited. 'Tom? Jamie McAlister. I've found your missing motor-car. The satellite dish too. And the rest that goes with that. It's not TV, Tom. Communications equipment. All of it. American. Very sophisticated. Very special.'

'I'm not understanding but I'm still listening.'

'If I told you your perpetrators were Russians what would your reaction be?'

'You say *American* equipment? Well, a few years back I'd say we'd an extension of the Cold War being conducted on our respective territories. But that's all over, isn't it?'

'Not for someone living in the past.'

'You're losing me.'

'I realize that. Tom, listen, I'm about to stick my neck out – way out – but you need to catch these people as much as I do. Get yourself to a fax machine.'

'What have you got, Jamie?'

'A sad tale.'

'I'm bloody Irish, we've enough sad tales of our own.'

'Not with this backdrop of horror.'

'I've seen enough horror today for one lifetime, thank you.'

'Tom, you want your man, I'm giving him to you – ID, everything, the whole sorry bloody awful story. *If* he's on your side of the border.'

'And if he's on *yours* will you hand him over? Jamie?'

'I may not be able to.'

Silence fell.

'It's political Tom. Heavily political. I'm certain of that, now. I *feel* it. The whole American thing right from the start. I don't think even London appreciates *how* heavy.'

'And justice, Jamie? Doesn't that come into it?'

'That could be out of my hands.'

'Jamie?'

'What?'

'We're hunting an *animal*. Drive him my way. That gets you off the hook and puts the evil bastard on my ground. All right?'

McAlister breathed. 'I'll quarantine the car – you send your people for it. Culloden Hotel, Antrim.'

'I'll be waiting on you, Jamie.'

McAlister closed the phone.

Ellis stood watching him. 'What now?'

McAlister tilted his head at the hotel. 'We do our bit for Anglo-Irish relations.' He reached into the glove box for the faxes.

'What about Anglo-American relations, Mr McAlister?' Ellis pointed at the filled boot of the car.

'For as long as I'm allowed to be I'll be what I am. A

194

policeman. I'll worry about the politics when it's bearing down on me.'

'Leave yourself room to jump, then, Mr McAlister,' warned Ellis.

S HE LAY against him. Not in his arms, not held by him, barely touching, but there. His presence was all she needed right then.

'Just walk away, Marcus. Tonight. Take the children and walk. Leave any anger you have behind.' She turned, faced him. 'Leave it inside me if it makes it easier.'

He had his eyes closed. Had slept a little. Mainly he had just lain there, relaxed, body rested, mind switched off; even without sleep he would be refreshed.

'Would you make that offer under other conditions?'

'No, probably not.'

'Then don't now. Rest, you've got to be better than you've ever been before.'

'A better liar.'

'More. You have to pretend Patrick told you everything. Everything he said to them. Everything they wanted. Everything he could give them.'

'I don't know any of it.'

'You know some. The rest is up to you. I told you once already – back in that house when Melsham took me away – use your lawyer's mind. You'll have to think on your feet. Work it out from their questions – and their answers to yours.'

'That's a razor's edge.'

He opened his eyes and looked at her. 'Once in everybody's lifetime they have to walk a razor's edge for the ones they love.'

She smiled. 'Yes.'

He nodded. 'Yes.'

They slept a while, side by side; she held his hand.

He awoke when the light from the city-grimed window with its scrupulously clean flowered curtains and white net on the inside, and curled barbed wire against sectarian attacks on the outside, faded.

'It's time,' he murmured.

# Chapter Eleven

————◆→◆←◆————

R OSE MURPHY wanted to die. Now. Before she must face the reality of the nightmare running before her bulging eyes. Face it for herself. Feel the hell of it. Hell was what it would be. Eternal torment. Not eternal in reality – but what was reality any more?

He had promised it would seem eternal and at that moment – which seemed to be the only moment in time she had ever occupied – *he* was all.

No one else existed for her; not even the fair, troubled one who averted his eyes not from horror but shame.

Only *he* existed.

And herself.

And the gross thing that once was her husband.

The half-skinned object that lay before her like some long unrecognizable animal carcass. Raw, red meat, nothing human about it at all.

Except below the waist.

The skin that had been him was peeled back, hanging from the waist like a slack shirt. *The* waist; not his waist. This thing, no longer her husband; no longer he – despite the heavy genitals she knew and which had pleasured her well. It. Warm meat. Only thus could she keep her teetering sanity which too much of her had already relinquished.

Rose was lost. Damned for ever. Watching, waiting for her own torment. Except she would be alive. *Alive!* Would see herself peeled like soft fruit, her juices draining away; not fast enough to kill, not quickly, not mercifully. Mercy was not a word to the damned – and *he* and she, both, were damned. He by love of death, so strong he had to prolong its coming like a lover holding back the moment, and she by her failure to rush into oblivion.

He had promised he could keep her conscious and Rose believed him. Believed everything he said. He was – now – her only belief and now was for ever. There was nothing more. Only absolute fear and expectation of agony and the glow in his eyes which told her he would enjoy her torment, live it with her, draw life from her like an expert yet eager lover, leaving her blood-naked, stripped to the flesh and screaming.

It had begun with love.

What, in comparison, was love.

His taking of her.

That way.

The way Murphy had attempted only once; she striking him harder than she had struck anyone – even the bastard Brit soldier who had strip-searched her in her teens at a checkpoint.

*He* had taken her. Painfully, brutally; easily. No protest, no fight offered – none possible with her hands bound tightly behind her, lying bent and exposed over the heavy garden chair which, upturned, in the chill basement seemed like some crude medieval torture apparatus.

That pain, now, was sweet. All pain was sweet against what was to come.

She had done whatever he wanted. Been whatever he wanted. She would do anything for him. If he would kill her. Kill her first.

She had told him everything he wanted to know. Shown him every secret place that Murphy had made or used. Given him all the pillow talk, every operation, every name she could remember hearng and some she could not remember but which terror threw up from her subconscious like small gifts of hope.

There was no hope. He had all of their secrets and all of her. It was not enough.

He wanted pleasure. He wanted pain. Her pain.

'Kill me,' she whimpered.

He looked up at her. Up, because now she was sitting, naked, bound with Murphy's belts to the righted garden chair: legs to legs, arms to arms as if for execution.

'There's time,' Rick said.

'Mercy. I beg you, mercy.'

'Mercy doesn't exist. It's a lie made up by dreamers.'

'You can make it real. You can do anything.'

'Yes.'

'Please!'

'No.'

*'Holy Mary, Mother of God, pray for—'*

He reached out and thrust fingers into her brutally. 'You can't pray when you're being defiled.'

'Kill me.'

'Eventually.'

She turned away, gasped. 'Stop him!'

Dave sat on the floor, knees pulled up to his chin, arms crossed over his lowered face, shutting out all of it. He might not have heard.

*'Stop him!'*

Rick smiled. 'It's not possible for Dave. Dave can only hide – sometimes he can watch.'

She was laughing now; reason slipping away, yet still she clung to the cold stone face of sanity. 'Why? What have we done to you?'

Rick laughed with her. The sound echoing wildly off the hard basement walls. He stood, moved away from her, stripped himself; his naked body perfect, lean frame loose limbed and flowing, musculature clearly defined. A dancer's body.

He turned, swiftly, stopped, looked at her over his shoulder.

She gagged.

The reverse of him was like his soul: ugly, raw, perfection destroyed. His flesh had been flayed to the bone; healed it was discoloured, puckered, ridged, more reptilian than human, with cruel diagonal stripes where white-hot metal had struck like whips.

She squeezed her eyes tight, dropped her chin, forcing it deep into her collar-bones. His strength was too much for her. He lifted her face, prised her eyes open with his thumbs, looked into them and let her see hell.

His hell.

THE OPERATION had to be carried out immediately.

Too little preparation, only the barest Intelligence, dangerous in the extreme.

Classic KGB thinking: find the politician brought across the border into the mountains by rebels eager to demonstrate their courage against the Soviet superpower, adding another voice to their plea for more funding from the mighty USA, kill him, fake evidence so that the assassination was seen as rebel inter-faction rivalry, an everyday bloody occurrence in that vicious war, forcing Washington to reassess its financial and logistical commitment.

The two *Spetsnaz* teams had no illusions as to the urgency of their task: Moscow was already stretched to breaking point in its commitment to the war and extra US funding could be critical.

They were the best; would do the job whatever the difficulties; but none had any doubt as to the mortal danger of entering rebel territory. The fierce, cruel enemy knew every crevice of the mountains since childhood: could operate there blindfold; hide where no apparent cover existed; slit throats as swiftly as the swoop of the hawk to the dove's jugular then vanish into rocks like wisps of smoke in the chill high-altitude winds.

Also, they could take a man on a journey of pain he would never return from. Not whole. Not the same. Changed for ever, bared to his soul, exposed for what he truly was – martyr, coward, beast – never hero for no glorious light could shine in that last dark room whose door opened only to death.

The first team were captured to a man by nightfall: CIA money once again proving treachery was the cheapest weapon to buy.

In the darkness the second team heard every dreadful scream as they climbed nearer, the pain theirs too for they were all comrades bound by secret candlelight barrack-room blood-rites.

Rick was Karelin then, the best of the best, and their leader. The failed principal dancer the KGB had made their own, recognizing the soft lying eyes of the silent killer set like dark jewels in all that grace of movement.

When finally Karelin's team reached the peak, they gazed down on hell. Or an entrance to hell. A deep, wide crevasse which split the mountain; invisible from the air because of rock overhang. Fire seemed everywhere, like a glowing carpet across the rock floor, smoke blurring its edges, spilling it from one blazing brazier to the next. Through icy gusts they could see their comrades, hanging heads down over the braziers, military crops now singed to black stubble against deeply scorched skin; eyes dried out, opaque and blind, torsos glistening wetly as men worked on them with short curved knives, like flenchers working on carcasses. Except these were still alive.

Karelin knew he should have waited, should not have allowed the agony of his comrades to affect his judgement, but something snapped, broke for ever inside him. He swept down the rocks, ran amok, machine-pistol blazing, killing whoever was in front of him until he reached the fires and killed his own.

They swarmed over him the instant his weapon jammed.

At first, when they pulled him into the firelight and saw him clearly, there was great argument which neither he nor the shaken politician understood though the second big quiet American, who spoke their language, knew their ways, knew what was likely to come.

He watched, still as a vulture, the chill wind flapping the tribesman's robes he wore as cover, standing beside a grey satellite dish, his weather-browned hand resting on it, like some twenty-first century warrior with his weapon: his electronic trident and shield which could direct attack or defence, linking him via the stars to the secret heart of the superpower far beyond the roof of the world and placing him, in rebels' eyes, somewhere close to God.

For once the handset hung impotently from the tripod. He knew no call bounced off heaven to Langley, Virginia, that night could halt what was to happen.

It was inevitable. They had seen Karelin's beauty. Could not resist it. His pale perfect skin; the dark, liquid, woman's eyes, the slender form. These were fighters without women. Also, until betrothal, women were forbidden, so their need was great. And that night their blood was hot.

The argument went back and forth for a while – which was their custom.

*He was theirs and should be used in any way they wanted. It was fitting and also served a purpose.*

*No! He must die horribly and it should begin instantly. The American politician would not be impressed with carnality, Americans had strong views on such matters.*

*Cha! Americans make whores of their women – we don't accept their judgement!*

In the end they did it anyway; the politician led aside, disgusted, appalled but heeding the measured warning in his ear by his big fair countryman: Do nothing, show nothing. This is a different culture where future considerations are easily lost to present, urgent passions.

In plainer, life-preserving terms: *Stand back and smile; you don't have to mean it.*

Karelin lost count of the number.

After the first it ceased to matter.

When it was over, the questions began from one of their number who had some Russian.

*Where were his comrades?*

*How many?*

*Where were his comrades?*

*Russians never came alone. Russians worked in groups, needed each other like girls clinging hand-to-hand for comfort.*

He had only one answer for them, throughout: He was alone.

*No! Not possible.*

*He was alone.*

Pain.

He was alone: alone with three comrades out in the darkness, face down on their bellies, evading the scouts who had been despatched to seek them out because that's what they were trained to do. Watching with indecision freezing them to the cold rocks, weighing the odds, knowing they too could end where he was so doing nothing, sitting it out, waiting to whisper in the Mil Mi-24 gunships at dawn's cold rise over the peaks. Or had they run down the mountain when they had seen his own mad run into the flames, abandoning him?

Whichever, he was truly alone.

Alone with his torturers, his violators, swarming over him and the tall, still American watching him fixedly, standing back from the fire-glow, fair hair and half his face concealed by the local head-dress but sky-blue eyes clear, detached, their message unequivocal: What is happening to you is not my concern. We may share this space, this time, but not this moment; that is yours alone.

Karelin was glad to be alone.

He was awakening.

Deep inside, so deep he never knew such a part existed in him, there was rising pleasure.

The knowledge was terrifying.

201

And thrilling.

A deep itch he wanted to tear at but could not reach.

Only by stripping away layers of himself would he ever get there, ever find relief.

So he said nothing.

Let them do all they felt they had to do.

Did all they made him do.

Even chewing the charred flesh they stuffed in his mouth, chewed it, swallowed it, ate it.

Ate his comrades.

At that moment it was right. Consummation. He was becoming them, as they were becoming him. Fighting to keep it down, gagging, swallowing deep to hold it all in. Hold them in. Their strength. He was Karelin but he was all of them too. He was powerful. He would survive and be extraordinary.

It was his destiny.

He knew.

He felt an awareness, an opening of himself that was unworldly, lifted his face to the stars, felt the rush inside, the explosion, the release from all bonds that might control him, the intensity overpowering. He knew nothing would ever be the same again. He would have to shape everything to his will to get even half the way there. And he could.

Alpha and Omega, the beginning and the end: he had passed the Omega point and was reborn.

So when comrades with their gunships came in the cruel red light of dawn and ripped the mountains apart with a million bullets – none touching him – he stood, bound to his torture frame, laughing amidst the carnage.

Even when the medics carried him away – on his belly because the back of him was lying shredded on the rocks – he laughed.

He laughed for a long while afterward, safely back in the motherland, in the hushed cool white room they provided, until he realized that they would never use him again until he stopped. So, instead, he laughed inside and smiled outside, a very small smile that he kept from his eyes because no one should see anything inside him. What was inside was for him alone. And naturally the others. The

202

others also inside him. Inside, was dangerous. Black. Black as burned hanging heads and impenetrable as opaque blind eyes.

It was then, when they were pleased to see his small smile and trust his cleared mind, that his incantation came to him. Secret, silent, never uttered:

*I am fear. Chaos and destruction are images of my creation and I of theirs.*
It was not long but he would add to it in time.

In time they made him Rick. All of him they could see and hear: dressed, tutored, praised, scolded, examined, honoured; the latter quietly because he was a great secret. Not, of course, as great a secret as the comrades inside him.

Then they showed him what they had accomplished with his old comrades from the mountains. The watchers. They had done well. Not as perfect as Rick. But good. He smiled in congratulation and the creators were pleased. They valued his judgement. They were insecure people whose time was running out.

Then they set him free with the others.

Almost free.

And they became nothing. Faceless. For too long. Time passing for Rick like the ticking of a great stone clock upon which each second was a mountain he had to climb. Only the occasional gifts of blood – and the power these released in him – kept him from being crushed by his existence.

Then, as he had known they would, his masters passed into history, poorly, like an unsound structure collapsing, chunks falling from it before the remaining mass slumped into rubble.

He smiled. Smiled too for his new masters – through the subhuman Krotkov who alone saw their faces, stated their will, passed their rewards and promised their protection. He tolerated Krotkov, tolerated his masters, old and new. He had to. He had to have the things they wanted him to do.

So Karelin slipped deep inside with the others and Rick was now.

And now was everything . . .

'KILL ME,' Rose Murphy whimpered.

'Enough,' Dave gasped, like a man run into the ground. 'Just finish it, Rick.'

She heard the spring of steel, felt his hand clamp her mouth and even as she bit into it, he smiled.

'For you, Dave.'

She felt the needle-prick at her navel.

She screamed. Mostly in her mind.

CARTER DROVE the old Jaguar MKII hard, the 3.8 engine responsive and sweet despite its age, kept in perfect tune by Aunt Doris's mechanic nephew.

He had been stopped once at a road-block, the RUC officers admiring the car.

'Nice. Yours?'

'Borrowed. Distant relative, here in Belfast. Really keeps it sweet. Maybe I'll buy it from him, take it back to the States.'

One had indicated the obviously new boots and stuffed backpack on the rear seat. 'Got yourself kitted for some serious walking, then?'

'Great country for it.'

Smiles. 'Get yourself up to the Causeway, nothing like it anywhere.'

'Count on it. You know the bridge at Carrick-a-Rede?'

Laughter. 'Bridge! A rope and a few planks inviting you to gamble on the strength of cross winds and the depth of the water over the rocks eighty feet below? You stick to the cliffs, sir, leave the bridge to the fishermen who know it. And don't miss out on Bushmills, best whiskey in the world right where they make it.'

They had not searched the car, not found one million dollars in crisp $US100 notes taken from a relieved Frankel's opened safe and now jammed tightly into the new backpack he had purchased with the boots earlier that day from a Belfast sporting shop.

The aroma of the Jaguar's leather and wood and its twin cams' distant growl soothed him, focused his mind, kept that part of him which needed to be sharp and quick sheathed, passive, deliberate.

The time would come when he would need speed, need instant reactions to counter the ripping blade he knew would be readied to gut the life from a child before his eyes.

*Tell Carter if he even looks at me aggressively tonight I will kill your children before his eyes. Beginning with the little girl. I shall split her like a peach: anus to navel. Primitive but satisfying and ecologically sound – giving her life's juices back to the earth. Then I'll kill him. He's dangerous. I'll do that quickly. Tell him.*

He had no doubt at all the mind was insane. Not the madness born of jumbled, uncontrolled thoughts that came out as deranged ranting. The kind of insanity that made absolute sense. Made threats thought out to the finest barbaric detail. Threats *meant*, not simply uttered.

He drove harder but remaining relaxed, his resolve clear, his purpose fixed, his judgement made.

You do not negotiate with such a mind. You obey or you destroy, no middle course, no enlightened, compassionate, liberal view. No compromise. You are not dealing with a human but an *evil* being from which human values have been stripped or in which these have never existed. Death was necessary.

He had already condemned the beast. If he could not out-think, out-match, out-fight him then his own death awaited instead.

The children's too.

*Don't do anything to him, Carter. Give him the money and bring me my children or he won't have to kill you. I will. I swear.*

'I believe you, Kate,' he murmured. But will *he* believe I'll obey?

He drove on, not thinking now.

He smelt the sea and lowered his window to draw it in. Darkness had crept over the land and only the sky, seaward, was bathed in light from the slipping sun. Time meant nothing. It felt like the last day.

He saw swinging torches and bright reflective clothing and slowed, the still smoking devastated inn silhouetted hard like a burned out vessel against the violet-bruised horizon.

'Where are you going, sir?'

'Finding a bed for the night. Your tourist shop gave me some addresses in Bushmills.'

205

'You'll need to go inland a bit, then.'

'I know. Wanted to take a few shots of the Giant's Causeway at sundown first.'

'Follow the coast to Causeway Head, you won't miss it.'

'And Carrick-a-Rede? The bridge there?'

'Further on. Park at the National Trust Information Point, then it's a three-quarters of a mile walk. Take care now on those cliffs. I'd leave the bridge until tomorrow – when the light goes you're best away.'

'I'll do that. What happened here? Fire?'

'This is Northern Ireland.'

Carter drew away.

Mentally, he checked through the arsenal of innocuous weaponry he had compiled before leaving Aunt Doris's spotless room: one bunch of keys, one cheap ball-point pen with the ink-fill removed and replaced by a similar length of stiff wire snapped from a hanger – for strength; a small aerosol of perfume taken from Kate's handbag. Little enough with which to defy a monster but all he would be allowed to keep when they gave him the hard search.

There would be more than one.

They would be well armed.

All he needed was one of their weapons to even the odds, and anything he could use to achieve this – more than just his bare hands, his speed, his wits, his training – was a bonus.

He thought he heard the throb of a helicopter, far above, ducked his head and peered up through the windscreen but saw no lights – though that meant nothing in Ulster.

They would be reacting to the bomb, of course. Or maybe he was imagining it. He had spent most of his life hearing, avoiding or being launched into one battle or another from helicopters; sometimes he dreamed about them, usually the falling type which shook him badly because too often this had almost been reality.

He remembered the fierce rifle-blow which turned his head to ice – and the deep throb above echoing, fading slowly in the cold aching after-blackness.

*They weren't IRA, McAlister.*

He was about to find out what – who – they were.

206

About to face *him*.

The Headhunter.

◀•●•▶

E LLIS SAID: 'Trouble.'

McAlister switched on the overhead interior light, slowed easily, rolling to a gentle stop, his warrant card already at the window for the probing torch to fall on it.

'Careless? Or the other thing?' he enquired, tilting his head at the burnt-out inn, turned into a film set by police floodlights.

'Big one, sir. Army bomb people reckon there'd been a major stash down in the cellars. Wouldn't have thought it of the old feller!'

'Then don't expect to draw your pension. Think it of *everyone*.'

The face below the tall RUC peaked hat fell gloomily. 'Yes, sir.'

'Anything left to go on?'

'They're doing their best. You know how it is, sir.'

'Don't we all.'

The RUC Constable ducked lower, nodding briefly at Ellis, taking in the hard, set face and the stocky body. He looked again at Ellis. 'You on business, sir?' His eyes flicked to the floodlights.

'Not this one. Four men, late thirties but fit – couple of them might look like squaddies. Army haircuts. The others – when last seen – were completely opposite: stubble beards, longish hair, leather jackets, jeans.'

'Sounds like a couple of Provos?'

'They might want you to think that.'

The Constable gave McAlister a look. The description given could equally have fitted an SAS – or other Army – undercover group. Special Branch officers in Ulster often hovered on the peripheries of some of the harder-edged operations, usually when they had informers to protect.

'Not seen any matching that description,' he said. 'Some unidentified remains in there though. I mean *remains* sir. Tweezers and plastic-bag job. Can't say how many. Army reckons there was probably Semtex in there as well as the usual fertilizer mix.'

'I'll have a word.' McAlister nodded and pushed the gear-lever forward. 'Oh, they might have just a touch of the foreign about them. We know one of them had a bit of an accent.'

'Had a Yank drive through not long ago. Now *he* looked fit. Sometimes you can really see the hard ones. It's in the eyes.' Involuntarily his eyes flicked to Ellis.

'Carter,' Ellis growled, leaned over: 'Drove a flash Merc, big one – the five hundred, silver grey?'

'Jag. Real old, sixties, but looked after. Dark green or maybe black. Dark green I'd say. British Racing, chrome wires.' The Constable's arm indicated as if he were directing traffic. 'Going to the Causeway. Photographs – sunset – usual thing.'

McAlister said, easily, 'Think hard. What else did he say? Everything you can remember.'

The Constable looked worried. 'Not much. Had addresses in Bushmills for over-nighting from the Tourist Board . . . wanted to photograph the Causeway and Carrick-a-Rede – the fisherman's bridge, you know? I warned him, those cliffs at dusk—'

McAlister gripped his arm. 'Alone? Was he alone?'

'Just him.'

'You're certain?'

'Front passenger side empty for sure. Rear had some climbing boots and a big fat haversack chucked in. Looked new. I thought, that lot's not going to do the leather any good.'

Ellis said: 'He's paying them off. Quid to a farthing. The boots are for the march they'll make him do to sweep his back. Classic.'

'Or for climbing up behind them,' said McAlister, thoughtfully. 'I can't see him complying meekly.'

'You still want to check those remains, sir?'

'I'll check the living first,' said McAlister and floored the throttle.

# CHAPTER TWELVE

K ATE BRANNIGAN had watched Carter drive away in the old Jaguar, his call to Frankel made, the pick-up arranged. She would not see Carter again until it was over – though she knew he'd be there watching with Frankel from a distance for the black cab to pick her up before driving hard for the money, then please God, her children.

She felt desperately alone. Terrified. She stood, unable for that moment to go on, the wild swings in her moods taking over again, pitching her now to the bottom of the pit.

Aunt Doris came up behind her. 'He'll be back. Love's a hurting thing. Come and have some tea.'

Kate smiled. 'It's not love.'

Aunt Doris's eyes twinkled. 'Next best thing, then. That's better, a nice smile.'

Kate followed, watching the ample hips shift under the flower-patterned dress, seemingly cut from the same cloth as the curtains in the bedroom. Kate would have given anything to be her now; able to walk, talk, think freely; no black cloud above, no pressure, no pain.

No fear.

She could not seem to hold fast to any memory that bore no fear. Peace seemed another lifetime before; might never have existed; might have been dreamed and all she had ever had was torture.

*Think of something good, something positive, something that'll keep you going.*

She thought of their Vermont home, the beauty of it, the elegance, the fun – all dissolving as Patrick's blue, lying eyes smiled at her and her children's laughter turned to screams.

*Carter, if you bring them back to me alive and whole you can have any part of me – all of me – for as long as you want.*

But Carter did not want her. Carter wanted revenge. Wanted his name back. And that was almost as terrifying as the smooth, cruel voice on the telephone promising to cut the life from her little girl.

She did not hear the telephone ring, just saw Aunt Doris holding the receiver, stretched too far on its coiled wire, in front of her.

'Wouldn't give her name, said you're expecting the call. You tell her *courtesy* costs nothing.' Aunt Doris turned and poured tea.

'We know where you are,' said the same school teacher dry as chalk and as brittle voice as before. 'You walk to the end of that road. The south end. That's *right*, when you get out of the gate, got that?'

'I'm not a complete idiot!' snapped Kate, angrily.

Aunt Doris smiled.

'Tell that woman there she's to let us take the car without trouble. Any problems from her and her Prod nephew gets a second navel.'

'I'm not telling her that!'

'Tell her what you like, then. You just leave the Mercedes' keys in the ignition and we'll sort it out.'

'If anyone is hurt you can forget any co-operation from me.'

A sharp, laugh. 'Go fuck yourself. Who do you think you are? You *want*, you'll do. No more talk. Do it.'

'You people really are ugly.'

The voice sneered. 'That's why when it's bad for you wonderful Yanks you have to come to us.' The line clicked and purred.

Aunt Doris turned. 'Sounds like you have some problems there, dear.'

Kate laid the Mercedes' keys on the table. 'Some people will come to collect these. I've no idea why they want the car. I can't say any more. They're not pleasant people. I want you to understand that. Please trust me. All I can tell you is that I'm trying to protect my children. I *have* to do what I'm doing. I just don't want anyone else hurt. It's bad enough already.'

Aunt Doris sat opposite, fat arms planted before her heavy

210

bosom on the scrubbed pine table, studied her, nodded. 'Your man was shot. The one bringing us jobs. Didn't recognize you till now. You've lost the glamour.' She paused, sighed. 'You don't *say* what you did on the TV, dear – not here in Belfast. That's what this is about, isn't it?'

Kate nodded. 'It's what started it.'

'What do you want me to do?'

'Whatever they tell you.'

'Or they'll hurt me?'

'Your nephew.'

'Ah! They would put it that way. They think like that. Bent. Twisted. You see what it's like to live here?'

Kate felt tears start, sucked in breath, reached out for Aunt Doris's cigarettes and took one.

Aunt Doris pushed her lighter across. 'You go ahead, dear. If it helps.'

She struck the lighter, saw the flame trembling. 'I'm frightened.'

'We're all frightened. It's part of our lives. Every day.'

She slapped the lighter down, crushed the cigarette, looked at the shreds in her palm. 'Someone's taken my children.' She broke, sobbed.

Aunt Doris came around to her, held her, soothed her hair. 'The Provos? They've got your little ones?'

'I don't know. It's too complex. I'm sorry, I shouldn't be telling you any of this – it puts you in danger. Just do whatever they ask. Let them take the car. What's a *car* matter, goddamnit!'

'But you're going to them? *You* matter.'

'I have to. It's part of it.'

'And afterward?'

'Afterward I come back here and I wait for Carter to return. Please God, with my children.' She pulled herself together, found tissues in her handbag, dried her eyes.

'I'll wait up for you.'

Kate smiled. 'You're very kind. There's no need.'

'There's every need.'

Kate stood. 'They'll be here soon. They're picking me up at the end of the street. I'll get ready.'

211

Aunt Doris looked up at her. 'Don't fret, I'll do my piece, won't cause any problem. You get along now. It'll all work out.'

S HE OPENED the front door, stepped on to Aunt Doris's neat path and immediately saw the Jaguar further down the street, saw Carter's head dip with a small nod and felt overwhelming relief. She had insisted Carter leave his gun. Had hidden it from him while he slept, refusing adamantly to hand it back, he finally having no choice but accepting her decision.

*The money is the only weapon you'll need, Marcus. Use it, bring them back, bring them back safe.*

Now, despite Carter's small gesture of assurance that all was well, part of her felt as if she had condemned him to death, stripping him of his means of protection, but what choice had she? With the gun he would be tempted to use his expertise, to give rein to the deep anger she felt simmering inside him as he had lain beside her. Anger that had stopped him taking her – instinct telling her, and lifting her, blunting the feeling of rejection.

She walked to the gate.

*Damn.* You're just seeking reassurance. Do what you have to do! You don't need a crutch to lean on. You don't *have* a crutch to lean on. There's you and only you and you'd better walk out there and face them.

*You've got the money now, you don't have to go,* a small, pleading voice urged; even protested.

Don't and they'll kill you. Not the IRA. Your own beloved countrymen. Protectors of all you hold dear, or fear; from Mom's Apple Pie to Atomic Demolition Munitions.

And my children will be orphans with only a failed bodyguard between them and any extended wrath the great bald eagle might decide to vent on them.

She walked, south as directed, away from the safety of the Jaguar and the man inside sworn to protect her, prepared to fight another wearing battle in her personal war, against all odds, all enemies, all flags, even her own.

She knew that when it was over, if she lived through this, whatever the outcome she would carry her fight to its conclusion. Not on the bomb-blasted streets of Belfast but through the sprawling wire-bound secrecy of Langley and along the wide avenues of Washington. She would use her attorney's mind and training; her own awakened drive; her experience – *this* experience – to ensure that expediency, even dire expediency, should never drive against their will nor crush the people its design was meant to protect.

She heard the muted growl of the Jaguar creep closer, heart banging she studiously ignored it. Lit a cigarette from the pack Aunt Doris had given her, drew smoke deep, closed her eyes and looked at the dirt-grey sky. She crushed the cigarette under her toe.

Her pick-up was late so she had time to see three men climb from a grubby car, walk swiftly up Aunt Doris's neat path, lean on the door bell until the gloss-painted door was opened, push past her, the last through grabbing her fat arm, dragging her along the linoed hallway.

*Don't hurt her,* she whispered.

She saw no more because the cab arrived, black as a hearse but filthy, little shine on the bodywork, vibrating, throbbing, the woman inside opening the door and pulling her in fast.

'Drive,' the woman barked and leaned back into the seat. 'You look terrible,' she observed. 'TV made you into a film star. That what losing a man does to you? You can keep them.'

Kate saw herself in the glass partition. She's right. Aunt Doris was right. I look seventy. And dying. Which most of me is. And will continue to until I get my babies back. So *fuck* you! She glared at the woman.

'That upset you, didn't it? There's some comfort in being ugly you see, Mrs bloody Brannigan, no one ever notices when you look bad.'

Kate could see the plain face in the glass: bitter, pinched lips, eyes sunken, staring, angry, a large mole disfiguring her forehead so that one eyebrow appeared permanently raised insolently.

'Shut up,' Kate told her. 'Just take me to whoever makes your decisions for you.'

'There'll come a time when all your money will get you is a bullet in the back of the neck. It won't be long coming.'

213

*What money?* Kate almost blurted. *It's all gone. Never was.* But kept it in, kept looking away.

The woman snatched at her hair, drew her head down hard. 'Your money killed some of our boys. One was my baby brother. Who'd you pay, bitch? Some wild SAS pigs out for a little bit on the side? What did you ask for? *What?*'

The driver pushed back his glass. 'Leave her *be*, Moira.'

'What, bitch? *Heads!* That's what! *And they fuckin' took them!*'

'That's enough!'

'*It's fuckin' not enough!*'

The cab swerved as the driver fought to watch both road and the conflict behind him. 'You let her go or I swear to God I'll stop the cab and give you a fist you won't forget.'

The woman pushed Kate to the floor of the cab then spat on her.

'Fuck!' the driver swore and slammed the partition closed.

Kate looked up at her. 'I'm sorry your brother was killed. If he was innocent of the murder I'm sorry, all right!'

'He was *innocent*, all right. Your man didn't get it from *us*, bitch. The Brits put him down because they know he'd talked to us. You want to meet ugly people you talk to Brit fucking Intelligence. Green Slime, the squaddies call them, and that's what they are – except they're *yellow*, not the glorious colour of Ireland. Yellow coward bastards who hack off kids' heads when they're sleeping. Nineteen – and such a committed bloody Catholic he hadn't had himself a woman. Can you believe that? Jesus!'

'He was one of you – that doesn't make him an innocent.'

'What do you know about any of this? You should just keep your opinion to yourself. You've no idea what any of it means. Blood, that's what it means, decades of it. You don't give up when blood is spilt, you fight, we fight. We'll fight till every last Brit is gone – or dead.'

The cab halted, vibrating madly now, the interior lit balefully by ghastly white halogen light from the building outside. A fine drizzle hung, swirling in the air like a million minuscule insects, framed by the juddering windows. Kate looked up from the floor seeing the murk of the sky and the *flick-flick, flick-flick*, of an aircraft's lights. She wanted to be inside it, softly cocooned, belted in tight, secure – then remembered the last time she had been and felt as if a fierce blow had struck her middle.

*I don't believe this is happening. Please let me wake up in Vermont with the mountains outside and love inside and all of us alive and safe.*

'You're here, bitch,' said the woman and kicked her hard with her thick-soled boot.

Kate pulled herself up, anger burning cold now. 'You'll never win,' she said. 'Because you haven't the courage or the brains to admit you're beaten. Do that and they'll give you *everything*. All of it. The whole damn God-forsaken country! Then they'll march away, pipes swirling, flags flying. The British always do. Don't you read *history*, you stupid woman?'

She stepped from the cab.

The street was bleak, a rough wall running along one end, breeze-blocks hurriedly thrown up, ill matched, temporary but permanent. An enforced divide to keep warring tribes apart. Razor wire curled wherever there was a surface someone might mount or climb: houses, garages, everywhere. She might have been in Berlin before the Wall fell. On the wrong side.

She stood before a solid impregnable-looking door set into a concrete stipple-fronted building built like a bunker, windows barred and grilled, no view whatsoever to the inside because the wire-reinforced glass had been painted black. It bore an air of violence. Blind violence.

There was a sign on one corner, partly broken. *Green* something. It has to be Green, she thought. If this were the other side it would read the *Orange* something. The crushing banality of it all was mind numbing.

She wanted to be away. Away from this dreadful place.

*If I ever come out I'll see the world through different eyes.*

The driver came around and stood beside her. He turned briefly to the cab. 'Sorry about her, she's hurting.'

'We're all hurting.'

'That's a fact,' he agreed, knocking in sharp rhythms, then pressing a button, then saying quickly: 'OK, it's Sean, she's here, open up, it's fuckin' pissing down out here.'

'Is this where you brought my husband?' she asked.

He nodded.

'Where are we?'

'Doesn't matter.'

'I want to know. I want to know where his last hours were spent, damn you!'

He glared sideways at her, his face shining with wet, big droplets already formed on his thick brows. He shook them free. 'Wasn't here. He didn't get it *here*, OK? And it *wasn't* us!'

'But he came here. You drove him.'

'All right! It's just a place. Part of Belfast. Turf Lodge, if it really matters that much to you. What do *you* know about this city? Jesus!'

'Enough to want to leave it.'

'Tell your Brit friends that, maybe they'll catch on and join you!'

'I don't have any *Brit* friends – the one I might have had you just killed. Alan Reardon.'

'Aye, well, he was a legitimate target. Government minister, you know.'

'He was an *economist*!'

'Same thing.'

The doors opened with a bang, a heavy bar inside dropping with a gallows sound.

Inside a fat man sprawled on a wooden captain's chair, a revolver pushing back the folds of his belly, spilling it out either side like squeezed, parted dough. He tilted his head backward. 'He's here.'

Kate noted the change in the driver; felt his apprehension.

'They're all here, then?'

'Fuckin' matter about the others, does it?' smirked the fat man and shifted his pistol, dislodging his belly. 'Best get in there with her.'

The driver nodded and eased her forward through a second heavy door where, puzzlingly, she saw beer crates filled with concrete stacked against one wall.

Here a second gunman waited, this one standing, the weapon he carried squat, angular, fully automatic, altogether more serious. Kate had seen one in the movies spraying lethal bursts of fire, turning a set to matchwood in seconds. In reality, before her in the man's hands, it looked absurdly small and toy-like, the metal scratched – not pristine, gleaming, oiled, as on the screen. It seemed more dangerous this way.

*Well used. It's killed people. It could kill me.*

'Along there,' the gunman said, the snout of the weapon giving the direction along a plain corridor further away.

She had expected trappings: banners, icons, the panoply of revolution. All there was was a grubby bar, men drinking, very quiet, no music. An air of expectation. Expectation of violence.

She noted more of the concrete-filled beer crates she had seen in the entrance – these stacked high blocking the emergency fire doors. It's a fortress, she thought. No one gets in. No one gets out. Alive.

'Faster,' snapped the gunman.

And the corridor before her. Like walking to the gallows, she thought, remembering the sound the door has made.

Then it happened.

For the first time since it had begun, a strange peace fell over her, like a soft light cloak. She did not fear dying. She felt at ease; strangely calm. She was where she was and nothing she could do could aid or save her. Everything was preordained. She would live or she would die and nothing would make any difference. She knew instinctively it was her mind coming to terms with death and wondered if everyone – at the stage where it was suddenly, imminently, possible, even probable – felt this same calm. It was as if a storm had suddenly subsided and she floated on her back on soft warm supportive water with a gentle breeze playing over her limbs, her face, her hair. She smiled. Almost happy. Her children would be safe. Marcus Carter was a good man; a strong man. He would never abandon them.

'Who do I have to talk with?' she asked.

'No names,' said the gunman and pushed her lightly ahead to yet another door. He knocked, opened the door, pushed her again, said: 'Go on,' and withdrew closing the door behind her.

She heard bolts and the locks go. *One, two, three, four.* Then silence. There had been none visible on the door. He's a magician, she thought. Or someone in here is.

217

The room was absolutely dead, no reverberation whatsoever. Flat. No one greeted her. They all sat. Smoked. Ashtrays overflowed. Cigarette smoke waited in layers for extraction near the ceiling.

One man headed the table and, unspokenly, the meeting: tall, fair but greying hair, tight curls, his face vaguely familiar. His pale eyes seemed dead, like a fish on the slab: she guessed he had killed too many people. *Nothing can shock you. You've gone beyond it, lost how to feel.* She felt pity for him, as she might for a brutalized child, but sensed he would kill her out of hand if it suited their purpose so crushed that emotion instantly.

Survive, she told herself. You're supping with wolves: show them your lamb's coat and they'll devour you.

Their leader said: 'Sit down, Mrs Brannigan, we've some travel arrangements to make.'

She took the vacant chair. 'Travel arrangements? I don't understand.'

'There's been a change in plan. Your husband's murder – not our doing by the way – has made things very difficult for us. Movement is restricted. The Brits have clamped down hard. And right now we need to be . . . *fluid.* Is that the right word? You're an American, one they would like to keep sweet, so it will be easy for you. We need you to make a delivery for us. We have your very nice Mercedes in one of our workshops right now having a few structural changes made to the petrol tank. The one we'll put in won't get you the length of the street outside. That's an exaggeration of course, it'll get you to the docks – but don't worry about that because there's little or no driving to be done once you're off the ferry at Liverpool. A few yards to a crane, that's it. Then it's up and over and you're away. You'll enjoy the sea air.'

She started, bewildered: 'I understood the arrangements my husband made were—'

'*Changed*, Mrs Brannigan, like I said. You want what we have very badly. You may think we're stupid but we're not. Your people have been listening to too many jokes about the Irish when they should have been listening to the sound of our bombs.'

She kept her face calm, though she worried about her eyes. 'My people?'

His dead eyes almost smiled. 'Look, the Brits infiltrate us and we infiltrate them, it's how the game is played over here. Amazing how a little Irish blood rears up and destroys established loyalties! Still, they always say blood will out, don't they? And if the blood's too thin, or not there at all, we can always rely on ideology. I mean with the East finding democracy there's few options left for the committed, is there? We're happy to give them a place in our hearts.' He showed teeth with expensive American-looking bridgework.

'Just tell her what she's got to do and let's get out of here,' growled the spectacled one on his right who might have been an accountant.

He sighed. 'This is an intelligent woman here. She needs to *understand*. Otherwise her mind will be cluttered with questions and we won't get the performance we need from her.'

Kate watched him, terrified, feeling everything slipping from her, all the things she had planned to say, all of Armitage's briefing, the whole charade dissolving; nothing to replace it with except Carter's warning: *Once in everybody's lifetime you have to walk a razor's edge for the ones you love.*

She breathed deeply. 'So you know my husband and I have some backing in our business dealings. All right, *government* backing. I admit that. Not so unusual these days. You don't need informants! You could have got your information from *Time* or *Newsweek*. Government-backed arms deals are old news. I don't see how any of this changes our agreement?'

'Mrs Brannigan, we *know* you're no wheeler-dealer with an under-the-counter line in high-tech weaponry. I'm not saying you *can't* arrange the deal, I'm not saying the deal's off, I'm just making it clear we know we're not dealing with you personally. *You*, independent of the trappings of your great but tearing itself apart nation. Indeed we now know we were never dealing one to one with your husband from the start. There was him, and behind him a cart-load – maybe I should say limo-load – of government employees of the type you don't see listed in your public phone book – all feeling, how do you say it over there . . . *stressed out?* Panicked is more like it. Wasn't hard to work out why once we knew what information you were after.' He leaned forward, impatient now. 'We need this extra service done. It's simply been added to our price. Not asking you, you understand. Stating.'

'The agreed price was Stinger missiles.'

'Still is. Call this a surcharge. Call it whatever you want.'

'I'll have to consult on this.'

The spectacled one said: 'No. We have dealt with your husband as the principal throughout. You have presented yourself in his – absence – as being in the same position. No consultation.'

*Now*, she told herself. Your security, your children's future hangs on this. *Ask now*. She said it woodenly, though she had practised it a thousand times in her mind. 'You have the information we require? The terrorist group in the United States who've been supplied with these weapons?'

'We even know the dates they intend to use them, Mrs Brannigan. But you'll not get a word until after you've driven your lovely German motor-car where we want it. The captain of the ship will have it in his safe. It will be there, we keep our word.'

She froze, realization of the truth halting even her breathing. There was ice in her stomach. She gasped. 'I can't.'

The man smiled. 'I knew you were a perceptive woman. You will.'

'No. I won't go. You can't force me.'

'Mrs Brannigan, there's a man outside that door whose one task – and pleasure – in life is playing executioner. You complete the bargain or we'll take payment in blood. It's not the way we want it but it is a way we've done business before and it works, I assure you. You understand me? It's your choice.'

'There is no choice.'

'You're very wise to see that.'

She stared at the faces. Whispered: 'Oh, God.'

'God is dead, Mrs Brannigan. *Causes* have taken His place. And all the causes in the world put together don't kill as many in a decade as He does in one year. We're just trying to catch up on the Old Feller a bit.'

Someone laughed, the rest followed.

She stared at the impassive, surprisingly ordinary faces. 'How can you even contemplate this?'

'We're not interested in giving reasons, only in achieving results,' answered the one in spectacles. 'We'll be watching you every step of the way, Mrs Brannigan. Close enough to hear, to see, close enough to kill. If you make any attempt to communicate with crew or security people before or after you board the ferry we'll kill you and everyone within shooting distance. It will be a bloodbath, I assure you. Remember that. So you'd better decide which you want to save – London or New York.'

The one who had laughed snapped: 'She'll not be saving *either* if she doesn't go along. She'll not be saving herself. Or her children – if we wanted to make a clean sweep of it.'

She felt her anger and her terror rise. 'What do you know about my children?'

Their leader smiled, confident. 'We don't know where you've hidden them, Mrs Brannigan, but there's nowhere in Ireland, North or South, you can hide them from us for long. But that presupposes you'll be alive to find out how long? Which you won't unless you co-operate completely.'

*They know nothing*, she thought wildly, glad it wasn't them. Then, horrifyingly: My God, there are people out there worse than *this*!

# CHAPTER THIRTEEN

D<small>AVE HAD</small> protested that another fire would draw attention at a time when, critically, they needed to be in the shadows.

'Fire cleanses,' Rick had stated. Nothing would shake Rick once he was set on something.

Rick meant to destroy everything in Murphy's house. Complete destruction would include everything pertaining to the IRA, and specifically, to an imminent operation so secret they had no name for it. Evidence of its existence was in Rick's possession. Travel documents and schedule – every step of the way, every meeting, every contact, every pick-up – for a certain Frankfurt-based Czechoslovak called Miloslav Kopecky, codenamed Housefly. Rick had spent childhood summers in Prague with his beautiful mother, he spoke Czech as well as he did Russian, both now sleeping languages inside him but which could at a moment's notice be awakened and used.

Rick had decided that Kopecky should forfeit his place in history.

To him.

All he had to do was make adjustments to the travel documents with the surprisingly sophisticated equipment in Murphy's secret room.

There was no new identity for Dave. Dave was slipping away, fading, like an old photograph: now dulling, now sepia, now pale, soon gone.

He smiled as they drove from Murphy's house – this time with no immediate explosion behind because Dave had discovered timed detonators in the secret room with a small quantity of Semtex – smiled, because anyone who would accept a codename like Housefly deserved everything he got.

Rick had also decided that America deserved all the suffering that could be heaped upon it. Any additional weight he might personally add was a pleasure. This was not a new decision but the thrill it brought now – the thought of *action* – gave it all the freshness of new birth.

'Will he bring the money, Rick? The Yank?'

'Dave, you've never understood the weight women put on to a man. She's weighed him down with guilt, conscience, responsibility, and probably because she's bereaved he's gained nothing for himself. Taken nothing which is his due. Women are at their best when they're vulnerable. They'll do anything. Take any treatment, because they were born to suffer. They accept the role.' He held the back of Dave's neck, not gripped, nor a caress. 'Women have a grave responsibility for the chaos in this world. They should be used and discarded. Remember I said that. It's worth noting and keeping inside you. You can gain from that.'

Dave grinned, warily 'I don't understand all that deep shit, Rick. I just fuck them.'

'So do I, Dave. I just don't see heaven flowing around them afterwards nor feel they will be eternally in my soul. I wish them hell. And sometimes I'm allowed to send them there.'

Dave turned, too quickly. 'Allowed?'

Rick stared ahead. 'Don't try and hear too well, Dave. Don't try to know too much. Sometimes to know is to die.'

'I don't understand, Rick?'

'Innocents never do. *The innocent and the beautiful have no enemy but time.* Someone wrote that. Could have been just for us.'

'We've got enemies, Rick.'

'*Mortal* enemies, Dave. You didn't hear what I said.'

'I'm sorry. You know I don't see things the way you do.'

'It doesn't matter.'

Behind, strapped on the rear seat in Murphy's Range Rover, one of the children suddenly wailed. Rick turned, stroked the small drugged face. 'Not long now,' he murmured.

'Don't give them any more, Rick. It's dangerous.'

'They don't need any more. Either Carter is there with the money in which case we don't need them any more, or he isn't; in which case we need them even less.'

223

'What will you do with them?'

'Feed them to the sea. Ecologically sound. I promised their mother.'

'You don't have to kill them, Rick. You could just leave them.'

'I don't have to breathe but if I don't I'll die.'

It was dark now and Dave was scared. More than ever before. Worse than the night of hell on the mountain. He drove on in silence, Rick poised, black and still beside him in the red-gold glow of sunset like the Devil Incarnate. There was no escaping him; he owed him, needed him, loved him, would do anything for him; had done, too many times. He felt, inside, his debt finally was close to being paid. When it was, Rick would kill him. Rick set nothing free. Rick let nothing live that once belonged to him.

'There,' said Rick. 'Carter will be there. The headland at the farthest end of the bay – past the chalk quarry.'

He took the silenced Browning from the battered leather grip at his feet, checked magazine and mechanism with his hands only, eyes still forward to the horizon, then laid the long weapon across his thighs. The stiletto clicked once, the silver blade flashing gold in the strange light, then withdrawn. He slipped it beneath the thick leather strap at his wrist.

'No enemy but time, Dave. Think about it.'

'I'll try, Rick.'

'You always try, Dave.' Rick smiled, lifted his foot on to the Range Rover's dash, took off his shoe and massaged his calloused toes, grimacing. Shoes were torture for a dancer.

THE SUN gulped one last breath of day and was gone. Burnished gold water and burnt-brown tilted basalt stacks along the fault line out toward the distant bay became suddenly dull pewter and black as a pale moon hung weakly in the new night, lighting a scene as old as its own existence.

The wind was getting up in gusts, bringing rain; fine needles of it piercing the air, hitting the old Jaguar in quick ripping sheets as Carter drove into the deserted car park.

He parked away from the cliffs, backed up against the weather, swung his legs out, quickly tied on the new boots, zipped on a weatherproof jacket, distributing his small collection of improvised weapons into various pockets, hefted the backpack out of the car, locked up, strapped it around on to his shoulders and started briskly but cautiously along the cliff path.

They'll be there already, he thought, breathing lightly under the hood of his jacket. Though they may not appear to be. They know about cover, know about ambush, know about surprise. They had taken him once. Not again.

He had to get close. That was the key. Closest would be the hand-over. There would be one moment when it just might be possible. Only one or none at all, because they were good.

There *would* be one.

Nobody's perfect.

He had to see it, take it, use it.

*Kill.*

The moon was stronger now, its dull light good enough for him to see some distance ahead despite the gusts of rain. Which, he knew, worked both ways.

*They had the night-sights on the SA-80 assault rifles.* One of which was responsible for the stitches in his scalp.

He felt suddenly exposed but pushed that aside. He had the best hand for the present – while he had the money. The bad time was when he threw it down and picked up the lousy hand: three children who maybe had seen too much or, simply, were expendable.

He jogged now, his night vision growing, going through the logistics of it: three children, frightened, struggling or completely cowed and quietly weeping, either way a distraction for the kidnappers. If the numbers played as he thought they did, there were four. Two who had stopped him on the airport road, two who made the hit on Brannigan. Neither of the two who played soldiers was the *crazy*. A hunch only, but strong. The *crazy* would have wanted to be there at the kill. Wanted to be the shooter. It was in his voice. The *crazy* would not have measured the rifle-butt blow; he'd have followed through – past bone. Now, he'll make himself known; won't hide, his ego will want to do the talking. He'll front it. He might even get close.

He'll kill first so he dies first.

Breathing a little stronger now, not just from the exertion or the weight of the backpack. Easy. Roll it back a bit. Don't let *him* see. He'll be watching for it. He's laid out the warning already.

*Tell Carter, if he even looks at me aggressively tonight . . .*

He.

*The Headhunter.*

It was time.

'LISTEN,' ELLIS said, suddenly, breaking the long silence. 'He's not right. No one would be after that.'

'Karelin?'

'I had a mate once. Had a bad time – *bad*. Not here, Middle East. Quacks put him together again after. Tried anyway. Seemed to do the trick – all that listening and the drugs. You know.'

'I know.'

'Couldn't have him back in the regiment because of the risk – well, stands to reason, doesn't it – but he got himself together, decent job, married, couple of kids, *settled*. Went to see him a few times. He looked straight.'

'But he wasn't.'

'He bloody killed the lot. *And* his mam who happened to be around for lunch. Sunday it was. All back after chapel. I saw the photographs after. Evidence. Bloody abattoir. Gone at 'em with the carver. And he knew *how*.'

'And afterwards?'

'Wasn't any afterwards. Fell on it himself. Like some bloody Roman – except there was nothing honourable about it. Just a mess. The quack hauled me in – well, natural that, me being the last of our bunch to see him like – told me it had always been possible. I said you should have told him that and he could have told the sodding family. Maybe he wouldn't want a family – I wouldn't! Didn't seem to hear. Went on with the big *why*: he couldn't distinguish between those who hurt him and those who loved him. Blurred. Couldn't see straight. They'd closed in on him. He didn't see the faces, just felt the . . . what's the word?'

'Oppression?'

'*Oppression*. So he dealt with it.'

McAlister nodded. 'So what are you trying to tell me?'

'Maybe we're walking into something here that's not *straight*.'

McAlister glanced quickly at him. 'My God, *I* know it's not straight! I saw inside that box, remember? Sleeping boys, dreaming probably, cut off – literally – from all they had going for them, however little, however good or bad that might have been. It was the callousness of it. The utter brutality. I sensed then that the perpetrator was himself brutalized. I just didn't know how much. I *know*, Ellis.'

'Look, if it comes to it I'm going to put him down, all right! You have to understand that.'

'Who's talking here? You or Hereford?'

'I'm fucking talking. There's two of us and four of them . . . no disrespect meant, Mr McAlister, but you're not in the same league.'

McAlister glanced at him. 'It wasn't meant to be this way – you know that! I was following a lead. Things have moved too fast. If I'd called in the whole shooting match back there when we heard about Carter being here too that's *exactly* what we'd have had. You know who they'd have called out if I told them the background of what we're dealing with – and I'd have to, make no mistake. Bloody Hereford. Can you see four backs-to-wall bloody forgotten exiled *Spetsnaz* handing over their weapons to a fully kitted bunch of your heroes? They'd go down guns blazing and to hell with any kids caught in the crossfire. Anyhow, it's academic, there's no time to call in the cavalry. We're here and we're it. At least Carter will come in useful if it turns sour.'

Ellis stared at him bleakly.

McAlister sighed. 'Look, I need to talk to them – to let them know there *is* an alternative to their present existence. Ellis, they've nowhere to run. Haven't had for a very long time. Maybe we can even get them home – if that's what they want?'

Ellis shook his head. 'The other three maybe – just maybe – you can talk them down, negotiate, offer them bloody Christmas every day of the year if you want, but him – Kara-what?'

227

'Karelin.'

'Beyond the bloody pale. You tell him: *All is forgiven, come on in, we're the best thing that ever happened to you*, he'll maybe nod, smile, give you the big Russian kiss on both cheeks like they do, and he'll be feeling for where to slip the blade while he's doing it.'

'That's why you're here, Ellis. To watch my back.'

'Yeah, and who's watching mine?' Ellis growled.

McAlister ordered, firmly: 'If it comes down to it we don't do a damn thing. The safety of the Brannigan children is paramount. I don't want to take corpses back to their mother – wherever she may be! Carter's safety is vital too. We don't want another American killed within these shores.'

A vast area of limestone slipped past, gleaming white in the moonlight.

'Quarry. Larrybane Bay. Almost there,' said McAlister.

Ellis nodded, turned and pulled his Heckler and Koch machine-pistol from out of his canvas bag. Checked it, held it across his chest, relaxed but very still.

McAlister's voice was stern. 'Use it only to save life. You hear me.'

'I know what I have to do, Mr McAlister.'

'Good.'

Ellis turned as if to look out toward the coastline and the sea but his eyes were fixed, hopefully, on the sky.

THE BRIDGE was constructed of rope and wood, a narrow section for walking – only single file possible – no solid sides, only simple rope rails. It looked and was temporary, being set up for only part of the year by the salmon fishermen. Caution and strong nerve were needed to traverse it in broad daylight. To cross at night with a baleful moon as the only natural light could be suicidal.

Carter saw it: stopped, breathed deep and long. He could hear the sea churning in the chasm beneath. He didn't know the state of the tide but from the sound of water on rocks it didn't sound up. A fall could lead straight on to the rocks eighty feet below.

Carter would happily parachute from miles up but high flimsy structures attached precariously to the ground were places he avoided.

If he had to lay everything he owned on which side of the bridge they would want him for the hand-over he would bet the middle – because life always played hardball.

He remembered the guide book he had picked up, reading: 'Standing by the swaying rope bridge, trying to muster courage to cross, is perhaps not the appropriate time to be told you are at the lip of a volcano. But fear not, this is long extinct.' *It's still goddamn high.*

He peered through the murk seeking the small island used by the local salmon fishermen but the swinging bridge seemed to fade into gloom, the promised island no more than a promise.

A light glowed green from the other side.

*Night-sight.*

He breathed in deeply once more.

Hardball.

A voice called something, then a child squealed, both sounds ripped away in a sudden gust. He tore off his hood, the rain flailed one side of his face, stinging his straining ear.

'*Carter!*'

He had a small torch. He turned it on, aimed it at the opposite side.

Something whipped close to him, hard, fast, whining off the grey volcanic rock.

He dropped, tried to gauge the calibre of the round. Not high velocity. So not the assault rifle. Heavy but not a magnum load. Nine millimetre, maybe even a forty-five, heavily silenced. Aimed to miss, but be heeded. He had the message, his torch already, immediately, switched off.

'*Come to the centre of the bridge, Carter!*'

'*I want to see the children before I move one goddamn inch!*'

A glow grew in the darkness bathing three small huddled figures in ghostly light. They lay on a rock edge, each with a broad leather belt around their necks, the ends looped through the buckles then gathered and gripped by a pale disembodied hand. Behind them one black-clad leg seemed poised ready to sweep them into the chasm. In the light-spill he saw the oily gleam of a long-barrelled weapon. A handgun, held relaxed, hanging at arm's length.

'*You've seen them. Follow the command!*'

Command. Yes, thought Carter. You.

'*That thing is dangerous, you might lose the money if I fall!*' he called.

'*You fall, they fall. Don't fall.*'

'*Don't you care about the money?*'

The belts tightened around the small necks, the heads jerked, floppily, like marionettes.

'*What's wrong with them, you son-of-a-bitch!*'

The bullet whipped through the dropped hood of his weather-proof. He felt the heat of it on his cheek. Knew he was dealing with more than a mere marksman. He was facing a genius with a firearm. One of the rare ones who could point a weapon and hit precisely where he sighted and do it every time. He knew only one in a thousand could shoot like that. In this light, this visibility, these gusts – with a handgun, he thought – maybe one in ten thousand.

He heard his own firearms instructor say: *There's some guys can think a bullet home: you're gone before they've even drawn their weapon. Don't argue; run, pray they've hit an off-day.*

He called: '*I'm coming!*'

The laughter was chilling. Empty.

*The Headhunter.*

THE WHINE of the bullet, distorted by the gusts and the rock formations, might have been a bird's cry.

For Ellis it was a familiar, unmistakable signature. He ducked fractionally, instinctively, grasping McAlister and hauling him down to the ground. 'Stay there,' he commanded and darted forward to the rise, mounted the rocks and peered below to the bridge. He turned, waved McAlister forward. 'There,' he whispered, grasping McAlister close, his mouth almost to his ear. 'Look, the glow, night-sight.'

'I need to get down there to talk to them.'

Ellis gripped him hard. 'We move down there, it's a duck-shoot and we're the ducks. Wait for Carter to show. They're not firing at us. If it's a hand-over they'll get him out in the open. Have him on that bridge – guaranteed – vulnerable as shit, couldn't do a thing.'

A voice yelled. '*Carter!*'

'Bingo,' breathed Ellis.

'Listen!' snapped McAlister straining for the words echoing across the chasm.

Finally he saw the bulky outline of a figure mount then start across the swaying bridge; clouds shifted from the moon leaving the figure exposed suddenly seeming very bright.

'Carter,' McAlister murmured.

'They'll kill him,' said Ellis, flatly.

'Why?'

'Because he's come after them.'

'He's come with the money. Look at the haversack. She raised the money. That's why she dropped out of sight.'

Ellis shook his head. 'That's part of it. Given half a chance, he'll go for them. I would in his shoes. It's important. He needs it evened up.'

'He won't risk the children's lives.'

'Maybe not. But once he's got them, he'll go for it.'

'I'll stop this.'

'You call out they'll kill him straight away – and the kids – reaction, OK? Wait. Let them do the business, let's get the kids over this side.'

'*Far enough!*' a voice called.

A dark figure wearing a fisherman's waterproof cape broke from shadow on the opposite side and walked toward Carter on the bridge, stopping six feet from him at the centre.

'What's happening?' hissed McAlister.

Ellis was silent, eyes wide, watching, allowing his instinct to take over, to feel what passed between the two. He whispered. 'He's sodding *daring* Carter. That's *him*. Only a nutter would take the chance.'

The fisherman's cape lifted, the moon caught gold and the quick slicing flash of silver.

'Oh, dear God!' blurted McAlister.

CARTER HAD moved cautiously on to the swaying bridge, placing his feet one before the other, barely lifting them off the planking, aware that either side on the narrow centre strip were only spaced struts and nothing else. Suspended there, in the clouded moonlight above the chasm, he felt as if he were trapped in the cold heart of a nightmare with no waking to come. He reached the centre, the clouds shifting, moonlight stronger, the opposite side clear now, the shadows becoming a bulky shape who stepped on to the bridge, moving toward him as confident and poised as a high-wire walker.

Cold terror froze Carter as he realized he had been manoeuvred into the worst possible position – his adversary was in his element and he was floundering. A fatal error that could cost him his life.

Then he saw the pale hands no longer held the silenced automatic.

Rick smiled, tossed back the oilskin revealing the golden curls of the child. 'Welcome to the dance, Marcus Carter.'

The eyes opened in the small face, fought to focus, widening as they saw him. The whisper was weak but clear: '*Marcus.*'

The stiletto flashed erect, arced, then settled at the corner of the child's eye.

Carter pleaded. 'The money's all here. There's no need to hurt her. Hurt any of them.'

'Listen to yourself, Carter? You're not the man I read about at the start of this. Such detail! She's changed you. Tamed you. You'd have tried to take me – child or no – *before.*'

'Not me,' Carter said, icily. 'They gave you the wrong script.'

'You're human again, what a tragedy.'

'Take the money. This isn't a game to me.'

'It is for me?'

'You sound like you're enjoying it.'

Rick took a pace back. 'Take off the pack – very slowly – then push it along between us with your feet. The slightest aggressive movement and the child goes over the side. I'll blind her first. Begin now. *No!* Don't hold the ropes Carter, I want you off balance.'

The child wailed as the bridge swayed.

Rick smiled.

Carter stood back, his breathing shallow, he could feel terror weakening him, felt he could never move from that spot, wanted to close his eyes but knew if he did he would lose balance and he would plunge into the chasm. He swallowed. 'What now?'

'I said I wanted clearance for the money. You have it? Signed?'

Carter reached for his zip.

'*Careful.*'

The bridge was settling, the swing becoming gentle. 'You want it or not,' growled Carter.

'Take it out slowly, show it to me – one hand, arm's length, fingertips only – hold your torch underneath with the other so I can read. You blind me she goes over, you move toward me she goes over, you let the paper slip she follows.'

Carter obeyed, the small torch shining from below the paper.

'Not witnessed. *Do it.* You do it.' Suddenly there was agitation in the cold voice, like the first trace of bubbling in water readied to boil.

Carter patted his pockets.

'Do it!'

'Pen . . .' He delved in his pockets.

'Careful, Carter!'

'Here.' His hand flew up, something sprayed, Rick yelled, blinded, Carter tossed the perfume away and struck with the reinforced ball-point, the stiletto flashing up defensively, the pen driving through knuckles and palm – but still the blade did not fall.

Rick stumbled back and threw the child away from him, Carter flinging himself out over the ropes, feet slipping, one leg plunging into the gap, yet somehow he had the girl's wet dress gripped in iron fingers – even after his testicles struck the slats and the crushing pain hit him.

Through his agony he heard Rick scream: '*Shoot!*' and frantically dragged the child over the rope like a rag doll, covering her with his body.

The sun exploded above him, from nowhere, falling fast, white and hot, bringing a hurricane that tore at him, preparing to blow him off the wildly pitching bridge.

The scream of the girl in his ears was worse than his own agony. He had failed Kate Brannigan, cost her the life of her husband and now her children.

One more swing and he and the girl would be gone.

233

He no longer cared.

He wished he could have saved the girl.

ELLIS SAW the torch gleam upward beneath whatever Carter held stretched before him. '*Shit!*'

'What's wrong?'

Ellis rolled instantly on his back, eyes searching the sky.

'*What's going on, damn you?*' hissed McAlister.

From the bridge came a cry, McAlister turned, saw a blurring of the two figures, a flash of something thrown and Carter heaving himself out crazily, dangerously, grasping, falling, crying out himself, somehow dragging the limp rag-doll shape back on to the bridge.

Someone yelled: '*Shoot!*' and the unmistakable red needle of a laser sight pierced the night seeking its huddled targets at the centre of the swaying bridge.

McAlister fired his pistol rapidly at the start of the line, not aiming, blasting, forcing the marksman back before the trigger was pulled.

Ellis swung over fast, fired into the same area – then immediately dropped his aim, firing two bursts at the figure clutching the haversack on the bridge.

The figure staggered, tripped, pitched over the rope still clutching the haversack and was gone.

The huge blast of noise from above was like an express bearing down from the sky, a glaring unbelievably white light piercing McAlister's brain despite his shielded eyes.

*Set-up!* he thought, fiercely. Everyone knew but me. He glared at Ellis.

'*Fucking don't lay it on me – I'm just a squaddie who obeys orders, all right!*' screamed Ellis over the helicopter's rotor blast.

McAlister saw bulky black-clad heavily armed figures leap from the aircraft, fanning out fast for positions, one group heading straight for the bridge, others establishing borders.

No one gets past, thought McAlister. No one sees, knows, nor ever will. Why? Who needs reasons? It's policy. That's reason enough.

The helicopter lifted fast, hovering again, somewhere high in the night.

McAlister stood.

Ellis dragged him down, hard. 'You want to get fucking killed?'

McAlister hit him, pushed him off. 'I want the truth before they kill that too.'

'Jesus!' Ellis crouched, grasping him again. 'Come on, then, at least they know my face. *Ellis!*' he barked. '*Coming in! OK?*'

THE CHILDREN had already been carried across to the mainland side of the bridge, one of the black-clad figures tending silently to them with medical instruments. Carter sat doubled over next to them.

McAlister came up, touched his shoulder, bent to him. 'Where are you hurt?'

Carter smiled wanly. 'No comment. You called in the SAS? You had surveillance on us all the way? How'd I miss all this shit?'

'You missed nothing that I set in motion,' McAlister said, tightly.

Carter looked up at him, grunted. 'So they shaft people this side of the pond too.'

McAlister looked across the bridge. 'How many? Should be four.'

The SAS trooper tending the children lifted his blackened face: 'Just two.' He pointed upward. 'Picked them up with the heat-seek. Saw Ellis and you, sir, the kids and Mr Carter. There's no more. Guaranteed.'

'They're both dead, naturally?'

The eyes in the black face were steady. 'One on the bridge took a hit then fell down there, he's gone for sure – other one went down from Ellis's fire too. You missed him completely, sir.'

'I intended to,' growled McAlister.

235

'Yes, sir.'

'So he's dead?'

'Not yet, sir.'

McAlister arose quickly, Carter following, crouched, hand clutched to his groin.

Ellis sat on rocks, watched them go. 'Shit.'

'And you're in some, boyo,' said the SAS trooper. 'Should have finished him when you had the chance.'

'Chopper fucking blinded me, didn't it! Why didn't one of *you* finish him?'

The trooper looked down. 'He's done anyway. I gave him a heavy shot of the happy-stuff to help him along. What's a couple of minutes?'

Ellis sighed, heaved himself up wearily and marched across the bridge.

Dave lay propped against a squared concrete arch at the top of rough steps, McAlister beside him holding his hand, Carter sitting turned away staring at the sea.

'He's gone?' Dave murmured. 'You're sure?'

Carter said, not turning. 'If the bullets didn't kill him the fall did. Or the sea.'

'What are you?' Dave asked McAlister.

'A friend.'

Dave closed his eyes, drifting with the drug. 'Even our friends were our enemies.'

'I'm not your enemy. Trust me.'

'You want me to tell you?'

'Will that make you feel better?'

'I feel better he's dead.'

'Karelin?'

Dave sighed. 'Karelin died on a mountain long ago. Karelin climbed the mountain, Rick came down.'

'I know about the mountain.'

'Then you know everything.'

236

'No. I don't know about all this. Who started it? Why?'

Dave opened his eyes and stared as if seeing into some other world, silent for a while, McAlister patiently waiting, gently stroking his hard hand. 'You know anything about the Soviet Union?' Dave asked finally.

'Not very much.'

'No one knows who starts something . . . you only know the last person to give the orders.'

'Krotkov? Now called Kramer? Who gave *him* his orders?'

Dave smiled, coughed, grimaced, looking deathly pale in the moonlight. 'Krotkov passed them to Rick. Who knows before that? Maybe it was you?'

'No.'

Dave shrugged wearily.

'Rick killed the woman in the Republic?'

'Rick always killed the women. I killed the man.' He indicated Carter. 'I thought it was him, sleeping.'

'Melsham,' said Carter, not turning. 'Langley's finest. CIA.'

Dave seemed to gather strength from somewhere, speaking quickly, his breath coming in gasps between his words. 'The dish was CIA. Rick knew. That's why he killed. He would kill CIA on sight. There was one on the mountain. The dish. A man with it. Might have been Brannigan. Same hair, same eyes. Rick showed us the photographs of Brannigan. I knew we had trouble.'

'Yet – if he was Brannigan – he killed him cleanly?'

'Rick did what he wanted. He had no rules.'

'I'm glad he's dead too,' admitted McAlister. 'Is there anything you want me to do for you?'

Dave smiled. 'Do something for Arnie. You know about Arnie and Max?'

'Where are they?'

Dave let his head flop sideways. 'The explosion – up the coast? In there.'

'I passed it. What can I do for Arnie?'

'Had a girl . . . baby coming . . .'

'He called us, said something about a garage. They're there?'

'Bayswater. Kawolski.' Dave closed his eyes. 'Your people will know where. *Jesus.*'

'They're not *my* people, whoever they are. I'll find out and see she's taken care of. Anything else?'

'Send me home.'

'Where's home?'

Dave smiled. 'Georgia. Sukhumi, Black Sea coast.'

'What is your real name?'

'Yakov Lobjanidze. You'll remember?'

'I'll remember.'

Dave sighed. 'Then I'll tell you.'

'Tell me what?'

'How the IRA will destroy London.'

Ellis climbed up to them, his weapon readied.

McAlister turned, saw him.

'I've got orders.'

McAlister glared. 'Ellis, you carry out those orders and Hereford's worst punishment will be nothing to what Downing Street does to you.'

HE FOUGHT the clutches of the bag net, refusing to release the fat rucksack which had saved his life twice, once when the bullets struck and again when he crashed into the shallow water before being taken out to sea and swept along the salmon course until, like them, he ended where he was now, trapped, the life slowly going from him.

*No!*

Using the immense strength of his lean, muscular body he twisted himself into a position where he faced the net, the stiletto still in his hand, almost pinned there by the pen through his fingers and palm. He drew it out, eyes and cheek bulging, uncaring about the pain, survival the only thing on his mind. Survival and retribution.

He cut swiftly, pushing the jostling fish away until, with nothing left in his lungs, he tore through and kicked up for the surface.

He swam hard for the shore, dragging the bag with him. He had weapons, money, documents. And he had knowledge. All he needed was time. And there was not much left. On the beach he checked the haversack, relieved to find genuine US banknotes – most dry because of the waterproof covering and stout zips, despite the bullet holes. He smiled when his hands found the spent rounds, tossing them wildly into the sea, laughing.

He strapped the rucksack to his back and began running to where he had hidden Murphy's Range Rover. It was a good strong car with a powerful engine. He would need all its power to reach the ferry in time. He had his bag with dry clothes in the car. Shoes too. The water had taken those he had worn. He tore off his socks, curled his toes in the sand, exhilarating in the feeling of freedom. There were some rocks to traverse on the way to the car but that was no problem, he had hard feet.

He wasn't Rick any more. Nor even Valentin Vasilevich Karelin – or Richard Steven Cain. He was Miloslav Kopecky. And he could do everything poor Milo the Housefly could do, even arm an obsolete atomic mine. He would do it personally – for history's sake – and his own pleasure – then walk away afterwards with the beautiful Mrs Brannigan and do things to her at his leisure. First he would make her eat the information the *Irish* were prepared to sell like the subhumans they were. Then he might eat her. And the real Milo? He smiled as he ran. He had *ceased to be* the second I became him. Milo was an irrelevance. Milo was already dead – it was only a question of time.

It was all a question of time.

He ran harder.

Leapt obstacles as Nureyev might; like the great principal dancer *he* might have been had they not awakened the killer in him.

# CHAPTER FOURTEEN

◆

KATE HAD no choice. The Mercedes had been brought to her and all she could do was get in and drive as they had ordered, which she did, numb with terror, her eyes constantly moving to the rear-view mirror and the following car, suspecting correctly that a large saloon holding position in front was also with them.

There was no way out. She was as trapped as any animal. Worse. She was locked in with the awesome power, the horror, of a nuclear device, there, behind the rear seats, seeming almost alive.

Boarding the ferry was simple, maddeningly easy, she might have been completing or beginning a vacation for all the attention she was given.

She wanted to scream: 'Search the goddamn car, rip it apart like the movies, arrest me, jail me if you must until you're certain of the truth – just don't leave me in here with that *thing*.'

They had booked her a cabin, which she went straight to, needing to just think. Even if there was no action she could take without risking her own or other lives on the ferry. She had to focus on her predicament, face it hard; shake the dreadful lethargy, the numb uselessness she felt.

Surely she could do *something*?

What?

How?

She had no idea who was watching her – every face turned even halfway toward her seemed dangerous but she knew that was her imagination out of control – had no idea how many of their men were aboard.

Could they smuggle arms on to a vessel with all the security she had witnessed?

This was Belfast. Half the crew might have been sympathizers for all she knew.

She sat on the lower bunk feeling wretched. She had a picture of her children in her handbag. She took it out, placed it on the small shelf, stared at it, no tears left to shed. The feeling of inevitability was still with her, yet the thought of the carnage which would occur in London lifted the fight in her. *She* would be taking the awesome weapon right into the heart of a heavily populated metropolis. She, personally, would be bringing death to – what was it Carter had said when she had asked how many would die? *After the first thousand who keeps counting?*

She prayed. Actually, physically, prayed on her knees, elbows on the bunk, like a child. She had not prayed for years. Had almost forgotten how. She stared blankly at the cabin wall, feeling enclosed in the tight space btween the upper and lower bunks, feeling momentarily safe, hidden from the horror in the bowels of the ship, trying to find the strongest possible plea to offer up.

In the end she just said, aloud: 'Please stop it. If it has to be it has to be. But I ask you *please* stop it. Give me back my children. *Please* give me back my children and I'll do anything you ask of me. *Anything.*'

There was no more she could do. She lay on the bunk. She slept. Mercifully she did not dream.

A KNOCK woke her with a start, her heart banging, still lost in a half-world unable to comprehend where she was until a steward's voice called: 'Liverpool!'

It all came back like a recurring nightmare.

She flopped back, closed her eyes, murmured: 'Oh God, no!' Then hauled herself up, infinitely weary, dowsed her face with cold water from the basin, collected her small photograph from the bunk and made her way to the car deck.

She felt like she wanted to die; believed she would, soon.

She started the Mercedes' engine and followed in line as cars disembarked, noticing a sticker positioned clearly on the windscreen, impossible to read from inside the car, and the line was steadily moving forward to Liverpool's grey morning.

At the bottom of the roll-off ramp a crewman in uniform signalled her to swing out of line.

'Transfer,' he said leaning down to her. 'Follow that vehicle.' He pointed.

She nodded, dumbly. Friend? Foe? Is his uniform genuine? Stolen? Rented? He could have been a Hollywood extra for all she knew.

The entire scene was unreal. The glare of floodlights; the ship behind, decks and portholes still glowing; lines of cars and people going about the business of life blithely, wearily, excitedly, while she sat in their midst with the means to destroy every one of them; vaporize the whole unreal setting in a single blinding flash.

She almost laughed and had to clamp down hard on herself, recognizing the first crack of hysteria.

Drive. Don't just sit. Sitting will kill people.

So will going forward, she thought. Except movement gave hope.

She drove, wondering, trivially, if there *would* be enough petrol in the Mercedes' modified tank.

*A few yards to a crane, Mrs Brannigan, that's it. Then it's up and over and you're away. You'll enjoy the sea air.*

I'll never enjoy sea air again. I'll hate the smell of it. And the smell of motor-cars, and ships, and of my own fear. That's if I ever get the chance to hate anything again. Or to love.

The car in front slowed then stopped, the driver stretching across the seats, speaking to a man in workmen's clothing. Something exchanged hands.

Behind this she saw a man. Darkly handsome; dressed entirely in black: black zipped up soft leather jacket, black jeans, small leather shoes, light as pumps, waiting, leaning with languorous grace against the rising structure that divided the grey morning sky with an arm that seemed to stretch for miles. She watched him as one arm lazily grasped metal. He could swing himself up the crane with ease, she thought.

The driver put his arm out, flat-palmed, signalling her to stay

242

where she was, then drove off slowly. No one's in a hurry, she thought. Or is it all running in slow motion in my mind? I'm treading water while around me there's rapids and I'm too exhausted to tell.

The man who had taken something from the driver walked past her, face turned away. She wondered if he was the crane-driver and who would drive the crane?

The man in black walked over, tried the door handle then rapped the passenger window.

She lowered it.

'Open the doors,' Rick ordered.

'Who are you?'

His eyes seemed impenetrable, nothing there for her to plead to. No compassion. Empty. Frightening.

'Open the doors!'

She obeyed.

He tossed a bulky backpack and a small black leather grip through the rear door on to the seats then sat beside her.

Close to, his eyes were dark, soft, sexual. The hard sodium dock lights, she thought, still alight despite morning. That's what made them seem the way they were.

Get a grip on yourself! she scolded. You may have to use this man. Do whatever is necessary.

'Who are you?' she repeated.

He looked behind, seemed to muse on his answer, then flipped the glove box open, felt inside, then pressed buttons on the radio and stereo, making them work briefly.

'What's wrong?'

He said nothing, scanning the car with his searching eyes. He breathed out, glanced quickly again through the window, this time seaward, then said: 'I'm supposed to be a Czechoslovak ex-Army captain paid to arm and time-detonate what's behind us.'

She stared at him. 'What?'

He repeated himself, quickly, agitatedly.

She couldn't grasp what she was hearing. 'You said *supposed* to be?'

'I'm an agent with the British Secret Intelligence Service. You may have heard it called MI6. I've just taken Milo's place. That's his name. Milo Kopecky. We've been watching him for months.

Intelligence confirmed he was to meet with members of an IRA cell here in Liverpol. We lifted him earlier today, got the whole story. The story about – that.' His eyes flicked backward again. 'It was decided I should substitute myself for Milo.' He showed a passport, opened at his picture. 'Bloody awful, isn't it. Had to be done fast.'

She shook her head. 'I don't understand? Are you telling me this is over? It's all over!'

'Sorry, no. Look you have to understand, we need to follow this through all the way. Need to get the big fish. Can't stop it now, that would blow everything. Months of work – a couple of lives lost too, I'm afraid.' He looked uncomfortable, agitated.

She glanced around her. 'Are there people – like you – out there? We're being watched?'

'Not too close I'm afraid – but yes, we're under close surveillance. Don't worry, everything's under control.'

She shook her head hard. 'Have you *any* idea what I've been through?'

He looked down. 'A pretty shrewd one, actually.'

'What's wrong? Something's the matter. You're holding back on me. What is it?'

'Better wait until we can get you out of this. Somewhere safe. Home would be best.'

'Goddamnit, tell me what's happened? *My children!*'

He breathed deeply. 'I'm afraid your countryman went haywire.' He looked away. 'There was some – interference – by your Central Intelligence Agency.'

'I *know* there was interference by the goddamn CIA! That's why I'm here! Now tell me what's happened!'

'CIA mounted an armed raid on the people who had taken your children. The IRA.'

'But they said they didn't have them?'

'I'm sorry, but they would say that, wouldn't they?'

She stared, utterly numb now.

He said: 'One of your Special Forces units was at the sharp end – not sure which, Delta probably – but of course Langley pulled the strings. They generally do. Carter is with them, I'm afraid. I know you trusted him . . . but he was the trigger, set the whole damn fiasco

244

off. He decided to pre-empt everything. They might have succeeded if he hadn't – acted independently.'

'You're telling me they're dead? *You're telling me they're dead!*'

'I'm sorry. When it came down to it Langley really had little interest in your children's safety. They were simply caught in the crossfire. You must have seen yourself how your military can act. Iraq . . . Somalia . . . ?'

'*Shut up! Damn you, shut up!*'

Hawsers suddenly arose all round the car, tightening, straining. The Mercedes lurched, tipped over, throwing Kate hard against the door. She screamed, frantically working the central locking as the car lifted and swung high, first over a warehouse far below, then out over gleaming black oily sea water, then hung poised swaying gently over the gaping hold of the coaster below. She screamed again just from the awful stillness of it, certain they were going to be dropped at any moment.

He reached over for her, held her, pushed her head deep into his chest, burying her face in the soft leather of his jacket. She clung to him madly.

The crane lowered the car swiftly, the suspension compressing deeply as the tyres hit the steel deck.

'I want to die,' she whispered, grasping him, head buried. 'Kill me, please kill me.'

Rick smiled. *Eventually.*

HE HAD abandoned Murphy's Range Rover in Belfast docks car park, purchased a return ticket, which was always safer, boarded the ferry, then made his way upward to lean on the rail with other envious foot passengers watching the line of cars being driven aboard.

He agreed with the man next to him that the Mercedes 500 coupé – one of which they could see on the ramp – was an exceptional car, ruefully admitting the chance of him ever having one was about the same as the ship sprouting wings and flying them all over to

Britain and smiling inside while doing so because he had his foot squarely planted on one million dollars in used one-hundred-dollar bills which needed no laundering whtsoever.

He looked forward to enjoying the money.

Afterwards.

He might even own a Mercedes 500 coupé just for the irony of it. But with a complete petrol tank so he could travel for as long as he wanted. Free.

Bidding his fellow passenger farewell he made his way to where the drivers emerged, saw *her* then let her be for the journey. He would have his time on board ship with her soon. They would study the stars together. She would welcome his presence, his strength. She would need his strength. He was going to inflict more pain than she could bear. With two long leisurely days together he could spread the pain. Mental and physical. In that order. He would make her his. Become her lifeline when she was drowning. Then cut it. And her.

He bought a sandwich and cold milk, ate, drank, then slept as lightly as ever on a lounger, his head rested on his grip, his bare feet stretched forward on to the haversack; a fly coming too close would have woken him. He had no fears whatsoever about being robbed.

He had killed a thief once. On a deserted train, very late. One blow – when the man bent over him as he dozed. Killed him, bloodlessly, tossed him from the train and forgot about him, not even bothering to follow the story in the papers. Krotkov would have had to have squared matters with his London masters if somehow he had been tracked down but nothing happened. He knew that would be the case: the police would close their investigation of a dead nobody as soon as they could. It would be listed as an accident. The fall would have obliterated the bruise from the killing blow.

He awoke with the change in the ship's engine note, gathered himself up and made quickly to where the duty-free shops were closing up, recognized the face he had seen in Murphy's files and walked up to the man, his accent hard Belfast.

'I think I've been made. I need to be off without going through the routine out there. Can you fix it?'

'Who're you?' the man snapped, alarmed.

'Jesus, I'm delivering!'

'How do I know that?'

246

'Christ, look *here!*'

The man looked down, panicking, but managing to grasp and open the passport thrust at him, low.

'Shit.'

'Shit is right and if I don't get off soon I'm in it – and so are you mate 'cause if they lift me they'll tear this tub apart and look fuckin' hard at everyone who works in it. That's *your* cushy number gone!'

'Below. Quickly.'

'Come on then!'

There was a door at dock level, and a railed gangplank, men in kitchen porters' uniforms unloaded waste on to the quay in sacks.

Rick took the grubby clothes he was offered, put his bag and the rucksack into a bin-bag and walked off without a word.

He became what he had always been: a master at blending into his surroundings, drifting away from all the frantic end of journey activity, becoming a sylph, moving closer to where he would no longer be Rick, where he would become Milo.

Milo died as fast as the intake of his last breath. Died knowing nothing. Waiting as had been planned for weeks to meet an IRA contact off the ferry in that precise place at that precise time.

Rick took nothing from him. Milo had nothing Rick did not have already, including his identity.

Now everything was right.

He stepped out to wait for her.

And watch her break.

As Max and Arnie and Dave had watched him.

He had not broken, he had *become*.

THERE WAS only one free cabin, cramped; very basic: double bunks, one up one down, a curtained hanging space – with clothes already in there, pushed aside – a narrow fold-down table and two metal chairs, also folding.

The Captain had showed them the way, his manner brusque, eager to be done with them as fast as he could: 'You'll be cramped and you'll have to share. That's how it is.'

Kate didn't care. Didn't care about anything. Had stopped caring about the bomb in the hold. Had even stopped fearing it.

She had crept into the lower bunk, curled herself up and pulled the pillow over her head. She wept and after an eternity with the deep thud of the coaster's engine pounding muffledly through the mattress into her ear from below, sheer emotional exhaustion slipped her mercifully into unconsciousness.

When she awoke and turned over, feeling ill and old, he was sitting on one of the small folding chairs, watching her.

'What happened to your hand?' she asked dully.

He glanced at the grubby binding around the wound inflicted by Carter's improvised weapon. 'Milo resisted. He had something hidden. It's nothing.'

She arose from the bunk, prepared to do anything just to keep moving, stop thinking, feeling. Remembering.

'Where are you going?' he asked.

'That bandage is filthy. It isn't even a proper bandage. There's a medical kit in the corridor on the wall.'

He looked at her. 'Bulkhead. On ships they call that part the bulkhead.'

She shrugged, went out and returned with a first-aid kit, unfolded the second chair, took his hand and laid it on the lowered table between them, untied the binding and gasped. 'What did *that*!'

'A kind of spike.'

'That must hurt terribly.'

'Pain is in the mind.'

'I'm sorry.'

'Why are you sorry? You didn't cause it. You didn't hurt me.'

She shrugged. 'Someone has to apologize for others' violent actions.'

'You're not responsible for the whole world.'

'Aren't we all just a little bit responsible for everything that happens?'

'That's nirvana,' he murmured.

'What exactly *is* nirvana?'

'The cessation of individual existence. A Buddhist concept.'

'You've obviously studied it.'

He stared at her. 'Maybe I've felt it.'

248

Her eyes met his. 'How?'

'It doesn't matter.'

She cleaned the wound with antiseptic, wondering: Is this how some women fall into nursing? Tending others' pain while salving their own?

'What's your real name?' she asked him.

'Pardon?'

'Your real name? You're not Milo whoever? So you're who?'

He blinked. He hadn't considered another person. Hadn't invented him. There was a blank there where someone should exist. It was more than a blank, it was failure. *You're tired.* That was an excuse. He did not acknowledge excuses; his own or others.

'Aren't you allowed to say?'

He looked at his hand. 'No, not really.'

'You don't look like someone called Milo. I'm surprised they believe you.'

'They?'

'The IRA.'

'They don't know Milo, he's part of another terrorist group – in Germany. They wouldn't share identities. Anyway the IRA aren't here. They come aboard in London. They've planned it to keep well back until the last moment. The men on the docks in Liverpool believe this is a drugs run. So do the captain and crew.'

He didn't feel comfortable with her questions – not while she was tending his wound – she was making him say too much. Too much truth. Murphy's truth anyway. The truth of an operation so secret it had no name.

'And what then? In London? Will you kill them? All alone? You got hurt badly just arresting one man?' She looked up at him. 'There *will* be others to help?'

He was lost, striving with the need to have an identity to face her with. There was only Rick, no one else flowed from inside. 'Richard Cain,' he said. 'I'm Richard Cain.'

She looked up at him. 'Richard. That fits better. You're very English.'

*I'm not!* He blinked, the anger inside jolting him.

She worked steadily, expertly on the wound, bound it, curled his fingers over, gently pressed his hand and pushed it back to him.

'You do that like a mother.'

She blinked at him, the tears flooding her eyes.

'I'm sorry.'

She shook her head. Turned to the bed for her bag and found tissues. She noticed vaguely that her perfume spray had gone.

'I took a course,' she said. 'First aid. That's a bad wound. Have you had a shot? Tetanus? You should have.'

'No.'

'They must have something like that on board, I'll check. If they haven't, you'd better do something as soon as . . .' She looked at him grimly. '*If* your people can stop this madness.'

'If they can't it won't matter. Will it?'

'You're amazingly calm considering the position you're in.'

'I told you there are no terrorists on board. We're in no danger. We're free to do what we want.'

'Except escape.'

He smiled. 'Do you want to jump over the side? Steal a lifeboat? I can't come with you.'

'How long before we get to London?'

'Two days – if the Captain keeps good speed, which is what he's paid to do. He can go straight through to the Pool of London – right to Tower Bridge – no stopping for a pilot, he has dispensation. Makes the trip regularly. Brings animal feed from Rotterdam.'

'And Mercedes-Benz automobiles with atomic weapons welded into them.'

'Never before.'

'Your people really know a *lot* about this, don't they?'

'It's our business.'

She looked at him, steadily. 'And how much did they know about my business? My husband's business.'

He shifted, tested the knot on the bandage.

'They had to have known *something*? Tell me! I deserve the truth.'

He stood. 'The weather is good. Why don't we go on deck.'

She looked up at him. 'I don't want any more lies.'

'We'll see truth dawn together,' he told her.

'When?'

'When it's over.'

250

She stood and because – desperately, right then – she needed the warmth of another human being, she held him. They clung together and for a brief moment she wondered who was in most pain. Then as his dark hair fell against her face she had the strangest sense of smelling her own, missing, perfume. So faint and, oddly, mixed with the smell of the sea. She knew she imagined it. It was all part of her confusion.

# EPILOGUE

'THERE SHE is,' McAlister murmured.
They were crouched on the cold pavement, ducked below the Embankment wall, dawn still an hour away but its growing presence evident in the occasional bright, small square suddenly appearing in the grey-black ramparts of the many riverside blocks and in small movements, small sounds: the whine of electric motors and the clink of bottles as milk-carts glided under fading street lamps.

Carter said: 'Have to go.'

'Do what you can for her. You know what he can do.'

'He's probably done it already.'

McAlister shook his head. 'I doubt it. Even a bunch of pirates like the crew on there wouldn't stomach what he does to a woman. If he had done his business they'd have heaved him over the side with all the evidence. They're smugglers not killers. Well, I'm sure not that kind of killer anyway. They certainly wouldn't want to go down on *that* charge. Solitary for life? Fair game for prisoners and screws alike? They'd be crazy and criminals rarely are. I think she's alive, all you have to do is get her away from him – fast.'

Carter tipped his head at the big black operation co-ordination vehicle further away along the Embankment. 'I don't understand why they haven't evacuated the area.'

'How big an area can you evacuate without chaos? And there would be chaos, believe me. People don't listen any more. Don't obey blindly. They argue, get bloody minded. They stick. No, it's better this way. Even with the risk. The SBS are the best there is – they'll get in there, do the business and God willing we'll be able to share the best mug of morning tea you'll ever have at that mobile café I told you about. You just make it down-river with her. I'll be waiting.'

'Make that coffee – with doughnuts – and you've got a deal.'

'This is London, you drink tea and like it. Good luck.'

'I'll be back.'

Carter grasped the outstretched hand, squeezed it hard, then darted away, dressed identically to the Special Boat Service units crouched further away behind the river wall: black from Balaclava to body armour to boots, the same Heckler and Koch machine-pistol on a sling around his neck.

'Good luck,' McAlister breathed again, watching him move into position, then turned to watch it unfold.

SHE HEARD him climb down from the top bunk.

'Where are you going!'

'It'll be time soon,' he whispered.

'We're *there*? London?'

'Yes.'

'What have you got to do? Signal them? Your people?'

'Yes.'

'Richard!'

'What?'

'Be careful.'

'Yes.'

'You are coming back?'

'Yes.'

'How soon?'

'We'll leave together.'

Then he was gone.

She lay back, still in the twilight of half-sleep. She had never known anyone like him. Had never known a time like the last days. Had lost touch completely with all reality. Certainly any reality she had ever known – even if half had been a lie. Vermont might never have existed. The children . . . the children were as if from another existence. The pain was there, but dulled. She assumed it was all due to shock. Suspected she was close to a breakdown – even having one already.

She was grateful to him. He had been the perfect English

253

gentleman. It was almost as if he were playing that role. To the hilt. A little over-the-top at times but she guessed that was to keep her from worrying; to suppress her anxieties. She felt he probably suffered guilt – from having to be the bearer of such dreadful tidings. Like poor Reardon. Only worse.

He had not touched her. After that moment of them clinging together he had kept his distance. Slept on the top bunk, swinging up there as easy as a circus artiste – and with all the grace of a dancer.

Not at all like an English gentleman.

She had not even seen him unclothed. When he showered in the booth down the corridor outside their cabin he went and returned clothed. She could see no reason he might feel ashamed of his body – on the contrary, he seemed superbly fit – so she assumed he simply felt uncomfortable with women. Perhaps just with her?

Or was it the danger? Their perilous situation? Was he focused totally inwards, shutting her out? She sensed a struggle. She was good at *feeling* people. She felt for him. He seemed such a lost soul.

She had friends in Vermont who were Russian *émigrés* and occasionally, like a veil falling, she saw something of them in him. That same stern, austere quality. That Russian *heaviness*. Also a stillness when she wasn't looking at him or talking with him that made him seem not *invisible* but away, somewhere else – or at least trying to be away.

But then he would look at her, smile in that English self-denigrating way and be comfortable again. She accepted both faces. As far as she was concerned he might be the last human being she would be close to. For those short days he was as close a friend as any she had ever had.

Perhaps that is the nature of dying? she wondered. Accepting. *This* is all. Make the best of it. Look for the best. Smile, and if there is sorrow let it only be a soft shadow that lay to the side of you, not falling upon you or others close to you.

She definitely saw him as a dancer. Classical, of course. Ballet, which she adored. She smiled, imagining him in tights. Black, naturally. He had the figure, she could see that despite his remaining clothed.

254

His habit of going barefoot all the time – even when they walked up to the deck to watch the sea and the stars – added to the image. *Not* terribly English, she told him. He had no answer; continued scanning the stars as if he hungered for them.

He had seemed – as the hours passed into days – to have less and less to say; fewer answers to her questions. Like a liar who had run out of lies.

Except she believed him, implicitly. He was risking his life for her – or at least *with* her – so belief in him was natural. Was fair.

In an odd way he reminded her of Carter: the same deep reserve; holding back of emotion; a dam, solid as stone and as unyielding. She supposed it was to do with possessing great courage. Perhaps it was the *cost* of possessing courage?

More intense than Carter, she thought, dreamily. Carter could survive anything; Richard she wasn't at all sure about. Survive *inside*.

She lay back, perhaps slept again, woken only by the strange sound of pillows being thumped rapidly and she wondered who was making beds. Or were there children aboard having a pillow fight? Then there was commotion and she was wide awake and sitting up, heart banging against the roof of her mouth, and fear like half a million ants crawling up her because she knew, she simply knew, that the monster in the hold was primed and ready to blow her into atoms.

She squeezed her eyes shut.

The crash as the door exploded inwards was, she knew, the end.

H E HAD mounted the ladder and started the climb out of the hold, his bare feet gripping cold crusted iron, moving catlike to the open square above where he could see a few stars still hanging emptily in a blueing sky.

*It's over. Dawn comes without truth.*

There was sickness in the pit of his stomach. Fire in his eyes. The world was afire and he saw it inverted, as if the square above was the pit and he was climbing down into it. He kept on because that was how he lived. Whatever the next torture, it was no greater, nor less, than his own.

He climbed to the lip. He stepped over. He breathed, looked at the sky, spread his arms, said: '*Zvezdy, berite menya!*' Stars take me.

The shock was astonishing, the force irresistible, even his great strength made powerless; he clutched the rail but his steel fingers were boneless flesh and flopped uselessly so that, overbalanced, he staggered, tilted and was falling before he could grasp the reality of taking the full burst of the Heckler across his body.

At first the water was cold, so cold he felt the fires die inside him, then warm around him, warm as blood, his urgent rush downward slowed, calmed. He felt suspended; air lightly blowing across him like a mellow breeze from some forgotten summer when every sensation seemed new and lasted almost for ever. He drifted face upward to the stars.

Death is only letting go, someone said. He thought it might be his beautiful mother.

He did.

CARTER TUGGED back the Balaclava to silence her screams, then grasped her, lifted her, took her out on to the deck running hard for where they had the rubber assault craft hitched below and with her over his shoulder now, limp, unprotesting, leapt the last feet into the craft, yelling: '*Go! Go! Go!*'

It was only afterward, farther down-river – along which they had careered, bow lifted, stern biting deep, powerful engine destroying the silence – that he asked her: 'Are you all right? Did he hurt you?'

She could not understand.

When he explained she wouldn't believe him.

She didn't believe him until she saw under the river lamp by a mobile food-stall, the tall figure of McAlister, one golden-haired child grasped close to his chest, two others standing beside him, firmly protected by his other arm.

She screamed and cried and kissed Carter and McAlister and

hugged the children who were wide awake and bright eyed and excited, their tears only reflections of hers which soon became smiles and laughter as day broke around them gloriously.

HIS PRIVATE line rang. The Prime Minister lifted it.

The Home Secretary sounded annoyed. 'I've just heard. This raid on the ship in the Pool of London? SBS called out? I knew nothing about it. I'm sorry but why wasn't COBRA convened? A major terrorist incident—'

'Drugs,' corrected the Prime Minister, placatingly. 'Not terrorism. Apparently not as much of a haul as hoped but a major transporter has been arrested – the captain – and he'll implicate a few others, they're certain. Could have been bigger, but there we are! Nothing requiring COBRA.'

'Oh! Well in that case I'll make sure there are commendations handed out. Build it up a bit. Get some good press out of it. We could do with something positive on the law and order front.'

'Good idea. You can mention Rotterdam as the source.'

'I *should* really have been informed.'

'MI6 provided the intelligence,' the Prime Minister lied smoothly. 'You know they don't give much away. Protecting sources, I suppose. I've only just learned myself.'

'Well it's *something* to justify their new Vauxhall gin palace, I suppose.'

'Since you've raised the matter . . . the debate on the Service is coming up. I think we may have to be *seen* to be curbing some of their excesses – and their autonomy. A discreet but firm shake up won't do any harm. How do you feel about that?'

'I agree. Can't have them spreading their net too far. Without the Red Threat they'll be spying on *us* next!' A chuckle came down the line. 'Mind you the way things are with Washington one doesn't know quite who one's enemies are any more.'

'It's a funny old world.'

'Famous last words!'

'But a lesson learned. One must always protect oneself. I'm

afraid that has become a vital principle in high political office these days.'

'"Protection is not a principle, but an expedient," Disraeli.'

'Well, he knew a thing or two.'

The Prime Minister put down the telephone, gazed for a moment at the document that had been rushed to him by motorcycle from the coaster. He reached for another line and lifted it.

'I realize the hour over there but I'd like to speak urgently with the President.'

He listened patiently to the aide's excuses.

'Well, if you feel it really is *too* difficult to wake him I must accept your good judgement. However, if he does wake for any other pressing reason please be so good as to let him know the Prime Minister called from London. I have a list for him which I understand he needs rather urgently. Indeed your Central Intelligence Agency has been trying desperately to get hold of it – or so I'm informed. Oh! You will wake him? Of course I'll hold on.'

He sifted desultorily through the contents of one of his red boxes, the telephone held loosely at his ear.

He smiled as the familiar – though now eager, if shaken – voice came on the line.

'Good morning, Mr President!' he began, brightly. 'I'm so very glad we are able to help each other once again . . .'